# ACCIDENTAL SORCERESS

# ACCIDENTAL SORCERESS

DANA MARTON

ISBN: 1940627117
ISBN-13: 9781940627113

# DEDICATION

With my sincere gratitude to all who provided encouragement and their special skills while I was writing this story: Sarah Jordan, Diane Flindt, Linda Ingmanson, Toni Lee, and all my wonderful readers in the Dana Marton Book Club on Facebook. I appreciate you more than words can say.

Many thanks to Sami Jordan for giving Bloodstorm his name.

# CHAPTER ONE
## CONCUBINE REBELLION

"We may lose the ones we love, but we do not leave them behind, Lady Tera," the Guardian of the Sacred Cave said.

"They are a thread woven irremovably into the fabric of our lives. Because they were, we are." He patted my hand as the two of us walked the parapets in the dusk, the Kadar fortress city of Karamur spread out below us. "If you miss their voices, listen deep inside your heart."

My heart hurt. We had lost too many good men and women in the siege.

The smell of wood fires filled the air; locked-up hunting hounds bayed in the night. The hem of my cape swept the worn stones with a soft whoosh as we walked. I drew the cape tighter around me. Fall had barely ended, but halfway up the mountain as we were, the chill of winter was already in the air.

A small shadow on our path caught my gaze and brought me to a halt. A shudder ran through me. I stared down at the dead bird, and said without meaning to, "A journey through darkness."

The Guardian stopped next to me. He had lost much weight. He might have counseled me in my grief, but he too suffered greatly from our losses. He had aged. His shoulders sloped, the set of his mouth grim, his face drawn, but his eyes radiated endless wisdom and kindness. In the voluminous folds of his robe, he looked like an ancient figure out of myth.

1

He peered at me. "What did you say, my lady?"

I expelled a small sigh, wishing I had not spoken. I could not tear my eyes away from the slight, broken shadow at my feet. "The Kadar believe a dead blackbird means a journey through darkness for the one who finds it."

The Kadar had many superstitions. My people the Shahala, who lived on the southern half of the island, believed not in omens. Neither did the Guardians, so the Guardian of the Sacred Cave stepped over the bird without giving it much notice, and continued forward.

I drew a deep breath and pushed away the sense of foreboding that tried to settle on me. No sense in becoming as superstitious as a Kadar kitchen maid. I tore my gaze from the bird and hurried after the Guardian, as the city around us prepared for sleep behind the safety of the walls.

Karamur clung to inhospitable cliffs that protected the city from the back, while the city wall guarded the front, the damage from the siege fully repaired at last. Everything about the fortress city spoke of the warrior nation that had built it: sturdy, stark, battle-ready. The top of the walls we walked were wide enough to drive an oxcart on, no adornments, only sheer, intimidating strength.

But no fortress was impregnable.

"How holds the Gate on the other side of the mountain?" I asked.

"The Gate holds." The Guardian of the Cave folded his gnarled fingers together over his brown robe that hung on him. He sounded confident, perhaps for my sake.

"Any news of the new Guardian of the Gate?" I held my breath for the answer.

The old man shook his head, looking out over the city as we walked, at the lamplights that blinked to life behind windows. "He has not returned."

We had repelled the fall siege and triumphed over the Kerghi horde. But sooner than we had expected, new troops broke through the island's Gate, and the old Guardian of the Gate had bespelled the Gate to seal it, cutting off the larger enemy force from reaching us.

Our island of Dahru was the largest one of the Middle Islands that dotted Mirror Sea where all could safely sail. The Outer Islands edged the sea, also within reach by ship. But surrounding our small corner of the world spread the wild ocean, ruled by hardstorms that allowed no passage.

Island groups like ours dotted the wild ocean, with a bigger stretch of land here and there, one even large enough to be called the mainland. We could reach those kingdoms only through Gates, the portals of an ancient people whose lost knowledge we could not recover. We could use their Gates, but if a Gate was destroyed or damaged, we could not repair it.

Of all the islands of the Mirror Sea, only Dahru had a working Gate—and it was a special one. But that Gate was now sealed, and we were thoroughly cut off from the rest of the world.

"At least we are saved from immediate occupation," I said, only too aware that we had paid a most high price for the protection. The strong binding spell had required the life of the old Guardian of the Gate.

The three old Guardians—the Guardian of the Gate, the Guardian of the Scrolls, and the Guardian of the Cave—had been like grandfathers to me. Of the three, only the Guardian of the Cave still lived.

When a Guardian dies, his son takes over his duties. But the son of our Guardian of the Gate had been traveling to other Gates, still learning, when his father had died. And with our Gate now sealed, we feared he would not be able to return to us.

I drew my cloak tighter around me against the wind. "Do you think the enemy troops that squeezed through might steal down the mountain and attack when the weather worsens, thinking it is what we would least expect?"

The Guardian considered my question for a long moment before answering. "For now, the strength of our forces is equal. As long as the Kadar warriors remain in the fortress city, the enemy cannot overpower the defenses. The attackers would be disadvantaged out in the open, standing before the city walls."

And our army could not march to attack them at the Gate on the other side of the mountain. We could not overtake them as they sat behind their makeshift stone and wood-spike fortifications. Our warriors would be disadvantaged there. Several skirmishes had proved this, and now the two forces sat at a stalemate.

The Guardian said, "Likely they are settled in where they are for the winter."

"Can the enemy reopen our Gate from afar and send more troops through?" Emperor Drakhar, who sought to conquer the world, had a sorcerer in his service, the knowledge of which had me steeped in worry.

"It would be best if our young Guardian of the Gate could return," the Guardian of the Cave admitted, then stopped. "I should be leaving. I still have a long walk ahead of me tonight."

He lived even higher up the mountain, in the Forgotten City. For centuries, people believed that the Forgotten City had been lost, their Guardians and their people, the Seela, relegated to myth. Until I had found them…or rather, they had found me.

Our island of Dahru was inhabited by three nations. In the south lived the nine tribes of my people the Shahala, a peaceful nation of healers ruled by their elders. In the north lived the warrior nation of the Kadar, ruled by their warlords and their High Lord. Up the mountain above Karamur hid the Forgotten City, the small enclave of the Seela—the descendants of the First People—protected by their three Guardians.

And around us, the world at war.

"Will you talk with Batumar before you leave?" I asked as we turned around and walked back toward the palace.

The High Lord had spent the evening meal discussing something with Lord Samtis, another powerful warlord whose lands lay to the west of Karamur. The Guardian and Batumar had only had the briefest of exchanges.

But Guardian said, "I have come only to see how the city fares."

I had the odd sense that his sentence was unfinished, as if he had meant to say more. And that more I could almost hear as: *one last time.*

Did he feel his own end? Did he wish to follow his friends to the realm of the spirits? Of course, I could not ask such question. But my heart worried.

We reached the spot where the dead blackbird had lain earlier, and I searched the stones in the falling darkness. I could see no trace of the small, broken body.

"A hungry cat," the Guardian suggested.

A shudder ran through me once again.

We walked on in silence, then took the stairs that led to the bottom of the wall where the Palace Guard waited to escort me back to the High Lord's palace—four sturdy men dressed in red and gold, the High Lord's colors.

The premonitions that had assailed me on top of the wall would not leave me, so I asked the Guardian, "Has the Seer seen something?"

But the Guardian only said, "Remember your mother's words. And hold on to your light."

*Spirit, be strong. Heart, be brave* had been my mother's last message.

The Guardian looked at me with great kindness and the warmest affection, his gnarled hand reaching out to touch my arm in farewell. Then he turned and shuffled away from me, down the cobblestone street.

I watched his progress for some time in the light of the flickering torches before I turned in the opposite direction and hurried off toward the palace.

The Palace Guard escorted me straight to the High Lord's Pleasure Hall, the concubines' quarters, a nest of luxury—in the middle of military order and simplicity—as could scarcely be imagined by outsiders.

Had anyone told me of such a place, back when I'd been a sunborn Shahala girl impatiently waiting for her healing powers to manifest, I would have thought the descriptions a tall tale. Never would I have thought that one day I would end up among the Kadar as their High Lord's favorite concubine.

*Only* concubine, until recently. My heart gave a painful squeeze as I pushed the door open, hoping against hope that the others would be back in their chambers, settling in for sleep.

Instead, they all waited, gathered in the round center hall, every displeased, suspicious eye on me as I entered.

"You poisoned the High Lord against us." Lalandra spat the words instead of a greeting.

The slender beauty of amber eyes and full lips stepped forward from among the rest of the concubines, the silk of her emerald gown rustling as she moved. Her golden hair towered in an elaborate design of looped and folded braids, making her look like a carved temple statue of some ancient goddess. Even the look she shot me was as cold and hard as marble.

I winced at hearing the word *poison* from her lips. In that regard, the High Lord Batumar's Pleasure Hall had a most unfortunate history.

I squared my shoulders as I stood my ground, between us the sunken pool in the middle of the center hall, its heated water filling the air with the scent of lavender oil that floated in glistening drops on the surface. Fur-covered benches lined the walls; silk wall hangings adding color, depicting couples in loving embraces. Low, octagonal tables offered fruit and drink: mosan berry juice, grapes, apples, pears.

In her lord's Pleasure Hall, a concubine could find anything she ever desired. Anything but peace. The Kadar saying had it right—a warrior *was* safer in battle than a concubine on her pillows.

Since merely holding my ground would not do, I took a few steps forward. I had meant to go to my sleeping chamber, and I would do so.

I faced the women head on. "This is nothing but a misunderstanding."

They had disliked me from the moment of their arrival, but this was the first time they openly challenged me. I had to find a way to turn us back from this road of becoming enemies.

*An unhappy concubine dries out a man's bones like the desert wind; but two unhappy concubines are twisting storms that can blow down a whole castle,* according to a Kadar proverb. I did not wish to find out what havoc more than two dozen unhappy concubines could wreak.

"You do not want us here," Lalandra accused, the light of the oil lamps glinting off the scented morcan oil she used to soften her hair.

Her emerald gown had been made to accentuate her perfect, curvaceous body, the silk high sheen. She practically shimmered as she said, "You used every excuse to keep us from our rightful place. Lord Gilrem died *before* the siege. Yet mooncrossing after mooncrossing, you found an excuse to keep us away from his brother, the High Lord, to keep *him* away from his lawfully inherited concubines."

Even in her anger she was regal, as graceful in posture and movement as a queen. She had ruled Lord Gilrem's Pleasure Hall, and the other women, for all her adult life. They owed their allegiance to her.

Out of all of them, I had only Arnsha on my side, whose life I once had saved when she'd nearly died in childbirth. But even she was too afraid of Lalandra to support me openly. At least, she stood aside and did not nod at Lalandra's every word like the others.

I filled my lungs. "I could not have you come sooner. After Lord Gilrem died, the High Lord left to avenge his brother's death." And I had gone after him. Shortly after our return, the enemy lay siege to the city, most certainly not the right time for moving the women and children here.

Lalandra scoffed. "The High Lord's Pleasure Hall stood empty with only you here, and you wished it that way."

I would not lie by denying her words. I *had* been the High Lord's only concubine, and I had foolishly convinced myself that life could remain so forever. Unlike the Kadar, my people, the Shahala bonded for life to a single mate.

I offered Lalandra a firm but friendly smile. As the favorite concubine, I was responsible for keeping Pleasure Hall's peace, and I *would* find a way. "After the siege the High Lord gave these chambers to Shahala healers to heal our wounded."

Room was plentiful here, heat and water readily available, which made healing work much easier.

Of course, Lalandra knew that. Even while concubines did not move outside the palace walls, they tended to know as much about the comings and goings in the city as if they sat all day at the city gate, every bit of news rushed to them by their servant women.

A concubine's days were long, little to do beyond the endless purification and beautification rituals. In any Pleasure Hall, gossip had more value than jewels.

Lalandra's voice dripped with venom as she said, "You kept us away as long as you could. And even now…The High Lord has not called for any of us but you."

I blinked. Batumar had summoned Lady Lalandra just the day before, the knowledge of which was a dagger in my heart. But I could not refute her words. This was not the best time to call her a liar.

Most of the children played in the back, watched by the older girls, but Lalandra's two were stuck to her side. When she took another step closer to me, so did they. She was reminding me that she *had* children while I had none.

Her beautiful eyes narrowed to slits. "You deny us even servants."

The rest of the concubines murmured in agreement, a wall of support behind her. They were mostly daughters of warlords, wrapped in silk and satin, used to the finer things in their fathers' houses and then in Lord Gilrem's, used to servants fulfilling their every wish.

I did not like the bustle of servants around me all day, nor did I need assistance to bathe and dress. Lalandra and the others considered my reluctance to order an army of maids to take care of us an insult most grave.

"You were brought to our lands as a lowly slave," she taunted. "And now you sit beside the High Lord at the nightly feast. He prefers you above all others." Her gaze grew frostier and hardened even more as she leveled her final accusation. "What else can this be but sorcery?"

The women gasped, reaching for their charm belts.

Lalandra's words, like ice-tipped fingers, crawled up my spine. I wished Leena, the High Lord's mother and my friend, was in the palace, but she was on a pilgrimage to the Sacred Pool of the Goddesses. She had gone under heavy guard to thank the goddesses for reuniting her with her son. She would not be back until tomorrow evening.

Of course, that Lalandra would confront me when the High Lord's mother was absent was no coincidence.

"I am a healer," I repeated firmly. "All of Karamur knows it."

Lalandra snapped back with, "All of Karamur knows that you enslaved the High Lord's attention. Because of you, he has forsaken his duty."

Those words I could not rebut. Spending time with his concubines was indeed a warlord's responsibility. The making of sons was required of him. A lord's sons became warriors, and the realm needed warriors to replace the great many men we had lost during the siege. All men who survived the attack—lords, warriors, and servants alike—had the sacred duty to fill their women's bellies.

"You are not Kadar." Lalandra pronounced the words like a judgment. "You wish for Karamur to fall in the next fight."

"I served the city during the siege with my healing," I reminded her.

Lalandra lifted her chin, and her cold gaze turned scolding. "Kadar warriors are the best fighters in the world. I do not think they needed help from anybody. I did not see this great deed of healing that you claim."

Of course, she hadn't. During the siege, Lalandra and the others had been barricaded in Lord Gilrem's palace with their children.

"You wish to rule us all," she accused.

I wished for nothing but peace. A child's wish, I thought with heavy heart, when the whole world was at war.

She kept her chin up as she demanded, "Where are the High Lord's other concubines?"

"You well know where they are, Lady Lalandra." *Dead.* The most dreadful story I'd ever heard, jealousy leading to the murder of innocents. None of that had anything to do with me.

"Some say you killed them." Menace hissed in Lalandra's words.

By *some*, I was certain she meant herself. I prayed to the spirits for patience.

"Strange how you always manage to live," Lalandra went on. "During the siege, did you not fall into fire? You protect yourself with an ill-gained power," she said the words as if she was the High Lord himself, pronouncing judgment.

Clutching their charm belts, the other concubines nodded in agreement, their elaborately arranged braids bobbing up and down like a flock of chiri birds pecking for worms.

Lalandra stepped closer to me yet—we stood but a few steps apart—and pronounced her final judgment loudly enough for her voice to fill the hall. "Sorceress."

Even as I moved forward too—I would *not* yield—the small hairs rose at my nape. To be charged with sorcery was the greatest sin among the Kadar.

But before I could defend myself against Lalandra's charge, the carved doors guarding Pleasure Hall rattled. One of the servant girls, Natta, entered and hurried to me, her twin braids flopping behind her. Her wood-bottom shoes clop-clopped on the stones, then fell silent when she reached the thick carpet.

She nearly tripped on her long linen dress, but caught herself and curtsied smartly. She looked straight into my eyes and smiled, a familiarity for which most other concubines would have slapped her. I smiled back.

9

Her words echoed off the walls in the sudden silence as she said, "The High Lord requests your presence, my lady."

Hate filled the room like smoke rising, twisting, reaching every crevice.

For a moment, as Lalandra's gaze flared with fury, I thought she might reach out to claw my face. I *would* have to address her burning hatred when I returned. And I *would* address this budding concubine rebellion with the High Lord in but a moment.

I stood my ground long enough to make sure they understood I was *not* fleeing, then followed Natta, knowing I was leaving smoldering embers behind me, embers that could at any moment burst into dangerous flames.

We hurried down narrow hallways lit by flickering torches. Shadows danced on the wool tapestries that depicted great Kadar battles.

Natta left me at the High Lord's quarters with a small bow and a big smile, hurrying on to finish her evening chores. She was a happy girl through and through, quick and smart, proud to be serving in the High Lord's palace.

Batumar kept no slaves, unlike some of the other warlords. All who served the High Lord served him of their free will.

I had seen little discord within the palace walls until the concubines had arrived. On that thought, I pushed the door open and stepped inside.

# CHAPTER TWO
## BATUMAR

"Lady Tera." Batumar awaited me in his antechamber.

As always, his obsidian gaze made me feel like he could see inside my heart. The color of his eyes matched his heavy mane of hair. His shaved face was sharp angled. An old scar ran from the corner of his eye to his chin, unbalancing the line of his lips. Newer scars, from the siege, broke up the pane of his cheek on the other side. Power sat on his shoulders, which were wider in his wool tunic than any other warrior's in full battle armor.

He was a fierce warlord through and through. I used to think he was the most fearsome man I had ever seen, but now the quickening of my pulse had nothing to do with fear.

"My lord." My heart stammered as his dark gaze slowly traveled the length of my body.

Did he like my gown of red satin? Red and gold were the High Lord's colors. The seed pearls that decorated the bodice caught the light of the torches, giving the whole dress a soft glow. The gold-embroidered hem swept the stones beneath my feet as I stepped forward, knowing that even in my finery I was not half as beautiful as Lady Lalandra.

The High Lord's gaze reached mine at last, and I saw hunger flare. He reached for me. I went to him and he pulled me into his strong arms, burying his scarred face in my neck and inhaling deeply, as if searching for the scent of our long-past summer.

The winds blowing across the cliffs of the fortress city had turned cold of late. Even the High Lord's palace walls couldn't keep out the early winter chill. But heat radiated off Batumar's great body, his arms around me a safe haven where I gladly rested.

A long moment passed before he raised his head and brushed his lips over mine, lingering, tasting me gently. My bones were melting by the time he withdrew.

"You looked troubled just now when you came in. Is everything well, my lady?"

His voice reached straight to my heart. I wished for nothing more than his lips back on mine.

"Fine well, my lord." But then I remembered what I had meant to talk to him about. "The concubines have...concerns."

His forehead furrowed. I ducked my head in shame.

He carried the weight of an entire island on his shoulders. Was I really so consumed by a small power struggle among concubines that I had forgotten the whole world was burning? I would handle the Lady Lalandra.

But before I could change the course of our conversation, he said, his voice suddenly weary, "Should I send them gifts?"

Concubines gained their status from the silks and satins and jewels that their lords gifted them with for their good service.

I stifled a sigh. "That might help. Maybe some furs for the winter."

I hated the base ugliness of jealousy, that it could so easily set up tent in my very heart. "And southern wine," I added.

Batumar's expression softened. He reached up and brushed his thumb over my bottom lip. "And what would you wish for, my lady?"

The easiest of all questions. "Only you, my lord."

He offered a rare smile that rearranged the scars on his face. My bruised heart responded. How could it not? His features were too stark, his scars too numerous to ever call him handsome, but he was most precious in my sight. I loved him with all my heart.

He took my hand and drew me into his bedchamber, to the bed where we lay on top of the furs, reclining on tapestry pillows against the headboard, fully clothed. We often began our evenings that way, talking in the warm glow of the fire that burned in the hearth.

To my shame, my gaze searched the chamber for signs of Lady Lalandra's presence the day before. I did not know what I expected to find, a veil or a silk stocking, but I saw nothing and swallowed a groan that I could be so foolish as to look.

Batumar gathered me against his side, my head resting on his wide chest. His heart beat strong and steady under my ear, his chest hard with muscles under my palm. I burrowed against him, trying to find the sense of peace that had eluded me all day.

The High Lord's quarters were as simple as any warrior's: a wool rug warmed the stone floor, a plain wooden chest at the foot of the High Lord's bed, a small table covered in maps. Yet I felt more at home here than in my own luxurious chamber in Pleasure Hall.

Before I could ask Batumar about the maps, he kissed my hair. "I must leave in the morning for Ishaf."

Had the mystical three-headed talking warthog of Morandor trotted through the door, I could not have been more startled.

I raised my head to look at him. "My lord, the Gate cannot be reclaimed. You cannot leave the island." Even if the Gate could be reopened, Batumar could not reach it through the ring of enemy soldiers.

He caressed my cheek with a finger callused from sword fight. "I mean to go by ship across the ocean."

That had me sitting up fully. My heart lurched hard against my ribs. No one sailed the wild ocean.

Batumar turned away from me and reached over to pull one of the tapestry maps off the table. He laid it over us like a blanket and dragged his finger along the route he planned to take. He started on Dahru, our island, the largest of the Middle Islands, charting a course across the Mirror Sea to the Strait of Ghel that led to the wild ocean.

Then he dragged his finger over a wide expanse of blue, all the way to the largest landmass on the map, Felep, called the mainland by its inhabitants that were of many nations, from the city states of Ishaf and Ker to the kingless kingdom of the Selorm, and many other countries.

Most of these realms had already been taken by the enemy and were part of the Emperor Drakhar's growing empire these days.

Batumar nodded as if satisfied with his course. "The trip must be made quickly, before the season of storms begins."

"There is no season of storms," I cried in distress. "The storms do not cease at all."

Endless hardstorms ruled the wild ocean throughout the year. Some believed the storms were at their quietest at the beginning of winter, but even so..."Nobody who has ever sailed the ocean has lived."

"They did once."

"Not since the hardstorms have come."

Before that, the ocean had been calmer, if legends could be believed, but that had been so long ago as to be at the very edges of human memory.

Batumar ran his large hand up my back in a gentle caress then down again, letting it settle at my waist. "I shall go with the pirates. I have it on good account that an Ishafi merchant turned pirate is even now making repairs to his ship in Barren Cove. He will be leaving to return to Ishaf within a day."

I stared at him, speechless.

The pirates were little more than a myth—a few scraggly ships now and then in a cove possibly hidden somewhere under the cliffs of Karamur. From time to time, they supposedly circled the Middle Islands and raided smaller merchant vessels.

Some merchants swore they had heard pirates brag about having crossed the ocean. *Nobody* but children believed those tales.

I searched Batumar's gaze. "Why would the Ishafi let a pirate ship come into their harbor?"

"Because this pirate doesn't attack Ishafi merchant ships." Then he added, "I must go. I shall hire a thousand mercenaries in the free cities of the north. The bank of Ishaf holds some gold coin for me."

A thousand mercenaries sounded a reasonable force. Yet I still did not like Batumar's plan in the least. From what I had heard—mostly servants' gossip—pirate ships were small sloops, built for speed.

"A pirate ship cannot carry a thousand mercenaries back to us." The plan was madness. All of it.

I considered the courses served for dinner, whether one of the herbs might have been accidentally switched by the cook, replaced with something that could cause this kind of loss of sanity.

I surreptitiously checked Batumar's pupils and laid a hand over his heart to see if his heartbeat was still steady. If I could puzzle out what herb he had eaten, I could give him the antidote. *What did he eat that I did not?*

He covered my hand with his. "The Landrians have a navy."

A laugh escaped me.

Dozens of small island cities made up Landria, their people living in grand isolation to protect the secrets of their dye-making industry. They produced a startling purple color—somehow with the help of sea snails—that was their prime export and the basis of their wealth. The older their king grew, the more suspicious he became of foreigners, seeing them all as spies.

"A foreigner approaching one of their city gates is as likely to be shot through with an arrow as let in." I repeated what I had heard from a wine merchant in the kitchen.

Batumar nodded. "*If* a person can even reach as far as setting foot on one of their islands. They have a full fleet of warships to ensure their isolation." Then he said, "Yet I must try."

I wished he wouldn't.

"Landria is far south from the free cities where you mean to hire your mercenaries." I marshaled my next objection. "And the lands in between are held by the enemy."

Batumar pulled another tapestry map off the table and laid it on top of the first, then pointed out the journey from Ishaf to Landria. "I mean to free the lands in between. Starting with Seberon. I pledged Lord Karnagh my assistance. He and other Selorm lords fought for us in the siege of Karamur with their battle tigers."

"But Castle Regnor has been taken. Lord Karnagh is thought to be slain," I said with a heavy heart. The last we'd heard of Seberon—the kingless kingdom of the Selorm—their lands had been overrun, but a warrior queen had risen in the south, a foreigner, holding their last free city.

"Last Lord Karnagh had been seen, he was on the brink of death," Batumar corrected, "and nobody has heard of him since. But death has a fair wide brink, my lady. You and I have both been there and have managed a return journey."

I could scarce argue with that.

Batumar said quietly, "I must help the Selorm, if I can. Our honor demands it."

I threw my hands up in defeat. "Oh, why not then the whole world, my lord. Easily done while you and your new mercenaries stop for your midday meal."

And from the somber look in his eyes, I could see that he *was* thinking it. "Not nearly enough men, and no time," he said at last. "We must cross the ocean with the Landrian warships during the spring lull."

The spring lull was yet another myth, a handful of days at winter's end, at around Yullin's Feast, when the hardstorms were thought to weaken ever so slightly.

How I wished I could make him see reason. "You cannot mean to sail the ocean, then cut a swath through enemy troops, freeing castles as you go, then negotiate with the King of Landria for use of his navy and sail across the ocean yet again, all in a few mooncrossings."

He tugged one of my braids free and wound a dark lock of hair around his finger. "Surprise will be on our side."

"For certain." I huffed. The enemy would not expect such a leap of insanity. "But how will the Landrian warships cross the wild ocean? Only the pirates know the way." *If* even that much was true and not a myth they themselves created.

"I shall hire the Ishafi pirate to lead the Landrian navy," Batumar said with confidence.

I could only stare at him as I imagined what the King of Landria would say to the suggestion that he turn his navy over to a *pirate*.

The whole plan was preposterous from beginning to end. The distance alone that would have to be covered...*Impossible.*

I ran my hand over the map that usually hung with all the others in the antechamber where the High Lord sometimes worked in the evenings, writing his letters or meeting with some of his most trusted advisors. I'd noticed some days ago that the maps had moved into his bedchamber. He had been planning this trip for a while. I thought he needed to plan it a good while longer yet, but I did not want to offend him by making that suggestion.

"You do not think my plan can be accomplished." He loosened another braid, then another, dissembling the intricate arrangement Natta had labored over that morning.

I shook my head.

Batumar's dark eyes seemed bottomless in the flickering light of the fire. "It is our only hope."

"And if Emperor Drakhar's sorcerer somehow reopens our Gate from afar while you are away? If more enemies arrive, they could destroy not only Karamur but all the Kadar strongholds, along with the Shahala lands."

And, the spirits forbid, what if the enemy entered the Guardians' Forgotten City? The Seela were the few remaining descendants of the First People, the custodians of the last of the ancient wisdom. The Forgotten City was the beating heart of our island. I feared that if it was destroyed, the whole island would simply sink into the sea.

Batumar relinquished the lock of hair he'd been playing with, took my hand and brought it to his lips. He kissed my knuckles. "The Gate will not fall."

And I heard the rest in his voice. If the Gate fell, it would not matter whether he had left or stayed. If the Gate fell, we were doomed. All of us would perish.

"You cannot go on a journey through war-torn lands as a lone warrior," I protested as I went into his arms. "Everyone will think you a spy. You will be pursued every step of the way."

"I mean to go in disguise."

*As what? A lonely beggar?*

Short of cutting off limbs, nothing could make him look anything other than what he was, the most powerful warrior of the land.

"As a merchant," he said.

Better than a rattle-bone beggar, but still…I looked up at him. "Without trade goods? Without servants?"

He frowned. "I cannot take trade goods. The pirates would seize them."

I laid my head back on his chest, while he returned to running his hand up and down my back. I desperately tried to think of something I could say to convince him to take me with him, and nearly fell off the bed in surprise when Batumar said in an even tone, "I wish to take you with me."

My gaze snapped up to his once again. "Why?"

"As perilous as the journey might be, I wish you under my own protection." He watched me carefully. "The Emperor knows of the prophecy that you are the one who will turn back the war."

His voice tightened. "The Guardian of the Cave told me that the Emperor knew of the prophecy even before you were born. He sent a man to your mother to kill you upon your birth. The Guardian seems to believe your mother softened the man's heart, so he could not kill you in the end. He sold you into slavery."

By the time Batumar finished, his jaw was so tense he could barely get the words through. But he managed to add, "You did not think this important enough to tell me."

I thought his anger most unfair. And worrying. Was this why he had sent for the Lady Lalandra the day before? Because I had displeased him?

If I were lost, he would still have a palace full of concubines, I wanted to tell him, but cast aside the childish impulse. "The Emperor wants to kill us all. If he desires me dead, a small measure more than all the others, what difference does it make?"

Batumar glowered. "It makes a difference to me. When Shartor came over the wall so close to you during the siege, that was not by chance. He meant to capture you. Or worse."

I shivered. Shartor, Karamur's soothsayer, had always wished for my death. But he could no longer hurt me. He had perished in the siege. *Best not to think of that now.*

I kept my silence for a while to let Batumar's anger lessen. I lay next to him without a word for as long as I could.

"In truth, I am to go with you?" I asked then with care, needing to hear the words again.

"You are not to leave my sight," he said roughly, and gathered me against him even more tightly, his strong arm holding me willing captive.

My heart thrilled. "We could go as a traveling healer and her guard."

And after a moment, he nodded. "But nobody can follow us to Barren Cove. Nobody can know that we left the island to cross the ocean. We must go in secret."

"How?"

His wide chest rose and fell. "There is a way."

I waited, seeing, for the first time, a small measure of doubt in his eyes.

At long last, he said, "We shall go through the mountain."

I stared at him. "A secret passage through the mountain to Barren Cove, then a journey on a pirate ship across the uncrossable ocean?" I shook my head. "Have I fallen into a children's tale, my lord?"

The corner of his lips twitched, and his hold on me relaxed. "Let us hope not, my lady. As I recall, many of those tales end most grimly."

"So there *is* a way through the mountain?" I never heard but the most superstitious servants talk about that before. To hear the High Lord of the Kadar utter such words shocked me more than a little.

"The tales are true."

I stared at him. "Everything?"

"They say dark spirits and old gods live deep inside the mountain."

"And you do not fear them?"

"Can they be worse than being overrun by the Kerghi?"

*They very possibly could be.* I did not say the words.

He let me go and sat up, undressed for sleep. When he unlaced my gown in the back, I undressed too, leaving on only my shift.

When we were under the furs, he gathered me back to him. He kissed the corner of my eye, then the corner of my lips. But even as I craved his touch, I thought, *did he kiss the Lady Lalandra yesterday?*

I pressed my lips together, hating that thought with every fiber of my being.

He leaned his forehead against my temple and expelled air from his lungs, his warm breath fanning my neck. "We might not get much sleep for a long time to come. I should not take advantage of you this way. Tonight we rest."

*Because Lady Lalandra was here yesterday?* The bitter taste of jealousy bubbled up my throat. I swallowed it. *Think of something else.*

The fire popped and crackled in the hearth.

"Have you been inside the mountain before, my lord?"

He did not answer at once. He closed his eyes for a moment then opened them again. "Vooren's grandfather has. And he lived to tell the tale."

Vooren was one of the High Lord's stewards. Since Batumar's last words sounded hesitant, I waited, and when he said nothing more, I prodded. "My lord?"

"He did not come out as he went in."

"How so?"

"He went in with nine other warriors, all men in their prime. He was the only one to return, aged to an old man in a mooncrossing's time, his hair white, his back stooped, his eyes blind."

Unease slithered up my spine. "What did he say?"

"He did not talk much for the rest of his life, but once or twice to his eldest son. Before he died, he passed on the secret of safe passage. And his son, on his deathbed, told his own son, Vooren."

*Impossible*, I thought for the dozenth time.

Yet I found I could not worry about our journey, for I found it far out of the realm of all possibility. One perilous threat I could have feared. But the plan had so many as to make comprehension impossible.

In truth, I only half believed there would be a journey. I would not have been surprised if we set out and found no path through the mountain. And even if we somehow found our way through or around the mountain and found the hidden cove, I could not fathom finding pirate ships in it, certainly no ship that would brave the hardstorms of the wild ocean.

On all that, I was wrong. Were that I were right. For never have I regretted anything as I grew to regret the dawn when we left the fortress city.

# CHAPTER THREE
## DARK PASSAGE

*"They say dark spirits and old gods live deep inside the mountain."* Batumar's words echoed in my dreams. Troubling images haunted my sleep, dangerous caverns that threatened to swallow me up, invisible eyes watching.

The High Lord woke me before the first light of dawn with a gentle kiss, but I could not shake my dark premonitions. Even in his arms, I shivered.

He dressed quickly, plainly like any ordinary warrior, not that he could ever look ordinary. He was a man born to lead, strength evident in his every move.

My own Shahala tunic and pants, along with a pair of scuffed, fur-lined leather boots, waited at the foot of the bed. A quilted wool cape would keep out the chill of winter. Batumar had even my healer's veil brought in.

"I mean to take some herbs," I said as I pulled on my clothes. Having my herbs near me always made me feel better, and we would likely need them on our journey. Even if we did not, I needed them for my traveling healer disguise to be complete.

I caught Batumar's gaze on me, and I thought I saw hunger flare in his eyes, but it might have been a trick of the dim light.

He looked away, draped a heavy fur cloak over his own shoulders, and picked up the lone candle to inspect the maps one more time. The scars on his face were more pronounced in candlelight.

That light was a small circle around us, nothing but darkness outside it, as if we were already in the belly of the mountain. I shivered.

"My lord," I began, then hesitated. What use was it to tell him that I felt danger all around?

He looked up, waited. Then, when I still said nothing, he set down the candle. "We must make haste."

So I hurried to the kitchen, where I wrapped bunches of herbs in cloth and hung the little bundles from my belt. Since the belt could not hold everything, I took a paring knife and cut small holes in the inside quilting of my hip-length tunic and stuffed more herbs in there. And then I did the same with my wool cloak, loading even more herbs into the lining.

When I thought I had everything I would most likely need, I found a simple leather sheath for the knife and tied that to my belt as well.

I did not go by Pleasure Hall; I hurried straight to the High Lord's quarters, where the steward, Vooren, already waited in the antechamber.

He was a gaunt man, with a scrawny neck and one lazy eye, but with much kindness in him. He had greatly helped me with my healing work after the siege by providing all the supplies, no matter what he had to do to obtain the items I needed.

"My lady." He bowed deeply, torchlight glinting off his bald head. When he straightened, worry lines crisscrossed his narrow face. "Are you certain?"

"Most certain. You need not worry about me, Vooren."

Batumar strode from his bedchamber, fastening his sword belt, with the great broadsword he carried to battle, not the ceremonial, jeweled sword of the High Lord.

He attached two water flasks to the belt on his other side, next to a food sack already hanging there. When he finished, he stepped over to me and looped two more water flasks onto my belt, which were immediately lost among the bunches of herbs.

As the last step for our preparations, he picked up the coil of rope the steward must have brought, and looped it around his torso, diagonally from shoulder to hip, over and over, until he reached the end, which he tucked in securely.

I thought all this most sensible, except maybe the size of the food sack.

Batumar caught my gaze. "More would be difficult to carry through the mountain. But the pirates will stop at Rabeen before sailing out to the open sea. I shall purchase more supplies at the market."

I relaxed a little. Maybe he *had* planned the journey more carefully than I had thought. Rabeen was the last small island before the inhabited rocky Strait of Ghel, through which we would sail.

Batumar nodded at Vooren, and the steward grabbed the lone torch from its sconce and led the way.

We moved down hallways and stairs rapidly, for the servants would wake any moment. The lowest levels of the palace waited, and we cut through storage rooms, then the dungeons, mercifully empty, then down more dark stairways.

We were in the very lowest level of the palace, a level I had not known existed. No sconces had been hammered into the walls. I did not think the servants ever came down here.

At the next turn, a sack waited with unlit torches, and another with more food and water the steward must have prepared for our journey. These we took with us, but not far.

Vooren reached a dead end where old flags leaned against the wall by the dozen, their colors faded, their fabric moth-eaten. For a moment, I thought he had lost his way, but he and Batumar moved to set the flags aside, and, as we all choked on the dust, a rock wall appeared with a heavy cast-iron door in the middle.

The chain sealing the door was as thick as my arm, gleaming darkly in the flickering light, secured by iron loops in the bedrock, fastened with a cast-iron padlock the size of my head.

The steward handed Batumar the burning torch, then lifted an ancient key from his belt and forced it into the ancient lock with considerable trouble. He had to use both hands to turn the key.

Then Batumar handed the torch back to him and, straining and grunting, pulled the enormous chain free, dropping it to the ground in a heap. The three of us were needed to open the door that creaked on its hinges, the sound like a warning scream from an ancient spirit.

My heart clenched.

The darkness that gaped beyond the door was absolute, the stale air that rushed out so cold as to be unnatural. It had a taste I could feel on my tongue even after I pressed my lips tightly together, a coating like thin slime made out of fear.

A shiver of apprehension skittered up my spine, prickling my skin like a needle-legged centipede. For no reason at all, I suddenly thought of my great-grandmother the sorceress. I had a strong sense of something coiled at the heart of all the darkness, lying in wait.

I was awash in a premonition that by crossing the threshold, we were doing something that could be never undone.

I watched with dread as Vooren stepped in first, torch held high. Batumar gestured for me to follow the man. I could not hesitate. If I did, if the High Lord knew I had fear in my heart, he might yet change his mind and leave me here under the protection of the Palace Guard. I gritted my teeth and moved forward. Batumar followed close behind.

*Sprit, be strong. Heart, be brave.*

I drew small breaths of the frigid, stale air, thick with the smell of mold and long-dead things. The goose bumps on my arms became permanent when, after but a few steps, the passageway widened into a great cavern.

I could only judge the size by the echoes of our footsteps. Our torchlight touched neither the walls nor the ceiling. As we progressed forward, I had the strong sense of being watched, but when I closed my eyes and reached out with my spirit, I could sense no other life beyond the three of us.

"What is this place?" I asked Batumar, barely daring to breathe the words.

Vooren answered me instead. "An ancient temple, my lady." He too kept his voice to a whisper, as if here lived things best not disturbed.

"Whose temple?" The question slipped out without thought, and I wished I could call it back.

But Vooren had wisdom enough not to answer. Dark spirits and old gods were best not named in a place like this. To name them would be to call them.

All sense of time and space disappeared as we felt our way forward on uneven ground. Nothing existed but the three of us and our small circle of light.

I knew of distant people who believed that a man's spirit journeys through a dark underworld after death, to be reborn again in light. I thought now I knew what such a journey might look like. And hoped we would indeed someday again see the winter sun.

I could not fathom how the steward knew which way to go. We could have been walking around in circles. If we suddenly reached our entry point again, I would not have been surprised.

But, as if knowing what I was wondering, Vooren stopped and lowered his torch so I could see what I had missed before.

A black handprint on the stone under our feet.

I blanched with recognition. *Old blood.*

*Blood sacrifice?* All the fine hairs on my body stood straight up.

But the steward said in a voice laden with gratitude, "My grandfather had marked out a safe path."

We proceeded forward, then suddenly reached the end of the cavernous space and entered a narrow corridor carved into the rock, the passageway here low even for me. Batumar had to duck his head as he followed.

And then the walls closed around us even tighter. Soon we were on our hands and knees, crawling forward, sharp rocks cutting into my palms. Vooren before me stirred up ancient dust, making even breathing difficult.

When a more spacious passageway opened to our left, the steward passed it by. I barely caught sight of a black mark on the wall by the opening before the torchlight moved on. My body ached to straighten. I opened my mouth to beg the steward to take the easier way.

But before I could have uttered a word, he said, "That passageway is where my grandfather lost his sight. In there, my father told me, poison weeps from the walls."

I shuddered as we crawled forward.

And crawled and crawled until my arms and legs shook from exhaustion, my back cramping. Despite the cold, sweat beaded on my forehead.

"Night must have fallen outside by now," Batumar said behind me. "We should rest."

He was probably only stopping for my sake and the old steward's, but neither of us protested. We collapsed where we were, then rolled onto our backs. The ceiling of our tunnel was so low that I could have easily reached out and touched it.

Batumar passed forward the food sack. "Something to eat."

I took a chunk of bread and dried fish, then passed the sack along to Vooren. We each had our own water flasks.

We ate and drank, then tried to sleep, but sleep would not come. The belly of the mountain was not a place to close our eyes, even with the torch still burning.

Wailing screams sounded in the distance, otherworldly shrieks. Nothing but the wind blowing through crevices in the rock high above us, I told myself, but I could not make myself believe it, and my stomach clenched with every new sound.

When an eternity later we began moving again—it might have been morning outside by that time—I was more exhausted than when we had stopped.

We scarce spoke on that second day, not even when the ceiling dropped yet again. We slid forward on our stomachs in silence, except when we were coughing from the ancient dust. I crawled with extra care so I would not lose my bundles of healing herbs.

Our water flasks banged and scraped along the rock, and so did the sheath of Batumar's sword, making our procession a noisy one, regardless of whether we talked or not. If any dark spirits guarded the mountain, they would have no trouble finding us. I shivered at the thought.

Then, at long last, we reached a cave where we could straighten. The air had the smell of rotten eggs.

"The sulfur caves," the steward said, lifting his cloak to cover his nose. "We must have taken a wrong turn. Hurry on."

We all but ran, stumbling forward.

And *then* the dark spirit found us.

One moment I was between Batumar and Vooren, following the steward's bobbing light. The next I was alone in the darkness, the smell of sulfur was gone, and I was colder than if I had been encased in ice.

The spirit hissed in a deep tone. "Why cometh you, Sorceress?" The sound, slimy and sticky, slid along my skin.

He was so close I could feel his fetid breath on my face. Cadaverous fingers caressed my face, seven or eight on one hand, all ending in sharp talons. I shuddered at the touch.

I had to work at gaining enough courage to speak.

"I am no sorceress, great spirit." My voice trembled.

Courtesy required that I say, *I am your humble servant*, but I did not dare speak the words, lest they gave the spirit power over me.

He waited, then issued an impatient hiss when he realized I would not be so easily tricked. "Cometh you to ask for power? What have you brought to trade for it?"

I wanted naught to do with dark powers. "We are but passing through. We did not mean to disturb you. We beg you to forgive us."

The spirit dragged his talons across my throat. I could feel the sharp tips scoring my skin and held still.

"Have you brought a sacrifice, then, to pay for your passage?" he demanded.

Numb with fear, I thought of all I had, my little paring knife the most valuable thing upon my person. Offering so meager a sacrifice would have been an insult.

Then I thought of the price that had been exacted from Vooren's grandfather: his sight. Suddenly I felt as if the cold and the darkness were inside me, swirling in my stomach. Nausea rose in my throat.

The spirit laughed. "No sacrifice?" He howled. Then he whispered, and the sound was more frightening than the howling. "No matter. Kratos takes what he will."

I could not move. Fear was all around me. I had gone temporarily blind from an injury during the siege. *To live life in that darkness*—the thought closed my throat. But the next thought scared me more.

*What if the toll is taken from Batumar?*

A warlord could not lose his strength, or his sight, not in the middle of a war.

"Take what you will from *me*, great spirit," I begged.

"Of your free will?" he whispered with dark delight.

My stomach clenched with dread. "Of my free will. Only let us leave the mountain."

The spirit said no more, but his terrible laughter echoed off the cavern walls as he left me, the sound of otherworldly hyenas.

Complete darkness surrounded me. I did not know where I was. I felt terribly lost, as if I could never possibly find my way back to light and those I loved.

When, out of nowhere, taloned hands clamped over my shoulders, I screamed.

But then Batumar called, right next to me, "Tera!" his voice filled with urgency.

My eyes fluttered open. I did not know they had been closed. We were in a new passageway. I was lying on the ground, Batumar and Vooren ashen-faced on their knees, peering over me.

Batumar had his hand on my shoulder, not the dark spirit. I drew a ragged breath. "You found me."

"I will always find you." He gathered me up and held me to him.

"Let her breathe, my lord," Vooren advised gently.

And Batumar drew back, just enough to look me over, the muscles in his face tight. "You fell ill from the sulfur."

Had I? The dark spirit's heinous laugher still rang in my ears. *Had he been real? Was our bargain?*

I blinked. I could most certainly see. The spirit had not taken my sight. In a panic, I struggled to my feet, nearly knocking Batumar over.

Relief cut through me. I could stand. The spirit had not taken my strength either.

I filled my lungs with musty, ancient air, no trace of rotten eggs here. Maybe the dark spirit *had* been a hallucination from the sulfur gas.

But then I reached up to my throat, and I could feel the droplets of blood where the sharp talons had raked my skin.

Batumar stood and moved the light closer. "You must have scratched yourself while you thrashed." Then he added, "We shall stay and rest."

My heart racing, I shook my head. I wanted to be away from this place. I wanted to be out of the mountain.

"Best not." The steward agreed with me and was moving forward already.

I followed. Then, finally, so did Batumar, staying even closer to me than before.

Soon we reached another low passage. I went to my knees and hands without complaint. I would have done anything to keep moving.

We passed other passageways, wider and taller than ours. But the steward did not alter our course for some time, and when he did, our new path was as tight as the last.

I heard water running in the distance, and fear filled my bones at the thought of that water coming into our narrow tunnel and drowning us. But instead of water, other things moved in the darkness here, things that slithered and scurried by us, on top of us.

*Living things.* These I did not mind half as much as the bloodless, hissing dark spirit.

"Just a little longer, my lady," said the steward up ahead, breathless from effort.

He was right. Soon our passageway expanded enough so we could stand once again.

As we stumbled forward, over the loose rocks that now covered the path, I heard bats swarming above, disturbed by the noise of our passing. Then I could see light ahead at last, *the spirits be blessed*, and could smell fresh, salty air.

My relief was so sharp, it nearly hurt. "The tunnel's end!"

I rushed toward the circle of light, passing Vooren. Then had to halt when I saw that the opening led to a sheer drop onto rocks below, the gray sea churning furiously, like boiling metal. Even as I leaned forward to look, the wind pushed me back, my cloak flapping.

Batumar's strong arm caught me around the waist, and he pulled me against his chest. "Careful."

But his voice held relief, enough to make me wonder if he had been as certain about the mountain passage as he led me to believe.

"That gust will help us stick to the rock face," he said over my head.

And, after a moment, he pulled away, shed the rope from his shoulder, then shrugged off his fur cloak and laid it on the ground a few steps inside the opening. He pointed at the sun, low in the sky, half-lost in haze. "It is early in the morning still. We are in time. We will rest before we climb down."

Now that I could see the sky and smell the sea, I could agree. I settled down next to him.

Vooren shed his cloak and sat a few paces from us. He offered us biscuits from his own food sack, and we accepted with thanks. He still had enough for his return, and we had enough to reach the markets of Rabeen, if indeed any pirate ships waited in some hidden cove. If not, I silently swore to go the long way around on our way back to Karamur. I did not ever want to journey through the mountain again.

I ate enough to sate my hunger, but not so much that I would be too full to climb down. We drank sparingly. When we were done, I leaned against Batumar, for the heat of his body and for the sense of well-being his touch gave me.

He put his arms around me, and we relaxed against each other. I took my first easy breath. We were out of the mountain, and the dark spirit had not swooped in to take what he willed from me. His mockery and menace had been nothing but a dream.

Yet even as I thought that, I felt a cold invisible talon caress the side of my face.

# CHAPTER FOUR
## THE DOOMED

*Kratos,* the dark spirit had called himself when he had held me in thrall. I did not dare ask Vooren as we rested, for I did not dare speak the name.

As if sensing my unease, Batumar tightened his arm around me. "We best not rest long. We must reach the ship before it sails."

I drew away from him to stand, more than ready to be away from the mountain. If we missed the ship, all we had gone through so far would be for naught.

While I inspected my bundles of herbs and retied some to be more secure, Batumar set up the rope, tying one end to an outcropping of rock inside the opening, then testing the strength of the knot.

When he was satisfied, he dropped the rest of the rope over the ledge to unfurl on the side of the cliff. "I shall go first."

He rolled his fur cloak into a bundle and tied it onto his back, stepped over the edge without hesitation, then began lowering himself, hand over hand. I peeked over the edge, my heart in my throat as I watched him.

He stopped and looked up. "Come carefully."

*Heart, be brave.* I bundled up my cloak and tied it to my back as he had. I kept reminding myself that I was good at climbing, had climbed all the tallest trees in my childhood to collect the healing drops of moonflowers.

Vooren said, "May the spirits keep you and bring you back to us."

The words were heartfelt, but as I turned, I could see in his sunken eyes that he did not expect such a happy reunion. I thought he was most noble-hearted for worrying about us. He would now have to return through the mountain all alone. I would not have traded places with him for all the world.

"The spirits keep you," I responded as I gripped the rope. Then I stepped over the ledge.

*Spirit, be strong. Heart, be brave.* Those words had been my mother's last message to me. I planned to hold them close on our journey.

The wind hit me at once, coming in from the sea in an angry squall. I held on tightly, glad to be wearing my Shahala healer's clothes that allowed for climbing instead of the billowing dress of a concubine the wind would have used as a sail to blow me clear off the cliffs.

The rough rope bit into my hand. I ignored the burn.

The first stretch of rock was a sheer cut, no crevices for foothold, slippery from the moist sea air, like walking on ice. I lowered myself carefully, handhold over handhold at least a hundred times before the surface turned more scraggly. Once I could find a foothold, I moved my feet from the rope to the rock, but held on to the rope with my hands as tightly as I had before.

Old bones littered the larger crevices, both animal and human, nearly petrified. I had to move to the side to avoid stepping on a grinning skull bleached by weather and time.

Buffeted by the winds, our climb was slow and seemed to take as long as the endless journey through the dark belly of the mountain. Countless times my feet slipped, but I held on to the rope, and that saved me. I hung on by sheer will and for fear that if I fell, I might knock Batumar down with me.

By the time my feet touched the rocky shore below, my muscles were shaking, my face was chapped, my eyes all teared up, and my hair had come fully undone, whipping around me in the wind.

But Batumar looked at me with nothing but pride and approval in his eyes. "Well done, my lady."

His words warmed me, but he meant to warm me further. He unwrapped his fur cloak and fastened it onto his wide shoulders, then drew me against him, tucking me under. I burrowed against him and soaked up his heat, clinging to him with my arms around his waist, grateful to be standing on solid ground once again.

"The people who lived on the side of the mountain before the Kadar came," he said into my hair, "used the passages of the mountain as their temples. They sacrificed greatly to their god, casting below even some of their children."

I had a dark suspicion who that god might be.

"Kratos?" My voice was muffled against his chest, so I tilted my head up to him.

Batumar nodded, an eyebrow lifting in surprise that I would know. "Rorin's father."

Rorin was the god of war Kadar warlords and their people worshipped.

I turned to look up at the opening we had come through, now impossibly high above us. Our rope was moving up, re-coiled by the steward.

Batumar said, "We have managed fine well thus far, my lady. We are probably the only people ever to leave through The Mouth of the Mountain and live."

He was right. The first step of our journey had been taken safely. I gave silent thanks to the spirits.

When the rope and Vooren disappeared, I extricated myself from Batumar's heavy cloak, stepped back, and checked him over, seeing his disguise for the first time in the full light of day.

The success of our next step depended on not being recognized. If the pirates discovered who we truly were, instead of transporting us across the ocean, they would hold us for ransom.

Batumar's cloak was old and worn in patches. He wore a simple wool tunic under it. His winter boots, treated leather on the outside that would not allow water through, warm fur within, were scuffed aplenty. At his side hung his broadsword, no different than any warrior might take to battle, the kind of sword that fathers handed down to their sons.

His dark mane was shaggy now from the wind, like any warrior's, not like a proper lord's who had concubines to comb it. The siege had sewn silver threads through that once ebony hair. His face unshaven, with his scars, he might yet pass for the type of soldier who would hire himself out as a guard for a dangerous journey.

"Where do the other warlords think you have gone?" I asked as I combed my hair into order with my fingers, then drew my healer's veil from under my tunic and wrapped the length of yellow satin tightly around my head.

"They think we are journeying to your Shahala lands to assess the damage and loss of life. And to negotiate the purchase of oil, in case of another siege."

During the siege of Karamur, we had poured burning oil from the top of the walls on the attacking enemy below. Nary a drop was to be found now in the city, not even in the High Lord's palace.

Batumar glanced to the sky. "Only Lord Samtis knows the truth. I left him in charge of protecting Karamur in my absence."

I wanted to ask more, but Batumar led the way around an outcropping that reached into the sea, and here the waves were too loud for us to talk. Each step required our full attention, so we struggled forward in silence for a while.

No ships bobbed on the water along the shore, nor farther out at sea, but as we rounded the outcropping, a hidden cove did appear as Batumar had predicted. And there, in calmer waters, sat a quick little sloop, along with a much larger merchant schooner, seabirds circling around their red sails. Both ships were manned, both looking ready to cast off.

I stared, feeling as if I had walked into a children's tale. "Pirate ships both."

"Merchant ships do not visit pirate coves, if they can help it. Rorin be blessed, we are not late."

I shared Batumar's relief, but not without some trepidation mixed in. *Will they take us? Why would they? Why not slay us here? Or take us into slavery?*

Now that I could see the pirates with my own eyes, they suddenly seemed frighteningly real and our plan poorly thought out once again. But despite my misgivings, I hurried behind Batumar, even as I struggled to hold my cloak closed so the wind wouldn't whip it around me and tug me off-balance, watching my footing on the rocks that were slippery from sea spray.

I could see how Barren Cove earned its name. Nothing but rocks, not a blade of grass, not a single spot of green.

Once we reached closer, I understood why pirates would choose this particular cove. Beyond a quiet spot to repair storm damage, the far end of the cove also provided fresh water from a stream that trickled forth from among the rocks.

Four men were filling a row of oak barrels. They wore snug, black wool pants and shirts, their long hair tied back with colorful rags. Curved swords hung from their wide belts, an assortment of daggers stuck in the back. As those men paid no mind to us, I turned my attention back to the ships.

Only a handful of men worked aboard the sloop, but the merchant schooner was better manned. Dozens of swarthy men hurried with their duties on and around it. I took in the two tall mainmasts and a shorter foremast, the red sails marked with symbols and patterns of faraway lands I did not recognize.

Some of the crew were making last-minute repairs, others prepared the schooner to set sail, and yet others were rolling water barrels—lids nailed down—up the plank that connected the ship to shore.

The pirates regarded us with sideways glances, keeping track of our progress, but as a single warrior and a woman presented no threat, they did not interrupt their preparations.

Batumar strode to the merchant schooner as boldly as if he were an expected guest, his stride strong and sure, yet not the regal stride of a High Lord. His gait and posture transformed into that of an ordinary foot soldier. He ignored the pirates coming and going and eyed the tallest man on board, who wore a round hard hat decorated with seagull feathers.

Batumar called up, even his tone different, sounding as if he'd grown up on the docks of Kaharta Reh. "Greetings to the captain."

The man measured him up with a cold glance. Then he looked me over and smiled, showing a single black tooth on the bottom.

"We wish to book passage," Batumar said with the deference of a man talking to someone he is asking for a favor.

I could but stare at him, so changed was his entire demeanor.

The captain scoffed. "Ye got yer eyes up yer arse?" He jerked his head toward the red sails above him that clearly designated them as pirates. "We take nay passengers."

Batumar reached under his cloak and retrieved a small leather pouch. "Ten blue crystals for taking us across the ocean."

No sooner had he said the words than he was attacked from behind. One pirate grabbed his elbows and jerked them back; another held a knife to his throat. Before I could decide what to do, the third pirate divested him of his coin, then tossed the pouch up to the captain. I was left standing there, gaping, my hand closed around the small paring knife that hung from my belt, hidden by my cloak from the men.

"Twenty blue crystals," Batumar said without fighting back. "It is all we have."

"'Tis what I got. Ye got shite." The captain jerked his head toward his men.

They released Batumar, one eyeing his cloak, the other his sword, no doubt picking out what they would take once they managed to subdue him and tied him up to be sold at the nearest slave market, or planning to cut him down if he fought too hard.

But Batumar did not move to fight. Instead, he pulled back his cloak and showed our food sack. "We have our own food. We will not be any trouble. I can help on deck."

Batumar was a strong man, and a ship could always use more muscle. But the captain shook his head, returning his gaze to me with a speculative gleam in his beady eyes that I did not like. I had been sold into slavery before.

I stepped forward and held my head high, tucking in the edge of my Shahala healer's veil so it would not flutter in the wind. "I am a traveling healer. The passage is a dangerous one. You might yet need my skill."

He sucked his black tooth and narrowed his eyes at me. "Why are ye leavin' Karamur?"

I was certain he already had my worth calculated, and Batumar's, along with how many men he would lose while subduing my guard.

Yet his ship was our only chance to bring help for our people. I stood tall before him. "The siege is long over. There are few to heal, and those prefer the Lady Tera. No room for a simple traveling healer now."

He watched me for a long moment. "And the Gate is broken. Bloody Kerghi bastards." He spat, returning his gaze to Batumar. "Ye nay have the look of a fool. 'Tis a mighty foolish thing, seekin' passage with pirates."

The two men spent a tense moment staring at each other in silence, each measuring up the other all over again.

Batumar spoke first. "Tatip the Cutthroat said you were the most honest pirate he knew."

The captain spat over the railing into the sea. "Insulting me will nay get ye on my ship." He spat again. "Never did like mine idiot brother."

"He said you might say that. He said you owed him a favor." Batumar kept his tone easy, even jesting.

"How's that?"

Batumar's lips twitched. "He said he will give your woman a good poking whilst you are at sea. Teach her about the ways of real men."

For a moment, none of the pirates on board or on shore drew a breath, and, in the sudden tension, I couldn't either. Then the hard expression on the captain's face dissolved as he broke into laughter, and the others laughed with him.

He shook his head, the feathers in his hat waving madly as he called down, "I'll take ye to Ishaf." He flashed a dark, terrifying grin. "Ye'll be as safe with us as on mine mother's own lap."

I sighed a breath of relief, although I had doubts about how nice the pirate captain's mother had been if she had produced a son such as this, and another that had *cutthroat* for a nickname.

Batumar kept his hand near his sword as we walked up the plank. I followed a few steps behind to give him room to move, should this be a trap. The roughly hewn wood swayed perilously under us, cold waves churning below, as if hoping for our misstep. But we made it aboard without incident.

Some of the men watched us openly; others paid as little attention to us as they did to the seabirds. Two pirates, right in our path, were having

37

a contest over who had more injuries. They were measuring scars, stripping off clothes. The taller one was nearly naked.

We stepped around them.

When Batumar walked straight up to the captain, I stopped a distance away, once again giving the High Lord room to defend himself should he be set upon. I prayed to the spirits for our safety.

"I am Umar," he said, using a common name he had no doubt picked out for the journey beforehand. "The mistress's hired guard."

The captain spat. "How do ye know my shite-for-brains brother?"

"I did some small favor for him during the siege."

I knew nothing of this. Since no imminent danger seemed afoot, I moved up next to Batumar, which I immediately regretted since I could suddenly smell the captain, four full steps away.

"I am Mistress Onra." I used the first name that came to mind, that of the first true friend I had made on Kadar land.

She had suffered with me as a slave, then suffered more during the battle. But she was safely inside Karamur's walls now, married to a kindly baker. She oft visited me at the palace.

The pirate captain watched me. "One-Tooth Tum." He ran his tongue over his black tooth. "Was born with this one, I was. Chewed mine way out of mine mother with it." He flashed another dark grin.

I did my best to look half-frightened, half-impressed. I suspected pirates were fond of their terrible reputations. But I had birthed enough babes to know that none had chewed their way anywhere. They were all pushed into the world the regular way, which was difficult enough without adding any horrors to it.

He must have been satisfied with my reaction, because he turned back to Batumar. "We'll stop at Rabeen tomorrow before sailin' out into the storms. If this floatin' tub cannay get ye through the storms, naything will."

The man puffed out his chest. "Welcome onboard the *Doomed*." Then he gestured toward the sloop with his head. "And that would be the *Damned*. They but sail round the island." He spat again. "Bunch o' fair-weather rats."

Batumar glanced toward the dark hole that led belowdecks. "Would there be a cabin for us, Captain?"

The captain laughed, a bellowing sound that came straight from his belly. "Ye think yer on some southern king's barge?" He sucked his tooth, then scratched his chin. "Ye cannot sleep onboard in a storm, fer damn certain."

He called a ragged boy of about twelve summers off the mainmast next to us. "Show 'em below, Pek. Past the grain sacks. Be quick with it, ye wee bastard."

Pek shot across the ship, quick as an eel.

Entering the dark belly of the ship made my skin pucker.

I had once gone aboard a slaver to heal their sick cargo, but they locked me in a cabin instead and sailed with me to a cold Kadar port, sold me as a slave to a hard lord. Before Batumar claimed me, I had lived some difficult times under the rule of a cruel concubine, and I had the scars of flogging on my back to prove it.

But on the *Doomed*, we were not set upon in the dark passageway. Our only inconvenience was the rats that scurried along without paying us much attention. We had to step over them when we crossed paths. They seemed disinclined to move out of our way.

"A ship full of rats is a happy ship," Pek said with a sinister chuckle.

I did not understand his meaning then. I came to understand it later.

We headed aft, following Pek's wiry frame. His clothes were dirty and rent, too large on him, likely hand-me-downs from the other pirates. He pointed over his bony shoulder toward the prow. "Best ye dinnay stray near the captain's cabin up there. He might think yer after his treasure."

He made a sharp, cutting gesture over his throat with his grimy hand, his face lighting up with mirth when I blanched.

He led us to a cramped, dank storage room filled about three-quarters of the way with potato sacks. Already, some of the sacks were covered in mold and rot.

I poked the lumpy cargo. "Are we to sleep on top of that?"

"Aye. Best watch 'em in a storm when they roll about," the boy said with no small amount of glee. "Likely ye'll be crushed to death."

*A strange boy.*

When he left us, whistling, I climbed on top of the stacks that reached to just under the porthole.

Batumar stayed in the small clear space in front of the door, his hand still on his sword. "If they are to attack us, they will do it either as soon as the ship is clear of the island or just as we reach Rabeen."

My heart clenched.

He watched me with an unfathomable look in his dark eyes as the ship began to move slowly out of the cove first, then faster once it reached open water and all the sails unfurled. The sound of them snapping above in the wind reached us below in the cabin.

I smiled to make sure the High Lord did not think I regretted accompanying him on his journey. Then I shifted, trying to find a spot comfortable enough for settling in. The bags made a lumpy bed. We had room to sit but not to stand.

"Here." Batumar laid his fur cloak down, and that helped matters once I rearranged myself anew on top.

He opened the thick-glassed porthole for me, and I watched as our island grew smaller, then soon disappeared. Sadness washed over me, and an odd sense of grief.

We had fought hard in the siege and lost many good people. The stone walls of the city had been repaired, but we barely had warriors enough to man those walls. And the enemy had learned our weaknesses, would use them against us when they attacked again.

We had to return with help. Eventually, the enemy would find a way to open the Gate from the other side. If Karamur fell, the whole island would fall. All of our people would die, or worse, become slaves.

"Why is the Emperor so set on taking our island?" I asked. "Dahru has no great treasure. The Shahala live in their huts and heal. The Kadar are great warriors, but truly, just soldiers when it comes down to it, with no special powers. Between us, the Desert of Sparkling Death, with its poisonous minerals."

"He must have discovered that our Gate is the Gate of the World," Batumar said, tight-lipped.

My breath caught. The hardstorms made sailing the ocean nearly impossible—if not altogether impossible; that remained to be seen. Only the Gates allowed transport from kingdom to kingdom. Each Gate opened a portal to nearby Gates. But the Gate of the World, a well-kept secret on Dahru, could reach all other Gates. If the Emperor possessed it, he could conquer the entire world with his darkness.

"He wants to be the Emperor of the Four Quarters." Batumar's words confirmed my thoughts.

I swallowed painfully. *We must not fail.* "All has happened according to your plan. We left the palace unseen, we found our way through the mountain, and we are on a ship."

Batumar kept guard, dipping his head toward the door to listen for sounds outside. "Boarding a pirate ship is not the hardest part, my lady. I fear that leaving it on our own terms will prove the greater difficulty."

# CHAPTER FIVE
## RABEEN

Safe for the moment, we both slept, exhausted from our journey through the mountain. I awoke the next morning in good spirits, but then suddenly remembered that Rabeen had a renowned slave market. Would our journey end there?

Before I could ask Batumar, who was already awake and sitting up, he held out our ravaged food sack toward me with a grimace. "The rats ate our food in the night."

I blinked to see better in the dim light, then stared at the holes in the burlap. My stomach growled in protest as I silently cursed the rats and sat up to stretch. "Why didn't they eat the potatoes?"

The great, lumpy pile under us did not appear the least diminished. After a moment's inspection, I found that the potato sacks' strong fibers had been soaked in some kind of substance that I had mistaken for mold and rot the day before.

I rubbed my fingers over the mystery coating and held it up to my nose, sniffed. I detected no scent. "I wish I knew what it is. It would serve well at the palace. And it might be useful for other purposes."

Batumar watched me with mild amusement. He often teased me that my first thoughts were always herbs. I suppose that was common enough for a healer.

I pulled our own destroyed burlap sack on my lap, fingering it as my stomach growled again. "Do we have any crystals to purchase food, my lord?"

On our island, people still used blue crystals in trade, mined with great effort in the poison desert, as was our ancient tradition. But in most of the world, gold coins were exchanged, a material not as precious, the coins easily struck.

"Our coin should be enough until we reach Ishaf," Batumar said.

I nodded. In truth, going hungry for a day or two was the least of our worries. I tugged at a loose thread of burlap until it came free. "I wish I had a needle." Now that I had thread.

Batumar reached into his boot and pulled out his dagger. He turned to the wall and cut a sliver from the rough plank, then pressed his blade into the thicker end, splitting the wood, but not all the way.

He handed it to me on his palm, sidling closer. "How is this?"

I grinned my answer and wedged the end of my thread into the split that gripped the thread tightly. And then I went to work on our food sack to repair the damage.

He leaned toward me as if to watch, placing a large hand above my knee, then caressing my thigh up and down in a soothing motion.

Boots slapped on wood outside as the crew went on with their work. Then people stopped by our cabin, talking in whispered voices. I could not make out the words but could hear the anger behind them. I did not like the way those men sounded. But, after a few moments, they hurried away.

"Should we go up on deck?" I asked when I finished with the sack.

Batumar nuzzled my ear as he pulled me into his embrace. I set aside my mending. His familiar scent relaxed me. He even smelled like a warlord: leather and steel.

I pressed against his body and let his heat warm me. "Should you not be helping?" Not that I wanted him to leave.

He ran his fingers over my hair. "We should stay out of sight as much as possible. Best they do not even remember that we are here."

His warm hand moved down my arm. "If the captain needs me, he will send for me. His crew should be able to handle easy sailing like this. They are more likely to need help once we reach the storms."

43

Already the winds were heavier, the waves tossing the schooner up, then dropping us down. Yet, so far, the sacks of potatoes beneath us stayed firmly anchored in place, thank the spirits.

I shifted away from a big lump that dug between my ribs. "At least we shall have more room as our journey progresses. These potatoes will be eaten by the men."

Batumar kissed my neck. His strong fingers massaged my back, then moved to my side, then up until they rested under my breast. Suddenly I was breathless, my whole body tingling with anticipation.

The evening of Lady Lalandra's summoning, he had not sent for me afterwards. The night before we left Karamur, he had insisted that I had enough rest. Then, in the mountain, we spent the night without being able to touch, wedged in a narrow tunnel. Now I was suddenly starving for his hands upon me. When his large palm covered my breast at last, I arched into its warmth.

He deepened the kiss, fully claiming my mouth. Then his hand trailed down, slipped under my tunic, his fingers moving to the waistband of my thudi. Heat rushed through my body and pooled low in my belly.

"Someday," he said between kisses, "after the war, I shall take you on a sailing trip around the islands, on my own flagship."

I enjoyed that thought very much. But only for a brief moment before I remembered the way I had left the High Lord's Pleasure Hall.

*Me and all the other concubines?* I wanted to ask.

I would not. The High Lord owed them his protection and more. They were his duty, according to the ways of the Kadar. He had brought *me* on this journey, and that would have to be enough, even if he only brought me because he believed the enemy sought to kill me.

I wanted to ask what would happen when we returned to Karamur, but I had given in to my jealousies too much already. He loved me. I knew he did. *But why will he not say it?*

Suddenly, I realized that he had drawn back a little and was watching me.

"Are you unwell?" he asked, the heat in his eyes turning into concern.

He would think me such a fool if he knew all I had been thinking. "We should store up on rest. We will not have much once we reach the hardstorms and the waves start pitching under the ship in earnest." I glanced toward the door, wishing I could leave for a few moments until I collected myself.

He misunderstood the gesture.

His lips twisted into a rueful smile. "Next time, my lady, we shall travel in a cabin with a lock on the door."

A sharp rap on the door drowned out the last of his words.

"Up on deck!" Pek shouted outside. "Captain's orders!"

Batumar reached into his boot and retrieved his dagger, handing it to me. "Block the door with potato sacks behind me. If anyone comes in…" He wrapped his fingers around mine as I held the dagger. "Aim for the heart."

He leaned forward, mindful of the dagger, and brushed his warm lips against mine one last time, lingering but for a moment, then he was gone, leaving me alone in the cabin.

I did as he instructed, barring the door, then settled back on our uncomfortable bed with little to do but worry about him up on deck. I refused to go back to my thoughts of jealousy and be like a child who picked at a sore until it bled.

When the hunger grew worse, I drank. I had emptied one of my flasks on our journey through the mountain, and now, to ease my grumbling stomach, I kept drinking until I nearly emptied the other, but I knew we could refill our flasks from the freshwater barrels we had seen being loaded.

To relieve myself, I used the old bucket in the corner as we had before, then dumped the contents out the porthole. I preferred that to squatting over the side of the ship in full view of the pirates.

The rest of my time was filled with worries about how we would fare at the market of Rabeen, whether we would leave it as a free woman and man, or be left behind as slaves.

Dusk neared by the time Batumar returned, calling through the door so I would let him in.

When he said, "We reached Rabeen. I will take you to see the island," I relaxed a little. At least he had not yet been seized. I straightened my clothes, then followed Batumar up to the deck, both of us alert for an attack.

45

But the pirates ran about their tasks, barely sparing us a cold glance. The *Doomed* was nearly in port.

In front of us, mud-brick dwellings mixed in with market stalls, covering most of the island, barely any land showing, so Rabeen looked as if the islanders had built their houses on top of a surfaced whale that could at any moment dip back under the sea.

I did not draw an easy breath until the ship had docked and we were on firm ground, still uncaptured. Only then did I allow myself to fully inspect our surroundings. The whole of Rabeen was but a single city, and the whole of the city was but a marketplace.

Batumar briefly placed a hand on my arm. "We must not draw attention to ourselves."

On this, we fully agreed.

Beggar children ran around in flocks like honking geese. Seeing us depart a pirate ship, at first they did not approach, only watched us closely. But once they convinced themselves that we did not look like pirates, they swarmed around, begging for food. Two had no eyes; others had missing limbs.

Batumar had our food sack under his arm. The little beggars grabbed for that, then cried out with disappointment upon finding it empty.

I gave the ribbon from my hair to one little girl. The small, grimy hands of the others were everywhere. When they discerned that we had no more to give, they ran off for their next target.

I stared after them, wishing we could take them all back to Karamur. *Maybe on the return journey.*

"Were they left behind here by slavers because of their injuries?" I guessed that feeding them through a sea voyage would cost more than a slaver could get for them at the nearest city.

"Or else, their beggar lord maimed them himself." Batumar scanned the colorful sea of people around us. "Good health in a beggar is a disadvantageous calamity."

I could not fathom such cruelty. I shivered, but not from the wind that blew from the sea.

We passed a man in threadbare clothes, leaning against a pole, sleeping standing up, both hands missing from the wrist.

"And him?"

"A thief," Batumar answered. "The first time, they cut off a hand, the second time, the other hand, the third time, they cut off the head."

I stared at him.

"That is why you never see a beggar child with only the hand missing. Beggar lords are always careful to remove at least half an arm, so the little beggars are not mistaken for thieves. Nobody would toss a coin to a thief."

We walked on in silence, my mind spinning. I had seen many dark things in war, but the customs of Rabeen made my heart sick. "Are many cities like this?"

Among the Shahala, those too sick to work were fed by their neighbors. Those caught in a crime were taught by the elders to do better. At worst, a criminal might be cast out. My people did not go about chopping up others.

Among the Kadar, each warlord made his own law. In Karamur, under the High Lord's law, theft had to be twice repaid, even if it meant servitude for the thief.

"Why is Rabeen so barbaric?" the words slipped from my lips.

"No market town is kind to thieves." But then Batumar, his gaze scanning the crowd, added, "Rabeen was not always like this. Once, they had a smaller market but grew all the most exotic fruits here on the island, in hanging gardens. They traded only food back then. They had ways of irrigating their crops and growing tenfold in raised containers, one atop another, as clever as if the gods had invented it themselves. Once, the merchants of Rabeen were more than merchants. They were inventors and philosophers and poets."

I longed to see such a place, a shining contrast to the now overcrowded island that teemed with a wide range of goods but also with the mutilated. "What happened?"

"War. Their old ways were lost. Now they grow little. Ships bring merchandise, and other ships take it away." Batumar turned toward the market stalls. "Let us purchase what we need."

I glanced back toward the handless beggar and caught sight of Pek instead. He seemed to be watching us, but he ducked his head when he realized I had seen him.

As I followed Batumar into the labyrinth of passageways, staying close to him, I tried to shake off my unease.

The market buzzed like a nest of hornets. Not even the sounds of the sea could overpower the noise that rose and fell like the waves. Here on the outskirts, merchandise was sold in open stalls, canvas stretching above to protect the tables that offered fruits, meats, vegetables, and spices.

Various smells assailed us, some pleasant, others stomach-turning. I had never before seen so many things fermented.

We bought hard-fleshed ican fruit that would last the long journey. Batumar also purchased some sweet mosan berries, which we ate at once. Then cheese, which we sampled. And strips of dried meat. We ate some of that too as we moved on, our stomachs filling at last.

The farther we progressed, the more substantial the stores became, square, high-walled tents first, then mud-brick houses stuck to each other. In these houses, colorful clothes and furs were on display on the lower levels, or carpets standing in tall piles. At the top of stairs that led to the second, private, level, children sat, playing, chewing on sugarcane, watching their fathers work, already learning the trade.

We stopped at a candlemaker, and Batumar selected six large tallow candles. Then he tugged off his left boot, shook out a coin, and paid.

He added the candles to our sack.

A droopy-mustached merchant called to us as we passed his shop. "Silk for the mistress."

"I have the finest perfumes in the world. Try my musk and jasmine," another offered, wiggling his sizable nose like a rabbit smelling clover.

"Soft kid boots."

"A jewel to match her eyes."

All this we passed by. Soon we were nearly across the city. Straight ahead was the sea again and another port with a long wooden dock. To our left, animal pens stood near the water so they could be easily cleaned.

The fowl merchant listed his entire inventory in a singsong voice. He had everything from purple-plumed nefel that lived on swamp frogs, to curved-beak emerald machup that nested on high cliffs. Next to them chickens and ducks were packed two dozen to a cage, but the roosters were kept separately from each other.

"Fighting cocks," Batumar said. "If they were packed together, they would kill each other."

As we passed the fowl merchant, I glanced to our right, toward the sprawling slave market.

My breath caught when I saw Pek again, talking to a slaver.

# CHAPTER SIX
## THE TIGER

Before I could point out Pek to Batumar, the boy was gone, and my attention was drawn to the shocking sight of women and children kept penned in, separated from the men, all huddled against the cold. In another area, I saw two dozen other children in individual cages like the fowl merchant's fighting cocks.

The cages were not much bigger, entirely too small for the children. Their feet hung out between the bars on the bottom, their arms to the side, a hole allowing their heads to stick out on top.

Their bodies had conformed to the shape of the small cage, unable to grow past it. I envisioned their bent and stunted bones, and could only imagine how much pain their little bodies must be in.

My spirit sickened. My heart pitched in my chest like a ship in a storm. "Are they deformed by design to make them better beggars?"

But Batumar said darkly, "Dwarves are for entertainment, not for work. One of them is worth twenty times the coin beggar lords pay for a beggar."

He turned me from the sight and kept talking as we moved away. "The Emperor Drakhar has a fondness for dwarves. There are not enough of them naturally. Some slave masters try to breed them for the Emperor's court, but it is slow work and does not always bring result. The slave masters of Rabeen invented a different way."

I truly and well hated the slave masters of Rabeen. I could see a handful as I glanced back, standing together and talking with each other, wearing fanciful clothes decorated with beads and shells, the lower portion of their faces wrapped, but not as with a healer's veil.

Their wrapping was much more substantial, the cloth ending on the top of their heads in some sort of a turban. Only their eyes showed, and I thought it fitting that they would hide their faces in shame.

As I returned my gaze to the children in the cages, I was shaking with anger and grief. I could not imagine how so much darkness could live in a man's heart as lived inside the Emperor. How could he be amused by such cruelty? As we walked through rows of animal pens, I kept thinking how we could possibly stop such a man.

I turned to Batumar. "Those children...On our way back?"

He held my gaze. "When we have our mercenaries. I promise."

As I had never known the High Lord to break his word, the ache in my heart eased a little as we moved on. Once we had the children, I would see what I could do about healing them. I prayed to the spirits that I would get the chance.

Sheep and goat bleated side by side as we moved forward. Cows, horses, then other great animals I had never seen before, the color of desert sand, long-legged, taller even than Batumar. They must have been used for dragging carts, for I could not see how a person could sit on one's back where a giant hump took up all the space.

Batumar stepped closer to pet one. "Camels."

A portly man—fat as a harvest mouse, in truth—immediately rushed up to us with an earthenware jar. "Camel milk, mistress. The healthiest of all milks. It will cure any disease. It will strengthen any weakness." Then he smiled slyly at Batumar. "It will increase a man's strength in bed."

I nearly choked on my own spittle at his brazen suggestion. The High Lord of the Kadar certainly did *not* need help between the furs.

But Batumar laughed at the small man and clapped him on the back. "We will take a flask."

"A taste, mistress?"

I accepted the cup. The camel milk tasted saltier than cow milk, and richer. Likely it did have some medicinal benefit.

"Very healing," he said again. "Camel piss too. A cask of that?"

I knew urine was used in the tanning of furs, but I never heard of it used as medicine. Batumar was ready to move on with the flat flask that had an interesting knobby topper, but I asked the merchant, "How does this heal?"

The man went on about wounds and infections, but he was no healer, so he could not tell me what I wished to know. And then I saw a large cage far ahead, apart from the others at the edge of the market, and something about the majestic animal inside drew me forward. I forgot all about the camels.

"It is not the same one," Batumar said as I passed him.

Eight men were attempting to move the tiger cage, struggling to hold the four long carrying beams—two in front, two in the back—as the tiger roared inside, snapping at them with her fearsome teeth and swiping at them through the bars. I could see scars on her side. I knew those scars.

I grabbed Batumar's arm, my heart pounding with excitement. "It is she."

A year earlier, I had been sold into slavery at the port city of Kaharta Reh but was later taken to Karamur, the High Lord's seat. On that journey, our traveling group had come across a tiger. She had come too close to me. Batumar's warriors filled her side with spears, but I had healed her afterwards. I had understood that she'd meant us no harm, had only been defending her young.

She had been fearsome then, but now she was truly terrifying in her fury. Between the tiger and the rest of the market, warriors stood on guard at a distance with their bows and arrows, others with lances, in case the cage could not hold her.

Batumar and I stopped at a safe distance.

"Where are you taking her?" he asked the workmen.

The tallest of the ragged men answered without looking at us. "One-Tooth Tum bought her. He's taking her to the fighting cages of Naresh." He grunted as they heaved. "She is worth her weight in gold there." He grunted again. "If we can get her to the ship. Thrice the size of our island tigers. A Selorm battle tiger, I wager."

52

She was powerful and powerfully enraged. I did not want her blood to be spilled on Rabeen's rocks. I fastened my eyes to hers and hummed a spirit song in my heart.

*Oh great mother, I greet you as a friend. Oh great mother, I bring you no harm.*

Her gaze sharpened. She shook her head. Could she hear? Did she recognize me?

*Oh great mother, think of the forest. Think of the wind in the trees. Think of the water of the creek. Oh great mother, think of sleep.*

Her eyes found mine. The tiger blinked once, slowly. She stood still now, did not try to swipe at the men through the bars.

*Oh great mother, think of the forest. Think of the wind in the trees. Think of the water of the creek. Oh great mother, think of sleep.*

She lay down with a great heaving sigh, which nearly unbalanced the crate, but the men steadied it again, grunting under the weight. All the while, she was looking at me.

Some of the men caught her gaze and glanced toward me with fear, others with speculation. I paid them no mind.

*Oh great mother, think of the forest. Think of the wind in the trees. Think of the water of the creek. Oh great mother, think of sleep.*

And the tiger closed her eyes.

More people were watching now, wondering why all that roaring suddenly stopped. As more and more eyes turned in my direction, Batumar tugged me away.

I followed with reluctance, consoling myself with the thought that I would see the tiger again on our ship.

"What happens in the fighting cages of Naresh?" I asked Batumar.

"Whatever pleases the Queen of Naresh. Female warriors fight each other, bears, lions, and tigers. The gladiator cages of Naresh draw men from the far corners of the world. They fill the cages with a mixture of fighters and beasts, and the fight goes on until only one warrior remains. The women fight naked, with a single double-edged blade. It is considered a great attraction."

I could not imagine such a place.

I did not wish for the tiger to go to the fighting cages. But neither did I want her to remain on Rabeen, this rock in the middle of the sea.

I could see no escape for her here. I consoled myself with the thought that we had a long journey to the mainland. I would think of something before we reached the port of Ishaf.

We meandered back toward our ship, taking a different path through the warren of passageways. Shaking another coin out of his boot, Batumar purchased a blanket made out of camel hair to increase the comfort of our cabin. I tied it around me like a second cloak. The blanket smelled like the camel had, but it did block the wind.

Then we bought dried fruit, smoked sausages, and more cheese, and flat, hard bread that would have to be sawed to bits and soaked in water before we could eat it.

"I would spend the last of our coin on pickled eggs," Batumar said, and I nodded in agreement.

We had passed by those earlier. Sealed tight in their earthenware jars, the lid made of metal, that would be one food the rats could not attack. Pickled eggs might save us yet if we lost everything else.

The beggar children did not bother with us again, as a new ship had come to port, but a little girl sitting aside by some sacks of wheat grabbed my ankle as we passed.

"Food, blessed mistress. A bit of food please, or a little coin," she begged in a singsong voice laden with pain. Dark circles of suffering framed her eyes. She winced as she shifted.

Batumar reached into our food sack and came up with a chunk of cheese, which the girl grabbed greedily.

She was moving her arm with difficulty. And she could not move her bony little legs at all. As her clothes shifted, her scars became apparent. She was deformed from having been badly burned.

While Batumar inspected a bag of oats, I reached my hands out to her without thinking. I would have naught to do on our long journey but lie on top of a pile of potatoes. I would have time to recover.

She startled but did not pull away.

I could feel her damaged skin and the muscles that had been destroyed beneath. Then I felt for the good skin and good muscles of my own body, and I sent my healing spirit into her. I gasped as her pain flooded me, but held on until she was fully healed.

Her gaunt face cleared and her emerald eyes flew wide with aston-ishment, even as I had to steady myself against the pole that held the canvas roof of the stall next to us. She moved her arms and legs, laughter bubbling up her throat as she jumped to her feet, losing her balance and falling down again. She hung on to the wheat sacks behind her and pulled herself to standing once more, eager to learn to walk again.

"Tera." Batumar managed a growl that was at the same time angry and concerned.

I tried to breathe against the pain I had drawn, watching the girl move in every direction in jerky twists, like a dancing drunkard. Then she suddenly stilled, staring past us before collapsing to the ground and wrapping her arms around herself, her laughter replaced by a gasp of fear.

A wizened old man was running toward us with a dark storm on his face. "What have you done?" He sucked in air. "Heathens!"

He reached us and began to strike me with his fleshy hands at once, but Batumar shoved him back, looking ready to cut him in half.

The man turned to the merchants behind their stalls, and, having caught his breath at last, began loudly complaining for all to hear. "A full gold piece it cost me for the blacksmith to burn them just right. My grandson I lost to infection, but this one lived. Now I have to have her burned again. Who will pay for that? What if she dies? She will probably die, I tell you."

He waved his arms and stomped his feet as he turned to Batumar. "I demand payment."

The vendors around us nodded in agreement.

"It is right." A tall man with pockmarks on his face spoke up. "You damaged his property. If you do not pay for it, you are committing theft."

The sea of angry faces scowled at us as if we had stolen a side of mut-ton off a table.

I let the pole go and stepped closer to Batumar, leaned against him for support as pain coursed through me. We could be swallowed in this crowd and never be seen again. One-Tooth Tum would not come looking for us or be overwrought by our disappearance. He already had our crystals.

The crowd moved in closer. A few daggers appeared. One man hefted an ax. I hid my hands behind my back, fearing what would happen if they branded us thieves.

Batumar shot them a warning look, pulling to his full height, squaring his shoulders.

"Can we take her with us?" I whispered, my heart pounding.

He stepped between me and the angry mob, measuring up the men, his stance ready for fight. "We will be traveling through war-torn lands crawling with enemies. She would be no safer with us," he told me under his breath, his gaze on the crowd.

I knew he had little if any coin left, which we might need to pay the captain to let us off the ship in Ishaf. We might have to buy our own lives yet. And the lives of every man, woman, and child on Dahru depended on our success. But Batumar did reach under his doublet and pulled out a gold piece.

The old man's eyes glinted with greed as he snatched the coin with a speed that belied his age. He bit hard on it, then gave a satisfied nod as he quickly hid it in a secret pouch behind his belt. Then he stuck his chin out toward us. "Where is the rest?"

I could not have moved had I tried, just breathed against the pain as I waited for the men to finish bargaining.

"Do not burn her again." Batumar's voice had a cold edge. He held out another gold coin. From the grim look he shot me, I understood that this coin was our last. "On the next merchant ship, send her to Karamur to serve."

He stood and spoke like a warlord. He put his hand on his sword.

The old man grabbed the coin, bit this one too, then hid it as quickly as the first. "Yes, my lord. On the next merchant ship, I shall send her to Karamur to serve."

Batumar looked around at those who had gathered around us. "You are the witnesses."

Some men put away their daggers with disappointment as they eyed us, probably wondering if we could possibly have some coin left. But a few of the more honest-looking men nodded.

Then Batumar turned to the old man again. "I shall come back this way. When I come to Rabeen again, she better not be here. When I reach Karamur, she better be there waiting, or I will come to find you."

The old man nodded rapidly. "There are two merchant ships in port right now, my lord. I will put her on the one that leaves first for Dahru. I will even send one of my servant women with her to make sure she arrives safely to the palace." He grabbed the girl and dragged her along, realizing now that Batumar might be a man of some power.

She was smiling back at us as she stumbled after her grandfather. She might fear being sent to a distant land, but she feared more the blacksmith's fire. I hid my pain and smiled back at her. I prayed to the spirits to let us see her again.

A few stalls behind her, Pek stood by a pile of sugarcane, watching us with open curiosity on his face.

As the crowd dispersed, Batumar lifted me into his arms and carried me through the rest of the market, all the way to our ship and into our cabin. Even being carried hurt.

He settled me down gently on his fur cloak, then covered me with the camel-hair blanket. Every muscle in his body was stiff with anger. "You should not weaken yourself like this."

"I do not like the market of Rabeen." I gasped out the words.

His large hands brushed the hair back from my face, frustration and concern in his gaze. "How long will you suffer?"

"Not long," I promised.

His chest rose, his displeasure all over his face.

"I am a healer," I reminded him.

"I like it best when you are locked up in my Pleasure Hall." He climbed onto our platform next to me. "Nay. I like it best when you are in my arms," he corrected.

Soon we heard the rattle of the great chain as the sailors raised anchor; then we sailed around the small island to drop anchor again so the tiger could be loaded. Batumar opened the porthole so I could look out and so that fresh air could come in.

The cage waited at the end of the dock. The tiger was still lying down, although she growled as the men lifted her. I sent my spirit song to her to make her transfer easier. I did not wish for her to be dropped into the sea while locked in the cage.

After the tiger had been loaded, the servants carrying her returned to shore and quickly returned with a dozen black-and-white goats before leaving the ship for good.

Then I caught sight of a man nearly as tall as Batumar, his head and face wrapped in a black scarf against the wind, hurrying toward our ship with nine beggar children running behind him, much like the ones we had seen earlier—here an arm, there a finger or an ear missing.

The children squinted against the sun. Some even closed their eyes completely, hanging on to others for guidance, as if until now they had been kept in a dark place.

I could not see them past a point, but they did not reappear on the dock. The scarfed man must have been able to negotiate passage with our captain, despite One-Tooth Tum's protests that he did not take on passengers.

"A beggar lord," Batumar said and closed the porthole. "They come to the slave markets to replace the little beggars that they lose to abuse or disease."

I hoped we would not be forced to spend much time with the beggar lord during our journey. I thought it likely that the children had been maimed by the slavers on the man's orders to make them better beggars. My heart shivered inside my chest. I hated the man already.

# CHAPTER SEVEN
## HARDSTORM'S FURY

As we left Rabeen, I rested while my body rapidly healed. Batumar brought in a bucket of seawater so we could wash and he could shave with his dagger.

Night had fallen when the captain sent word with Pek that we should go on deck as we would be entering the hardstorms early morning. I left our cabin with Batumar, walking on my own two feet. The thought that this would be our last chance for fresh air, for standing under the open sky for a while, drew me forward.

*Our last chance forever if the ship sinks*, a little voice whispered in my head, but I shooed that voice away. I would not let fear rule my heart.

We walked down the passageway, and I could see in the moonlight that came down through the open hatch that the tiger cage was now lashed to heavy iron rings in the walls in the open area that led toward the captain's cabin. The tiger roared and swiped at the sailors passing by. But her ears perked up and she sniffed toward me when she saw me coming.

I was happy to see her well, but a sailor kicked one of the four carrying poles of the cage just to rattle the animal. He spat at the tiger. Other men scowled at the beast too, with hate and fear.

"For the captain, the tiger is a source of gold," Batumar said next to me. "For his men, she is a threat. If the storm tosses the cage around and breaks it, the tiger will kill every one of them. In the close quarters of the ship, no man could stand against her."

I watched the men a moment longer. They went about their tasks with a dour determination. The loud joking and fighting of the previous day had disappeared. It seemed the thought of sailing into the hardstorms at dawn filled even the most grizzled pirates with dread.

I nodded toward the tiger. "On the island, what did the men mean when they said she is a Selorm battle tiger? Where is her lord warrior?"

Batumar shrugged. "The Selorm had come to our aid centuries before, not just at the last siege. I heard tales told of it. When a Selorm lord dies, his tiger fights to the death. But if the battle ends before that is accomplished, the tiger goes off, becomes wild again. She might be the offspring of such tigers."

I thought about that as we went up on deck and moved to a spot where we would be sheltered from the wind. The full moon glazed the ship in silver glow, making it look as if we had just sailed out of a myth.

On other ships I had seen, the deck had been filled with merchandise, bales, and barrels. On the *Doomed*, nothing was stored abovedecks. Our red sails were patched many times over. Much of the rigging appeared new, as if a recent trip had torn most of the ropes. I stepped on deep gouges in the planks we stood on. The whole ship looked like a warrior who had barely escaped with his life from a brutal battle.

And the men looked no better. As if they were once the beggar children of Rabeen, now grown, nearly all of them had some visible injury: battered faces, limps, lost teeth, lost eyes, even lost ears.

They inspected the ship with grim looks, and worked on the rigging and the sails. Some prayed to their gods. I saw one tossing a handful of dead rats into the sea, muttering something after them. I wasn't sure if he had been cleaning up below or giving an offering.

Batumar and I stopped in the aft, out of the way, looking slightly deformed, the both of us. Our food stores were tied to our bodies, some under my tunic, the rest under Batumar's doublet, with the reasoning that if the rats came in the night to rob us again, at least we would wake and could fight them off this time.

He pulled me to him and enfolded me in his cloak so only my face was showing. "Are you warm enough?"

"I am." I leaned against his hard chest and soaked in the heat that radiated off his body. I watched the ship and the men around me like some baby bird from her nest.

Batumar rested his chin on the top of my head. "Are you truly well enough to be up and standing?"

"I am fine well." The way we stood just then, I thought I could handle anything.

I thought how far we had already come in our plan. We were nearly at the hardstorms' edge. In but a few days, we'd be through the worst. Then we would reach Ishaf and could begin gathering a mercenary army.

For the first time, instead of the hundred ways we could fail, at last I could see our victory. Even the dark god of the mountain had let us go without taking what he willed, and I swore never again to return to his mountain temple.

Angry shouts pulled me from my thoughts. I turned toward the foot of the mainmast, where two pirates quarreled, then came to sudden, vicious blows. Nobody paid them any attention, and the fight ended when one broke the other's nose.

I moved forward, but Batumar held me back. "You are not strong enough."

And I leaned back against him after a moment. The broken nose *could* heal on its own. Most every man on deck had suffered such before, judging by their faces. They seemed to carry their scars as badges of honor. And indeed, even though they all knew I was a healer, the injured man never even looked my way but shuffled off to work.

As I stood there in the warmth and safety of Batumar's arms, the little beggars popped up from below one by one, the beggar lord close behind them. At least he did not keep them tied up. Their fair hair was matted, sticking out every which way. They were scrawny from first to last, their faces pallid, scratching as if they shared their sackcloth garments with fleas.

The five boys and four girls huddled together wherever they went. The youngest, a girl, might have seen six summers, the oldest, a boy, no more than ten. I looked at their injuries and could not bear to think that their deformities had been caused on purpose.

The beggar lord watched them closely. He was as tall as Batumar but leaner, somewhere between myself and Batumar in age. He wore all black, from his boots to his quilted doublet and his cloak. His head was still wrapped in his headdress. His hair, what I could see of it, was the color of a camel. His eyes were the gray-blue of the turbulent sea.

He looked toward us.

I turned away.

When I turned back, he was sitting on the deck with his face into the wind and the children all gathered around him.

Batumar said pensively next to my ear, "Every beggar lord I have ever seen was old and fat. Maybe he is a merchant, making delivery."

"Why risk a pirate ship?"

"The same reason we do. It is the only ship that will cross. He might have come through the Gate before the war, gone around the islands, trading. Maybe he lost everything he had in the war, invested whatever he had left in these little beggars. And now he has to get them home, whatever way he can."

The children sat quietly around the man. They barely moved, as if too scared to even breathe. They did not look around like their master. They kept their gazes down. They did not talk to each other or even squirm as other children would have.

The youngest of the girls coughed a deep, tortured cough. I could feel the pain in her lungs through that scraping, gurgling sound.

I moved forward, but Batumar's iron arms would not allow me to step away from him.

The pain I had taken upon me on Rabeen was lessening. I could have borne the pain of this little girl's chest and her fever. Once we went belowdecks, I would have no need to move from our cabin for days. But I knew Batumar would not hear any of that, so I said, "At least some herbs."

And he nodded.

I had a small tin flask hanging from my side, half-filled with water. I parted Batumar's cloak around me, then my own, and checked the bundles hanging from my belt, selected the right herbs—feverfew, sour birt, and sweet, fragrant bambler—added the right amount to the water, then stuck the flask under my clothes, against my skin, between my breasts. Then I drew the cloaks back around me again and let the herbs infuse into the water that was warmed by my body.

We stayed on deck until the wind grew bitter cold. The waves churned under the ship, stronger and stronger. When the merchant gathered his little beggars to go below, we followed. We might as well try to catch some sleep, for I suspected there would not be much sleep in our future.

I pulled the flask from my clothes and approached the beggar lord in the passageway below. Batumar stayed close by my side.

"For the little one." I held out my offering. "I am a healer."

I spoke in the merchant tongue used throughout most of the world, a simple dialect with words borrowed from near every language.

The man responded the same way, with a thick accent. "What is it?"

"Herb water."

Behind him, the children gathered around the tiger cage. The tiger watched them as if mesmerized. They were about the same size as the goats the pirates had stocked for the tiger for the journey. I could scarcely look away for fear that one of the children would step too close to the cage.

But even when a boy did, the tiger simply watched, cocking her head, pricking her ears.

Pirates moved around us, performing their tasks. The schooner held about seventy of them, from what I had seen so far. Rarely did one pass the tiger without at least spitting toward her. One man cursed the animal. The other one cursed the captain, then looked around quickly and ducked his head.

"Thank you, mistress." The merchant took the flask with a sharp nod, then clicked his tongue at the children, who left the tiger and hurried down the passageway behind their master.

Their cabin was past ours, all the way in the aft. I heard the faint bleating of a goat from that direction. I suspected the pirates had put as much distance between the tiger and her food as possible, so the goats' smell would not overmuch tease her.

Batumar and I retired to our cabin, climbed the pile of potatoes, ate a quick dinner, then slept through the first half of the night. The other half, we clung together as the ship pitched worse and worse.

By the time morning dawned, the ship rolled so hard we could not go up on deck. When we emptied our bucket out the window, twice as much water splashed in as what we threw out, wetting the potato sacks.

We crawled to a dry spot and bundled up together. Neither of us ate, although the rats had not taken any of our food overnight.

My stomach rolled with the ship. Since barely any light filtered through the thick glass of the porthole, I lit one of our tallow candles.

"Watch that we do not set the cabin on fire." Batumar sounded tired.

"I shall not let go of the candle," I promised and moved the light toward him.

His face had a greenish tinge. His lips thinned. Agony sat behind his eyes.

"What is it?" I asked in full alarm.

He tried for a smile and failed. "I was not made for water."

I blinked. He was shipsick. Some people could not bear the movement of the sea; their bodies rebelled. And, of course, of all sea passages, crossing through the hardstorms was the worst. The toughest sailors dared not even to attempt it, only pirates who did not care for their lives.

"Why?" I asked, stunned and worried. Why would he take a journey such as this upon himself? Oh, I knew the answer. He would have done anything to save his people. So then I asked, "What hurts?"

He did manage a rueful smile this time. "If you could only remove my brain and stomach, my lady, it would be a merciful service." And then he grabbed the bucket and heaved up his sparse dinner.

I took his flask, warmed water in it over the light of the candle, and made an herb tea I used to settle the stomachs of expecting women. I did not tell him that. He was too proud a warrior to drink women's tea. Although, maybe not too proud right at that moment.

He drank and sighed. "You should not have come, but I cannot regret having you here with me."

The ship pitched even harder.

I cleaned up the vomit, letting in as little sea spray while doing it as possible, then blew out the candle and curled against him in the darkness.

Pirates shouted outside our door, running down the hallway. I could hear heavy footfalls on the deck above us as well. Time passed, the ship rocking so hard, every moment could have been our last, timber giving to water, then a cold, deep grave.

The tiger roared.

I sent my spirit song to her.

She roared nevertheless.

Then the weather turned worse.

Wind howled outside; rain and waves lashed against the side of the ship. The schooner lifted up and up, high into the air, then came down with a bone-rattling crash.

The sacks of potatoes shifted in our cabin. We rolled with them.

Batumar groaned. I only heard it in the din because my ear was so near his lips.

"Are you well, my lord?"

"Never heard anyone die from being shipsick." He pushed out the words with effort. "I wager I shall live."

Maybe we would, maybe we would not. Being shipsick was turning out to be the least of our worries. With every passing moment, I was becoming more and more certain that the ship would sink. No shipwright could make a ship tough enough to withstand these waves' battering.

I had been in a siege not long ago, but this was worse than the battering ram at the gate. Unlike a human enemy, the relentless and brutal waves never tired.

My stomach too rebelled at last from the endless onslaught. We could not have eaten if we had a box of the palace's best venison roast and cake.

Indeed we did not take any nourishment on that first day of the hardstorm, nor on the second. On the morning of the third, I was thrown so hard against the wall that I thought my arm broke. It did not, thank the spirits, but ached with a throbbing pain.

"Hold on." Batumar sliced the camel-hair blanket into strips with his dagger and strapped down the potato sacks, strapped us to them so we wouldn't bounce around in the small space.

Our candles had rolled away and were hopelessly lost. We could see nothing. We could hear nothing but the waves and the storm and the tiger. Once I heard a man scream. The sound seemed to come from right outside our porthole.

"A pirate washed into the sea," Batumar said in a flat tone.

We could do nothing to help him.

When night fell again, Batumar untied himself. "We must eat."

I had no great desire for food, but I agreed.

"Here," he said a while later, then rolled into me the next second as the ship pitched. "Dried meat."

I searched blindly for his hand, then found him, just as something hit me in the head. I snatched after it—the flask with the knobby topper. "I got the camel milk."

"You eat all the meat. I do not think I can," Batumar said.

I offered him the milk, and that he accepted.

I chewed in silence, nearly biting off my tongue more than once as the ship rattled and shook. I heard the flask clink against Batumar's teeth.

"I shall walk off this ship looking like a twin to One-Tooth Tum," he said dryly. "Will you still wish to be my lady, then?"

"I will," I assured him. "I might look the same."

He chuckled, and I smiled into the darkness. Despite my misgivings, having food in my stomach again made me feel a little better, a little warmer.

The spirits be praised, Batumar's stomach did not heave up the milk. Maybe the camel merchant had been right and the milk did have some medicinal value. I hoped I could ask somebody about that again someday.

"Will there be camels where we are going, my lord?"

"There will be camels aplenty."

Reassured of that, I tried to sleep some, but sleep was impossible.

"How do you feel?" Batumar asked after a while.

I opened my eyes. "As if someone had stuffed me in a barrel and rolled me down a mountain."

I feared we had not seen the worst yet. I feared what would happen when we did.

Then a loud banging came on our door, and Pek shouted, "Up on deck! We have a loose sail."

Batumar went at once, leaving his fur cloak with me.

"I shall go too." I tried to move after him, releasing the restraints that held me in place.

"No."

"I am a good climber."

But his voice hardened. "I will not allow it."

The door opened, then closed. I dropped back onto the potato sacks and prayed to the spirits to keep him.

I no longer tried to sleep. Every time I heard footfalls nearby, I hoped he was returning. But a full day passed before he came back to me, wet and half-frozen, shaking with exhaustion.

He drank the rest of the camel milk and ate some bread and cheese. I held him close to my body afterward to warm him.

From then on, he spent more time on deck than he did in our cabin, and each time he came back more drained. He had a potato bag open and was lining up potatoes on the small square of floor that stood empty. He kept track of the stars every time he went up at night and was trying to map our journey by them, in case he could not buy the Ishafi pirate to lead the Landrian navy on the way back.

We spent some time memorizing the potato jumble, not easily done, as the potatoes rolled around, then disappeared each night when the rats came to scavenge. Then I had the idea to stitch the map into the lining of Batumar's cloak. That way we could take it with us when we left the ship.

Ten days of misery did we spend in the storm, growing weaker and weaker in body and spirit. I despaired for ever seeing the sky again. Then suddenly, on the morning of the eleventh day, the storm noticeably quieted.

Leaning on each other, we staggered up on deck. I was hoping to see land, but we saw no such thing, just endless gray waves.

Most of the pirates were on deck. The captain was inspecting the ship for damage. We had two loose sails, and some rigging was missing.

"How many men?" the captain snapped at his second in command, a one-eyed man called Grun.

"Twelve overboard." Grun shrugged. "And Drunkard Pete."

"He was half a man, anyway," another pirate joked.

But the captain did not laugh. He ordered the men to hasten the repairs. "The storm will hit us again."

The tiger roared below deck. Then I heard a goat's bleating, and soon after, the tiger quieted.

The merchant and the children did not come up that first day, but we saw them the day after. Once again, the little beggars huddled around their master. They looked worse than before, if possible, sitting on the deck listless and beaten. But the little girl no longer coughed.

The merchant was looking at the damaged rigging the pirates were busy fixing. He was probably wondering, same as I, whether repairs could be made in time. The loose sails still had to be rolled tightly back up before the storm returned, or the winds would shred them and possibly tear the ship apart in the process.

At least the sail hung flat at the moment. The wind had died completely. The captain paced the length of the schooner, his hands folded behind his back, his face to the sky, his eyes searching the horizon without rest.

He stopped by us for a moment, and I hoped for some encouraging news, but instead, he said most gravely, "We're in the lull, the dead wind. Aye. Breaks apart more ships than the storms. Some get stuck fer a mooncrossin' or more. Men starve. They go mad."

# CHAPTER EIGHT
## THE LULL

The schooner sat in the lull for twelve long days, adrift. The potato sacks disappeared one by one to feed the crew. When we were down to the last quarter, the captain ordered the rationing of food and water.

The men growled and snapped. So did the tiger, whose last two goats the crew ate.

We could have slept now, the sea smooth, but we were too hungry. And at night, the rats attacked. We had but dry bread and some apples left and were determined not to lose them. Batumar guarded our food sack like gold treasure.

One night, he killed a full dozen rats with his dagger. In the morning, I fed them to the tiger. Two pirates saw me and looked at me with such hate that I shrunk back.

In another two days, we ran out of the last of the food. Two days after that, we ran out of water.

"There are fewer and fewer rats," I said to Batumar one morning. He had caught only three during the night.

"The crew is eating them," he said.

As my stomach growled, I could not blame them.

The captain ordered the empty oak barrels brought on top so we could catch any rain should it come, but the spirits did not send any clouds our way.

The men talked of sacrificing the tiger to their sea god. The captain forbade it. They shouted at each other in one language, then another. Then punches swung. At the end, the captain ran one of his men through with his curved sword. The others stalked away, leaving the body where it lay.

By the next morning, the body was gone. Most of the men were abovedecks. I counted fifty-five or so as they came and went. The storm had taken over a dozen.

Three more days passed. The tiger roared without stop. I no longer had rats to feed her.

At least two dozen men had lines in the water, but so far, nobody had caught a single fish.

The pirates stopped talking about sacrificing the tiger. They started talking about eating the tiger and sacrificing one of the children.

"Give us the little one," the one-eyed man, Grun, demanded loudly as he stood in front of the merchant. At least a dozen pirates stood behind him, their faces and stances brimming with menace.

"No," Batumar said under his breath next to me before I could have pushed to my feet. We were sitting by the empty barrels, with me leaning against him for heat. His arm, a band of steel, came around me to hold me in place.

I could but watch as the merchant unfolded his long frame and stood in front of his merchandise. Instead of a broadsword like Batumar's, he had a narrow rapier at his side, about the length of his arm.

He pulled it from its scabbard, the metal glinting in the gloomy light. "The little beggars are mine."

The one-eyed pirate was the largest of the bunch, heavyset. Muscles bulged from under his worn wool tunic. He stepped toward the merchant and attacked without warning.

His great curved sword was much heavier than the rapier, and far more deadly looking. But the merchant danced out of death's way over and over again as they fought.

More pirates gathered around to watch, while others stayed at the side of the ship with their fishing lines, holding out against all hope, half-mad with hunger.

As the merchant fought on, I could feel Batumar's muscles tighten, relax, tighten again, as if he too was fighting.

I wanted him to help the merchant save the little girl, even if the merchant's motive was less than noble. He was only protecting his profits. But if Batumar joined the fight on the merchant's side, the rest of the pirates would join their mate.

Just the two men fighting was the best we could hope for. The merchant and Batumar could not kill all the pirates. And if they did, there would be nobody to sail the ship once the storms circled back to us again.

The little fair-haired girl looked at me with fright in her eyes.

I smiled at her with encouragement and reached out toward her. *Come.*

She broke away without warning and scampered to me, stopping quickly before we would have touched, huddling down by my feet. Then the rest of the children followed a moment later, all in a frightened bunch, as if indeed they were roped together.

That gave the merchant more room to move, and the fight picked up speed.

I glanced toward the captain. Would he not stop the fight? But, in the prow of the ship, he seemed otherwise occupied, looking at his charts and instruments, calculating something.

The two men kept on hacking at each other as the children watched with wide-eyed fear. None came close enough to me to touch, but close enough to place themselves under our protection, should the swordplay turn out badly for the merchant.

Since I could not help the duel or the children, I turned my attention to the men fishing. Maybe I could at least cause a distraction. I closed my eyes and reached out with my spirit, looking for the spirits of the fish under the water.

I did not find any.

I reached farther, sending my silent song along the waves. *Oh little sisters, oh little brothers, hear our plight. We are starving, little friends. Will you not help? The sea feeds you. Please give us nourishment today. We beg you for this noble sacrifice. Little sisters, little brothers, come to us, please.*

I sang my song over and over while swords clanged and clattered a short distance away.

And then suddenly a man shouted, "Fish!"

Then another. "Fish!"

In but a moment, they were laughing and cursing, yanking silver fish up on deck one after the other until they had enough to fill a barrel.

The fight stopped as Grun abandoned the merchant in favor of food. Both men were bleeding, but neither was mortally wounded. My first thought, of course, was to heal.

Batumar flashed me a hard look.

I flashed my best hard look back, but he was right. I was so weak from hunger, had I taken any injuries upon me, I wouldn't have lived. If the captain ordered, I would have to help, but the captain, like his men, was too distracted by the sudden appearance of food.

Some of the fish were eaten raw, the men mangling them like animals. Then, after the first rush, they began gutting them and skinning them, frying the meat on the braziers that were brought up on deck and lit.

During the storms, we had no fire on the ship, but now, with the calmer seas, the captain had allowed heat once again.

We had nothing to trade for food, but he allowed us some fish nevertheless, his eyes narrowed as he watched me. His one tooth flashed black as he spoke. "I've ne'er seen fish in a lull."

I smiled at him innocently, as even Batumar looked at me with suspicion.

The merchant had taken his charges belowdecks and carried food to them, one whole grilled fish wrapped in an empty potato sack. They did not return for the remainder of the day, but they came up again the day after that.

Fish kept coming. I thanked them for their sacrifice, and thanked the spirits as well for their kindness.

But by the end of that following day, I was beginning to think that calling the fish might not have been the wisest act. The small fish—the size of a man's arm—were followed by the bigger fish that hunted them. Dark fins filled the water.

Then the big fish were followed by even larger fish that hunted those. They jostled our ship almost as badly as the storm, as if the *Doomed* was a mere boat. They crashed into us so hard at times in the feeding frenzy that I worried they would break the hull. Even the captain was casting concerned looks toward the water.

I did not think matters could get much worse, but then, in the dim light of dusk, the great fish came.

Its glistening black bulk, many times the size of a whale, rose out of the water slowly, like an island. If Rabeen had indeed been built on the back of a fish, it was one like this, I thought, dazed.

Some of the pirates stared with mouths agape; others ran down below. One man jumped into the sea on the other side of the ship and tried to swim away from us. His screams echoed off our limp sails as the finned predators of the sea devoured him.

No one paid his death struggle any attention. We were all transfixed by the great fish that rose from the waves until he was taller than our ship, its two monstrous eyes staring at us unblinking.

Then suddenly the pirates ran, all toward the hatch that led below deck, some still with sword in hand, beating others out of the way, some of their mates tossing their swords and cowering.

I stood still, my limbs frozen by the sight of the giant monster in the sea, my mind furiously churning. I had reached out to the little fish. Could I reach this one?

I tried to feel what it felt, see what it saw, think what it thought. I tried to feel the cold water that half submerged its great body, as if I was submerged myself. I tried to feel the intermittent, slight breeze on my back, tried to see our ship the way the monster saw us as he stared blankly at us.

Since I was in the prow of the ship, I was closest to him. Batumar stood with his sword drawn next to me. On my other side, the merchant came up with the children, his rapier in hand.

I sang silently in my heart to the monster. *Oh great lord, forgive us for disturbing your kingdom. Great lord, please let us pass in peace.* I sang and sang, putting my very heart into every word.

I could heal men and animals with my spirit, but I could only reach animals with my spirit songs. Animals were pure in spirit, knew no hate or treachery. They wanted to eat, and they wanted to live. For the most part, their hearts were quiet. Not so with men drawn forward by all the things they endlessly wanted. They wanted those things so much and so loudly, they could not hear my spirit songs.

I hoped and prayed fervently that the great monster could hear me.

And maybe he did, because he suddenly sank into the sea, splashing up a wave so tall it nearly overturned our ship. We all fell to the planks and hung on to each other, Batumar to me so I would not be swept overboard, while I clung to some of the children, and their master hung on to the others.

By the time we scrambled to our knees, sopping wet and freezing, the great monster had vanished.

And the other fish went with him.

But that night, we had some rain, enough to fill a handful of water barrels when poured together.

For many days, our fortunes were restored and peace ruled the ship. But the wind would not rise, and soon days of hunger came again. Men were fighting, arguing night and day.

"They will turn against the captain soon," Batumar said as we lay in our cabin one night, starved again and weak. "If there is a fight and something happens to me, stay close to the merchant."

This I did not promise. Nothing was going to happen to Batumar. If he was injured in a fight, I would heal him, even if I had to give my very life for his.

And I would never put myself under the power of the merchant. *Never.*

In any case, mutiny was averted. The next morning, the hardstorms returned. We were once again all too busy, from one day to the next, fighting for survival.

I prayed that the spirits would let us see the end of our journey.

# CHAPTER NINE
## BACK INTO THE STORM

Days passed, nights, sometimes with Batumar, sometimes without. Once again, he helped abovedecks as much as he could. We were all weak from hunger, but at least his shipsickness diminished.

I lost track of time. Most days were as dark as the nights. The roar of the storms was near constant. In the rare pauses, sometimes I could hear the tiger roar or a child scream.

I feared the children were sick, so while Batumar was abovedecks, I tripped and rolled myself to the merchant's cabin one day, banging on the door until he opened it.

I had heard the children call him Graho up on deck, so I greeted him as such.

He gave a small bow. "My lady."

"Mistress Onra." Courtesy demanded that I give him my name.

His head was uncovered at last, and, for the first time, I could see his face, although not much of it. Barely any light came through the porthole, but I saw enough to know that he had a terrible face, all hard lines, his eyes rimmed with dark circles, his chin too sharp, his nose too big.

The front of his shirt was covered in vomit, although what he or the children could heave up, I did not know. All we had was rainwater we had collected, but we were running out of even that, back on water rations.

"Do you need my help?" I asked. "I freely give it."

"They are frightened," he said after a tense moment. "They cannot sleep from the hunger and the storm. And when they can sleep—" He looked away. "They sleep poorly."

I looked at the missing ears and the cut-off fingers, the burn scars. A little boy of seven or so was missing an eye. The children had plenty of material for nightmares. I blamed the merchant for all their afflictions, which, in the interest of him letting me stay with the children, I did not say.

Even in my miserable state, I was so angry at him, I could barely look at him.

I wanted to step by him with my head held high, but as I stepped inside the room, the ship rolled and tossed me to the floor. I did not bother to rise.

The children gathered around me, some even close enough this time so their arms or legs touched against mine. I was sure they missed their mothers. I was a grown woman, and I missed my mother still.

"Do you have a candle?" I asked the merchant.

He shook his head. "We had tallow candles. We ate them."

I nodded. We had eaten ours when we had found them at last. Tallow was animal fat. During the storms, the ship tossed by waves and battered by winds without stop, the candles could not be lit anyway.

"Do you have a water flask?" I asked next.

He nodded and handed it to me.

I added the right herbs to settle stomachs, then handed the flask back to him. "Warm it against your skin."

The medicine could infuse in cold water, but it would infuse faster with some heat.

Graho lifted his black shirt, and, even in the dim light, I could see the odd-shaped tattoos crisscrossing his skin. *Owner's marks?* I'd heard they were used by some slave masters. I looked away. Maybe he had been a slave before he became a master. Some continued the trade they knew the best, after they were freed.

I knew the slave trade was so, but I could not understand why. He knew what the whip felt like. How could he do it to others? How could he have these children harmed so he could sell them to the beggar lords on the mainland?

My jaw clenched. I fervently prayed for our arrival at the port, but I dreaded it too. On the ship, the tiger and the children were still safe, still near me. What could I do to save them once our journey ended?

I set that despair aside and turned my attention to helping them in the present moment. I could not feed them; I could not bathe them; I could not give them back to their mothers. But maybe I could take away their fear, even if for a short while.

"Have you ever heard the tale of the wise beggar and the foolish prince?"

They all snuggled closer, little faces turned up, listening.

"In a faraway kingdom were once two brothers. When their father died, he left them all his wealth and all his houses, and all his vineyards and fields, but one brother soon stole the other's inheritance by treachery. So that the betrayal could never be avenged, he had his hired swords cut out his brother's eyes. Then he used his brother's wealth as a gift to court the king's daughter. In good time, he married her and became a prince, while his blind brother became a beggar.

"Soon, hard times came to the kingdom," I said.

"War?" one of the little boys asked.

"War," I told him. "While the treacherous brother, the new prince, moved into the palace, the beggar brother went from town to town. The good people fed him; the bad people beat him. As he journeyed through the land, he met many men, lords and lowly shopkeeps, craftsmen and servants, and got to know their hearts.

"If he got two heels of bread in one day, he gave away one to someone who was hungry. If he passed an old woman whose donkey couldn't pull her cart, he helped. Because he could not see, his other senses grew sharper until he could hear as well as an owl.

"Once he came to a village where the people were in great sorrow, for they had lost a child. But as the beggar listened, he could hear the child call weakly from the bottom of a narrow well.

"Nobody could go down to help the little girl, but since the beggar was always walking and rarely eating, he was lean indeed. Even though he could not see, he told the people to tie a rope around him and lower him. And he saved that little girl."

The girls all seemed very happy with that outcome, but one of the boys put in, "What happened to the prince?"

"The prince lived lavishly, ate stuffed pigs, drank wine, and gobbled up cake." I made a gobbling sound.

Some of the children smiled for the first time.

But the oldest of the boys frowned. "There is no cake in war," he said with great certainty.

I supposed none of them had seen much food in a very long while. Certainly not in the slave pens, and definitely not here on the ship.

I went on with my story. "His people saw the prince day after day, eating and drinking while they fought and starved, and the people began to hate him."

The children nodded.

"Even the king despaired. He was old and sick. He hoped the prince would lead his army, but the prince refused to leave the palace. He did not become prince to be killed on a battlefield, he said. He did not become prince to starve. So he stayed home and feasted while the country and its people fell into despair.

"Even the king's best friends began to betray him, knowing that soon his kingdom would fall. The palace was full of spies. Some men tried to poison him. The king fell into such dark sadness that he walked out of the palace, down to the edge of the water, and he fell onto his knees to beg the spirits.

"'This man I chose for my daughter, this man I chose to be my son,' he cried. 'I did not choose wisely. Oh merciful spirits, send me a hero to save my country. I do not know who to trust. I have not been a good king. But for my folly, do not let my people perish. Send me a man who is worthy, and I shall give my whole kingdom to him.'"

I had to raise my voice to continue as the storm grew louder around us. We all clung together so we would not be tossed around the cabin.

"The blind beggar walked by just then," I said, "and heard the king cry about not knowing his people and not knowing who to trust. At once, the beggar strode up to the king and fell onto his knees in front of him.

"'Your majesty,' he said. 'If it pleases your grace, I can tell you who the good men are and who are the ones you can trust.' And then he told the king about how he had lived year after year, what lords had been kind to him, what lords had tried to force him into slavery. Many people do not even see a beggar. He had heard much that he had not been meant to hear. He knew what lords were thieves, what lords were cheaters, what lords talked treason."

"Did he tell the king that he was the prince's brother? Did he tell the king that his brother was a rotten egg?" the littlest girl asked.

"No," I told her. "Even after all those years of suffering, the beggar did not want his brother to come to harm."

"What happened next?" One of the older boys spoke up, impatient with the interruption.

"The king invited the beggar into his chambers. That night, the king himself wrote letters, all night, for he could not even trust his scribes. And in the morning, all those letters were sent to his trusted lords with the last of the king's trusted soldiers. And those trusted lords hastened to the king's side. And do you know who was invited along with the lords to the war council?"

"The blind beggar!" a couple of the children shouted.

I nodded. "The blind beggar was a wise man indeed. Once, he had managed his father's vast holdings. When he gave advice, the lords saw his wisdom and accepted it. They could see that he was a man blessed by the spirits in some regard, even while cursed in another."

"Did they defeat the enemy?" Another little boy piped up with the question.

"Indeed they did, and after the war, the king had his people gather in front of the palace. He took the prince and the beggar with him to the palace balcony that overlooked the crowd.

"First, he addressed the lords who waited in the front row, sitting on their prancing horses. *'I have grown old,'* he told them. *'I ask you to choose a new king. Who do you choose to rule this country, the beggar or the prince?'*

"*'The beggar!'* the lords shouted. They remembered that he was the one who vouched for them with the king. They remembered his wise advice at the war council. They remembered how the prince cowered, caring only about his own comfort and safety. Better a king without eyes than a king without wisdom and courage, they murmured amongst themselves, and shouted again, *'Let the beggar be king!'*

"Next, the king turned to his people. *'I have grown old and sick. If a new enemy comes, I fear I might not be able to protect you. Who do you choose for your new king? The beggar or the prince?'*

"*'The beggar!'* the people shouted. They all remembered the beggar walking among them, helping when he could, sharing what little he had with those less fortunate. They remembered his stories that gave them hope, and they remembered his kindness. They remembered the child he saved from the well. *'Better a king without eyes than a king without a heart,'* they murmured to each other, and shouted again, *'We choose the beggar!'*

"The blind beggar was crowned the next day. But when he sent for his brother so his brother could sit by his side at the feast, the prince and the princess could not be found. They had run away in the night."

The children pressed even closer, smiles on nearly every face. Whether because they had not heard a tale in a long time or because they liked the idea of a maimed beggar becoming a king, I did not know.

The two youngest ones were sleeping, half curled up on my lap. I was glad for their peace.

The merchant's blue eyes looked black in the dim cabin. I did not like the way he watched me. I had been sold into slavery before, and selling people was his business. Maybe he was already calculating how much coin he could earn for a healer.

I gently set the sleeping children aside and struggled to my feet. "If any of them start heaving, let them drink the medicine," I said, then half lurched, half crawled back toward my cabin.

But instead of going in, I visited the tiger. Her eyes were glazed, her great side caved in. She had sores and open wounds on her skin. I suspected that the men poked and tortured her when the captain wasn't looking. She was but fur. Even if the pirates decided to slaughter her now, there would be nothing to eat.

I sang her my spirit song to comfort her. She pushed a great paw out between two bars, but not to swipe at me. She left her listless paw lying next to my hand. I reached out carefully to stroke her. The tiger closed her eyes.

Dizzy with hunger, so did I.

I stayed there, stroking her matted fur and singing to her, as much as to comfort her as because I had no strength to move. Then Batumar came down below, lifted me up, and carried me to our cabin.

# CHAPTER TEN
## THE RED TOWER

By the time the hardstorms spit us out, we had lost most of our sails, and the ship was taking on water. We barely had any rigging left. The only reason we drifted toward land was because the currents pushed us that way.

"How long before we reach port?" Batumar asked One-Tooth Tum.

"Two more days." The captain watched me. "We have nayver made it out of the storms with this little damage afore."

I sensed he suspected that I had called the fish, and now he was uncertain how far my powers reached. Not far enough to feed us again.

We were all on board, enjoying the fresh air, dazed and starved. We could see fish in the water, but we did not have as much as half a rat's tail for bait.

*Two more days*, I thought, and then we'll have survived the belly of the mountain, the hardstorms, and the pirates. I had never wanted anything half as much as I wanted to feel the paved streets of Ishaf under my feet.

One-Tooth Tum looked at me, then addressed his question to Batumar. "Have ye been to Ishaf of late?"

Batumar shook his head.

"Avoid ye the red tower," the pirate captain advised.

"What's in the red tower?"

"A sorcerer. The city fathers called him to the city to protect it. But he exacts a terrible price." The captain pinned me with a sharp look. "What ye have, he would take."

"Take how?" Batumar demanded.

The captain shrugged. "He leaves people empty."

Then the captain looked over my head at some of his men and moved off. His shoulders seemed stiff, his stride maybe a little too measured.

I glanced at Batumar. He was now watching Grun, the captain's second in command, who was standing in a circle of the most disgruntled pirates. The captain was looking out to sea, but I caught him checking the men now and then from the corner of his eye.

Casting insolent looks toward the captain, the men climbed down into the belly of the ship one by one. Tension took their place on deck, anticipation of something dark coming our way. Suddenly we were waiting for what would happen next, as we had waited for the hardstorms, the air filling with premonitions.

Batumar pulled me to the prow and put himself in front of me, keeping his hand close to his sword. Graho, the merchant, gathered the children around him in the most out-of-the-way spot he could find, behind a pile of empty water barrels that had been brought up again in hopes of rain.

Other pirates who'd been working until now sensed the unease and began positioning themselves in groups of twos and threes, no weapons in hands yet, but alert and ready.

I thought the men who had gone below might return with the captain's treasure, claiming it for themselves, but instead, when they appeared, they were dragging the tiger cage up to the deck, grunting and cursing.

The tiger kept shifting but did not fight them. Maybe she thought that being out under the sky again meant her freedom was near.

Then, with one more heave, the cage was up on deck at last. The tiger suddenly looked to the east, and her tail and whiskers twitched as if she could smell the forests from here. Maybe she was saving her energy for an attempt to escape once the pirates docked the ship.

But swords scraped against scabbards as the men drew their weapons, ready to stab the emaciated animal through the bars, jeering and shouting now to work up the courage.

Sensing the danger, the tiger rose to her haunches and roared, swiping through the bars, but she could not defend herself from every direction at once.

"Leave it!" the captain shouted as he pulled his own sword and rushed the mutinous pirates.

Metal clashed against metal in an instant. Men fell to his left and right, wounded. As the last of his faithful men hurried to back him up, he charged his first mate with a ferocious blow.

Grun's skull cracked, his spirit departing.

The captain and his faithful men growled and snapped at the rest of Grun's crew. But after trading insults, the two groups pulled back from each other.

"The tiger is worth gold," the captain shouted, and kicked the dead man hard enough so that Grun slid the width of a plank or two in his own blood. "He's worth nothin'. Ye eat *him*, ye bastards." He strode away, his chest heaving, his shoulders shaking with fury.

The men moved in around the body, their faces dark, emotionless masks.

My stomach clenched. I watched as the merchant herded the children down below. Batumar and I followed.

I glanced back at the tiger, which did not seem aware that a battle had been fought over her. She had her eyes on me.

Batumar kept as close to me as possible, even on the stairs. "She is safe enough now," he said. "What the men eat today will carry them through until we reach port."

I moved forward in the hope that he would be proven right, and that the captain would protect the tiger again should the animal face danger.

We closed the door to our cabin behind us, but soon the smell of roasting meat reached us anyhow—sweet and somehow foul at the same time, all wrong, turning my stomach more than the storms ever had.

We huddled on the floor in the corner, Batumar's arms around me. His great body seemed to me as a bulwark against the world, and I leaned against him, wishing now even more that we were finally off the ship.

Silence ruled belowdecks. In it, I heard crying.

I pulled away from Batumar. "I shall go and tell the children a story."

He frowned. I could see *no* forming on his lips.

"The merchant will not hurt me," I hurried to say. "He has no reason."

"There is danger in the air still," Batumar said carefully. "I do not like it."

"We will reach land the day after tomorrow."

"Until then, we shall stay in here."

He had not taken his sword belt off as was his habit whenever we were inside our cabin, but he had left his weapon hanging at his side.

In the end, I did talk him into letting me go. But he came with me.

Graho, the nine children, and I filled most of the room. Batumar's large frame took up the rest of the space as he stood inside the door, his feet braced. I could not tell if he was guarding me from the merchant or from the pirates.

The children gathered closely around me, unsure of what to make of the giant warrior suddenly in their midst.

I started into a story I learned from my mother.

"At the foot of the Mountain of No Top, where it meets Bottomless Lake..." My mother always began the story in a hushed voice as if telling me a secret never told before, and I spoke the same way. "Lived a beautiful young girl called Lawana."

"One day, a man came from far away to ask for her hand in marriage. Lawana folded up her clothes and veils and all that was most important to her and left her father's house to go to him. When she was halfway, she turned back. She did not want to leave her family. Then she turned to the man. She truly wanted to go with him. She turned back and forth faster and faster, unable to make up her mind, until she spun so fast she drilled a large hole in the ground.

"The hole, deep and wide, drank Bottomless Lake and swallowed Mountain of No Top. An endless swamp took their place, and to this day, it is called Lawana's Swamp."

*"What happened to Lawana and her parents and the man?"* I would ask my mother each time she reached this far in the story.

*"The swamp swallowed them,"* my mother would say, her voice deep and grave.

She used to tell me many such tales, sometimes even about the
Forgotten City of the Guardians, but mostly about young girls and all
the hardships they faced and what happened after the choices they made.
I liked that, the gentle way she taught me.

I finished the story for the children. They nodded with understand-
ing. They were not troubled overmuch by Lawana's untimely demise.
Children's tales were meant to teach, so they rarely had happy endings.
Most were tales of warning.

I tried to pick one next that spoke of happier times, and told the children about the merchant and the beggar boy, then the story of the faithful
wife, and ended with the Guardians and the Forgotten City.

"Do you know the Guardians, mistress?" the littlest of the girls
asked. Nala, I had heard the others call her.

I smiled at her. "I do, Nala. I have been to the Forgotten City."

Their sparkling blue eyes could not have grown larger.

So I talked to them about the Forum and the Seer and the Gate, the
Sacred Cave. They listened with rapt attention until no more light came
in through the porthole.

Then Batumar and I went back to our cabin.

He gathered me into his arms as we lay down on top of his fur cloak.
He caressed my jaw with the back of his fingers. I ached for his touch,
ached for more.

He outlined my collarbone with his thumb.

He dragged his lips over my eyebrows, then kissed his way down the
ridge of my nose. His fingers circled my breast. Then his mouth sealed
over mine.

The kiss was heartachingly gentle, then seeking, then mastering.
Every part of my body responded.

I tried to push my hand under his doublet over his flat stomach,
desperate to feel the warmth of his skin.

But he put his hand over mine to halt me.

All the jealousy I had left behind in Karamur flooded back into my
heart. He had never stopped my caresses before. "Because of the Lady
Lalandra?" I asked, my throat tight.

He stilled. "What is this now?"

86

I felt foolish beyond bearing for saying the words, but I could not stop myself. "You summoned her before we left."

Silence stretched between us, unbearably long. I grew dizzy, for I was holding my breath for his answer.

At last, he said, "To inquire how they all fared. I owe them my protection." He caressed the back of my hand with his thumb. "My brother's concubines and children have been at the palace for nearly two full moon-crossings. I could ignore them no longer." He tightened his hold on me. "I want no other but you, my Lady Tera."

My heart thrilled.

He let my hand go and ran the pad of his thumb along my jaw. "Before I met you, I did not know that it could be like this between a man and a woman."

Heat suffused my body at his softly spoken words.

He tilted my head up and kissed me in the darkness, starting all over again. Then he kissed me deeper. His large hand was covering my breast, its familiar weight unbearable torture.

As he explored my mouth and my body, my heart sang.

But too soon, he drew away with a tortured groan. "It is not safe. I must be ready if they come for us. But tomorrow we will spend a night at the best inn Ishaf has to offer, with a door that has a lock," he promised, his voice strained.

And then he held me as I tried not to moan with frustration.

He did not let me leave our cabin the following day. He did not trust all the racket on deck. But the noise died down at one point in the night.

In the morning, when we stepped out into the passageway, we found belowdecks abandoned. We went up the stairs to the deck, and the first thing we saw was that the tiger yet lived and land was in sight, a dark strip on the horizon. Oh, how my heart thrilled.

But the next thing we saw was that at the prow of the ship, the deck was covered in blood. Five mutilated bodies lay in crumpled heaps by the empty water barrels. I jerked my gaze from the grisly sight, up toward the sky, only to see the captain dangling lifelessly from the front mast. His men had used some of the rigging to hang him.

Pek peeked from the safety of the crow's nest, the lookout basket on top of the mainmast. The boy was a survivor if ever I had seen one, I thought for a distracted moment before I heard a soft cry and whipped around to see the merchant and the children in the aft, corralled by pirates with drawn swords. The merchant had his rapier in hand.

Next to me, Batumar drew his broadsword.

A dozen pirates immediately headed our way, their faces menacing, hate boiling in their eyes, words of murder spewing from their lips.

They now had the ship and their captain's treasure. They had never wanted passengers.

# CHAPTER ELEVEN
## SEA OF SORROW

Batumar sprang into the fight, taking on three opponents at once, swords clashing.

I pulled out my small knife and stood back-to-back with the High Lord, holding the knife out in front of me. I knew not what to do if a pirate attacked, but none of the men lunged for me. Mayhap they saw me, and the children, as spoils, merchandise to sell in Ishaf, since their captain hadn't let them sell us at Rabeen.

At least, while I was protecting Batumar's back, they could not attack him from behind.

He cut down one man, then another, his feet planted on deck, his arms moving swiftly. Metal clanged against metal, over and over.

I could see the merchant from the corner of my eye, defending himself with his rapier, protecting the children behind him. I was surprised to see that he also had bodies lying in blood at his feet now. I had not expected a merchant to fight like a warrior.

Then the tiger's roar drew my attention to the cage as several men stabbed at her. She swiped, then lurched from side to side, trying to turn in the narrow cage as men attacked her from the back, stabbing her hindquarters.

Blood ran down her matted hide. She roared again, a mighty roar, and swiped with her massive paw, throwing up her head. And even from a distance, I could hear a crack.

She stilled as if she knew what the sound signified. And then she attacked the cage itself.

My heart rate sped even faster. Could she? The endless jostling of the cage in the storms had to have loosened the lashing that held the bars together.

The men jumped back, but not all of them were fast enough. The bars cracked open the next moment, and the tiger sprang forward, bringing the nearest pirate down with a mighty swipe. Blood washed the deck.

This time, she roared so loudly, the sails rattled.

Most of the pirates abandoned us at that, and went to fight the tiger, knowing she was the most dangerous threat on deck. They needed numbers to take her down, and they knew they could come back to us later. Only three pirates remained with Batumar and the merchant each to keep them cornered.

One man sliced into Batumar's shoulder before the High Lord ran him through with his sword. I could feel Batumar's pain, although he did not allow it to slow him down as he faced the remaining two men. We were still back-to-back. Through that touch, I healed him.

He gave a warning growl deep in his throat, sounding like an unhappy tiger himself.

He had long before forbidden me to heal him with my own strength. He allowed me to help with only my herbs. I was prepared to withstand his displeasure in this matter. I stood ready to take upon me whatever injury his attackers would mete out. Batumar could not fall. If he did, our island would fall with him.

One of the pirates rushed forward to run him through, while the other lifted his curved sword and angled it to cut off Batumar's head. Batumar jumped sideways, avoiding one man while cutting the throat of the other. Then he finished off his last attacker.

I looked to the merchant, where swords still clashed. He had one opponent left.

Batumar ran toward them, and I followed. I did not want to become separated from him.

A roar drew my attention to the prow, where the pirates had cornered the tiger and closed in around her. She was bleeding from half a dozen wounds, baring her teeth, swiping at her opponents. She brought down a man with nearly every swipe, but she was tiring. She had been starved and weakened to begin with, and now stabbed and bloodied.

I tore my gaze from her as we at last reached the merchant—just as he slayed his last opponent.

"The barrels," he shouted. "We need rope."

Batumar jumped to help him. Then so did I, once I understood what they were doing.

We lashed the empty water barrels together with bits and pieces of storm-torn rigging that was lying on deck. Nine barrels in all, bottoms down, open mouths up, making a raft that looked similar to a honeycomb.

We heaved the raft over the side of the ship and balanced it straight, the two men holding it, one from each side, with the two longest pieces of rope they could find.

I desperately scanned the feeble-looking device. "Will it hold together?"

"It will," Graho said with full certainty, as if he was also a builder.

*No time for questions.* I filled the raft, quickly lifting the children one by one and settling each into a barrel.

Then Graho said, "You should get in with Nala."

"Quickly," Batumar urged.

The little girl was crying, frightened by the bloodbath on board, likely just as frightened by dangling high in the air above the ocean. Enough room remained next to her. I had always been slight of body, and was even slighter now after our days of starvation.

I climbed over the side quickly, then into the barrel, and drew her into my arms. "We are fine well. Hold on to me, Nala."

She buried her face against my chest and wrapped her little arms tightly around me. The other girls whimpered. Even the boys were staring at the churning water below us with wide-eyed fear.

Batumar and the merchant began lowering us hand over hand, keeping the makeshift raft even so we wouldn't tumble into the sea. *A few moments*, I told myself. A little longer and we'd be on the water, then drifting with the current away from the *Doomed* and toward shore. I expected that our light raft would move faster than the heavy ship.

But at this point, our escape was discovered.

Pirates shouted up above, and then they were right there, seven, fierce and outraged. They were predators, just like the tiger, not about to let prey escape.

Graho and Batumar each held the rope with their left hands now while fighting right-handed, trapped where they stood. We dangled in the air, too far down to climb back up, too high up still so that if the ropes loosened, the crash into the sea would break the makeshift raft apart.

Land was still at a great distance, beyond what I could swim, for certain, and hopelessly far for the children.

They all shrieked and cried now as blood splattered down on us. And even more so when a dead pirate dropped by us only to be immediately swallowed by the waves. *Spirits have mercy.*

I had not the time to reassure the little ones. I had to focus all my attention on the fight above. The cuts Batumar and the merchant suffered, I immediately healed, taking the injuries upon myself. We were in this desperate escape together. We all had to live for any of us to live.

Then the merchant suffered a fearsome cut between his neck and shoulder, and before I could heal him, he was heaved overboard.

The raft tilted, the children screamed, but Batumar caught the second rope before we could all spill into the waves. Tilted as we were, he held both ropes in one hand while fighting with the other, a feat beyond human strength, and yet somehow he managed.

He roared as loud as the tiger, in full battle rage.

Below, Graho treaded water, the ocean turning red around him. I healed his wound before he could draw predators, if the slain sailor hadn't already.

Our raft began to lower, and kept lowering. I looked up. Batumar was letting the twin ropes slide through his hand little by little while he fought the enemy.

My heart clenched as I watched him. He needed to move so he could outmaneuver the men, or they would cut him down. He fought at least four at a time, while holding the weight of the raft and all of us in it.

If he let the raft go, he could have grabbed another sword from a fallen enemy, danced away, set the rhythm of the fight. But if he let us go, the raft would break apart as it hit the water, and we would all drown.

He held on with a strength I did not know a man could possess.

I saw red staining the rope as it slid through his hand, and knew that the rough rope was shredding his skin and his flesh. The weight he held had to be unbearable.

Yet he did not let go.

I raised my spirit to heal the wound, but he was stabbed in the side the next moment, his liver run straight through, so I healed that first, then tried to catch my breath as blinding pain seared into my own body. Agony sliced through me. I felt as if I had been cut in half.

All through this, the raft dipped down and down, moving lower against the side of the pirate ship.

Soon we were nearly at the water, although at a perilous angle. If we did not touch down level with the sea and some of the barrels began taking on water, they would pull down all the rest and the raft would sink.

A sword sliced through Batumar's arm above. I breathed hard as I took in that injury and used my healing spirit to mend it in myself.

As Batumar fought the pirates above, I fought time below. Slicing a man to the bone takes but a blink of an eye. Healing that damage takes much longer. With four men surrounding him still, he was receiving his injuries at a greater speed than I could mend.

The closer the raft reached to the water, the weaker I became, my body a ball of agony. Even my mind sank into a fog. I could feel the severity of each of Batumar's new injuries on top of my own pain.

"Spirits save us!" I cried aloud.

But instead of relief, I felt every inch of the sword that ran Batumar through, as if the blade had sliced into my own chest.

His shredded fingers let go of the rope then, and the raft splashed into the water, wobbled violently for a few moments, then steadied.

I stared up, searching desperately for sign of life in him. He was still standing, braced against the side of the ship, but only for another breath. Then he was tossed over the side without mercy.

Already the waves pushed the raft away so I could not reach for him as his battered and bleeding body began to sink.

Then I was in the water, swimming down, searching for him.

I was too weak to send my spirit to him without touching.

*If I could touch him...* I had one thought only: to give my spirit and my life to him.

I saw the shadow of his great body, a black shape floating gently downward. I swam as hard as I could to reach him.

I couldn't.

My lungs burned, then threatened to burst.

Water filled my mouth. I was choking. Then I was drowning.

What air was left in my lungs buoyed me up, and I was too injured and shocked and broken to fight harder. My head broke the surface, only to be covered again when a wave slapped me.

The raft washed farther and farther away, the children crying, some screaming for me. I had not the strength to reach them. And even if I could have mustered the strength, I had not the spirit.

A new wave filled my mouth. What did it matter?

I wanted to float down into the deep with Batumar. I was his—heart, body, and soul. I could not leave him here. I *would* not leave him here in a cold, watery grave.

The sea chilled my bones. My limbs moved slower and slower. My eyes glazed over with tears and pain. I could no longer see the raft or the ship. All I could see was the murky depths, Batumar floating away from me.

I did not fight the waves.

# CHAPTER TWELVE
## DAYS OF DARKNESS

My head was underwater when the tiger splashed down next to me.

She licked my face with her big, raspy tongue, bringing it up, then grabbed me by the collar in the back—as she would with one of her cubs—and began swimming toward shore, her great paws paddling in the water.

My heart was dead, and my body would soon follow, I was certain, despite the tiger's efforts. I could not feel my feet from the cold. My whole body grew numb.

The port of Ishaf was too far for us to reach. I closed my eyes, waiting to sink again, waiting to join Batumar in the deep. My tears mixed with the sea.

But the tiger would not release me.

She swam for hours that seemed days. I felt as if a lifetime passed while she dragged me through the frigid water. Before that swim had been my life. After it, something else waited that I neither recognized nor wanted.

I had died in that water with Batumar. Some ghost-spirit had been dragged ashore by the tiger.

She dragged me up on rocks that cut into my skin and dug into my thighs. She dropped me and licked my face again. Her tongue felt burning hot compared to the water. She nudged me with her nose, then staggered away on shaking legs.

I shook even harder. I stayed on the hard rocks, shivering, staring up into the gray and dreary sky. I could not feel my body. I could not feel my heart.

Clouds rolled by like marching armies in an endless procession. Eternities passed. Then a seabird landed on my chest, perhaps thinking I was dead. It pecked at my chin.

That sharp cut of pain made me sit up at last.

The bird protested angrily and flew away.

I was on a rocky shore, the point of land that had been closest to our ship. The shoreline resembled that around Barren Cove from where we had sailed—a rocky beach backing to sheer cliffs.

The port city of Ishaf waited a day's hard walk away across a wide bay. I could see two dozen ships in the harbor, the *Doomed* among them, its tattered red sails rolled up. I could see the red tower and remembered the captain's warning about the sorcerer within. I had nothing to fear. I had but emptiness inside me, nothing left for the sorcerer to take.

Saltwater spray hit me in the face. I shivered, looking numbly out at the sea that was closer than when the tiger had dropped me. The tide was coming in.

For a moment, I thought about staying where I was. But something, perhaps my mother's spirit watching over me, perhaps Batumar's, made me crawl to higher ground at the foot of the cliffs.

I sat with my back against the rock and pulled my knees up, hugged them close to my chest for heat. The wind had dried my clothes, but it had also chilled my body that ached through and through with a vast variety of pain. I still carried Batumar's and the merchant's injuries.

The gray sun was dipping into the gray ocean, dusk settling on the rocky shore. I could not think of what I should do next. I felt empty, then suddenly as if I was filled with cold water—a vessel too small to hold its contents—a terrible heaviness and pressure inside my chest. I stared out at the waves, part of me expecting Batumar to somehow walk out of the endless gray.

He didn't.

The tiger returned at nightfall, bringing half a bloody fish and dropping it by my feet. She sniffed around, first checking the immediate area, then lifting her nose and smelling the wind. Then she padded back and lay down by my side with her back to me.

Soon heat seeped into me from her body and took away the numbness of the cold. I curled my aching body against her back and slept on our bed of stone while she snored.

Morning came. The tiger ate the half fish, then padded off.

I relieved myself on the rocks by the sea, then went back to my spot and lay down again. I stared up at the sky, hoping to see a cloud in the shape of Batumar's face, hoping for a message from his spirit.

Every part of my body hurt still, with an unending ache. My spirit was too broken to heal my injuries. I lay with my eyes closed. *If I could somehow go back*, I thought. *If I could do something differently.*

I did not know how much time passed as I lay there. Then a shadow fell over my face. I thought the seabird was returning to see if I was yet dead. But when I opened my eyes, I saw Graho bending over me.

"You live." The merchant sounded oddly pleased.

He looked haggard, his face drawn, his hair hanging in twisted locks. His clothes were rent where the pirates had stabbed him. I had healed his injuries, but his garments carried their own wounds.

Anger washed over me that a man such as he should live while Batumar was gone. Hot tears leaked onto my face in a spurt of fury.

Then the children surrounded me, their blue eyes large and haunted. Only six. My breath caught. Had the others been lost to the sea?

The merchant bent to me and tossed me over his shoulder, carrying me away as easily as if I was a child. He was strong for a merchant.

If he thought he could get coin for me at Ishaf, he was bound to be disappointed. No wise man would pay for what I was now.

Being moved hurt, but I did not moan.

He carried me to a gap in the rock wall, then up steps that looked man-made. At the top of the cliffs, after a stretch of rocks, a forest waited with bare trees.

He carried me into the woods, to a small campsite. I gave thanks to the spirits when I spotted the three missing children tending a fire.

The merchant laid me down on a bed of dry leaves, close enough so I would feel the warmth of the flames.

He offered me his flask of water and a handful of berries. "You must regain your strength."

I turned away and closed my eyes, shutting out the sounds of the children coming and going, talking in a language I did not understand.

When night came, the tiger walked up to the edge of our campsite. She lay down and called to me, chuffing softly, like a mother to her cub. I stumbled over to her and slept curled against her side. She was as warm as the fire.

"Thank you, Marga," I named her with the Shahala word for mother.

In the morning, Marga was gone, and the merchant was back, standing over me.

"Who are you?" he asked.

I did not have to think. "I am nobody."

I had once been a Shahala healer, but now I could not even heal myself. My belt of herbs had been lost in the waves. I had once been the favorite concubine of the High Lord of the Kadar. Batumar now rested on the bottom of the ocean.

"Lady Onra," the merchant started.

"My true name is Tera," I corrected on a sigh, in case he was the one who would recite the Last Blessing over my grave. If his people even offered a Last Blessing.

"Lady Tera." Once again, the merchant offered me berries and water. "You must eat and drink." He sounded brisk, like a teacher ordering his pupils.

A brittle laugh escaped my chapped lips. "For what purpose?"

I had no coin for travel. Even if I did, I did not fully know Batumar's plans. And even if I knew every last detail, kings and generals would not negotiate with a woman. I had no authority to represent the Kadar and sign treaties in their name.

Graho sat down next to me, crossing his long legs in front of him. Then he said, in a softer tone than before, "Eat so that you may live."

*So I can sell you at the market*, he meant.

I had been a slave before and had survived. Perhaps I could survive it again. But did I want to survive in a world where my people wouldn't?

Batumar was lost. Our quest was lost. As soon as the Gate opened, our people would be slaughtered.

"We shall stay here another day to rest and recover," the merchant told me, "then we shall go to Ishaf."

"I wish to remain."

Anger flattened his lips. His blue eyes flashed. "You wish to die."

I said nothing. What did I wish? I wished that Batumar and I had never left on our journey, but I could not turn back time. "I wish to return to my people." Yet another impossible wish.

"To be locked away in the next High Lord's Pleasure Hall?" The merchant snapped out the words.

I closed my eyes. So he knew the Kadar customs and had recognized Batumar. As a traveling merchant, he'd probably been on our island before.

I hated his words, but they held truth I had not considered. If I returned to Karamur, I would become the next High Lord's concubine. Batumar had no living brothers. Lord Samtis, the warlord who was in charge of Karamur in Batumar's absence, would likely be elected the new High Lord now.

I had seen Lord Samtis at the High Lord's feasts many a time. He was younger than Batumar, and, according to Batumar, a true warrior. He was built for battle, yet quick to smile. But to live in his Pleasure Hall, or any man's...*No.* In truth, I found death preferable.

"Why don't you heal yourself?" Graho asked, his voice back to a kinder tone.

I said nothing. I knew well the source of his sudden interest in me and concern for my well-being. He would receive more for a healthy woman than one half-dead.

"Why did the High Lord of the Kadar leave the island in the middle of war with no guard?" he wanted to know next. "On a pirate ship? With a concubine?"

When I did not answer, he puzzled it out for himself. "He was heading somewhere to make some kind of an alliance." Graho paused. "The High Lord should not have brought you. That was ill done."

He pushed to his feet with a frustrated grunt and strode away.

A little while later, the children scampered over. They brought water in a flask, berries in their hands, and a few sea mussels in a nest of seaweed, their large blue eyes watching me with worry.

I could not find it in my heart to send them away, so I ate, even if the food made my empty stomach cramp.

Afterward, they snuggled against me and lent me their warmth. How could I say no? For certain, they missed their mothers.

Soon the tiger returned, but the children weren't scared in the least, perhaps because they had seen her earlier with me. She brought a leg of deer and dropped it at my feet. Then she curved her great body around us as if we were her cubs. She looked bigger and stronger already, after two days of fishing in the sea and hunting in the forest.

I was pleased for her. I wanted one of us to live.

Marga's side rose and fell in a steady rhythm. The children slept, their soft breath a contrast to the tiger's snoring. Heat seeped into my aching body.

As I stared up at the night sky, I felt the first flicker of strength, my thoughts clearing at last. I could not save Batumar, I could not save my people, but maybe I could save these children. My forehead furrowed. What could I trade with the merchant?

I had my waterlogged boots and my ruined clothes. My cloak was gone, and so was my belt of herbs. On my leather belt I still had my empty water flask and my simple kitchen knife, both worth very little.

The tiger was worth considerable coin, according to One-Tooth Tum, but the tiger was not mine to trade, and even if she was, I would not have traded her. I thought hard for half the night, coming to the only possible answer with dread: I had only myself to give.

I sent a prayer to the spirits then and tried to heal myself again so I might have more value in the bargain. Nothing happened.

None of the pain or the soreness or the tightness went away. I tried again, without result. Deep in my empty heart, I cried out to the spirits. They did not answer.

A sense of heavy defeat settled on me once again. I closed my eyes and let the tears wash down my face.

I truly was nothing. *Good*, part of me said. If I was nothing, then nothing more could be taken away from me. This brought some odd measure of comfort that made sense to my grief-addled brain. I closed my eyes and went to sleep.

In the morning, I dragged the deer leg over to the fire, skinned it with my knife, and roasted it, ignoring the merchant's curious gaze.

The children liked the meat. I even caught a couple of smiles, and caught their names. Nala, Kera, Tana, Mora—the four girls. Petars, Mikal, Willem, Andrev, and Gregno—the five boys.

I ate with them, a little, not wanting to overtax my stomach that had been without substantial food for many days.

I could not heal myself with powers, but food was another kind of healing.

The merchant fried a fatty fish next that he must have caught earlier, careful to catch the dripping fish oil in an empty shell. He worked that into his boots and gestured for me to do the same. This gift I accepted gratefully.

The leather of my boots had been treated for winter to repel water. Walking through snow or even puddles would not have done much damage, but the extended swim in salt water had soaked the leather through, and it had dried stiff, chafing my skin at every step.

The fish oil helped some, but no matter how much I worked the leather, I knew those boots would never be the same again. Before we went anywhere, I would have to fill them with dry moss to make a long walk possible.

I walked into the forest and gathered that moss, then some herbs, made a strengthening tea, and shared it with the children, who, while taking turns drinking from the flask, shyly asked for a story.

I could not remember any.

Packing up to leave for Ishaf did not take long, as we had nothing but the clothes on our backs. Instead of the rocky beach that would have slowed us down and likely caused injury, we walked through the forest, the merchant in the lead.

He had lost his rapier in the water, but since the tiger walked with us, I did not worry overmuch about being set upon by bandits.

We progressed slowly, all of us still too weak, the children's short legs taking only very small bites out of the distance. Here and there, when I saw healing plants, I cut a few bunches without conscious thought and tied them to my belt. They made me feel slightly more whole. I wore them like the Kadar concubines wore their charm belts.

"At least there is no snow on the ground," the merchant remarked.

I nodded. No snow, but a stiff wind blew, and the leafless trees and bushes blocked little of it. Being cold slowed us further still.

By nightfall, we were only halfway to the city, according to the merchant. He did not berate me or the children for slowing him down. Instead, he made a fire and we sat around it, eating what we had foraged: more berries, some mushrooms, and wild grapes that had dried on the vine. We could not hunt without bow and arrows, and we could not even hope for eggs, for no bird laid eggs in winter.

Once again, our main, and only, satisfying meal came in the morning when the tiger presented me with the hindquarters of a wild boar. This we roasted and ate.

I did not broach my idea of offering myself for the children. I wanted to wait until I was more recovered. As we walked, I thought about the famous stone temple of Ishaf and its priests, the daily sacrifices they made for their gods and goddesses. I had heard that many orphans served at the temple.

If I could not return the children to their families, they'd be better off serving at the temple than serving a beggar lord, starved and forced to beg on the streets.

The merchant treated them well, even giving them food before he ate, but, of course, he wanted them in fine shape for the sale. The children did not seem afraid of him. But I knew well that slaves grew used to their captors and their fate. Still, at least he showed no unkindness toward any, no violent discipline, not even when one tripped on a root and wailed.

When we reached a wide stream, he even carried the children across one by one. And when I slipped in the middle of the stream, he came back for me and carried me out over his shoulder.

I looked back for the tiger, but Marga was off exploring some other corner of the forest. She often wandered away, then returned to check on our progress, soon padding off again. Maybe we were walking too slowly for her.

"Where were you headed?" the merchant asked, falling in step next to me as we took a wider animal trail.

*Landria.* But I no longer had need to go there. I would have no army of mercenaries to ship back to Dahru to liberate our island. I said nothing.

"What will you do when we reach Ishaf?" he asked then.

This I answered. "The spirits willing, I shall make a trade."

He watched me with a puzzled look in his blue gaze. When I added no further detail, he said, "I shall be taking the caravan to Muzarat. Come with me."

But the very name made me shudder. Muzarat was possibly the biggest slave market in the world, on the other side of the great Cetrean Desert. I looked away from him. He did not plan on selling his little beggars at Ishaf. He was taking them where he could receive top coin.

Or maybe he lived in Muzarat. I did not care enough to ask.

He kept watching me as we walked. "I offer you my protection for the journey."

*For the journey.* But not at Muzarat. He intended to lure me along, then sell me.

I said nothing.

We stopped to rest often and made little progress by the end of the day. I helped the children gather branches while the merchant cleared a spot for us to sleep and made sure we would not be lying next to any poisonous snakes.

We had no shelter, but in this, the spirits favored us at last, for it neither snowed nor rained. The night remained mild for the season.

At dawn, the tiger found us and gifted us with the shoulder of a brown horse.

"We must be close to the city," the merchant said later as he roasted the meat.

He was proven right. We reached the edge of the forest by midday.

The pirate ship was gone from the harbor. The port city spread out before us, its distinct red tower in the eastern quarter of the city proper, the white spire of their stone temple in the west. A multitude of peasant huts crowded outside the city's wooden walls, horses and cows and sheep milling among the huts with the peasants. Servants and soldiers passed in and out the city gate. The slight wind carried the scent of wood smoke and animal waste toward us.

*Ishaf.*

I stopped for a moment, and the tiger paused by my side.

I had reached Ishaf. Without Batumar. The dark void inside my chest felt large enough to swallow the whole city.

The merchant and the children moved forward, toward food and warmth and relative safety. I followed them. I would save the children if I could, I resolved again.

Marga stayed at the edge of the woods. She gave a mournful roar behind me. I turned just in time to see her disappear in a flash of gold.

*Thank you, great mother,* I called after her. *May the spirits keep you safe.*

Then I caught up to the merchant, who said, "I wondered what would happen if she tried to come into the city with us. I am relieved that she likes the woods better."

He sounded almost as if he cared for the tiger. Then again, in all that time we had been together, he had made no attempt to capture Marga, despite her trading value. I thought that odd for a merchant.

We followed wagon tracks to the city gate. The city guard did not question us but let us through. They must have seen their share of war refugees of late.

An oxcart rolled by us; narrow houses lined the road. To our right stood the City Gate Inn, a two-story building with a handsome thatched roof and green shutters. We stopped in front of it.

The merchant said something to the children in their strange tongue, and they ran off. He had probably sent them off begging.

To me, he said, "We meet here at nightfall," then strode off to pursue his own affairs.

I looked around. Ishaf was a great deal different from Karamur. The port city was more crowded, dirtier. The streets lacked the orderliness of the High Lord's seat—a city run by soldiers.

A rosy-cheeked woman came to the inn's door. "Wantin' a room, lovey?"

I had no coin. But I had an idea. "Greetings, mistress. Would you please tell me the way to the town healer?"

I had plenty of herbs to sell. I was beginning to look below the belt like a small hut with a thatched roof, the upper part of my body like a great chimney on top.

The innkeeper's wife furrowed her forehead as if not quite understanding, but a moment later, her face cleared. "Ye'd be lookin' fer Ina the herb woman, eh?"

I nodded with some hope. And the innkeeper's wife sent me on my way.

I found the herb woman on the outskirts. She was in the back of her small lot, harvesting what little she could from her winter garden. She was at least four times my age, in a wide black skirt made of layer and layer of material. She looked like the wind-ruffled crows who followed the plow and bobbed for turned-up bugs.

"Grandmother," I called out to her.

She peered up at me from her bent position, her face as crackled as the wall of her wattle-and-daub hut. Her fingers were knobby and gnarled, the small sickle in them halting over a bunch of thyme.

I had foraged all along our two-day walk through the woods, tying my herbs in large bunches to my belt. She looked them over.

"Ye a travelin' healer?" She straightened as much as she could, which wasn't all the way. "I am Ina."

"Tera is my name. I come from Dahru." I did not think I would need my disguise any longer.

She brightened at that. "Shahala?"

I nodded. "I was wondering if you might be able to use some of what I collected in the forest. My traveling companions and I are short of coin."

She shuffled closer and fingered some of the green and silver bunches I was offering. "I 'ave nay much coin mineself. These days, people are poor. They pay fer mine services in trade."

"I would trade for food, Grandmother," I said quickly.

Food would be most welcome now that the tiger would not be hunting for us. She had cared for us as if we were her cubs. I hoped she would not come to harm in the forests of Ishaf.

Ina turned toward her thatch-roofed cottage and gestured me to follow her.

"How is it that Ishaf is still free?" I asked.

Her expression tightened, multiplying her wrinkles. "The Emperor wanted to conquer the mountain countries first, befer their harsh winter reached 'em. He succeeded fer the most part, but his wars there took longer than he expected. Now winter is here. He might wait until spring befer comin' against us." She sighed. "Maybe some sudden disease will take 'im, the spirits be willin'."

I stared at her. No Shahala healer would ever speak those words. Ishafi herb women were a different breed, it seemed.

She had tea steeping over the embers of her kitchen fire. She pointed me to a chair, then filled a cup for me with the hot amber liquid.

I let the tea roll around my tongue. "Mersion pear, elne, penin grass. And sistan," I added. "A very good tea for winter. It will ward off colds."

She nodded with approval, then looked at my herbs again. "How much are ye sellin'?"

"Everything."

"These old bones…" she said after a moment on a sigh. "I cannay walk as far as I used to. I can give ye bread and eggs fer these, and nay have to go into the forest mineself. Mine hens have slowed down fer winter, but they are still layin'."

I thanked her most sincerely and asked if I could have the eggs boiled. She agreed readily to that. To repay her for her kindness, I helped her collect the eggs from pretty brown-black hens in a coop at the end of her garden.

"Tell me," she said, holding the basket while I handed out the eggs. "Do ye know the Tika Shahala, Chalee?"

Tika Shahala was a title of great respect among my people, signifying the best healer among healers.

"Yes, I knew her. She has gone to the spirits," I said, but did not betray that I was Chalee's daughter.

I was a stranger in Ishaf. I did not yet know whom I could trust. There had been Shahala healers kidnapped for their healing skills.

The old woman clicked her tongue and bobbed her head from side to side. "A sad shame that. If half the stories 'bout her are true, there will never be another like her."

After we took the eggs in, I offered to help in the garden. I yet had time before I had to be back at the inn.

"Are ye travelin' with family, then?" the old woman asked.

"With a merchant and nine children," I told her, and recounted our unfortunate voyage with the pirates, how we escaped with our very lives. I said nothing about Batumar or the true goal of our journey.

"Sailin' with pirates." She sighed. "I s'ppose it could nay be helped. The Gate is closed, I hear."

"It is."

"A shame fer the island people. Thank the spirits Ishaf is on the mainland. I cannay imagine to be stuck on an island, be cut off from the rest of the world ferever."

I nodded, but in truth, I thought if the Gate somehow reopened, it would be even worse. Emperor Drakhar's mercenaries would pour through then.

Inside, I helped her clean and bunch the herbs, hang them up to dry. I ground the seeds already collected and tied them up in pouches, marked them with their names.

When dusk fell, she boiled twenty-two eggs, two for each of us in our small traveling party, and gave me two loaves of round herb bread, much more than my work was worth. I gratefully accepted.

"Will ye come back on the morrow?" she wanted to know.

"I do not know, Grandmother." I did not know what the merchant's plans were.

She took my hand and peered into my eyes. "Ye have a shadow on yer heart, Granddaughter."

Her tone of compassion undid something inside me. So I told her the truth about the merchant, and how the children were little beggars, and how I intended to trade myself for them.

"Foolishness." She bobbed her head from side to side. "Ye cannot change the will of the spirits."

"The spirits did not will those children to be maimed. The merchant did."

"And ye would sell yerself to such a man?"

"I cannot go back to my home. And I have nothing here."

"Ye could come and live with me," she said after some thought. "I could use the help."

But I was not even a healer anymore. My gift had deserted me. I shook my head.

"Dinnay let that shadow settle on yer heart overly long, Granddaughter," she advised, true concern in her eyes. "A shadow like that can darken yer very spirit." She made some kind of warding sign with her gnarled fingers.

"Mayhap saving the children will lift some of that shadow," I offered, if only so she would not worry about me.

"Mayhap." She tilted her head. "If ye manage yer trade, send the children to me. They can help in mine garden and with mine chickens. Mayhap one of 'em will have a feel fer herbs." She sighed. "I cannay promise much. They might still have to beg. But I can offer shelter."

The children going to a kind woman was more than I had dared hope. For the past few days, the light had gone out of my world. But here she was, suddenly, a bright spirit.

I would rather have the children in the warmth of Ina's heart and hut than serving in a cold stone temple. I *would* save them. Yet I ached to do more, to save my people.

"I am but a woman." Frustration pushed the words from me. "I wish I had a man's power." I would challenge the merchant then for the children. And I would negotiate with kings for armies.

Instead of chiding, Ina shook her head. "Every man has been brought into this world by a woman. Ye have plenty of power of yer own, and no need to wish fer the power of another."

She hugged me so warmly, as if I was enfolded in my own mother's arms. Then tsked as we pulled apart. She was looking at my boots. "Ye dinnay mean to go on the road in those, do ye?"

She didn't wait for an answer but shuffled off and fished around under her bed with a broomstick until she nudged out an ancient boot, then another. "Mine old man's. He's got nay need of 'em nay more."

I thanked her with all my heart, put on the boots that felt as soft as a babe's breath compared to my old pair, then took my bundle of food and walked back toward the inn, ready to make my bargain.

# CHAPTER THIRTEEN
## NEVER A SLAVE AGAIN

Times being lean, Ishaf full of refugees already, the children did not collect much, but enough so Graho was able to secure a pile of hay in the inn's yard for the night, along with a couple of blankets.

The innkeep's wife smiled at the merchant, swishing her wide hips and tugging her doublet down so her oversized breasts could not escape his attention. Did she think him handsome? Did other women?

I could not, for I knew that greed ruled his heart, but I could allow that his visage had improved since we had left the ship. The meals Marga had provided us in the woods had filled out all our cheeks. And we had cleaned up in the creeks we had passed. Even the dark shadows were gone from around the merchant's eyes, and those blue eyes seemed to have acquired a sparkle.

But despite the woman's interest in him, Graho seemed to have no great interest in her. Once he spotted me, he bowed to her in short order, and strode to me and the children, a new rapier at his side. His mouth curved into a smile, as if he was relieved to see me there.

"I wish that you would share our accommodations, Lady Tera modest though they be," he said.

"I thank you for that kindness." I settled down by the children and laid out the food I had brought back for them.

The little ones were talking and smiling and seemed not the least tired from their day's work. They seemed to like the safety of the courtyard, the softness of the hay, and the warmth of the blankets. Those luxuries were a considerable improvement over our sleeping arrangements in the forest.

We each ate an egg and a piece of bread, leaving the rest for breaking our fast in the morning. Once again, the children asked me for a tale. Talking with the herb woman about my mother reminded me of some stories she used to tell me as a child, so I recounted a couple, tales meant to teach as much as entertain.

Shahala children's tales taught kindness, cleanliness, and honesty for the most part—different from Kadar tales that valued strength, bravery, and loyalty above all other traits. I used to think we were right and they were wrong. But the siege of Karamur had taught me that the world was a complicated place, and so I included a Kadar tale.

When the children fell asleep at long last, I looked up at the night sky, gathering the strength for what I meant to do next. For a moment, I thought I heard a tiger's roar in the distance, but it did not repeat, so I could not be certain.

I hoped Marga would not steal any more horses. She could stay hidden in the forest and live. But if she came to hunt among the peasants who lived outside the city, she would be hunted and killed. I asked the spirits to keep her safe.

Then I filled my lungs with cold night air and looked over at the merchant. He was lying on his back, his hands folded under his head, his eyes open. He was looking as intently at the stars as if he meant to count them.

The children slept between us. I slid from under the blanket I shared with two of the little ones, Nala and Mora, and went over to the merchant's side.

I crouched next to him, hugging my knees. "I wish to make a trade," I whispered.

He turned to look at me, his blue eyes as black in the darkness as Batumar's had been. He had that look of hunger on his face that Batumar used to have when we were alone in his bedchamber. Pain punched through my empty heart and banged around inside.

I swallowed hard, hugging my knees even tighter. "I wish to trade," I said again, willing my voice not to tremble.

The merchant waited. With his arms up, folded under his head, I could see the bulge of muscles as his shirt sleeve pulled tight. Merchant or not, he was built like a warrior. He was much stronger than me. If he meant to, he could force me to his will. Mayhap I was foolish to try to bargain with a man such as he. But I had to try anyway.

"You are taking the children to Muzarat to sell them to some beggar lord," I began.

He said nothing.

"You could leave them here. Ina, the herb woman, would take them in. All nine."

He kept watching me, his intent gaze never leaving my face.

"I will go to Muzarat with you instead of the children." Saying the words aloud left me breathless. I felt cold inside at the thought of the life waiting for me, and the cold spread through me, to the tips of my toes.

Graho's shoulders tensed. Anger narrowed his lips.

"I know one woman is not much to replace nine little beggars," I rushed to say. "But I am a hard worker. I have been a slave before. And I am a healer." I hoped my powers would come back to me. "I am a good herb woman." I swallowed. "You will journey easier with me. You will not have to carry me." He'd *had* to carry me before. I looked at my feet. "Again."

"No," he said, tight-lipped.

"I will gather herbs along the way. I will sell them. I will heal people. I can make baskets. I will earn as much as the children would."

"No." His shoulders stiffened even harder.

I was drowning in desperation like I had been drowning in the sea. Without thought, I reached for my knife and pulled it from its sheath, grabbed the handle tightly.

He saw but did not move. He held my gaze in the moonlight, his chest rising and falling evenly.

Despite the cold, sweat beaded on my brow.

With everything I was, I hated the man before me. But I could not reach out my hand to harm him. I slowly slid my knife back into its sheath, tears burning my eyes. I hoped he could not see them. The thought of this man seeing me weak and broken once again was intolerable.

But he did not laugh at me or mock my weakness.

"I fear for you, my lady," he said on a deep sigh.

I shook my head. How could he fear for *me*, when only a moment before I had the blade out to cut his throat?

"What would you wish to do," he asked quietly, "if all things were possible?"

What a strange man. We were without means, refugees in a world at war. Our possibilities were most limited. Truly, we were little above slaves ourselves. We had our freedom, but no shelter, no protection.

"I would give these children a loving home," I said.

"Beyond that," he pressed.

*I would save my people.* I did not dare tell him that, for fear that he might yet turn out to be one of Emperor Drakhar's spies. What better disguise than a traveling merchant?

"Do what it is you wish to do," he suggested. "We live in a time of war. We're all likely to come to a bloody end. We might as well meet that fate while doing something we believe in."

I barely heard the second half of his speech. *Raise an army?* I bit back a bitter laugh. "It is not possible."

"Who but you makes it impossible?"

"The world."

"You want this thing very much?"

With all my heart and soul. "Yes."

"Then you must conquer the world."

Spoken like a man who was used to power and riches. He must have been a very wealthy merchant before he had become trapped on our side of the Gate.

But he had neither power nor riches now. Now he sounded as if he had lost his sound mind.

"Come with us to Muzarat," he offered again.

He wanted it all, the children *and* me. No man was as greedy as a merchant. No doubt, he was in a hurry to build his wealth back.

When I said nothing, he pushed on. "Do you *want* to go back to the High Lord's Pleasure Hall? Serve the next Kadar barbarian?"

His cold tone turned the word *serve* into an insult. The denial that the Kadar were not barbarians was on my tongue, but I swallowed the words. Had I not thought the same, not that long ago? For certain, they were a hard people and given to war and violence. But I had also found much honor and nobility amongst them.

"I will never be a concubine again," I said. And, in that moment, I knew that I would never be a slave again either, not willingly. Never again would I meekly go along with my fate.

That thought filled me with sudden strength, more than I'd had in days. I felt as if I had been underwater all these past days still, only now reaching the surface, only now being able to breathe or open my eyes fully to see.

I stood and looked around, at the merchant, at the children, at the inn. Suddenly the night noises of Ishaf reached me. My lungs expanded.

Without making a conscious decision, I was walking. I walked out of the inn's courtyard, walked through the sleeping city, to the city walls. These I climbed and stood on top of the ramparts, looking past the ships in the harbor, out over the moonlit sea that had swallowed the warlord I loved.

The dark waves called to me still. But, no, I was not meant for the waves.

I looked into the night, my heart aching for my island of Dahru. And for a moment, I felt as if could see it, just on the horizon, behind the moonlit clouds, the lovely shape of home. I felt as if I could hear every heartbeat.

Batumar was no longer.

But I *was*.

Maybe I was no longer a healer. Maybe I was no longer the High Lord's concubine. But I was here. I was the only one who could bring help.

Batumar had taken many a life. But I had saved just as many. Was that not as powerful? What if I could, by myself, accomplish the goal of our journey?

I had not died in the waves. I had not died on the rocks. I had not died of the injuries I had taken upon myself. They were healing little by little.

I could live with Ina, be an herb woman here, and a healer if my powers came back. But had I been kept alive for that by the spirits? To be safe behind the city walls of Ishaf while my people were conquered and killed?

While the children were sold in Muzarat?

My mind raced along with the night winds. Muzarat lay far to the south. The caravans to Muzarat left from Ker, this much I knew. And from Batumar's maps, I knew that Ker lay a day's journey south of Ishaf. Muzarat lay at least a mooncrossing's journey by caravan from Ker.

Regnor, Lord Karnagh's city, had been lost to the enemy, but Seberon, the country of the Selorm, had yet a free city left, now ruled by a warrior queen, somewhere to the east of Ker. The Silver River began in the hills of Seberon and flowed to the South Sea, going right through Muzarat.

I could travel to Seberon's last free city, negotiate with the warrior queen. She was another woman, the most likely to talk with me. She would know much about strategy that I did not. She could teach me. She could advise me on how to free my people.

*Would she teach me?* What did I have to trade for her help? *Nothing.* Yet who else could I turn to?

*Lord Karnagh.*

If I could find him. He had disappeared when his lands had been overrun, but he had not been reported slain.

Lord Karnagh would come to our aid; he was Batumar's strong ally. He had aided us during the siege of Karamur, and we had become friends of a sort. I was the only woman in the castle who did not cower from his battle tiger. He was a Selorm, an ancient race of warriors who bonded with their battle tigers and fought as one. His people were great in courage and fame.

If I could find Lord Karnagh...I closed my eyes for a second and clenched my teeth. I *would* find Lord Karnagh.

With Lord Karnagh and what warriors he might have left, we would travel south, making more and more alliances.

I had to somehow earn coin on the way, then book passage on a barge, float down the river and reach Muzarat before the merchant sold any of the children. For good coin, as much or more than he would receive at the market, I thought he would make the trade.

I would have the children, and have a full army, and then we'd go to Landria to ask them for their ships. If the pirates could sail the hardstorms, so could the Landrian navy.

Batumar's cloak with the star map was lost, but I had embroidered it and I remembered every stitch.

*A plan for a fool*, a small voice said inside my head. Yet Batumar's plan had seemed no less impossible, and we had made it halfway through before tragedy hit. Mayhap another foolish plan would receive luck enough from the spirits to accomplish something.

Having a plan gave me a new sense of strength.

I looked up into the sky and thanked the spirits in advance for their help. Then, with one last look at the dark ocean, I returned to the inn's courtyard and crawled under my blanket next to Nala and Mora, who were still sound asleep.

The merchant watched me settle in before he closed his eyes at last.

Nala curled up against me. The thought of letting her go broke my heart. I hugged her as she slept. I might let them go for a little while, but I would come back to claim them, I silently promised.

# CHAPTER FOURTEEN
## THE HOLLOW

"Will you stay in Ishaf, Lady Tera?" Graho asked in the morning as we ate our last eggs and bread.

I made some fortifying herb tea for our flasks. "I shall go with you as far as Ker."

"And then?"

"I shall journey toward Regnor," I said, picking hay out of my hair.

I hoped to find Lord Karnagh along the way. If not, then I would go to the free city, to the warrior queen who held it, and throw myself and my people at her mercy.

After we ate, the merchant gathered up the children, which was all the preparation we needed. We had no possessions to bundle up and ready for the journey, although we did have blankets. These Graho had purchased, as it turned out, so they were ours to keep. I wore mine like a cape around my shoulders.

We left Ishaf through the same gate that we had entered. The merchant in the lead, then the children, myself bringing up the rear so I would notice if anyone tired and lagged behind, which wouldn't happen for a while. We marched at a good pace, filled with the energy of the morning.

The sun was barely up, but traffic already flowed into the city, traveling tradesmen, soldiers, and disheveled refugees. Oxcarts rattled on the cobblestones; overloaded donkeys brayed. I glanced back only once, at the red tower of Ishaf, glad that we had escaped the sorcerer's eye before it could have fixed on us. I sensed a dark presence in the tower that made me shiver, and I wondered if the Ishafi elders might yet one day regret the bargain they had made.

As I was turning away from the city for good, I was nearly knocked over by one of half a dozen youths that raced by me, grinning and shouting, skipping with excitement as only young boys can.

I looked after them, wondering what game was afoot, and realized that their excitement wasn't over a game. They had found prey.

One must have seen the dark shape in the ditch beneath the walls and alerted the others. Even as I watched, the boys surrounded the prone form of a beggar and began throwing rocks at him.

I gasped at this, even more horrified when I realized that no passersby would stop to help. They saw the assault but simply kept on walking.

I turned back and ran toward the boys, raising my arm. "Stop that at once! Away! Away!" If I sounded like a shrew, I did not care.

The boys started and looked offended at my interference but moved on as I reached them. They did not go far but waited in the shadow of the gate, ready to resume their heartless fun as soon as I went on about my business.

"Better fer it dead," a scruffy city guard called to me. "Let 'em finish it."

Instead, I stepped up to the beggar and took my flask from my belt, then filled a broken piece of a pot I found in the ditch near the man.

The city guard scowled at me and strode away.

I glared after him, then glared at others who were casting disapproving glances toward me. What was wrong with these people?

"Is this the charity of Ishaf toward its beggars?" I asked a fishwife who looked as if she was about to chase me off.

"Ain't no beggar," she scoffed. "'Tis a *hollow*. Nuthin' but a wraith." She glanced toward the red tower. "The sorcerer took the inner spirit. The poor body will be dead soon enough, nay sense in draggin' out its sufferin'." She spat in the dirt. "Sixth one, this one is. The sorcerer has taken one at every mooncrossin' since he'd come to the red tower. The rest of 'em died fast enough." She made a sign in the air, likely some local superstition for warding off evil spirits. "Harsh 'tis, aye. But seems to werk. The city is yet free."

I looked at the wraith at my feet. It wore a soiled, faded-black burlap cloak with the hood drawn deep over its face. Back bent, fingers—what little I could see of them—mangled and wrapped in bloody rags. Feet the same. I could see little of the wraith, in truth, beyond its general, broken shape.

"A hollow?" I asked the fishwife.

She scowled as if I were a foolish foreigner who understood nothing. "Empty inside. 'Tis a void. A wraith, I tell ye." Then she fixed me with a hard look. "Touch it, and it'll suck out yer spirit to fill itself. See if it won't." Then she turned and hurried off, leaving her dire warning hanging in the air behind her.

The boys in the shadow of the gate waited, stones in every hand.

I looked to the *hollow*. A shiver ran down my spine. I stepped back to make sure we did not touch in any way. It did not raise its head, but remained on the cold ground in a broken pile.

I could not save the man it had once been, yet I could not leave this shell of a body to be stoned to death in a ditch. Even if the spirit was already gone, the body was still here. And bodies could feel.

It would die soon, the fishwife had said. I wished to see to it that the hollow would be allowed to die in peace instead of in pain.

"Come," I said.

But it did not rise.

Maybe it could not hear. Or if it could, maybe it could not understand me. It had not yet even reached for the water I had poured into the broken pot.

Were the Ishafi right? Was the hollow beyond help?

I glanced over my shoulder at the road and could see the merchant and the children far ahead now. I did not want to lose them. But I did not want to leave the hollow to be stoned either.

I stepped toward the road, frustration cutting through me as I searched for a solution, looking back through the city gate and hoping to see Ina. Maybe she would know what to do.

But as I stepped away from it, the hollow shifted toward me.

"Come," I said urgently, and moved away again.

It wobbled to its feet, the uncoordinated effort eerie.

I walked down the road, one slow step at a time, looking back over my shoulder to see if it followed still. And it did come after me, its movements odd and ghostly. If its every step hadn't been a struggle, its following might have scared me.

"Just a short distance," I promised.

And it came.

I walked down the road, then off it, up the dirt path that led to the forest. I led him inside, to the shelter of a tree.

I pointed. "You could sit there."

He sank to the spot, if not understanding the word, then recognizing the gesture.

I watched for a moment, waited. Then I remembered Marga. I was not certain what she would make of the hollow—preferably not dinner. I chuffed for the tiger, then called for her with the roar she had taught me. But the tiger did not come. I hoped she had returned to the deep forest, away from the city.

The wraith huddled under the tree. It did not look up or make any sound. Was it hungry? How much longer would it live? How long could a body live without its spirit?

The Guardians of the Forgotten City would probably have been able to answer my questions, but the Guardians were far away, on the other side of the ocean.

I reached into my pocket and pulled out my last chunk of bread, placed it on a stone a safe distance from the hollow. Then I untied my smaller water flask from my belt and set it next to the bread.

"The spirits watch over you, whoever you were," I said, my heart twisting in sympathy. "Die in peace."

It showed no sign that it heard me.

I could think of nothing more that might help, so I turned and hurried out of the woods, breaking into a run as I reached the road, eager to catch up with Graho and the children.

I did not have to run far. The merchant had noticed that I had fallen behind and had stopped on the side of the road to wait for me.

"What happened?" He checked me over as if searching for injury. "We were about to come and look for you."

"All is well." And as we began walking, I told him about the wraith.

When I finished, Graho responded with, "I am glad to be walking away from such a city."

The wagon trail we followed ribboned along the edge of the forest, well trampled, dry, easy walking.

From time to time, when the surrounding area looked right, I strayed into the woods to look for mushrooms and dried berries. What I found, I tied up in a rag and hung from my belt. Here and there, I found herbs too. I picked as much as I could, and pinecones, for we would be able to roast the seeds once we had fire again.

On the third trip, Nala followed me to help.

"Barren berries," she called out, and hopped over to a bush I had missed.

She was much shorter than I, could see under leaves I could not. I collected twice as much with her help.

"Thank you, Nala." I kissed the top of her head as she added the berries to my bundle. And then I heard rustling in the undergrowth.

I turned at once, putting her behind me. But when the bushes parted, Marga's great head appeared.

She chuffed at us fondly.

I chuffed back.

For some reason, this made Nala laugh, the sound so pure and sweet, it set the birds trilling above us in the trees.

The tiger came over and rubbed her head against us. Her side was flat, her muzzle had no blood on it, so I had some hope yet that she hadn't eaten the hollow after I left it.

When Nala and I walked back to the road, the tiger followed but did not come out of the cover of the bushes, rather paced us while she still stayed hidden.

Maybe Marga had heard the dozen warriors coming up behind us. They seemed in a hurry, their boots stirring up the dust. We pulled off ahead of them, giving them no cause to mistreat us, and they paid us no mind.

They disappeared behind the next bend within moments.

Then a young man herding a dozen cows came from the opposite direction. He had a nasty gash in the middle of his forehead, red and infected, oozing yellow pus he wiped on his dirty sleeve, a grim look on his face.

I approached him carefully. "I am a healer," I started. "I am friend of Ina, the herb woman."

He stopped and clicked his tongue to halt his cows, which they did, setting to grazing on the roadside at once. Luckily, on the other side from the tiger.

"I could heal your wound," I offered the man.

"Cow kicked me." He scowled at one of the animals. "I 'ave nay coin," he said then. "All I 'ave is milk."

His master's milk, I thought, but I did not argue with him. The children needed nourishment badly.

I cleaned his wound by squeezing the pus out first, then washing the inflamed opening with water from my flask. Then I prepared a poultice and ripped a strip of cloth from the bottom of my undershirt to tie it to the gash.

I gave him more of the mixture of herbs. "Change the poultice to fresh every morning for three days. First wash the wound, then dress it."

He nodded, then took my empty flask, kneeled under the nearest cow, and filled the flask with warm milk.

We all thanked him before he hurried away.

After the cowherd, a wine merchant came with a wagon full of barrels. He slept on the bench while his servant whipped their two horses forward. I wished I could trade him for some wine I could have used for disinfecting wounds, but they had no visible injury or illness, and I had nothing but my healing to trade.

We let them pass too, then stepped back on the road, didn't pull off again until the sun was dipping below the treetops. I did not see Marga in the woods. Mayhap she was off hunting. She seemed to like the twilight hours best for that purpose.

We gathered dry wood and kindling, then I produced the dry moss and tinder mushrooms I had collected earlier. The merchant used his flint to start a fire.

The edible mushrooms I had we roasted; the berries we ate raw. Then we shared the milk.

We were about to add another pile of branches to our fire when the brigands came, three men, unshaven, gap-toothed, armed with swords and axes.

"Give us yer food," their leader demanded.

Graho stepped forward. "We have no food. We're but poor war refugees."

I stepped back and put my arms around the children, who pressed up against me.

The men moved closer. Soon they could see that we, indeed, had little.

"Give us the wee beggars," the leader said then, and made a rude gesture. "Ye can make more."

The other two laughed.

"The little beggars are not for sale," Graho said calmly.

"I was nay plannin' on payin' fer 'em." The brigand threw his head back as he laughed.

They moved closer another step, stalking us as if we were prey.

We could not outrun them with the children, so we stood our ground and faced them down. I was hoping someone would come along, maybe another troop of soldiers, but the road stood deserted.

The brigand's leader looked me over. "Give us the woman, then."

My spine stiffened, my hand going to the paring knife that hung from my belt, but I stuck close to the children. Graho drew his blade.

The three men attacked the merchant all at once. He parried well, light on his feet, his thrusts powerful. He ran his rapier through one man's thigh, and the brigand fell out of the fight.

But the other two just fought more fiercely as they cursed him. One stuck his foot forward to trip him so he might fall into the other one's sword.

"Watch out!" I shouted, my heart in my throat.

Graho jumped back and avoided the trap.

The taller of the two attackers hacked away with renewed vigor. While Graho defended himself from that, the other attacker managed to cut him on the arm.

I tried to reach out with my spirit to heal the merchant. I could not. Such dark and endless grief lived within me for Batumar, it drowned my healing spirit.

And even if I had any skill in fighting, I could not help with my small kitchen knife. The children were hugging my legs, hanging on to me in fright, holding me in place.

Then Graho moved on the offensive and cut off the shorter man's ear. He dropped out of the fight screaming, holding his wound, blood running from between his grimy, stubby fingers.

The fight continued one-on-one.

Graho's left arm was bleeding. Then suddenly his right side, just below his ribs, where the brigand's sword cut him.

The brigand wielded a heavy sword, Graho his lighter rapier, but I could tell he was tiring. He had already defeated two of the men. I prayed to the spirits that he would have strength for the third.

The brigand raised his sword and aimed a crushing blow at Graho's head, but Graho danced back so only the very tip of the sword caught him on the lips. Blood ran down his chin.

He lunged forward and pierced the brigand's sword hand. The man dropped his sword, lunged for it, but something moved on the road behind us. Other travelers were coming at last.

The brigand snatched up his sword with his good hand and backed away, his eyes narrow with hate. "'Tis nay the end." He spat toward us. "We'll meet again."

Graho kept his rapier up. "You best have more men with you. And better trained," he called after the brigands as they ran into the woods and soon disappeared.

As a healer, I could wish no man ill, but I wished they would run into Marga. I did not want them to be eaten. But if the tiger put some fear into their hearts…I would not have been much bothered by their misfortune.

The children loosened their grip on me. Graho grabbed up a handful of dried grasses from the side of the road to clean his rapier. I looked back on the road where I had seen movement earlier. I could discern now that the movement was slow indeed, just one solitary shape, a dark cape.

Graho sheathed his weapon but kept his hand on the grip. He raised an eyebrow. "The hollow?"

I shivered as the black wraith seemed to float toward us. "Why did it come?"

But before I could truly begin to worry that it had come to steal my spirit, it stopped and collapsed into a shapeless heap at the side of the road, well far from our fire.

Satisfied that it posed no threat, Graho moved his hand from his rapier and came to sit by the dying flames. I added wood to revive them. The children settled down around us.

Graho glanced back toward the hollow that was but a darker shadow in the darkening evening. "Maybe it is lost without its spirit. Maybe it follows the only kindness shown to it." He looked at me, open curiosity in his eyes. "The fishwife said it will die soon?"

I nodded, sitting down by the fire next to Nala, in a spot from where I could best keep an eye on the hollow.

The children too watched it, but didn't seem frightened. Then again, these were children who had seen more than most, having survived maiming and a journey through the hardstorms with pirates. They had accepted a tiger as our traveling companion. Now it seemed that they would accept a wraith.

Graho looked at it again, then back at me. "Maybe it wishes not to die alone. Even injured animals have instincts. It knows it's more vulnerable alone than in company."

Maybe. As long as it kept its distance, I could not see what harm an empty, fading shell of a man could do. As the fishwife said, it would probably soon be dead anyway.

Nala crawled back from the fire once the heat increased. Without her, I was sitting next to the merchant. I caught a glint of red on his face in the light of the flames. "Let me see to your wounds."

He shifted closer so I might look him over.

His top lip had been but scratched. I used his water flask to clean the shallow cut on his bottom lip. I could not do much more than that. The cut was in a place where I could not place a poultice, not without wrapping his whole mouth shut.

Our faces were as close as they had ever been, far closer than I wanted to be. He kept his blue gaze on me—black now in the darkness. I looked at nothing but the lip I was treating. I held a piece of cloth against the cut and pressed, held the pressure.

The children gathered closer to watch.

I wished Marga would return. The tiger made me feel safer, and I suspected she had the same effect on the children.

When I removed the pressure from the cut, the bleeding had slowed. Ruhni powder would have been helpful to ward off infection, but that I did not have.

I checked Graho's arm.

The cut no longer bled, needing only cleaning, which I saw to, kneeling in front of him. Then I dropped back to my heels, ready for the next task. "I need you to take off your tunic."

The corners of his lips turned up into an open smile, but he said nothing as he obeyed. A good thing, or I *would* have bandaged his mouth shut.

I dropped my gaze to his side, paying little attention to his odd-shaped tattoos. This cut was deeper. The injury needed not only to be cleaned but closed. If not treated right, this cut would become infected and bring on fever. This cut could kill him.

I let none of that show on my face. "Water."

He handed me his flask.

I cleaned the wound, wishing for ninga beetles. I had used them many times to close wounds, holding one up to the edges of a cut, then squeezing its body until it pinched the flesh together, then twisting the body off the head, and the pincers stayed in place.

But I did not know where the nearest creek was, and I did not know whether any ninga beetles even lived in the creeks of Ishaf.

I turned to the older boys, pointing in the opposite direction from where the brigands had disappeared. "I need you to go to the edge of the forest. I need you to find me a bush with long, slim thorns. Bring me a handful." That way, I could select the best one for my purpose.

As the boys went off, I revived our fire and boiled what water we had left in the flask. Then I pulled a long thread from the bottom of my tunic, put it in the water, and boiled it to make it as clean as I could, a trick I learned from my mother.

When the boys returned, proudly bringing me three thorns of good quality, I selected the thinnest, used the tip of my knife to make a hole on one end, then threaded my new needle.

"Hold still."

Graho's earlier smile was now nowhere to be seen. But he lifted his arm again so I could have free access to his injury. Cords of muscles bunched and shifted in the light of the fire. "I'm ready."

I pierced his skin without hesitation, paying no attention to the soft hiss that left his lips. I worked quickly and accurately. I closed the gash, then I tied off the thread.

By the time I finished, cold sweat beaded on both of our brows.

I added some herbs to the still hot water, let it infuse for a few moments, then I washed the wound again. Next I cut a strip off the bottom of Graho's shirt and bandaged him.

He kept both arms raised straight out at his sides, and I finished my work, touching him as little as possible. Then I pulled back to examine my work, but also to put some distance between us. I did not like being so close to him.

"You must check under the bandage for redness and pus." I gave him a bunch of herbs. "Make a potion from these and wash the wound every day. In a fortnight, you can cut the thread and pull it out."

His eyes went wide, but he said, "I will."

The children had watched all this with rapt fascination, looking at me as if I was some magical creature from a tale who sewed human skin just like their mothers darned socks. But they looked at Graho as if he was some immortal warrior out of myth.

He dressed. "We shall reach Ker tomorrow, but it will be a long walk. You best rest with the children."

"And you?"

"I shall be the night guard, should the brigands return or the hollow move closer."

I tried to convince him we could share guard duty, I could wake him if danger neared, but he would not hear of it, and I had not the strength to argue long. One moment I was settling down onto the hard ground, the children pressed against me; the next, the sun was coming up again.

My limbs ached. My body begged for yet more sleep. I could only imagine how Graho felt, sitting up all night, watching and listening.

Then I remembered the hollow and turned. It sat in its broken heap, had not yet fallen over. Its head dipped slightly. It yet lived.

"Never moved a limb all night," Graho said as he caught me looking. "That is one fate I would wish to avoid at all cost." He stirred the dying embers of the fire. "Do you know what the wraith had been? A trader? A soldier?"

I shook my head. Impossible to tell from its shapeless lump. Only by its size I could tell that it had been a man and not a woman.

Graho pushed a handsome wooden bowl toward me. And then I saw he had two more. He had spent the night carving.

I thanked him for the unexpected gift, even as the children woke around us. Seeing the bowls, they asked for food.

I stood. "Off we go, then." And took them to forage in the woods.

Graho followed us shortly.

Pine nuts were our biggest find on our way in. Then I came across a willow tree in a glen with a creek. We filled our flasks, and I dug for edible rhizomes. Then I cut a good bundle of willow branches and tied it onto my back. But the spirits blessed our foraging even further. On the way out of the woods, back to our campsite, Graho threw his dagger and brought down a squirrel.

Our breakfast was a feast.

As the children ate with big smiles on their faces, I used some of the squirrel grease and the rhizomes, with some herbs added, to make a soup for the hollow. I did not know if it had eaten the bread I had left the previous day or not. But it still had a body, and bodies needed food, I reasoned. I could not see it starve to death while we ate.

Graho cast me a dubious look but did not try to call me back as I walked to the hollow and placed the bowl on the ground at a safe distance.

"Eat," I said, but it did not move.

I did not think it could understand me. It seemed to possess but the most basic instincts.

Graho had already kicked dirt over our fire by the time I walked back. We started out for Ker, careful as we went, but no brigands jumped out at us as we progressed forward. Only Marga came by for a visit.

She did not seem to be bothered by the hollow. She gave it one good, long look, sniffed the air, then kept pace with us, walking at the edge of the forest. I felt better for having her. She would alert us if anyone lay in wait up ahead.

The wraith followed us, never dropping out of sight that whole morning. I had not seen it eat, but it carried the bowl, and I could see the bowl had been emptied. The flask I had left for him was hanging from his waist.

I did not spend much time on the wraith. I pulled some willow branches from the bundle on my back instead and began weaving a basket, keeping my hands busy as we walked.

A band of marching soldiers could easily cover the distance between Ishaf and Ker in less time, but the children took small steps and needed to rest from time to time. I used the breaks well. I had five baskets on my arm by the time the sun dipped low in the sky and we spotted the caravan town in a valley, only slightly smaller than the port city of Ishaf.

Ker was surrounded by immense grazing fields, crowded with cows, horses, sheep, goats, and camels. The tiger sniffed the air with more than a little interest but turned into the forest as she left us to go on her nightly hunt.

The hollow too halted and would advance no farther. I sent a quick prayer to the spirits to watch over it, then stopped for a moment to think. Had the spirits sent it into my path for a purpose? A test? A warning?

"Come," Graho called back, cutting off my thoughts. "Night is falling."

I hurried to catch up.

We entered the city together through the main gate, the guards paying us little attention. With all the children, we hardly looked like an invading force, more like a couple who overmuch liked spending time in bed together. *Is that what people think when they look at us?* My cheeks heated.

Graho turned to me once we were inside the city walls. "Come with us tonight. We will have lodging and food at the caravan yard."

He carried a sleeping little girl, Mora. I carried Nala.

After a moment of consideration, I nodded. The market was closed. I could not sell my baskets until morning. Our run-in with the brigands on the road made me wary of sleeping out in the open street.

We walked by a number of inns and guesthouses, down narrow streets, cutting through the town clear to the far side.

"Just a little more," Graho encouraged the children, who were asleep on their feet. To me, he said, "The camel yard is next to Camels' Field from whence all southbound caravans start their journey."

"How will you pay for your trip?" I asked, worried that he might yet decide to sell some of the children at the local market.

But he flashed an unconcerned smile. "There is a merchant here who owes me coin."

We turned another corner, and then we were at the camel yard that covered an enormous area. A large inn sheltered the travelers. I could see buildings where merchandise was stored, under guard, waiting for the caravan's departure. There were stables for horses. The camels slept in Camels' Field.

The inn had a common room below and individual chambers above, I saw as we stepped inside. A few men threw dice and wagered in the middle by candlelight; others slept draped over tables and benches.

Graho left us there in a quiet corner while he went off to find the caravan master.

He returned soon enough, with a spring in his step. "The caravan will leave in three days. Until then, our food and board will be provided at the inn."

Then he left us again and roused the innkeep, a portly grandfather with no hair and ruddy cheeks, who wore a red-and-blue-striped robe that reached the ground. By this time, the children were asleep on the floor by my feet.

The innkeep sent a yawning maid, Posey, to show us upstairs into a room that held a bed and a washing table with a tin basin. Posey started a fire in the hearth, then, at Graho's request, she hurried off and brought us an armful of blankets.

We used the bowl and water in the corner to wash our hands and faces. Being able to clean off the dirt of the road was a true gift, as was the fire we did not have to gather wood for. Much better than me sleeping in a cold doorway somewhere outside.

"Thank you," I said when I caught Graho's gaze. He had a dark heart, true, but even the darkest sky held a few dots of light.

"You take the bed with the girls," he offered in a gruff tone, and he settled down on the blankets on the floor with the boys just as Posey came back.

She was my age, more awake now, or at least awake enough to smile widely at Graho. She brought camel milk and bread, which we finished so quickly, mayhap we just imagined it. Then we each crawled under our covers.

Graho lay just inside the door with his rapier close at hand to protect us should we need it.

I could see his face in the light of the hearth. He was watching me.

He was not a good man. I did not want to like him. I looked away.

# CHAPTER FIFTEEN
## MAKMIN AND HIS CAMEL

The next morning, I began preparing for my journey east. I was at the market as soon as it opened, sold my baskets, and spent the coin on food and a used wool cloak to replace the one I had lost. This one had a hood and would be far warmer than the threadbare blanket I had been using for covering.

I also bought flint and steel so I would be able to start a fire. Next, I went to see about another source of income.

I had picked as many herbs as I could on our two-day walk from Ishaf, but now I returned to the forest to look for more. Not much could be harvested at this time of the year, but I searched out as much as I could.

I did not see Marga, but the dark shape of the hollow soon appeared behind me. I checked to make sure I still had my knife hanging from my belt. But as I worked my way through the woods, the hollow followed me at a distance and made no attempt to come closer.

Maybe it hoped for more food. But when I found a bush with berries still on it and pointed it out, the hollow did not rush to eat. Instead, it followed me as I moved on, almost as if guarding me.

I reached a thick stand of bushes and turned back to go another way, doubling back on the trail I had taken to that point. The hollow moved around until it walked behind me again.

The fresh blood on the path startled me. The red smears had not been there before.

I checked myself, but I wasn't bleeding, hadn't been scraped by thorns. I looked toward the hollow. "Is it you then? Are you hurting?"

It stood still.

I took a step closer. Its faded black robe wasn't bloody. No blood dripped from its nose or its hands. Then I saw its feet—covered in nothing but rags—soaked in blood.

The hollow had made the long journey from Ishaf close to barefooted. I winced.

"You could have said something," I muttered, even while knowing it could not have.

I pulled my knife and cut a strip off the bottom of my cloak, a hand width. I cut the wool strip in half and placed the two pieces on the ground. Then from my bundles I took shirl moss I had collected for bandaging wounds. I piled that on top of the wool.

I looked about but could not find what I sought, my gaze settling on his burlap robe at last.

"String you must pull from your robe," I said, and crouched to demonstrate on my own foot how to wrap a makeshift foot cover.

When I moved back on the trail, the hollow stepped closer and gathered all I had left, but simply carried the bundle along with the bowl I gave it earlier.

I sighed. Without being able to touch, I could offer no further help. "When you settle down for the night, do as I showed you, please."

I moved on, and it followed behind me.

Like the hollow, the spirits were with me all day. Beyond the most common herbs, I also found valuable smin mushrooms that shrank tumors of the abdomen, brittle berries that eased blinding headaches, and kven roots that helped digestion.

I only ceased my foraging when dusk began to settle on the forest. The hollow followed me to the tree line but no farther. Hoping it would see to its bleeding feet, I went straight to the herb woman with my bundles, directed by another kind innkeeper.

The woman I sought, Eryl, was a young mother with three little ones clinging to her skirt. When I tried to offer her my herbs for sale, she beat me off, shrieking that I was a charlatan trying to steal her trade.

Disheartened, I returned to the caravan yard. I walked around to see if I might find some patients among the travelers and earn a few coins that way.

The men waiting for the caravan wore the clothes of faraway lands, were of different color of skin, different build, different language. They gathered in small groups of their own kind, sitting around camel-dung fires. They viewed me with mistrust, as men who had seen war and were wary of spies.

In one such small group, a traveler coughed nonstop, a deep, barking cough. His friends had him sitting by the fire, but that did not seem to help.

I eased up to them, stopping at a respectful distance. "May the spirits bless you all. I am Tera, a traveling healer. I could make a tea for that cough."

They looked at me through narrowed eyes, chins down, none breaking their closed circle.

The oldest one shouted, "We do not need you here. Be off."

I politely withdrew and tried another group with the same result.

Then someone did come to me, but not for help. He was a tall, wide-shouldered man with slanted eyes and a ground-eating stride. He carried a great staff as tall as he was. On his round belly, two curved daggers hung out from the sash that held his robe together.

"I am Makmin the caravan master. You do not travel with the caravan." He towered over me as he examined me from the soles of my boots to my windblown hair that had seen better days.

"No, master," I replied with a bow that showed my respect.

"What are you doing in the camel yard?"

I kept my gaze down. "I thought I might be able to help some of the sick."

"You are not Eryl, the herb woman."

"I am a traveling healer, master."

He scoffed. "We do not like strangers around the caravans who come to spy out our cargo and report to the bandits in the narrow mountain passes."

"I am no spy, master," I said quickly. After learning the punishment for thievery in Rabeen, I did not wish to discover the punishment for spying in Ker. I suspected caravan masters were not kind toward those they thought would harm their caravans.

Makmin waved off my response as if my denial was nothing less than he would expect from a spy. "Where do you travel from?"

"The Shahala lands." Everyone had heard of Shahala healers, so I thought mentioning my birthplace would help. I drew aside my cloak to show him my many bunches of herbs.

His eyes narrowed to slits. "You were lucky to come through before the Gate closed."

I said nothing. He would never believe that I had come through the hardstorms with pirates.

Makmin spent a moment or two mulling me over. "And now you cannot return."

It was not a question, so I did not answer.

"Ker already has Eryl," he said, not unkindly now. "You best find yourself a small village without an herb woman and set yourself up there."

"I am headed to Regnor. I have a friend there I can turn to for help."

But Makmin shook his head, his tone filling with regret. "Regnor has fallen."

"I would still see if my friend yet lives." I did not name Lord Karnagh. Makmin might find it suspicious that someone like me would know a famous warlord.

The caravan master shrugged, his expression saying he thought I was doomed and not possessing half the sense the gods gave to field mice. He turned, ready to walk away, but then he stopped. "A Shahala healer, you say? What do you know about camels?"

"Very little, master."

He watched me for a moment with more interest than before, and then, instead of belittling me for my lack of knowledge, he laughed. "Might be you are the first honest woman I've met. I have seven wives in seven caravan stops. Perhaps I have become jaded."

He shook his head. "Come. My lead camel is sick. See if there is something you can do for him with your herbs. Eryl will not touch him."

I soon found out why. The camel was possessed by a dark spirit for certain, braying at everyone who came near, spitting at us when we were at an arm's reach, then biting when we moved in closer.

He was foaming at the mouth, his eyes bulging out of his head. Truly, he was a more frightening sight than the wraith.

"Save him, and I will pay you honest coin." Makmin squared his shoulders. "But harm him, and I will cut you down where you stand."

This I believed.

I stayed out of the camel's reach, wishing he had some external injury. Treating wounds was the same from man to man, animal to animal. But sickness on the inside was difficult to name and even more difficult to cure. What healed a horse might kill a cow. And I did not know what my herbs would do to a camel.

"How long has he been ill?" I asked.

"Seven days." The caravan master's tone turned grave.

"Did he eat anything the other animals didn't?"

The man shook his head. "They all graze together."

"How is his dung?"

The man shrugged. "All the dung is collected by the inns' servants. Once it dries, waiting travelers use it for the outdoor fires."

No help there, then. I tried to think what else I could do to diagnose the humped beast.

I never knew for certain whether my spirit songs truly worked, but I began to silently sing to the camel. Whether due to my singing or not, he stopped spitting and snapping at me and quieted down. I stepped closer and, after a moment, reached a hand out to touch his side. If he bit me, he bit me. I had slept next to a tiger; I could not shy away from a camel that was no animal of prey but a grazer.

The camel did not feel too hot to the touch, nor did he sweat. He did not shiver either. I thought maybe his side was distended, but I had seen so few camels thus far that I found it difficult to tell. Comparing him to the other camels was no easy task either, for he was larger than all the others, and the rest were either standing or lay in some other way, forming different shapes altogether.

When my gentle patting did not arouse his anger, I lay my ear against his side and listened. I did not hear the usual sounds of dangerous bloating.

"What do you think?" Makmin's harsh face softened. He was near cooing as he gazed at his animal.

Since I could not diagnose my patient at a glance, I decided on a longer observation. "I shall stay with him until I can determine what ails him."

Makmin nodded and hurried off but came back shortly with a bowl of goat stew. He handed me the bowl, then settled down next to me. "I have been staying out here with him since he fell ill. If he dies, it will break my heart. If he does not survive, neither will I," he added with enough drama for a Kadar concubine.

"And your wives and children?" I suggested, wanting to cheer him.

But he only looked at me with reproach. "Ryod is my lead camel!"

I nodded.

"Ryod means *treasure* in my people's language," Makmin informed me and hugged the beast.

I ate the stew, then shifted closer to Ryod for heat, glad that I had purchased a cloak at the market.

Makmin shifted into a more comfortable position. "I am considered a wealthy and respected man among my people. I have one hundred and nine camels. But if I lose Ryod, I shall be nothing."

He fell silent for a moment, then said, "When I was a young man of but three camels, before I had even a single wife, I fell in love with the most beautiful woman in the world."

His eyes glazed over as he stared off into the night. "She woke my heart up from its great winter. She made my soul sing. She was as slim as the gazelles of the desert. Her laughter was the sound of water in an oasis, the very sound of life. I knew that if I could have her, I would be happy for all the days of my life." His voice trailed off, as if he was lost in his memories.

I waited for him to continue and, after a while, he did.

"When I went to her father to ask for her, the old man wanted Ryod as part of the bride price." He gave a shuddering sigh and said no more.

The camel gave a pitiful groan. I patted its side and sang my spirit song.

The caravan master did not speak again, and we both dozed as we sat, me reclining against the camel, and him sitting up with his legs crossed in front of him, leaning on his staff.

After walking in the forest all day, I slept soundly and only woke to a faintly familiar movement inside the camel toward dawn.

"Are you sure Ryod is a male?" I asked Makmin. I had not yet seen the camel on his feet.

The caravan master was already up, standing and bowing to the four corners of the sky, performing some sort of prayers, mumbling, then clapping quietly in what seemed an ancient ceremony.

He turned to me when he finished. "He is the father of half my herd," he said with pride.

And yet I felt movement again, the same as I might feel with a horse ready to foal.

How was that possible? And then I remembered something and had an idea.

I selected some herbs off my belt and held the bunch up in front of the camel's mouth. He viewed me with distrust, but then he sniffed. And then he ate. Animals often knew how to heal themselves in the wild and sought out plants that would make them feel better. Whether driven by instinct or led by the spirits, I did not know, but Ryod seemed to sense that the herbs would help.

The camel ate as much of the herb as I would have given a grown man. Then I looked at his great bulk and decided he needed more. I gave him all I had.

The caravan master watched me closely.

I remembered his words from the night before, how my fate was now tied to the camel's. Despite the chill of the morning, I felt sweat bead on my forehead as I watched Ryod and waited.

Nothing happened. Not even once men woke in the inn and stables and came outside, restarted their dung fires. Not even when the sun rose high in the sky.

"I need more medicine," I told the caravan master.

He thought for a moment, watched his camel that looked neither worse nor better for my treatment so far. Then he nodded but added a warning. "If you run, you will be found."

I had no doubt about that, for I had seen plenty of men at the camel yard. Some were his servants, others his passengers. I knew all would heed his word and hunt me down if he was to ask.

As I was leaving the caravan yard, I met Graho waiting by the inn.

"How fares Makmin's treasure?" he asked.

"On his way to healing, the spirits willing. I am off to gather more herbs."

"I came looking for you last night and saw you sleeping by the beast." He sounded amused. "Do you need help in the forest?"

I shook my head. "Picking herbs is easy enough work. And I have the hollow for protection." Not that it could fight off someone with bad intentions, but it would frighten them off, I was certain. And I did not think the brigands would come this close to the city. I meant to stay within hailing distance of the fields. Marga too might find me.

Graho raised an eyebrow, but then he let me go on my way. I felt his gaze on my back as I walked away.

I hurried off into the woods, more so to generate heat for my body than out of urgency. The camel was not at death's door as yet. And I was not so certain of my cure that I wanted to hurry back. Rather, I wanted some time to think.

When the hollow appeared behind me, I was glad for his silent company. And I was most certainly glad to see its feet wrapped. *It must understand more than people think.*

"I don't suppose you know about camels?" For all I knew, it had once been a camelherd or, like Makmin, a caravan master.

But the hollow said nothing, just followed me through the woods once again. This time, I did see him eat some wrinkled berries the birds had missed.

I ate the same dry berries and some roots as I found them, collected an armful of the proper herbs for the camel, and returned past midday, leaving the hollow behind in the forest.

As soon as the caravan master saw me enter the camel yard, he came to walk with me. He watched as I fed the camel all the medicine I had brought.

We waited together.

Nothing happened.

But then, at long last, the camel stood with a frightful groan.

"He has not stood in two days." The last of the caravan master's hopeful words were drowned out by the loud moaning of the camel.

The sound intensified in pitch and volume, into a wide-eyed gurgling sound of terror.

Hot fury mixed with cold panic in Makmin's eyes. "What have you done?"

But before he could cut me down, the camel's other end joined the noisy disturbance. To call what the animal passed a wind would not do it justice. A hardstorm emerged. Even the men around the fires looked toward us with alarm.

Then liquid dung blew from the camel, spraying in every direction. The caravan master and I moved hastily to the head, the only safe place. He held on to the camel's neck so the animal wouldn't move around and spray in a circle.

For a while, it seemed the great flood would never end. Then the flow suddenly halted, and the camel made the most frightful noise yet, as if he was being butchered, a plaintive and at the same time outraged cry that would break the heart of the very spirits.

The look in the caravan master's eyes promised me death.

But something new emerged then, little by little, from the camel's windy end. A pale creature, wriggling, sliding, larger than the largest river eel I had ever seen.

Men gathered around.

The creature's head hit the ground, but its tail was still inside the camel.

"River monster," some men whispered, and they began to say how the camel might have drank a small thing in the river and it grew in his stomach.

But I knew it was just a worm, although more monstrous than I had ever seen.

"The other animals should not touch it," I said when it came out all the way at last, as long as the caravan master's staff. "It might be filled with eggs."

The men murmured with alarm, and even the fiercest of them shuddered. Instead of the prior day's suspicion, they were beginning to look at me with awe.

With sticks, they lifted the creature and carried it far into the field. At once they began building a fire, and when the flames reached waist-high, they tossed the worm on top of the burning dung heap.

It screeched.

All through this, Makmin hugged his camel with tears in his eyes. But the beast wanted the freedom of movement more than its owner's affections and ran off at last.

Then the caravan master turned to me, tears of joy running down his face. "You may work your trade in the camel yard of Ker now and forever," he announced solemnly. "If anyone challenges you, you tell them you are a friend of Makmin. And for the next two days whilst we are still here, I will pay your room and your food at the inn."

The food I accepted, but I told him I already had a room. I had no great wish to share lodgings with Graho, but these would be my last two days with the children until I found them again.

Makmin bowed to me and hurried off after his camel.

I returned to Graho's chamber.

As he was out with the children, I took the opportunity to carry a bucket of water upstairs, stand in the washing basin, and bathe. I even washed my clothes and held them above the tallow candle's flame to dry them a little. Since that was slow work, I tried hanging them out the window into the wind. That worked better, but the clothes were still damp when I put them back on. I started a fire in the hearth and crouched in front of that to finish drying.

When my muscles tired, I sat. And then I curled up on some blankets. I closed my eyes.

I woke to the children coming in, Graho behind them.

His gaze cut to me, some emotion glinting in his eyes as he watched me straighten myself and fix my hair. I turned my attention to the children's chatter.

141

They brought tales of the city, of all the wonders they had seen and all the gruesome tales they had heard from war refugees. They only stopped when Posey brought a large tray of food that the caravan master sent for me.

We all shared, saving the smoked meats—the merchant for his caravan trip, and I for my own journey.

"I heard you cast out a great monster," Graho said once we sat by the fire, sated. "There is talk all over town." A smile hovered over his lips.

And, of course, the children wanted to hear the whole grisly tale, not once but twice over. And then they wanted other stories of other monsters.

That night, the children slept, but since I had rested earlier, my eyes would not close.

"I might have found out who your hollow is," Graho said from the floor in front of the door. "A cobbler from Ishaf said the city guards' captain was against inviting the sorcerer into the city. The captain was a big man who recently disappeared. Gramorzo was his name."

I thought some on that. "Perhaps." Despite its stooped shoulders and broken walk, the hollow did seem like it might have been a big man once. My heart twisted as I wondered if it had left behind a grieving wife and children.

"Going east is not safe," Graho said next. "The refugees tell bloody tales."

"My path leads to Regnor."

"You will be going alone, in winter," he pointed out. "It would be safer to come south with us."

Suddenly, I had enough of his pretense that he cared for my safety. "Maybe safer on the road, but not when we reach our destination and you sell me alongside the children. Are you not heading to the slave market in Muzarat?"

Painful silence filled the room.

I waited. But Graho did not deny his dark plans.

# CHAPTER SIXTEEN
## THE HERB WOMAN AND
## THE SOOTHSAYER

I woke before the children and tried to leave the room quietly. Graho shifted away from the door so I could open it.

"Where to?" he asked as he sat up.

"I must earn coin for my journey." There. That should tell him that I was determined to remain my own person.

"Tera, I wish to——" He reached for my hand.

I quickly stepped through the doorway. "I best hurry."

I swung by the privy, then hurried down to the camel yard, where the travelers were already drinking hot tea and eating breakfast. The men around the fires turned to me fully instead of watching me over their shoulders, narrow-eyed, as they had the day before. One who looked old enough to be a grandfather many times over rose from the nearest fire, then shuffled toward me.

When he reached me, his head dipped in a small bow, a hopeful expression in his rheumy eyes that were nearly closed under the many folds of his eyelids. "Makmin says you are a true healer."

I gave the man an encouraging smile. "Where does it hurt?"

"My back." He touched the lower quarter of his spine, and his face wrinkled into a look of pain.

I had him turn, then I probed the area, listening carefully for his quick moans and where he hissed.

"Can you help, mistress?" he asked when I finished.

"I will need a small jar of pig lard," I told him, and he shuffled off with a nod to obtain it.

I had walked forward but a few steps when the next traveler stepped up to me, a young man with the thinnest lips I had ever seen, but eyes so large and dark, he resembled an overgrown owl, especially with his shaggy white sheepskin cape flaring out behind him like wings.

"I am Jano. Makmin say you help me." He spoke the merchant tongue with difficulty, and ducked his head as if embarrassed, but lifted his pants leg, showing me the fist-size boil on his shin, the skin red and shiny.

"I will need fire," I told him after a moment of inspection.

He gestured toward the fire he had just left, the dozen other men sitting around it, all wearing similar capes, eating small black sausages. They looked to be relatives or, at the very least, from the same tribe.

I pointed to a more secluded corner of the camel yard.

The young man called over a servant and sent him off to bring us some fire. I called after the servant, asking for water too and something to boil it in. While waiting for that, we walked over to the spot and sat down.

"How long?" I asked my patient.

He thought for a moment. "Eight days."

"What happened?"

"Thorn bush." Again, he looked embarrassed. "Do you think is it much ugly?"

I began to shrug—an abscess was an abscess—but he added, "I go bride claiming."

*Ah.* "When will you see her?"

"Twelve day time," he said miserably.

And I understood that he feared his bride might find him repulsive. "In twelve days' time, you will be healed and dancing with your bride. I promise."

His face split into a smile, his large eyes shining with pure relief.

A maid cursing at someone drew my gaze to the inn, and I saw Graho in the window. He was watching me.

I wished he was a different man. I wished I had a friend yet left in the world. All who had been my friends before were now far away, out of my reach. I did not even know for certain if they still lived. Mayhap the enemy already on the island had discovered Batumar's absence and had attacked the fortress city.

With a heavy heart, I sent a silent prayer to the spirits to keep my people safe. I kept the prayer short, since the loudmouth servant was hurrying toward us with an armload of dried camel dung and a bucket of water. He was still cursing someone under his breath as he started the fire for us, and I set the metal bucket in the middle.

I pulled my knife from its sheath and gestured for Jano's long linen shirt under his fur cape.

Understanding what I wanted, he extended the bottom toward me and held the hem while I cut off a long, narrow strip for a bandage. This I tossed into the bucket of water and waited until the water was hot.

"Let me see your wound again," I told Jano.

He pulled up his pants leg.

I grabbed the strip of linen and washed the wound. Then I dropped the cloth back into the bucket.

Next I cleaned my knife, holding the blade in the fire until any remnants of dirt burned away.

"The cut will hurt," I warned Jano while I waited for the blade to cool.

"I dance with my bride," he said and puffed out his chest, as if trying to tell me that was worth any pain.

But he did squeeze his eyes shut and ground his teeth when at last, in a quick stab, I lanced the boil.

The pressure under the skin pushed out thick yellow pus in a never-ending stream. I let it run to the ground and waited. When the flow stopped, I pressed my fingers on either side of the hole and pushed out more, squeezed until the pus was mixed with blood, then until only red blood came.

By this time, Jano was swaying and a dozen men gathered around us to watch, some gagging.

The water was boiling in the bucket, so I added carefully selected bunches of herbs and let them boil for a few moments until the brew turned dark brown. I lifted the bandage from the brew with the tip of my knife and let the linen drip and cool a little, but not overly much. While still hot, I wrapped it around Jano's wound.

"This will help the infection," I said as I tied off the bandage. "Take this medicine and put it in a flask. Wash the wound with it and rewrap in a clean cloth every time you stop to rest on your journey."

"I dance?" he asked again, his face a few shades paler but with hope in his eyes.

"You will dance," I promised.

His tribesmen had to help him up. One used the corner of his own cape to grab the bucket out of the fire and carry it away. The oldest of the men, maybe Jano's father, gave me a deep bow and a silver coin.

I bowed in response, my heart thrilling at the payment. A full silver coin would provide me with food all the way to Regnor.

As the men walked off, my first patient returned with white hardened pig lard in a small pot. I set this at the edge of the fire to melt and added four different dried herbs. The heat would help their healing properties to seep out. While waiting for that, I had the man take off his cloak, spread it on the ground, then lie facedown in front of me.

I tugged his tunic free and folded it up on his back, then held my hands over the fire to warm them before placing my palms over his skin. He sighed at the heat.

I worked his muscles softly for a while, then added the warm, infused lard and kneaded them a little harder. So many hard knots he had. Then I felt my own palms tingle, and I could *see* the knotted muscles as well as feel them. I could feel my healing power surge inside me, such a welcome sensation. I could barely stifle a cry of joy.

I let that power pour out into the old man and healed his back, his aching joints, even the hidden sickness of his bowels.

When I drew away, he sat up with a stunned smile. "You are the goddess come to earth." He pushed to his feet without struggle, then bowed. "You made me a young man." He too paid me a full silver coin.

He hurried back toward the men and their fires, and as he spread his tale, more and more of them came to me.

Once again, I caught Graho watching me, but I was too busy to pay much attention to him.

I healed cuts and infections, coughs, eased the pain of gnarled fingers and aching knees. I used my healing spirit sparingly and only when absolutely needed. I did not want to weaken myself for my long journey. But I did have my healing powers back and I did use them, my spirit soaring.

By midday, I had a handful of coins, three loaves of bread, and several chunks of hard cheese. By midafternoon, I had even more food and another blanket to take with me.

Since I helped all who needed my help, I decided to leave the camel yard and walk to the market. Graho waited for me by the inn's back entrance.

"Tera."

Thinking he only meant to persuade me to go to Muzarat, I moved to pass by him.

His blue gaze burned into mine. "You judge me harshly."

Embarrassment made me look away. He spoke the truth. And hadn't my mother told me a hundred times that healers were called to heal and not to judge?

I had trouble finding my voice. "Forgive me."

He placed a hand on my arm, his voice filled with tension and a strange urgency, and something else I could not name. "Tonight I would wish to talk with you, when the children are asleep."

I looked around. "Where are they?"

"Up in our chamber. Posey brought them sweet raisin biscuits." He would not let my arm go.

I sighed. Nothing he could tell me would make me feel differently about his dark trade, but a healer listened.

"I must go to purchase my supplies. But tonight we shall talk," I reluctantly promised, and he offered to take my bundle up to our chamber for me.

I hurried off to the market to spend my coin before it closed. Coin was no good to me on the road, through barren winter fields and woods.

I needed more food and another flask. And I wished to purchase a proper pair of boots, if used, for the wraith. In truth, he did not seem to be fading. Mayhap he'd been a stronger man than the sorcerer's previous victims.

As I walked down the cobbled streets, people watched me with interest. Word of my healing must have spread beyond the camel yard. Some frowned; others smiled at me. I smiled at all of them, a small nagging worry in the back of my head.

Then my thoughts returned to my odd conversation with Graho. That I was still with him was strange enough in itself. I fully disapproved of his trade and his person.

*"If something happens to me, stay close to the merchant,"* Batumar had said.

Had Batumar known something I did not? What? What was the merchant's secret? Mayhap I would find out later.

I was still pondering that when I saw a most striking man rushing toward me and shouting.

From his wild eyes and great beard, the boiling hate in his gaze, I judged him to be Ker's soothsayer.

His splendid purple satin caftan swept the ground, his forked, blue-dyed beard reaching his bright green, studded belt. Half a dozen men followed him, as richly if not as colorfully dressed, probably the city fathers. All appeared equally outraged.

"Sorceress!" the soothsayer accused me at once, pointing a long, knobby finger at me, then stabbing my chest with it repeatedly when he reached me.

People gathered around, even leaning from their windows above our heads.

"Sorceress!" The soothsayer spat the word with revulsion. He looked as wild-faced as Makmin's camel during my treatment. "One of your kind has already turned the weak minds of the city fathers of Ishaf. That will not happen in Ker!"

My limbs went weak. "My lord, I am but a traveling healer."

"You cast out the beast of darkness," he accused me with enough drama for a harvest play. "Only darkness can cast out darkness."

I hoped tales of my healing had not been exaggerated. I had been accused of sorcery before, by Karamur's very own soothsayer when Batumar was on a military campaign. People believed that sorceresses could only be killed by boiling them in tar, a fate I had narrowly escaped. I hoped the city of Ker was not overly superstitious.

"I but helped a camel pass a worm."

"A dark spirit in the shape of a great snake," he accused as if he had been there and I had not.

"A worm, my lord." I bowed. "Nothing more."

"You are the sister of dark spirits," the soothsayer screeched at me, stabbing me with his finger once again. His mouth frothed, his eyes rolled back in his head.

"I meant no harm. I shall leave the city at once," I hurried to say, wishing nothing as much as to be away from him and the mob that gathered.

"You shall not!" he shouted, red-faced. "You shall be tried for your dark deeds, and then you shall be boiled!"

Fear closed my throat. I could not speak. And even if I could, what would I say?

I bowed meekly, as if ready to give myself into the mob's hands. But instead, the next second, I tore away and darted into the nearest alleyway.

*Spirits help me.* I dashed forward. *There*, a narrow doorway. I flew through a kitchen, out the front, into another alleyway, taking turn after turn. I ran, changing direction again and again.

I was clear on the other side of the city, way past the market, before I dared to slow and catch my breath. I was on Eryl the herb woman's street. Up ahead, I could see her hut, pressing up against the city wall.

I saw two men by her gate, arguing, paying little attention to anything else.

But when I reached them, a screech came from Eryl's hut. "That's her!"

And the two men set upon me at once, grabbing me. Before I could protest, a potato sack was thrown over my head, and I was shoved, dragged into the hut where Eryl kept screaming. "Not here!"

So I was dragged back out. The two men must have been her brothers or her husband and a friend, for the whole while they were dragging me, they were threatening to kill me if I didn't stay away from Eryl and the city of Ker.

Our boots scuffed on stone, the sound echoing off stone walls as if we were in a narrow passageway. Little light filtered through the potato sack as I begged them not to harm me, my stomach clenched in a hard knot as I struggled in vain.

Then more light shined through the bag again, and I felt soft earth beneath my feet. The next moment, rough hands touched me all over, and I screamed, fearing the worst violation, but the two men only searched me, stripping me of all my earnings and belongings before one of them kicked me in the back of the knees and sent me sprawling face-first into the dirt.

A hard foot connected with my ribs.

I cried out, but so did one of the men. "A hollow! Look! A wraith!"

And in the next moment, I heard their footsteps retreating.

By the time I sat up, by the time I pulled the sack off my head, they were gone. I was outside the city walls, somewhere in the back of Ker, the east road in front of me. The hollow was stumbling forward from the forest in my direction, like a dark spirit from a children's tale.

And yet, that black shape was such a welcome sight to me.

It slowed, then stopped altogether. Had it come from the woods to scare off the men? To defend me?

Did it have thought still left? Reason in its brain? Or did the body simply move, guided by some animal instinct that remained after the loss of spirit? I wanted no harm to come to him on my account.

"Go back into the woods!"

While I checked my ribs, I glanced back at the small door in the city wall, fearing the men would return with help to chase away the hollow and finish me.

Eryl must have heard of my healing work in the camel yard but not that the soothsayer was after me. For if she knew, I was certain she would have instructed her brothers to hand me over to the authorities instead of tossing me out on my ear. I had a feeling she would have enjoyed seeing me boiled.

My stomach clenched at the thought, and I scrambled to my feet. No broken ribs, thank the spirits.

I glanced toward the city one last time, wishing I could return to the inn and say good-bye to Graho and the children, claim my food and blankets.

*Not if I want to live.*

I moved in the opposite direction. The hollow still stood out in the open. I had to lead it back into the trees. We had to stay hidden.

The cold bit into me. Once again, I was without a warm cloak or a blanket. Without food. Yet the spirits had provided for me until now. I had to trust them to provide for me still.

The enemy was out there, threatening my people. I could not stand here and wish for things to be different. I had to go forward and do what I could to bring about whatever rescue we needed.

Marga chuffed somewhere in the woods. I strode forward. Maybe it was better not to see Graho and the children to say good-bye. Maybe he would have tried to trick me or force me into going with him. Yet, I felt oddly alone without them. We had become traveling companions along the way.

*What did Graho mean to tell me?*

I sighed after a few hurried steps. No matter. Now I would never hear it.

As I passed the hollow, it just stood there, head hanging. But a moment later, when I glanced over my shoulder, it turned and followed me.

When I reached Marga in the woods, the tiger bent her head and licked my hand in greeting. Then, because she was tall enough to do so, she licked my face. I dug my hands into her fur and hugged her for a long moment before letting go.

By that time, the hollow caught up too.

"We better be on our way."

The road cut through the forest. We walked inside the woods so we would not be seen by other travelers should any happen by. And this way, I was also able to find some mushrooms and berries, which we ate on the spot.

We did not journey far that day, for darkness fell early in winter. We settled into a small clearing for the night. At least, since my flint and steel were in my boots, I had those to start a fire. I wished I had not lost my blankets and cloak, but between the fire and the tiger, I did not feel the cold of the night.

I fell asleep to the tiger's soft snoring and woke to the sensation of being watched. Morning had not yet come, not even dawn, plenty of stars in the sky. I sat up and yawned.

The tiger was gone. The hollow sat on the other side of the banked fire, as close as he had ever come to me.

I felt no fear. If the hollow meant to harm me, it could have done so while I slept. Maybe because I had protected it at Ishaf's city gate, it seemed to have appointed itself as my protector. I was glad for the quiet company and pleased that the hollow still lived.

Was it really flesh without a sliver of spirit?

"What are you?" I asked without expecting an answer as I stirred the fire to life. I wanted to warm up a little before continuing our journey.

The hollow's chin moved as if it was trying to talk. Then it did make some sound that startled me.

I leaned forward. "Orsh?"

The rusty, scratchy sound repeated from lips I could not see.

"Orz," I said, catching the word better this time. I took that to be his name.

He sat perfectly still, but his back was a little straighter, as if the sound of his name, spoken out loud, had somehow brought a small piece of his spirit back to him.

# CHAPTER SEVENTEEN
## ORZ

The unexpected conversation left me unsettled. Was he more than an empty shell? Was he improving? He certainly did not seem to be declining.

I remembered Graho's words. *"A cobbler from Ishaf said the city guards' captain was against the sorcerer. He was a big man who recently disappeared. Gramorzo was his name."*

*Orz.* Could it be him?

That question and a hundred others filled my mind, about Orz, about what Graho and the children thought of my sudden disappearance, about the journey that awaited me.

As warm as the fire was, I could not settle back into sleep. Orz did not lie down either.

Both moons were full, clearly visible through the bare branches above, the light dusting of snow reflecting back their light. A silver glow bathed the forest. Since we had not walked much so far, I was not overly tired.

The beauty of the night drew me forward. The woods did not scare me. I had suffered much more harm in the cities of men, than I ever had in any wild forest.

"We could walk some more," I suggested.

Orz stood without a word, his head bowed. His hood as ever remained in place. I had not yet seen his face. Even in full daylight, I could see no more than the tip of his stubble-covered chin.

I pushed to my feet, then kicked snow over the fire.

This time when we set out, he followed me from only a step or two behind. Maybe so he could hear if I spoke to him again. Clearly, he could understand me. I had been wrong about that before. Could he say more than his name?

"What did the sorcerer do to you?" I asked. Maybe if I knew that, I would know how to help him.

But Orz remained silent at my question.

"What were you before?"

He said nothing.

"Did you always live in Ishaf?"

He followed me in silence.

I resigned myself to this and plodded forward. My stomach growled. Behind me, Orz's stomach answered.

I had planned on leaving Ker with full provisions for a long journey, early in the morning so I could walk a fair distance before nightfall. But ever since leaving Karamur, nothing had turned out as planned.

I thought of Batumar, and my heart twisted. I walked forward. I could not look back. There waited such a dark, deep hole as would swallow me forever.

We walked a fair distance before I heard someone walking in the woods. I thought of the brigands who had attacked us on the road to Ker and reached for my knife, which my attackers outside the city wall had deemed too insignificant to take. But once again, it was Marga returning.

Her whiskers were wet with blood. She licked them with a satisfied growl as she padded forward by my side. She had not brought me a gift this time. Maybe all she had caught was a squirrel or some other small animal that she had eaten in one bite.

"To the city of Regnor," I told her. "We must find Lord Karnagh."

Lord Karnagh's people, the Selorm who lived in the kingless kingdom of Seberon, fought with battle tigers. If any people would accept me with a tiger in tow, it would be the Selorm.

No wind blew, but the night chilled me through regardless. I was glad I was moving. Lying on the cold hard ground in the woods would have been even more uncomfortable, especially if the tiger wandered off again.

She sniffed the air constantly. When we heard the howl of distant wolves, she answered with a warning roar. The wolves must have turned in another direction, for they did not come to investigate, and I did not hear them again.

When the sun rose, I stopped in a small glen but did not start a fire. I lay on the bare ground. The tiger lay next to me and warmed me with her heat. She even put a paw over me, as if I were her cub she was protecting.

Orz sat with his back against a tree, as if on guard duty. Truly, I could not remember ever seeing him sleep. He was so silent and still that, after a few moments, I forgot about him.

Since the trees had no leaves, I could see the sky through their gnarly branches. I looked up at the gray winter clouds and thought of Batumar. Grief flooded my heart. He had given his life for me and a handful of little beggars. He had lived with honor and had died with honor.

Someday, the Kadar would be singing songs about him at a feast, about him and the siege of Karamur. I'd had no great love for the Kadar when I had first come to them, but now I hoped with a desperate hope that they would survive to sing such songs.

I fell asleep to the sound of the tiger's snoring and dreamed dark and disjointed dreams, remembering none when I woke past midday. Yet I carried their weight, feeling anxious as we continued.

Any food I could forage, I shared with Orz, who would not touch me, not even for victuals, but accepted whatever I placed on the ground for him.

If we came across herbs, I gathered them and hung them from my belt, but the pickings were slim. As we walked in companionable silence, my thoughts turned to another journey, one I had made with Batumar's mother to free him when he had been captured by the enemy. We had walked through a similar forest to this. We had been nearly captured more than once. At night, to keep safe, we had slept in the trees.

But despite all the danger, we had reached Batumar. And we had all made it safely back to Karamur, the fortress city.

I had doubts aplenty when Batumar and I embarked on our journey through the mountain, but once we passed that test, I had gained heart and expected this adventure to end in success. I had expected the journey to be difficult and dangerous, but I trusted Batumar's great strength to achieve our goals. Why would the spirits send him on a quest just to fail?

I railed against the injustice.

We walked through the same kind of woods as the day before and kept going long after dark, staying in the forest but within sight of the road. When we came across a creek, we drank. At least we had the flask I had given Orz outside Ker. This he now returned to me, along with the handsome bowl Graho had carved.

I turned my attention to finding food. We ate roots and leaves, and the grubs I found under the rotted bark of a tree. I had the sack the men who'd attacked me had left on my head, but what little food we found, we ate, so the sack remained empty.

We crossed a large clearing of waist-high dead grasses. I collected an armful as we walked. More woods waited for us on the other side.

As the sun went down, I pulled deeper into the trees to start a fire, and Marga padded off to look for prey. Orz drew closer and sat on the other side of the flames. He cut a dark and tragic figure.

From the pile next to me, I took four or five strands of grass and rolled them into thin rope, adding and adding for length, then made a light but strong net from the grass rope, weighting the edges with stones.

"I can use this to hunt tomorrow," I told Orz.

He watched from under his hood as my fingers worked, without ever raising his gaze to my face. His fingers twitched on his lap, mimicking mine. He had lost the rags that had bound them before. For the first time, I saw that his bones were at all the wrong angles. Not as if they had been simply broken, but as if they had been broken over and over again.

My throat tightened with sympathy. Since I knew Orz would not answer, I did not ask how he had gained those injuries.

The tiger returned late, when all the stars were out in the sky. Her maw was clean, her side flat. We all went to sleep hungry, for the dinner of grubs Orz and I had shared had been nowhere near enough to fill our stomachs.

In the days that followed, we fell into a routine, walking in the woods, stopping at dusk so the tiger could hunt, then moving on at first light. She liked the dusk and dawn hunting hours the best, and was content to walk with us most of the day, then sleep next to me and keep me warm most of the night.

Each night, Orz sat leaning against a tree. Maybe his back was as damaged as his hands were and having the tree's support was easiest for him. Now and then, I did catch him sleeping.

Many times during the day, I caught him looking at me, which he could do without lifting his hood, since the burlap material was threadbare indeed. I still had not seen his face. What little his hood did not cover was hidden by a growing beard. I suspected that, like his fingers, his features were most terribly ruined.

We had been traveling for five days—during which time I caught half a dozen small birds with my net—when we saw the first group of refugees on the road, heading toward Ker.

The tiger had gone off into the deep woods to investigate some strange noise or smell. Only Orz was with me.

We stopped and watched from behind a stand of evergreen bushes as the group of seven staggered forward. Three ragged women walked in front, one staring in front of her numbly, one grunting with exhaustion at each step, the last one crying. Four men brought up the rear of the column, looking back frequently for danger, pulling loaded wooden skids behind them. There were no children.

Only when they passed did I spy a gray hand hanging out from one of their bundles and realized they were not pulling their belongings. They were pulling their dead. I counted the lumps. Six bodies lay fully wrapped in strips of cloth that were stained with dirt and old, black blood.

*Five dead*, I realized as they stopped. The sixth, an old man, was wrapped in a blanket, but his face was free. He still lived. As the group stopped, he moaned loudly. The women crouched around him while the men took up guard positions.

I signaled with my hand to Orz to stay where he stood. He shook his head. Another bit of new communication we had not had before. His jaw worked. I waited for him to say something.

When he did not, I said, "I must help."

He shifted forward, as if he intended to reach for me.

I stepped away.

His hand immediately dropped back to his side. He hung his head.

I wished I could somehow fully communicate with him, and swore to try when I returned. His tense stance, the bend of his head, the set of his jaw, said he was desperate to tell me something.

I would find a way to understand him. But for now, I turned my attention back to the road and the refugees.

Since the men all had swords, I hesitated another moment before stepping forward, but at last the old man's cries of pain pulled me out of my hiding place.

The men rounded on me.

I smiled at the group, stopping but a few steps outside the edge of the woods. "I am Tera, a traveling healer. I bring no harm."

The bunches of herbs hanging from my belt gave credence to my words.

"Are you alone?" the tallest of the men asked, his pockmarked face grim. He spoke a mixture of Selorm and some other language. Since I understood Selorm well, I could guess the meaning of his words.

"Yes." Admitting that was a great risk, for I just admitted that I had no protection and they could do with me as they wished.

They knew this also, understood my gesture of trust, and responded by lowering their weapons, a goodwill gesture of their own.

"We are in need of a healer." One of the women spoke from behind them. "Help us, mistress."

The men parted, and I drew closer. They all had the look of hunger about them, all lean bodies and chapped lips. I had no food to offer, but Ker was within reach, and they could forage on the way like I had. They would not starve now until they reached the city.

Water was another matter. I caught them watching my flask with open interest.

"There is a creek a short distance from here," I said in Selorm, and pointed out the direction from which I had just come.

They seemed to understand me without any trouble. Two of the men collected everyone's flasks and hurried off.

I stepped up to the old man. The women drew back. I folded the blanket aside, and I could see the source of his pain at once. His clothes had been burned away completely in places, melted into his skin in other spots.

His injury must have happened some days ago, because there had been time for his wounds to become infected. I uncovered him a little more to see the extent of the damage but found little to encourage me. His legs too had been burned.

One of the women crouched next to me, tears rolling down her dirty face. "Soldiers burned the village down. He was trapped in our hut. Please, mistress, help my father."

My breath caught. Emperor Drakhar's hordes had not settled in to wait out the winter, then. How long before they reached Ker? Before they reached Ishaf? Before they found a way to open Dahru's Gate?

"How long have you been on the road?" I asked.

"Ten long days." The woman took the old man's frail hand, patted the liver-spotted, wrinkled skin, the gnarled fingers that ended in yellow, brittle fingernails that still had black soot under them.

*Ten days.* In ten days, at most, I would reach the end of peace and cross into war-torn lands. From now on, I had to watch for marauding soldiers who would cut me down as soon as they set eyes on me. I would have to be thrice as careful as I had been up to this point.

But for now, I turned my attention to my patient, my heart sinking. I could not take on his injuries and still go on with my journey. I would need food and shelter to heal. I had neither. And I *had* to find Lord Karnagh. I needed him to help me save my people.

Batumar, if he were with me, would have told me not to even consider it. He would have forbidden me taking on the pain. I did not make the decision as easily as that, but I did have to make it at the end.

I had some jalik, an herb used on burns, but for this man..."He is too badly hurt to be healed," I said quietly.

The woman cried harder.

I reached for a different medicine. "All I can do is ease his pain and make his passing gentler."

She fell on her knees and took my hand to kiss it, covering my skin with her tears.

"We need to make a fire," I said.

Two women immediately stepped off the road to gather tinder and kindling; another tugged a bunch of dry branches into a pile. In a short while, I could see a flame, and soon we had a good beginning of a fire.

The men did nothing through all this time but kept their guard positions, looking backward more than forward. I understood. They lived in fear that the enemy would catch up with them.

I carefully selected my herbs, found two flat rocks in the road, and ground the dry leaves, then gathered the results into a piece of cloth. When the men returned from the creek, I asked for a flask and tied it to a green branch, then held it over the fire. While we waited for the water to boil, I showed the old man's daughter how much of the herb mix to put in.

"Make one flask of medicine each day," I advised, "and let him sip it throughout the day. You have three days' worth here." I handed her the small bundle.

She nodded with a sob, understanding that her father would not live past three days. In truth, I doubted he would live even that long. He was closer to the world of the spirits than to ours.

"We have nothing to pay you with," one of the men said, ducking his head in shame.

"No payment is required." My eye caught on their bundled-up dead. "But might you have boots you have no need of?" I winced, embarrassed to be asking.

At this, the old man's daughter tugged the boots from her own father's feet before bundling him back up in the blankets. "He will not need boots to walk with the spirits, mistress. He would want you to have them."

I accepted the gift with many thanks, then glanced toward the woods, wanting to go back to Orz before he decided to show himself. But even as I wished the men and women well on the rest of their journey, before I could take my leave, a group of soldiers rode up the road from Ker, raising a cloud of dust behind them.

The refugee men stood in front of their women in a protective half circle but did not draw their swords this time. They did not want to provoke a fight, just to be ready should we be harassed.

I hoped the soldiers would pass without stopping, but they halted as they reached us. The captain questioned the refugee men about the enemy, their numbers, and their whereabouts.

I listened with interest. I should have done this, I thought. Batumar would have.

When the captain was satisfied, about to leave, he looked over the women. His gaze halted over me. I was dressed differently, had dark hair that contrasted with their blonde braids. His gaze settled on the herbs hanging from my belt.

He looked to be a battle-tested man with more than a few scars on his face and the tip of one ear missing. He was stoutly built, thick-necked, wearing quality armor that combined metal chain with hardened leather.

"Who are you?" he demanded.

"Tera, the traveling healer." I hoped he would be satisfied with that and they would move on.

*Go, ride, move,* I pleaded silently with the men. And, with a last speculative look in my direction, the captain turned his horse back to the road, ready to leave us at last.

But Marga chose that moment to walk out of the forest.

The horses reared and tried to bolt, some succeeding, carrying off three soldiers. Another two were thrown from their saddles, their horses galloping back in the direction of Ker.

Some of the remaining soldiers pulled their swords, others readied their lances.

"No!" I cried, darting toward the tiger, stumbling on the uneven ground, catching myself and lunging forward again.

And when I reached her, I threw my arms around her.

# CHAPTER EIGHTEEN
## CAPTURED

Marga growled at the danger, her muscles tightening, ready to attack the men who were poised to attack her. Then somehow Orz was next to us. I blinked. How had he moved so fast?

*Never mind that now…*I stepped in front of them and shouted at the soldiers, my heart wildly scrambling. "Stop!"

But the soldiers were frozen already. They stared at me, stunned, eyes wide, breath held.

The captain gathered himself first. "Weapons down."

His men lowered their swords but did not put them back in their scabbards.

The captain watched me with renewed interest from atop his wide-backed battle horse. He rubbed the silver-shot stubble on his chin. "So, you are the sorceress they speak of in Ker."

"I am a traveling healer. A Shahala."

"The Shahala do not bond with tigers. The Selorm do. But you do not look like a Selorm." His tone said he best not catch me again at lying. "And even among the Selorm, their women do not bond with the beasts," he added thoughtfully.

I said nothing. He would not believe my words no matter what I said. I counted on the fact that he was heading away from Ker, obviously on some mission. He was unlikely to turn back just to deliver me for trial, no matter what accusations the soothsayer had brought against me.

"Where are you going?" he asked.

"Regnor."

He scoffed. "Through battlefields?"

"Around them if I can."

"Are you a spy?"

*Oh, for the spirits' sake.*

But his sword arm was relaxed. I did not think he contemplated immediate attack, so I relaxed a little too. "A moment ago, you accused me of being a sorceress."

His eye glinted. "I am now thinking a sorceress would make a good spy."

"I spent most of my time in Ker in the camel yard, and most of my time at the camel yard with the removing of a worm from one bad-tempered camel. What important information could I have gained from that?"

"A worm, you call it?" He contemplated my choice of word. "People say you cast out a dark spirit that possessed the camel."

"Did you see this great dark spirit?" I asked. It had been a fairly giant worm, the largest I had ever seen but, nevertheless, it *had* been a worm.

He shook his head. "I wish I had. But I heard terrible tales of it. It devoured a man standing too close. A hundred men had to subdue it to burn it in the fire."

I gaped at him. No such thing had happened! I had been right there. "The men who burned it are like fishermen with their catch."

"Mayhap." The captain nodded. "Some men do exaggerate their battles." He paused. "The city fathers did not like the tales. They ordered the camel burned this morning to ascertain that no part of the dark spirit remained within the animal."

My breath caught. Sadness flooded me, for the life of the innocent animal and for Makmin, the caravan master. He loved that camel more than some men loved their children.

The captain said, "Some think you put the dark spirit into the camel, then cast it out to gain some kind of favor with the city. Mayhap you thought the city fathers would set you up in a tower."

"I asked no payment," I pointed out, then shook my head. "What do *you* think?" He seemed like a sensible man, as old soldiers often were.

He shrugged. "The caravans are forced to new routes to go around the armies. The camel might have caught something strange from some exotic beast."

After a moment, he added, "I once had a horse that died. I cut him open to feed my men. We were surrounded up in the mountains, had gone without food for days. But inside the horse was a nest of white snakes, a wriggling mess. We did not eat any of the meat."

I relaxed a little more. The captain did seem to be a man of some sense.

Until he said, "I could believe your tale about the sick camel. But I see you now with the tiger. And you have a hollow for a companion. You have power beyond what is given to ordinary healers."

He raised his hand when I would have objected.

I respectfully held my silence, even as my heart beat faster, dread and fear nipping at my heels. Antagonizing him would not be to my advantage.

He turned from me then and sent the group of refugees—who'd been listening with rapt attention—on their way. As the bedraggled men and women moved off with their skids, the soldiers who'd gone after the runaway horses returned.

I stepped back toward the forest, and the tiger and Orz backed away with me. But the captain had other ideas.

"You are wanted in Ker for questioning by the city fathers. You will come with me to the border. When I return to the city in a few days' time, I shall take you back with me."

He nodded to the men, and they raised their weapons again. I wanted neither the tiger nor Orz hurt because of me. I could not see a way out of the trap in that moment. I thought of Batumar, of what I had learned from him during our nightly talks when he discussed with me everything from city matters to military strategy.

*"A warlord always looks for the position of advantage,"* he had told me once. *"If he cannot take the position of advantage, he must wait until the circumstances change, or do something to change the circumstances."*

The circumstances at the moment were not to my advantage. Changing them was not in my power. But the trek to the border would take at least another day. Our stay there a day or two. Then many more days back to Ker. All that time, the soldiers would not be facing me with their swords drawn, all eyes on me.

I had to wait for my circumstances to change.

I patted the tiger's neck and asked her in a spirit song to leave me. I gave an encouraging nod to Orz, my eyes begging him not to interfere, but I had been around warriors long enough to know that the fisted hands at his sides meant whatever blood he had left in him sang for battle.

I could almost see the warrior under his robes for the first time, his body subtly changing, making me consider once again whether he had once been Captain Gramorzo of the city guard of Ishaf.

"Orz? Please," I whispered. He could not possibly fight. He would be cut down within moments.

My breath caught even as I thought that. Was death what he wanted?

His head was down, his hood over his eyes and most of his face, but I could feel him hold my gaze through the burlap.

"I wish not that you would come to harm on my behalf. Or come to harm at all," I said quietly. As unusual companions as they were, Orz and Marga were all that I had left. "I will escape. I promise."

His fists would not unclench, but, barely perceptibly, he nodded.

I walked toward the captain, reached the boots I had dropped when I had run to protect Marga. I picked them up and threw them toward Orz. I hoped he understood that they were for him.

I glanced back only when I reached the road. The tiger had gone back into the forest. Orz stood where I had left him.

The captain said, "Whether a simple healer or a powerful sorceress, I have one warning for you. Should you try to turn me or my men into hollows, you will not long live."

I looked him straight in the eye. "His name is Orz. He was turned into a hollow by the sorcerer of Ishaf."

The captain must have accepted this, for he extended his hand to me. "We will travel faster with you on horseback."

When I accepted the offer of help, he hauled me up behind him. The horses needed little encouragement to move forward. They were anxious to put some distance between themselves and the tiger.

Orz still stood in the middle of the field between the woods and the road, his head turned toward me. He had improved, and his movements had grown faster and easier over the past few days, but I did not think he could keep up with the horses. Yet, I did not doubt that somehow he would find a way to catch up with me sooner or later.

In that dark robe, he reminded me of the Guardians who had been good friends to me, and even more—like grandfathers. Suddenly I wondered how old he was. Warlords were men in their prime, the strongest warriors of the land. But if Orz had been the captain of Ishaf's city guard, he could have been a man more advanced in age. Maybe even as old as the Guardians. He would not have had to fight in battle, just supervise his guards' training.

On an impulse, I waved at him.

He lifted his hand in a broken gesture that I interpreted as his way of waving back.

"Why are you going to Regnor?" the captain asked after we moved some distance down the road.

I did not want to lie to him. I could not see what harm he could find in my true purpose. It threatened him not, nor his people. "I wish to find Lord Karnagh."

He turned to look at me. "How would a Shahala healer come to know him?" he pounced, thinking he had caught me in a lie.

"Lord Karnagh came to Karamur. He was a friend and ally to the High Lord of the Kadar. I met him at the High Lord's feast."

The captain turned forward. "The Kadar cannot abide sorcerers."

"I am not a sorceress. I was the High Lord's concubine."

He spent a moment in silence at that. Then he said, "Concubines do not travel without their lords, and rarely with them."

He clearly was not a man to trust easily.

"I traveled with the High Lord. He was lost at sea." My heart bled inside my chest, those last five words sharp blades that slashed it into ribbons on their way up to be spoken.

"You sailed with the pirates?"

"On One-Tooth Tum's ship."

The captain was silent longer this time. But after a while, he spoke again. "Batumar, the High Lord of the Kadar, was a great warrior. If what you say is true, his loss will be felt."

We rode in silence for a while, both lost in our thoughts, before he spoke again, summing up my predicament. "You cannot return to your island."

I said nothing. He wasn't asking a question.

But then he did a moment later. "Are you in search of another protector lord? A comfortable castle? Not many of those left, I fear. Few freeholds survive. The best of our castles have been burned."

"I am not seeking protection for myself."

Another moment passed. "For your country, then?"

"For our people."

His head bobbed forward as he nodded. "No ordinary woman could do it. But you *are* a sorceress."

"I am but hoping to find Lord Karnagh and plead for his help to save my people. He brought his warriors and their tigers to aid us in the siege of Karamur. I am hoping he and his people might come to our aid once again. We have enemy troops trapped on the island, more to come as soon as the Gate opens."

The captain simply said, "He has not been seen," but from his dark tone, I surmised he thought the Selorm warlord dead.

"He might be injured or kept captive," I protested.

"He is no lesser man than the High Lord of the Kadar had been. He would not be easily killed," the captain allowed. "I do hope you will find him. This world cannot afford to lose all its great men."

We rode in silence for a spell.

He then said, "Other than the city fathers, there is a traveling merchant making much of your disappearance. He has searched every corner of the city for you."

*Graho.* I wondered how the children fared. I missed them.

The captain turned his full attention to the road, asking no further questions.

When we stopped at nightfall, I helped the soldiers make camp and cook dinner. In exchange, they shared their meal of thin vegetable stew with me. They offered me a place by the fire, but by then the tiger caught up with us and chuffed for me.

With the captain's permission, to keep the tiger from coming to me and scaring all the horses into running off, I walked to the tree line where she waited and made myself a nest of leaves that protected me from the worst of the cold radiating from the ground. Being snuggled close to the tiger kept me from freezing while I slept.

Orz did not catch up to us that night or by the following morning. We left at first light, and we reached the border around midday.

The army sprawled across fields of frozen mud on either side of the road, men gathered in clumps in front of fires, tents scattered in a haphazard pattern. Horses grazed in a nearby field.

The soldiers were of every age, from beardless youth to grizzled old men. Some moved soldier-like and carried swords. Others had hunting and even four-pronged fishing spears. A great barrel-chested mountain of a man wore a blacksmith's leather apron and carried a blacksmith's hammer.

But though I saw many hale men, I saw twice as many injured. Most of them wore garments of different cut and color than the locals, probably men of other kingdoms, fleeing before the enemy. They had likely joined Ker's army to make their last stand, hoping to stop the invaders from reaching the caravan yard and the port city beyond it.

Compared to Batumar's trained and experienced warriors who worked like a unit, what spread before me looked more like a refugee camp than an army camp.

Perhaps the captain caught the doubt in my eyes, because he said in a bellowing voice that carried on the wind, "We *will* stop the enemy. The Kerghi hordes will come this far and no farther."

Around us, men stomped their boots and rattled their armor in approval as the captain directed his horse to walk through their ranks. He sat spine straight in the saddle, shoulders wide. He looked suddenly like a much younger man, fed by the trust of his men and his vision for them.

He cast me a glance full of confidence. "What think you, Sorceress?"

"I am no sorceress."

He lifted a hand, palm out, in a gesture that said he meant no harm. "In the country of the Selorm, on the other side of this border, sorceresses are revered. Sorcery does not bother me either. I am from a border town. Did I tell you that? When I was a child, a Selorm sorceress once saved our harvest."

He slid from his horse and held out his hand, but I jumped to the ground without his assistance.

We barely took two steps before a commotion amongst the ranks up ahead drew our attention. A small crowd of men gathered around one of the fires. We heard them shouting in alarm. The captain hurried that way, and, since I could hear pain-filled groans and moans mixed in with the shouting, I followed him.

The captain pushed through the circle of bystanders, and I pushed right behind him, seeing the cause for the alarm as soon as we were through. A dozen men writhed on the ground around the cooking fire, their faces distorted with pain. In between grunts and moans, they were begging their fellow soldiers to kill them.

They were clutching their middles, but I could see no blood. They had not been stabbed.

The captain dropped to one knee next to the man who seemed the most coherent, and grabbed him by the shoulders. "What happened?"

I had a fair idea, and if I was right, every moment counted. I pushed my way to the cauldron on the fire and dipped the ladle into the bubbling stew. I smelled the steam. Nothing strange there; it made my mouth water. I fished through the contents: very little meat, some barley, and what roots could be collected in the woods, a few mushrooms here and there.

My hand froze when I recognized one of those mushroom caps. I'd seen those grow by the dozen in the Shahala forests. My people used them to fight vermin if they overran the fields to such degree that they threatened the wheat harvest.

I turned toward the captain, who had already moved on to another man. "Tennicap!"

I hadn't meant to shout the word, but I did, and my outburst brought all eyes to me. None showed understanding.

I had no idea what the mushroom was called in their language. "Poison."

The stew steamed in the ladle I held, but I reached in and picked out the mushroom, dropped the ladle back into the cauldron, then put the poisonous cap on my palm and held it out for them. I rubbed off the stew's glistening coating so they could see the distinct stripes and dots that looked like the back of a fawn. "Make sure nobody else cooked with these."

Word was passed around and, after each taking a good look at what I held, most of the men dispersed, running off to ascertain that the mushrooms did not make it into any of the other cauldrons that boiled over scattered cooking fires.

The captain barked at two of the remaining soldiers, ordered the stew to be carried off and disposed of. Then he turned to me, a desperate urgency in his gaze. "Can you save them?"

I had already been thinking whether I had the right medicine. Noten flowers would have been the best, but there would be none of those in winter. *What else?*

"Rapice," I said. "They must be made to vomit."

I searched through my sack until I found a bundle of rapice roots. They had frozen in the ground before I had dug them up, but that would not affect their power.

I sat by the largest, flattest of the stones that surrounded the cooking fire and chopped my small store of rapice into enough chunks that each sick man could receive a piece.

"They must swallow one each." I handed half the chunks to the captain, then grabbed a moaning man next to me and shoved the rapice down his throat, no matter how he struggled, holding his nose so he would swallow.

The captain followed my example, and we moved on to the next soldier and the next until they all received their share.

"We better step back," I warned as the men began to gag.

Even the captain turned a greenish shade from the copious amount of vomiting that followed. Some of the soldiers standing around vomited themselves, without having taken the rapice.

I paid little attention to all that, for I was already making my next batch of medicine. As the soldiers carried back the cauldron, empty and clean, I had them place it in front of me, and asked for a bucket of fresh water. Once I received that, I emptied the water into the cauldron, then used the bucket to scoop charcoal from the edges of the fire and added that to the water, stirring with a stick to make a thick but ingestible paste.

"The sick men must drink this as soon as they can."

The rapice would bring up and remove as much poison from the body as possible. Whatever stayed behind, the charcoal paste would bind, and the poison would pass the other way.

Already, the vomiting was subsiding.

"Move these men over there," the captain ordered his soldiers, and they immediately dragged the sick a few paces away so they wouldn't be lying in their own vomit.

Then, following my example and that of the captain, the soldiers began pouring charcoal paste down the throats of their unfortunate comrades.

I kept my attention on the sick, wiping sweat from their brows, but I could hear the gathered crowd talking about me. News that I was a great sorceress healer, half human, half tiger, in search of Lord Karnagh spread faster through the army camp than dysentery.

The soldiers who had escorted me into camp had heard everything I'd said to their captain on the road and now freely shared my words, heavily embellishing them with all they had heard in Ker. They had their chests puffed out, taking full credit for bringing a powerful sorceress into camp.

I busied myself with the sick, making them drink clean water after they finished all the charcoal paste. I bathed their sweating faces once again, then I set about cleaning the vomit off their clothes. Their concerned friends brought me as many buckets of water as I needed.

"Will they live?" the captain asked, his voice tight.

And only then did I realize that the young man he had been administering to looked very much like him.

"Your son?"

He brushed the wet hair out of the young man's face, deep furrows lining his forehead. "The only one left living out of seven. Will he live?" he asked again.

"He will," I said, in case the sick could hear me. "We removed the poison." I raised my voice. "They will all live."

And then I prayed the spirits would not make a liar out of me.

I stayed with the sick as day turned into evening, made sure they drank again. I lay among them all through the night, getting up if any of them moaned or cried out for help.

By morning, they rested more easily. Some had enough strength to sit, among them the captain's son. The captain clapped him on the back with pure relief on his face. Then he did the same to the other men, as if they were all his. I supposed, in a sense, they were.

"They will survive the poison." I could say that with full certainty by then. "But they must keep drinking water and eat carefully for a few days. Nothing too greasy. Nothing too heavy. And as for the others… Only those who are from around these parts should go off into the woods to gather mushrooms and roots for the meals."

The captain nodded. He watched me for a long moment. "You have done us a great service."

I did what I knew how to do. "Why did you trust me?" I asked.

He rubbed the stubble on his chin. "Because of the camel." He offered a half smile. "Many people said many things about what happened in Ker. But Makmin said you saved his camel. On this, I took Makmin's words over the others'. That caravan master loved his camel."

I sighed at that as I thought how heartbroken poor Makmin must be.

The captain said, "I am Captain Witsel."

I inclined my head, knowing what finally sharing his name meant. He had not when he thought I might be a dark sorceress, for giving a creature of magic one's name could give them power over that person.

He continued with, "I owe you my son's life, and the life of my men. I regret that I will have to take you back to Ker to face the city fathers." He paused. "On the other hand, you are a powerful sorceress. How could anyone be surprised if you enthralled the night guard and escaped across the border through the woods?"

On the last word, he turned and strode away, leaving me looking after him with mouth agape.

I wondered what I was to do next but did not have to wonder long. Two soldiers came and escorted me to a tent. Then two more soldiers appeared, one carrying blankets, the other food.

"Captain says you best not freeze or starve before you can be taken back to Ker," one said before they left the pile of goods with me.

*Three wool blankets!*

True luxury, even if one did smell like a horse. I ran my fingers over the incredible treasure. Then, like an impatient child, I picked up and sniffed the full loaf of bread I'd been given in a new food sack. Half a round of hard cheese. Goat jerky. Six carrots and a cabbage. Six tart apples.

I blinked hard at the captain's generosity.

I sat on the tree stump in the middle of the tent and ate, just a few bites of bread and cheese. I had to save the rest.

Nobody came to see me, although I was sure there were some in camp who could have used my healing. A simple herb woman they might have approached, even a healer. But they were wary of a sorceress. I imagined tales of me were growing more and more exaggerated with every passing moment.

When night fell, I hung my sacks from my belt, then tied all three blankets around my shoulders as a many-layered cloak. I bundled up tightly, as if against the cold, then poked my head outside the tent.

Two men stood guard. I recognized both. I had treated them earlier, one of them the captain's own son. They appeared weak and exhausted, but they bowed deeply when I stepped forward.

"I must relieve myself. In the woods."

"There is a tiger in the woods, my lady," the captain's son said.

"The tiger will not hurt me."

He nodded as if they had already heard that tale.

They escorted me out of camp but stopped short of the edge of the forest.

I kept on walking until I was well covered by the trees. Then I looked at the sky through the bare branches, filled my lungs with cold night air, and silently thanked Captain Witsel for setting me free.

I walked east by the stars. Here in the woods, there were no border markers as on the road. By the time I first stopped to drink, I estimated I was well on the other side of the border, inside the kingless kingdom of Seberon, Selorm land.

I was hoping that Marga and Orz would soon catch up with me. But a team of soldiers reached me first.

# CHAPTER NINETEEN
## A NEW BEGINNING

Six men. On foot. Fast runners. Captain Witsel's men. The two who had escorted me to the forest were not amongst them.

They surrounded me but did not draw their weapons, indeed the leader bowed his head with respect. "The captain sent us after you, Lady Tera."

I stood still. *Had I misunderstood the captain?*

"We are Selorm," the man said next.

That explained the lack of horses. The Selorm were foot soldiers for the most part. Their lords fought with battle tigers, and tigers scared even the bravest battle horses.

The man spoke again. "We heard that you wish to find Lord Karnagh."

I nodded. "If I can."

He shifted on his feet. "The captain said if we came to take you back but you enthralled us to go with you, we could not be blamed."

The others looked at me warily, but also with hope, as if their lives depended on my answer. They had volunteered to go with me to Regnor, I suspected.

They knew the land better, and they probably knew Lord Karnagh better than I. The journey would be safer with their protection.

As I tried to think of what to say, the tiger chuffed somewhere behind them in the woods. I chuffed back to her.

A few moments later, she chuffed from much closer. And then she was there, walking out of the trees toward me. The men parted to allow her passage but showed little fear. They were Selorm, accustomed to tigers.

She merely sniffed in their direction, did not growl or bare her teeth. Maybe she smelled their lord's battle tigers on their uniform, left from past battles.

She padded straight to me and rubbed her head against my cheek, nearly knocking me over. I had to slide an arm around her neck to steady myself. I was most relieved to see her.

When I looked up, the wariness was gone from the men's eyes. Now all their gazes held were hope and excitement.

"Tigers do not bond with women," their leader said. "You are a true sorceress." He bowed again.

"It does not scare you?"

"You are a good sorceress. Tigers do not bond with an evil heart."

I looked at the men, all of them nodding. I appreciated the vote of confidence—a welcome change from suggestions that I should be boiled in tar.

Marga sensed their ease around her and behaved accordingly, sniffing at them one more time, then ignoring them entirely, since I did not act as if they represented a threat. She chuffed toward the forest then.

I peered into the dark woods in that direction. Had she found a mate? I stiffened. Would her mate be as tolerant of people?

But when I finally saw movement, it wasn't a flash of amber. Orz walked toward us, his black robe melting into the black woods around him. He wore the boots I had left him.

As easily as the soldiers accepted Marga, they froze at the sight of the hollow. They clumped together now, every hand on the hilt of a sword.

"His name is Orz," I said, calmly, clearly. "He means no harm. He has suffered at the hand of the dark sorcerer of Ishaf."

Marga moved from me to Orz and rubbed against him as she had rubbed against me earlier. I stared a little too, at that. She hadn't done it before. Had they spent all this time together? Had she followed my scent and led Orz to me?

At the tiger's full acceptance of Orz, encouraged that the hollow did not try to move toward them, the soldiers removed their hands from their weapons. But they still eyed the hollow with dislike and suspicion.

I filled my lungs. "If we are to travel together, we must have trust in each other."

"My lady." The young soldier addressing me bowed his head. "Do you not fear that it will suck out your spirit?"

"I do not." Didn't I?

Marga had just rubbed against him, and nothing happened to her. Marga most certainly had a spirit. Without it, she would not have responded to my spirit songs. Yet her spirit remained intact.

I needed three steps to reach Orz. I did not hesitate but a moment before I took his ill-shaped hand.

And gasped as something passed between us.

My head swam for a moment.

I pulled back. He drew nothing from me, and certainly not by force, but my healing powers responded to his battered body on instinct.

I looked at his bowed head as if seeing him for the first time, not that I could see much in the night forest.

*Could I heal him?*

Yet even as I reached for him again, he drew away. I had taken him by surprise the first time. He did not seem to want to be healed, or maybe he could not understand that I could help him with his pain.

Little by little, he raised his head at last. I held my breath, but as much as I tried to peer at his face, I could not see his features, for he stood in the deepest of shadows.

I would have given much for a torch or even a small candle just then.

At least I'd accomplished one thing. The soldiers relaxed. Seeing me touch the hollow and suffer no ill effects went a long way toward making them comfortable.

"Old wives' tales," I said firmly. Then, as Orz stayed out of my reach, I turned northward again and strode forward. "Let us walk until we find a suitable place to rest for the night. Mayhap we shall find water."

We were in the thick woods, gnarly roots breaking the soil every-where, no place for us to lie down to rest comfortably. We moved forward.

We stayed in the forest and did not go near the road as we headed north. We were now in a country at war. The road up ahead might be crawling with enemy soldiers who would kill us on sight.

The Selorm soldiers all gave me their names as we walked, and pledged themselves to my protection. Tomron was the oldest and their leader. He was Batumar's age, strong in the arms and shoulders, his nose nearly flat after having been many times broken.

Fadden was a handsome youth, even younger than I, the only one who smiled as he talked. Baran was thick-waisted and thick-necked, a blacksmith before the war. Hartz was the strongest-looking of the six, his arms swollen with muscles.

Atter was missing both ears but made up for it by having the most melodious voice. I hoped he was a bard. I would have loved to hear him sing some Selorm stories. Lison spoke only his name, then gave a brief nod and fell back. He talked to me no more nor to the others as we moved forward. He seemed to have a dark cloud over him, or maybe inside him.

They were all large men. Whereas Marga's head was level with mine, it reached only to their chests. But despite their size, they walked silently through the forest, stealing forward in their leather boots as softly as the tiger.

"When did you last see Lord Karnagh?" I asked.

Tomron answered. "When he rode out from Regnor before the harvest. At first, when the enemy reached our lands, the Selorm lords gathered their tigers and their warriors to defend the border as one great army."

He paused as if the words to come pained him. "But the Kerghi hordes overran us, my lady." Then he added, "The Emperor has a sorcerer on his side, and the sorcerer has a horn. When blown, the sound drove half the tigers mad."

He looked at me expectantly as he walked next to me, matching his stride to mine. On my other side walked Orz. We were following Marga, who glanced back at us from time to time, as if wondering what was so difficult about keeping up. The rest of the men fanned out behind us, watching for attack.

Tomron said, "At the sound of the horn, the battle tigers fell to the ground in pain. Some ran off and abandoned their lords in the middle of battle." He glanced at me again.

Clearly, he wanted to know if I had heard of such a thing, and if I, being a sorceress myself, could somehow counteract this.

I would have to think about that. "Where did Lord Karnagh ride from Regnor?"

Tomron accepted that I wasn't going to answer his unspoken question, and he answered mine. "When the battle on the border was lost, each lord drew back to his castle to defend his own."

He gave a long pause that spoke of memories of dark times. "We drew back behind Regnor's walls on Lord Karnagh's orders. First we heard news of one castle falling after another. Then the enemy reached us, and we beat them back. They had the horn somewhere else. We slaughtered them. The fields around the castle ran red with blood, my lady." His words brimmed with pride.

"And then?"

"Lord Karnagh decided to ride out and lift the siege from his neighbor Lord Brooker's castle. He rode out with five hundred men and fifty tigers." Tomron shook his head. "We waited for his return, but he did not come. Not one captain came back, not one tiger, not one man."

"You?"

"I had been left behind to guard Regnor. When we had no news of Lord Karnagh in a full mooncrossing, I took a team of the most faithful men to find him, sixty of us." He gestured at his friends. "The six you see here remain."

We walked in silence for a moment before he continued. "We ran into a great enemy force. We could not go forward, and since the enemy surrounded Regnor once again, we could not go back. We awaited the night in the thick of the woods, then we crept down to the river. We hung on to bloated corpses and floated away."

"Then came to Ker."

"We wanted to find fighting men we could join," he said heavily.

"What do you know of the warrior queen who holds the last free Selorm city?"

"Only what I heard from refugees. They say the enemy nearly had the city of Ralabon when the Queen of Habor showed up with her royal guard. She had been pushed out from her own land. She was looking for shelter, somewhere to regroup her warriors, walls they could retreat behind to defend themselves. She cut through the army outside Ralabon in a surprise attack, and her warriors joined forces with those defending the castle."

I thought carefully as we walked. "Do you think Lord Karnagh might be in Ralabon, sealed in by the siege?"

But Tomron shook his head. "If a Selorm lord was present, the foreign queen wouldn't be leading defense." He paused. "Ralabon is to the east of Regnor, Lord Karnagh's seat. He had marched west with his warriors, to Lord Brooker's aid."

"Then we shall go toward Brooker's Castle ourselves."

At once, Tomron protested that they had already tried that and could not get through enemy lines, but I pointed out that they had been a force of sixty men then; now we were but eight. Our small group had a much better chance of proceeding unseen.

Soon the forest thinned, and we came across a dip in the ground and settled into it for the night. What wind blew through the trees blew over the top of us. I had spent more comfortable nights, but our discomfort was bearable.

Despite having a tiger along, Tomron set sentries.

Marga sniffed around and made her noises. And, to my surprise, Orz was making some noises back, guttural, deep sounds that rumbled up from his chest. Almost as if they were talking to each other.

The tiger did not go off hunting. She must have hunted well and filled her stomach the night before, for her belly appeared still rounded.

I slept next to her for heat, the men under blankets, all in a bunch. I gave one of my blankets to Orz, who kept himself apart.

We rose at first light, ate sparingly, then pushed forward.

Tomron sent Fadden and Baran to check the road. The first enemy soldiers, or rather their deaths, were reported back in a short while. Fadden and Baran dispatched the three enemy scouts. The element of surprise had been on our men's side.

The sun had long passed its zenith in the sky by the time we reached the first village, little more than a ruin. Most of the huts had been burned.

We saw no people, but some from the village must have survived, for the fallen had been buried. No decomposing bodies littered the streets.

"I met refugees on the road before Captain Witsel caught up with me," I told Tomron. "They might have come from this very village."

He stayed by my side but sent his men to spread out and check through the charred huts for things we might be able to use.

They returned empty-handed. "Stripped clean," Atter reported.

Marga had been sniffing around the well but suddenly lifted her head and gave a warning growl.

"There are people at the edge of the woods up ahead," Tomron said without looking that way.

I looked, but all I could see were yew bushes.

The tiger growled again.

Our small team pulled back to the middle of the main square, the men's hands near their swords. But when the bushes began to move and people stepped out, they were not enemy soldiers.

I sang a spirit song to Marga to keep her by my side. Her ears twitched. She did not attack. She seemed to have an uncanny ability to sense whether I considered someone friend or foe. But her thick tail swooshed from side to side in the dirt.

A dozen villagers limped and staggered toward us, mostly older men and women, two little girls among them. They were of shorter stature and darker hair than my Selorm guards, cheeks sunk in, clothes torn and dirty. They seemed greatly cheered by the tiger.

"They are Seb," Tomron told me under his breath. "From the native tribes of this land."

"Is the war over?" the oldest of the women inquired in the same language that the refugees I had met on the road had spoken.

She had a bent back and a shuffling walk, her joints stiff with rheumatism, her thinning hair in a stringy bun at her nape—that disheveled, desperate look of those whose lives had been upended.

Tomron looked to me as if awaiting my response.

"Not yet, Grandmother," I said, and stepped forward.

Marga moved with me, staying close, taking a protective stance.

The wide-eyed little girl who was hiding behind the old woman's skirts peeped up. "Why does the tiger go with her?"

She probably expected Marga to be bonded to one of the Selorm men.

But before I could explain, Orz stepped from the ruins of a granary he'd lumbered into earlier. The villagers drew back at his dark figure as he came to stand beside me, his head deeply bowed as always.

Some of the women backed toward the woods, looking ready to disappear.

But Tomron pointed at me and said with his voice full of authority, "The Lady Tera is a high sorceress. The hollow is her servant."

I was about to protest, but the fear was lessening on the gaunt faces around me, replaced by curiosity, then acceptance when I said, "His name is Orz. I did not create him, and I will not create others," I added, in case they worried that I came to suck out people's spirits for magic. "He will not harm you," I finished.

Orz backed away and dropped his shoulders, dipped his head even more than usual, and I stifled a smile, for I knew he was trying to do his best not to appear threatening.

Men and women came to me and fell to their knees, some kissing my hands, others my boots. They gained such joy and encouragement from news of my sorcery that I decided to wait at least a short while before I disabused them of the notion.

Instead, I gestured around. "What happened here?"

The old woman spoke again. "The Kerghi came. The men they cut down; the women and girls they chained up to send back to the empire as slaves. The boys they took to be pressed into their dark army."

Her eyes glazed over with grief. "Only those of us they left for dead escaped. We hid in the forest, but we do not dare light any fires. And we are all too slow to hunt, either too old or too injured."

I asked them about the small group of refugees I had met on the road who gave Orz his boots, but they did not know a family like that. There must have been many other ruined villages.

"We are going to Brooker's Castle to find Lord Karnagh," I said. "But we would like to rest here. Do you have a camp we might share for the night?" I did not wish to stay out in the open in the village. The main road passed too close by.

The villagers led me forth with deep bowing and many smiles. The two young children each grabbed on to a bundle of herbs hanging from my belt, as happy as if they were somehow blessed by that small connection.

We did not have to go far to reach the camp. I would have walked past it if walking on my own, for they had only the least they required to keep living. They had no tents or huts here but slept in holes dug in the ground, which they covered with branches.

They had no food that I could see.

They led me to the middle of their clearing and gestured for me to sit on a log. I glanced back at the Selorm, who had their own provisions, same as I. "Let us share what we have."

The men did not protest. If anything, they appeared relieved as if they had worried that I would not allow them to share.

After we ate, then drank fresh stream water, I washed my hands. "Let me see all who are sick here."

They lined up before me, all twelve, minding each other, those with the most severe injuries first.

I began by setting a dislocated arm that should have been set days before, my work made more difficult by the overgrown swelling. The old man did not cry out. I bandaged his shoulder as tightly as I could, then told him not to move it for several days.

Then I treated a young man's stump—he lost half of his arm in battle. After that came infected stab wounds, and way too many burns.

Night fell by the time I finished, having the satisfaction of knowing that the people around me were in less pain now than when I had arrived at their village.

Marga went off hunting. We set sentries. But when Marga came back a short while later, dragging half a mule deer to me as a gift, even the sentries lay down to rest.

In the morning, we shared some bread. Baran chopped the half deer into two quarters, then wrapped the meat in leaves. He tied one package onto his own back; the other was taken by Hartz.

We did not discuss the villagers joining us. They simply fell in step.

As before, we moved to follow the road from the woods, at a distance. Tomron and the others were soldiers. They had marched on roads; the network of roads was what they knew. They did not know the hidden creeks and valleys enough to navigate by them.

But the old woman, Hilla, said, "I know the pathways of the forest, my lady. That might be a safer way."

So I told her to lead us, and she did.

We reached the next village toward the end of the day. The huts here too were all destroyed. But this time, three times as many survivors eased forth from their hiding places to meet us. Here too, I had to assure everyone that Orz would not steal their spirits. Since they could see that all others in our traveling group were yet hale and not running in terror from the hollow, they believed me.

The tiger they accepted at once and without question.

"How did this many survive?" I asked the village leader, a miller.

"A child had wandered off into the forest, my lady. Many men and women ran to find him, spurred by the pleas of his crying mother." He pointed at one of the women, who held a little boy close to her chest.

Then he continued. "While we were searching for the child, the enemy came to the village but missed the rescue party as we had gone far into the woods. By the time we returned toward dawn the following day, all we found in place of our homes was smoldering ashes and scattered bodies."

These villagers had been living in root cellars and offered us shelter there. They even had fires, which they kept hidden below the ground. We roasted the deer, and all ate well.

Come morning, as we left, the new people joined us.

"If we meet enemy soldiers, I cannot protect these people," I told Tomron, worrying a bundle of herbs with my fingers as we walked. "Do they know that?"

"We are at war. They will meet enemy soldiers one way or the other. If they are by your side, my lady, you can heal what harm might befall them."

I would try, if I was not cut down myself.

We followed an animal trail through the woods. Tomron pointed out deer and wild boar droppings, which the tiger sniffed with interest.

Our growing rag-tag tribe walked in groups of twos and threes. Since we had children and old people with us, we did not move as quickly as I could have with the original six soldiers. But since the path through the woods was shorter than following the road, I thought we might yet reach Brooker's Castle even faster.

The Selorm soldiers and the tiger hunted as we went. The rest of us foraged. We did not have much food, but enough for each day, so that nobody went hungry, which was more than the villagers had had for some time. They were happy, one after the other coming up to thank me.

"I gave them nothing," I told Tomron when he joined me later.

"You gave us all a shared purpose, my lady." As he walked, he was sharpening a straight branch as long as he was tall.

The soldiers were making simple hunting spears so at least all the men could be armed. The spears were shaved to a point, then the point hardened in fire when we stopped to rest—not much, but better than nothing, according to Tomron.

"A good purpose can give a man reason to live," he said now. "A good leader can bring a soldier out of the very grave to fight again."

As he dropped back to check on the end of our long column, I pondered his words. If I gave people a shared purpose, they gave me a sense of strength. They were here because of me, so I could not be weak. I could not grieve for what was lost. I could not turn around or lie down to die when I thought of Batumar and my heart broke over and over again.

The people followed because they had someone to lead them. And I led because there were people behind me whom I could not leave to their fate.

Thus we went from village to village, collecting up the left behind, the maimed, the frightened. As we marched on, I talked to each and every person, asked them what they knew about Brooker's Castle, about Lord Karnagh, about the great endless woods, even about strange plants that were unfamiliar to me because they did not grow on my island.

In the evenings, I healed the sick, then told stories to the children. Most of the adults gathered around us too, which was becoming more and more difficult. After each village we passed, we needed a larger and larger clearing for our night camp.

The men and women grew strong from regular meals and regular rest. Some felt safe enough to sleep through the night for the first time in a mooncrossing or more. They were greatly heartened by having a sorceress and a tiger and a magically recovering hollow among them.

And Orz *was* recovering. His gait improved. He carried himself differently. I began to wonder if he was yet as old as I had first suspected him to be. He joined the men to help with tasks but never strayed far from me and never uncovered his face. He never spoke to me again either.

He was as big an attraction, especially for the children, as Marga.

Tigers were the symbol of the Selorm, the lords who kept the kingdom protected. The Seb villagers blessed me for bringing Marga among them.

On the fourteenth day after we crossed the border, we came across the ruins of an ancient city in the hills. No fallen-down huts here, but great buildings made of stone, towering walls, and towers, some still standing, most collapsed, covered in moss and vines.

A hush fell over us as we walked down wide streets that had enough room for several carts side by side, drawn by teams of oxen.

Some of the walls were heavily carved, depicting people and animals and wondrous contraptions: one that seemed to make cloth, but not like a weaver's frame; flames that burned in sconces without torches, not an oil lamp, not a candle, yet clearly a source of light.

"What place is this?" I asked, but no one could answer.

Yet they were the ruins of some great nation that had once ruled these lands. We found the outskirts of the city early in the morning and were still walking through the ruins that night as the streets went on and on, walls carved with gods and goddesses that time had forgotten.

I saw rows and rows of symbols and great shapes of squares, triangles, and circles, carved over and into each other. I had the strong feeling that they represented something, perhaps the builders' most important knowledge, meant to be passed down to those who came after.

Yet war had erased all their wisdom, even their memory. All that they had known, would we ever again discover?

Trees grew inside houses and palaces, buildings and nature mixed together, climbing lianas covering walls and holding up the few roofs that had not yet collapsed.

The city was larger than any I had seen in our Shahala lands, or among the Kadar, or during my travels since. I could not conceive that people this numerous and rich could disappear without a name, without a memory.

And if they could, how could small villages and my small island stand against such forces as the Emperor's dark armies?

I might have lost hope there, as we camped in what had once been a great temple, if not for the people around me. They looked to me for hope, so I smiled and told stories of the weak overcoming the strong, the few defeating the many, tales of survival, and tales of better times that would someday be ours again.

Later, as I sat on a pile of rocks, I watched the people sleep around me. More than one had smiles on their faces. Maybe they felt safe because we were in a sacred place. I wondered which god had once been worshipped in this temple.

A strong sensation that I was being watched brought me out of my reverie. I looked around, then relaxed. Of course, I was being watched. I was sitting in the middle of a large group of people. Many glanced toward me as they settled in.

If unease seeped into my bones, I wrote it down to the strange place, to the fact that the sky was darkening.

Tomron sat next to me. "Bad news, my lady. The three men we found by the creek this morn say they passed by Lord Brooker's castle a moon-crossing ago." He said the words as if they sat heavily on his tongue.

"Did they see Lord Karnagh?"

"No, my lady. But they saw Lord Brooker's blackened corpse hanging from the parapets."

My heart sank. Lord Brooker was dead. So could Lord Karnagh be, for all my hopes. Was I simply leading all these people to the enemy?

As if reading my thoughts, Tomron said, "The spirits brought you to us, Sorceress. What you order, we obey. Where you lead, we go."

I was no leader. I was no sorceress. I kept looking at the people who had gathered in this long-gone city around me, unable to understand how all this had happened.

"They are here, gathered all together, all safe and fed tonight, because of you," Tomron remarked.

I filled my lungs with cold night air. "I will take them to Lord Karnagh." But as I heard my words spoken out loud, I buried my head in my hands for a moment with a strained laugh.

"They are taking *me*," I blurted the truth to Tomron. "The Seb villagers are showing the way. The Selorm soldiers protect us. The men and the tiger do the hunting. The women do the foraging. All this could go on without me."

Tomron's forehead furrowed. "Here is my truth, if you do not mind my saying so, my lady. I have spent most of my life in military tents. The canvas keeps out the rain. The smoke hole lets us have a fire. The flap allows us in and out. The tent has many much-used parts. The tent pole just stands stuck in the ground. Until I bump into it in the night, I often forget that it's there. But without it, there would be no tent. You are what holds us together and holds us up."

I sighed. "I fear your opinion of me is higher than what I deserve, Tomron."

"You are a very young sorceress. Mayhap you do not see all yet." He ducked his head. "Forgive me, my lady."

I smiled at him.

He stood. "I best go see to setting sentries. The tiger is off hunting. She can give us no warning."

As Tomron strode off, I stayed where I was, watching the people. Standing in a corner like a sentry himself, Orz watched me. Not for the first time, I wished I could talk to him. I had tried, more than once, but he always backed away.

I thought about walking over to him and trying again. But if he wished for solitude, did he not deserve to receive at least that? So I stayed where I sat.

A fair while later, Marga appeared in the destroyed doorway, dragging half a wild boar into the temple. She dropped it at the edge of the open space in the middle, then padded over to me.

I stood to find a spot for the night, laid my blankets on the ground, then we settled down to sleep.

Again, the sense of being watched assailed me. *Orz,* I thought. Yet his gaze on me had not bothered me in the past. He watched me like the Palace Guard would watch a queen they were ordered to protect. I did not know who he was, but I knew he harbored no malice toward me.

I wished he was not so averse to my touch. I knew his battered body was in pain. I wished he would let me heal at least that much.

Baran, one of the Selorm soldiers passed in front of him, and I realized that without his back bent and his head in that deep bow, Orz was just as tall as Baran, and even wider in the shoulders. He had a hunting spear now, one of Tomron's, and despite his ruined fingers, he held the weapon well. He truly must have been some kind of soldier or captain before his tragic path led him to Ishaf's sorcerer.

I closed my eyes, forcing my mind from him and toward all I needed to do next.

Within a day or two, we would be at Brooker's Castle. Of course, as we were now, all of us could not sneak into the castle unseen. We would have to camp at a fair distance in the woods and send but a few. Tomron and his men would know the castle best. I would go with them. I could not risk their lives in place of mine.

Marga and Orz would have to stay behind. They would attract too much attention. Whether or not they would obey my wishes to stay in the woods remained to be seen. I often had the feeling that Marga was humoring me, like a mother would a favored child.

And Orz...I sensed that he had ideas different from mine. But he would always place my wishes above his own. So he might yet be talked into staying behind once again, one last time.

I was certain that someone inside Brooker's Castle would have news of Lord Karnagh. Lord Karnagh might even be there himself, injured, kept in shackles in the dungeons.

I would heal him; then he could lead what Selorm and Seb were still alive inside, while those who followed me would attack from the outside. We would retake the castle. Then Seberon would have two free cities. That would be a start.

Pressed against Marga's round side for heat, I went to sleep with that hope in my heart.

We were attacked at dawn.

# CHAPTER TWENTY
## THE GOD DEMANDS PAYMENT

Marga had gone off for another hunt. Since our numbers had increased, she hunted more, as if accepting the people as her cubs. Or maybe she felt sorry for us, thought us deaf and blind, lost little things in the forest without her strength and fangs.

I had once, at Karamur, seen a merchant's ferocious guard dog that was half wolf adopt a kitten whose eyes hadn't opened yet and feed the kitten among her pups. Perhaps so we were with the tiger.

I woke when she moved off, instantly missing her heat. She padded silently among the sleeping people, leaped up to a window opening, hesitated for a moment, then jumped out and disappeared.

I settled back to sleep, knowing that should the enemy find us, we had sentries to sound the alarm.

And some time later, indeed they did. The plaintive cry of a shepherd's horn rent the night. But the warning did not arrive early enough to allow us escape. We barely had time to come fully awake before the enemy was upon us.

The ruin had too many gaps, was too difficult to defend as the Kerghi horde charged. Most of our men had spears, but the rest of us could only throw rocks.

The stone temple, at least, was an advantage. The enemy could not burn us out with fire, then slaughter us when we rushed outside to escape the flames. The roaming Kerghi who found us were prepared for villages with wooden huts and thatched roofs. They were not prepared for a siege.

They had a few bows but no grand division of archers. They had to come up to the wall, climb up to the windows, and try to fight their way in. At which time, they were close enough to suffer injuries.

Orz was by my side suddenly. In his hand, a sword dripping with blood had replaced his wood-tipped spear. Had he taken that sword from the enemy?

My gaze searched for the children in the semidarkness of but two small fires burning, the flames nearly dead. I could see little, not even if we were winning or losing.

We were many. We had enough soldiers and Seb men to defend each opening, with the old and the women helping. As I rushed toward a wounded man, I spotted two of the little girls and called them. They ran to me, burying their faces against my body in fear.

Other children, hiding behind fallen columns and broken stone benches, dashed over to us. Three young mothers had suckling babes. They too scrambled over and followed me as I dragged the injured man to a staircase close behind me. At one time in the distant past it had led down to a lower level but was now half-filled with dirt, nothing more than a hole in the floor.

"Go down and stay down. Quickly." I stood on the first step, pulling the arrow from the injured Seb's thigh, taking his injury upon me where my healing spirit could mend it much more quickly.

Orz stood in front of me once again. Whatever came for us would first have to go through him.

Hartz, with a lance in his side, was dragged to me. I helped him, then others who staggered or were brought over.

As light dawned outside, little by little, I could see better. The enemy had maybe a third of our number, though they were all trained fighters with swords and lances, while we had only a handful of soldiers. But we did have the protection of the walls.

And soon we had an ally outside, for I heard the tiger roar.

I watched for her, my hand wrist-deep in an injured woman's side, but I saw a white-haired man, Ramu, fall at the door instead. An old woman dragged him bravely to safety, back to the staircase. I would see to him next.

As I turned, I glimpsed a streak of yellow through the nearest window, Marga striking down an enemy soldier outside. *Be careful, great mother.*

Her claws shredded the man's face into ribbons, and the Kerghi warrior's scream could be heard over the battle din as he fell.

I could not watch longer, for I needed to tend Ramu, who had a spearhead lodged in his chest. "I need hot water," I begged Orz.

The injuries I had taken upon me were beginning to weaken me. I had to mix traditional healing with my powers. The battle was far from over yet.

Orz wouldn't budge.

"It's Ramu's life. Please."

Orz grabbed a woman running by and held her until I repeated my request. She hurried off toward the fire that burned in the back corner where the oldest and the youngest had huddled together earlier for the night. She returned a short time later with a flask of water that wasn't hot enough but would have to serve.

I prepared a poultice before touching the spearhead. Then I drew the sharp wedge from the old man's body as he moaned, blood bubbling up and rushing forth like a crimson river.

I placed my hand upon the gaping wound, closed my eyes, and prayed to the spirits; then I went about repairing the damage, taking as much of it onto myself as I dared. But not all. I could almost feel Batumar's spirit there, watching over me, could hear his admonitions to be careful with my strength.

Once Ramu was healed enough so he could finish recovering on his own, I applied the poultice, then sat back, giving my own body time to recover. I felt as weak as a newborn babe, as dizzy as a drunkard.

Other injured staggered over. I did what I could for them, but as time went by, my power grew weaker and weaker, the injuries overwhelming my body and my spirit.

The enemy was cutting people down faster than I could heal them.

I could see the fallen at the feet of those who defended the walls, but I could not walk to them, and Orz refused to leave my side to drag them over. Then I saw Fadden fall, the youngest of the Selorm soldiers, his ever-present smile turning into a grimace of pain.

The children cried in the stairwell, sensing a turn in the battle. They had been through this before, had seen their parents and siblings cut down, their villages demolished.

The tiger roared outside, the sound mixed with pain. I could feel her injury, a battle axe in her shoulder, but I could not heal her.

*Spirits help her,* I cried in a spirit song. *Spirits help us.*

I thought of something Batumar had asked me once, if as I saved life, I could also take it. Could I reach out with my spirit and stop a heart instead of restarting it, burst a vein instead of healing it, bend some bones instead of straightening them.

I had said no, not ever.

Yet the cries of my people rang loud in my ears, the smell of their blood filling my nostrils, their pain battering against my mind as if to split my head. The thought that they would all be lost before the sun fully came up was unbearable.

*Spirits, give me strength!*

But instead of the spirits, something else answered.

I felt a dark stirring, something airless. Then a faintly familiar smell reached me, and I felt dizzy all of a sudden. The dawn stopped lightening. Indeed, the sky seemed to darken again.

I could barely see the people around me.

"Have you come for power, Sorceress?" a deep voice hissed into my ear.

I recognized then the voice and the smell of it. *Kratos.* The god who had been worshipped long ago in Karamur's mountain temple had once been worshipped here.

"Let us go in peace," I begged.

"Have you brought a sacrifice?" He gave a dark chuckle, for he knew the answer. "Or will you pay the price?" he asked next.

I had not yet even paid the price for the mountain, I thought, but then the truth sliced through me with so much pain that I fell. *Batumar.* I could not breathe. Batumar had been the price I had paid.

I had bargained Batumar's life away to a fetid old god.

Everything inside me screamed.

But over that, I heard the voice of my people screaming louder as the enemy breached our defenses.

"I will pay the price," I said hoarsely to the god.

Kratos had taken Batumar, and with him my heart. What else could the merciless god take from me?

"Give yourself to me, and I shall give you great power." A talon scraped down my chin.

And I thought, was this how my great-grandmother had received her powers?

"All I want is safe passage," I begged weakly.

He laughed, the sound like a pack of otherworldly hyenas. "Passage, then. But I take what I take."

Then the god was gone, and I could see again, Orz bent over me, his hands gripping my shoulders as a hoarse sound escaped his ruined throat. On his knees next to me, he lifted me and held me to his chest. I leaned against his strength, which, in a strange reversal, was greater than my own.

The sounds of fighting filled my ears. I felt the departing spirits of the dead, then the spirits of the animals watching this great massacre from the forest.

Suddenly, a wind began in the middle of the temple and blew outward.

And then a slow hum began in the woods, but soon the noise grew, the sound of a thousand animals. The ground shook. Midfight, the men stilled.

A dark wave broke out of the surrounding woods: birds, squirrels, deer, wild boars, wolves, as if running from some great hunt. But instead, they were the hunters. That dark wave rolled over the Kerghi, up and around the walls of the temple, then into the forest on the other side just as suddenly.

The din settled, silence filling the ruin, save for some of the injured moaning and crying out for help.

Orz released me but followed as I staggered to a window to look out.

The enemy were either trampled or torn apart or ran. Only those of us inside the temple had remained unharmed.

I stared out at the carnage, stunned. I had only seen such losses at Karamur's siege. Behind me, the villagers cheered. But I was so cold, I thought I would never be warm again. I heaved, my stomach twisting with pain as hard as my heart was twisting with fear.

*What have I done?*

I wanted all men to live in peace. That was the way of my people. I was willing to give up even my own life to save others. But here, in this ancient place, I had taken lives instead.

Blood flowed outside the temple walls, dead covering the ground. It gave me no pleasure that they were Kerghi. Sick to my soul, I turned away. Orz took my elbow, touching me of his own volition, but I could barely feel him. My entire body was numb.

The Seb villagers lined my path, all on their knees, some reaching out to kiss the bottom of the blanket I wore as a cloak, calling my name as I passed. They looked at me with gratitude, at least most of them. Some of the children had drawn back, hiding behind their mothers in fear.

I sank onto a block of stone, dazed, watching as people moved around me. I could see their lips form words as they called to each other, but I could not hear their voices over the blood rushing in my ears.

Bile rose in my throat. I was going to be sick.

So *this* was power. This was what men had killed and died for since the beginning of time. My limbs turned cold as if filled with ice water. *All I asked for was safe passage.*

I scrambled outside, unable to bear people's gazes upon me, unable to bear their gratitude. I craved fresh air, although certainly, the air outside was no fresher than in, not with half the temple roof missing.

I had to step over the dead. I blanched.

Orz bent and hooked a hand under my knees. And then he carried me forward.

I choked on a bitter laugh. What a pair we made, him without a spirit and me without a heart.

Behind me, I heard Tomron say to someone, "Not now. The Lady Tera must rest."

There were more injured, I thought, dazed, and wished I could help them. But my own spirit was sick. I let Orz carry me away from the smell of blood and the sight of the massacre.

He carried me in the opposite direction from where the Kerghi had come, toward a creek we had passed early the previous evening. The creek ran through the city, through dead ruins. Water pooled in a place where an earthquake thousands of years ago had broken the marble floor of a now ruined palace.

He put me down there.

"Thank you." I reached in and washed from my hands the blood of those I had healed. Then I washed my face. But I had blood in my hair too, and my clothes were covered with it. I heaved, a sharp cramp cutting through my middle.

"I want to bathe."

Orz's shoulders had that stiff angle they had when he thought I was doing something reckless.

"It is not too cold," I promised. "I shall be quick. I need to be clean," I added, then gasped as another cramp doubled me over.

Orz bent to me with concern.

The cramp passed. I shrugged off the blanket I wore as a cloak.

With a heaved sigh, Orz turned his back to me.

I quickly stripped and slipped into the crystal-clear pool and dirtied it up in an instant. But the cold felt good. It felt soothing. Until the next cramp came, as sharp as if invisible talons were tearing me in half.

The water grew bloodier and bloodier.

Was I bleeding? I checked around wildly. I had not been injured.

The following wave of pain was more than I could handle. I must have cried out, for suddenly Orz was next to me in the water.

He carried me out, laid me on the blanket, and wrapped me in it tightly, but not before I saw that the blood was gushing from between my legs.

"*I take what I will take,*" a fetid voice whispered in my ear as shivers racked my body.

Orz knelt next to me and gathered me tightly against him. I bled all over him, but he did not seem to notice.

I screamed, but no sound came forth from my throat, at least none that I could hear.

*No! Not this! Anything but this!*

For at last I understood, once again too late, what the god was taking from me.

Batumar's child, the child I did not even know I carried.

Orz rocked me as if I was a babe myself.

Drowning in the sea of grief, I lost time.

I did not notice when the fire was started. Or when a ring of sentries surrounded us at a respectful distance. Or when water was boiled, or when my sacks of herbs arrived, or when clean, dry clothes were produced, I do not know from where.

Orz dressed me, padding dried shirl moss between my legs. I could not even be embarrassed.

When he finished and brought me hot water in a bowl, I added the necessary herbs and drank.

I lay down. Marga came, covered in wounds. None fatal, thank the spirits, for I felt too weak to help her. She lay next to me on one side, Orz lay next to me on the other. A fire burned at my feet. I was surrounded on every side by warmth, but I could feel none of it.

*Sorceress,* Kratos had called me. I had *not* asked him for powers.

"I do not want this," I said through chattering teeth.

I did not want to be like my great-grandmother, about whom I knew little, beyond that she grew great in power and used that power for a dark purpose.

A quick wind brought the sound of people from the direction of the temple.

"Your people live," Tomron said.

I had not realized he had come.

He crouched by my head.

*Your people.* How had they become mine? I wanted to protest, but I did not. I knew most of them by name. Even if I was a Shahala and they were not, my mother had always told me that in spirit, all people were one.

"Some of the enemy escaped," Tomron informed me. "They will bring a larger force against us. We should move on as soon as you are able, my lady."

He sounded hesitant. I thought likely that he did not know the source of my sudden illness but wrote it down as the price of great magic. Which it was, in a way.

Orz growled at him, sounding much like Marga.

I nodded, wanting to stand, but couldn't yet. My knees were made of water.

The sentries drew closer, perhaps to offer help.

I filled my lungs to strengthen my voice at least. "Those who are hale, see to burying the dead," I called out. "The enemy too. And if anyone knows the words to the Last Blessing, I would have it said over the graves."

Nobody objected. As Tomron had said, as I ordered, they obeyed.

"I shall rest a moment here."

In the end, I rested more than a moment. I slept for two days, trapped in nightmares where I was back in the dark, narrow passageways of the mountain, alone, and the dark god shredded me with his talons, over and over again.

When I woke, Marga was gone, but Orz was sitting with his legs crossed by the fire, the sentries in their places. My body was healed. My heart that had been empty since Batumar's death was now ground into dust.

I asked for my herbs. I had paid a heavy price for all of us to escape the Kerghi. I would not have anyone die now of an infected cut, not if I could help it.

Marga limped in and padded over to me. When I touched my forehead to hers, she licked my face with her raspy tongue. I began my healing work with her, then I saw to the men and women. I could not send my spirit into any. My spirit was too broken, and I was not certain it could fully recover again.

Once all battle injuries were treated, we moved off, eating the first meal of the day on the path, handing around bits of cold meat. I chewed food I did not taste, unable to think beyond my regret over my ill-advised bargain with the god. I grieved bitterly the price I had paid.

I walked at the front of the line, the tiger on one side, Orz on the other, both a little closer than before, nearly touching, as if sensing the turmoil inside me. But I walked tall, walked with strength, and made sure that was all the people would see who walked behind me.

*The tent pole must stand.*

We had lost seven men and two women, but the rest were in good cheer. They had seen, for the first time, their enemy defeated, which filled them with the kind of hope that spurred the women to singing.

But that hope did not make our journey easier. Indeed the next few days turned more and more difficult each, for now the enemy knew that we existed, and they came hunting for us with a much greater force than we had before seen.

# CHAPTER TWENTY-ONE
## BROOKER'S CAVES

Each day, my body grew stronger. My grief I kept locked away. I had many children depending on me, other than the babe I had lost, so I could not curl up by the side of the road and cry myself into the grave.

*The tent pole must stand.*

We tried to move faster through the winter forest once we left the ancient city. The hills grew, the mountain that had loomed in the distance for as long as we had been marching was getting closer and closer, appearing nearly within reach.

All of us knew to be as silent as possible. Here we had no temple walls to protect us. Our strategy became to run and hide whenever our scouts reported that enemy soldiers were closing in. On one occasion, our entire procession climbed the trees, the old and the young tied to the backs of the able. We hid in the tall pines, among the needles—hands, faces, hair, and clothes sticky with pitch.

Enemy soldiers spread out below us. If one of the three babes cried, we would have been discovered, but their mothers put them on the breast even as they hung on to the branches. We waited, holding our breath as the enemy passed.

The next village we found had been completely demolished. A village of miners who dug for copper in the hills, one of the Seb told me. The dead lay in the streets unburied, their bodies putrefied. No survivors.

"The dead are not to be touched," I instructed Tomron, thinking to spare the people of disease, and his men spread the word.

We used the wood planks of the huts to cover the fallen, then gave them to fire.

A young woman's body floated in the village well. We left her there, the only one left unburied, and for that, I begged the spirits forgiveness as I recited the Last Blessing for the dead villagers.

We moved on in silence and with near empty flasks, since we could take no water from the well.

Snow fell.

One of the orphan girls, Cila, ran a fever. I made her tea, then, because her fever ran too hot, packed her in snow until she cooled off enough. She had to be carried and wanted Orz to carry her.

Her request made an odd kind of sense. Orz was the most intimidating of our group. She probably hadn't felt safe since her village had been attacked and her family had been killed. She knew that in Orz's arms, nobody would attack her.

The pines here grew thicker. We followed the miners' wagon trail without straying to the right or left. We could not see far in any direction, for the trail was winding, forever disappearing among the trees up ahead.

We sent scouts ahead to alert us of any danger.

But instead, Marga ended up warning us, stopping in the middle of the trail and growling loudly.

When I stopped at the head of the column, so did everyone else behind me. Orz and Tomron, one on each side of me, drew their swords. Orz easily held Cila one-handed, but I stood ready to take her should there be a fight.

"Who goes there?" a disembodied voice challenged us from the woods ahead.

The man spoke in Selorm, which set me at ease. At least we were not facing the murderous Kerghi.

"The Lady Tera, High Sorceress," Tomron answered in my name.

Silence in the woods. "On what business?"

This I answered myself. "In search of Lord Karnagh, who is a friend. He was last seen heading to Lord Brooker's castle."

After another few moments of silence, a dozen men stepped out of the woods. Judging by their armor, they truly were Selorm. One of them chuffed at Marga. Marga looked unimpressed with their knowledge of her language. Her tail swished in the dirt.

I sent her a calming song in the way of the spirits. She came back to stand by me, rubbing herself against my side as if saying I was under her protection and nobody better forget that.

The men moved toward us. When they stopped, the one in the lead, an older soldier in heavily scarred leather armor, looked us over, and noted the Selorm soldiers around me.

"Tomron," Tomron said. "I served Lord Karnagh as his captain."

"Ridet," said the other man. "Captain of old Lord Brooker who was killed by the enemy. Now captain of young Lord Brooker."

He eyed Orz. Other than a slight shift in his stance, he did not betray his wariness. He did not ask about the hollow either. He simply pushed out his chest. He seemed to be the kind of man who would not easily admit if anything unnerved him.

"I will show you to Lord Brooker," he said at long last and turned.

We followed him and his men. Then more of his soldiers came from the woods, holding our two scouts. They were returned to us red-faced. Tomron fell back to have a word with them.

I did not envy the dressing-down they would receive for allowing themselves to be captured. I felt sorry for the two youth, village boys not properly trained as soldiers, but I would not interfere with Tomron in this matter.

He returned soon but did not walk with me. Instead, he hurried ahead. He talked to the Selorm, who were showing us the way. When he was done asking questions, he came back to me.

"Young Brooker, Lord Brooker's only son, saved many of his people by secreting them out into the deep woods through a passageway under the enemy," he said. "He is sheltering his people in caves."

We reached those caves as dusk fell, and I was at once shown to the young Lord Brooker. Marga walked with me, staying close to my side. And no matter how they protested, Brooker's guards could not make Orz stay behind either.

Young Lord Brooker waited for me on the ledge in front of the opening to the caves, a powerful male tiger next to him, his great tail swishing from side to side, matching the rhythm of Marga's.

He was a handsome young man of wild blond hair and sparkling blue eyes, in full armor, chin out, shoulders squared. He was a leader, no doubt, but not quite used to being a lord yet, relying on his family armor and fancy sword to announce his position.

His tiger snapped and growled at Marga, and Marga growled back. Then they sniffed at each other. They made no attempt to fight, and after a moment, Lord Brooker spoke to me.

"Greetings, Sorceress."

He waved me past the opening, most of which had been blocked with a wall of woven branches, the gaps stuffed with moss and scraps of cloth, then covered with mud that had dried, then frozen hard. Inside, the first section of the cave was used for storing wood and other supplies. From this area opened many large chambers, where people sat around fires.

He walked me toward the fire in a smaller, empty chamber that sat to the side, as private as quarters could be had under the circumstances. The tigers followed behind us, then settled down, one on each side. We sat on stones covered with fur.

Cila was feeling better and went with one of the women. Orz came to stand behind me. The sword he had gained in the battle made his dark figure even more imposing.

"The hollow is bound to you?" Brooker wanted to know. He could not hide his curiosity as well as his grizzled captain had.

Was Orz bound to me? I had not done anything to bind him. But I thought Brooker's people might feel more comfortable if they thought I controlled the hollow, so I nodded. Orz rarely left my side, had followed my every order so far. He had made no attempt to harm anyone against my wishes. I did not think that with that small nod I was lying.

I glanced past Brooker, at his people, all of whom were watching us with much curiosity, every face turned in our direction.

"Are you a sorceress come to save us?" the young lord asked as he watched me through narrowed eyes, his legs apart, his right hand braced on his right thigh, his left elbow braced on his left knee, as if posing for a painting: The Warrior Lord at Rest.

"I have come to find Lord Karnagh."

"You claim you are his friend." Brooker's gaze dipped to my cape as if he tried to discern what I looked like under there. "I fear Lord Karnagh is with the spirits," he said darkly after some time.

My heart twisted. "You saw him die?"

"I saw his broken body carried up the mountain by his tiger." He fell silent again, picking up a stick and stirring the glowing embers. "Have you ever heard of the Beast Lords' Chapel, my lady?"

I shook my head.

He stirred the embers again, his gaze growing unfocused. "The original home of the Selorm, my people, was far to the east of here, centuries past. Our ancestors came to Seberon from there, fleeing a great enemy. We were city-building people, but here we found tribes living in huts, ruled by a feeble, weak king. Even as diminished as our forces were, we easily conquered the land with our tigers.

"Our leader at the time, Lord Torimo, divided up the conquered kingdom of Seberon between his twelve remaining faithful lords and charged them to build castles and roads, let the Seb tribes work the land as before, live in peace, and pay taxes," he recited evenly, as if reciting a history lesson from his teachers.

"Some of the tribes fought, most accepted us, for Lord Torimo was a good leader and he brought peace to the land. The tribes even sent their sons to join their lords' armies. Foreign hordes no longer swept through Seberon every couple of years, raping, pillaging, and setting villages afire. Under the Selorm lords' command, the land was well protected. We became the kingless kingdom.

"The tribesmen called the Selorm lords Beast Lords because of their tigers. Soon our people blended and became as one, our separate origins all but forgotten. No enemy could breach our borders and destroy our great cities. Until Emperor Drakhar," he added with a heavy sigh.

"And the Beast Lords' Chapel?" I asked.

He pointed up. "At the first peak above the snowline. The original twelve lords and their tigers are buried there, guarding the grave of Lord Torimo and his tiger Bloodstorm. Over the centuries, tigers that lost their lords were drawn to the mountain and its forests. They bred and took over. Some battle tigers go up there to die. I have not heard of any man climbing up there in a hundred years."

He sat up straight, forgetting his pose. "These caves are as high as a man can go safely on this mountain, my lady. The caves keep us safe at night from the wild tigers' hunting."

*Had Lord Karnagh gone up the mountain to die?* I thought about that long and hard.

"How many escaped the castle with you, my lord?" I asked Lord Brooker.

"A hundred warriors, three hundred women, children, and elderly. Then another hundred refugees found us and joined us since, mostly peasants from the villages." He looked at me with questions in his eyes.

"I brought around as many," I told him.

"How many battle-ready men?"

"About a hundred." Tomron had been training the village men every night we stopped for camp and every morning before we renewed our march. From every abandoned village we had come across, they had taken every hammer, scythe, and sickle they could find and had worked them into weapons to add to their simple spears.

Brooker nodded. "Two hundred warriors might be able to retake the castle if we enter it unseen through the secret tunnel that helped us escape."

I considered his words. Maybe too long, because he added, "These caves will not hold a thousand people. Nor will these forests feed them through the winter. We would be safer within the walls at least."

"And food?"

"We shall take the enemy's food stores when we take the castle. They have pillaged every village and taken every bit of the harvest, every sow, every sheep, all the oxen."

When I still would not commit to battle, he said, "My hundred warriors cannot do it. But two hundred warriors with the help of a sorceress..." He flashed me a winning smile that no doubt had worked on every maiden in the castle in the past.

I considered his suggestion carefully. I did not want to lead my people into battle. In truth, the thought of another battle made me want to weep. I was no warrior queen. I loathed the idea of sending men to die. Until now, all our efforts had been to defend ourselves. Yet I was in this land to gather an army and take it back with me to Dahru to save my people.

I sent a silent prayer to the spirits to give me strength for all I had to accomplish, then stood. "Lord Brooker, have you enough to feed all our people for a few days?"

He nodded with a guarded look. "We laid by stores for the winter." He paused. "Your people could rest a few days here to recover from their journey while we make our plans. Then we shall attack the castle together."

But I shook my head. "We shall ask Lord Karnagh's opinion on that when I bring him down the mountain."

# CHAPTER TWENTY-TWO

## BEAST LORDS' CHAPEL

I spent the rest of the day talking with Tomron and resting for the climb. The women, children, and the elderly moved into the caves. Our men slept outside around their fires.

At dawn, I wrapped myself in the furs gifted to me by Lord Brooker, packed as much food as I could comfortably carry, then started up the mountain at dawn with Marga. Orz followed, of course, but I stopped him.

"I wish that you would stay and help our people. Tomron will be busy talking strategy with Lord Brooker. I am concerned that Cila's fever might come back."

I had only been able to treat the orphan girl with herbs, and they did not seem to be working fully. "If her fever returns, pack her in snow. But not too long. As I did before. Do you remember?"

He nodded, but his shoulders were stiffer than ever.

I placed a hand on his arm. "The spirits have been with me so far. They shall not abandon me now. Marga will protect me. I would have you stay," I said as a request from a friend, not as an order from a sorceress.

He looked at my hand on his arm and stilled, his body completely motionless. Slowly, he drew me into his arms.

I did not know in what way he meant it. As a friend? As the Guardians when they embraced me? As more? But what more could there be?

I had lost my heart. He had lost his spirit. In that, we were similar indeed. I *had* come to care for him. And I did not think of him differently than I thought of any other man. But I could not think of any man as I had thought of Batumar.

Orz had protected me. He had held me through the darkest day of my life.

Part of me did want to be held again, even if the rest was too broken to accept that comfort.

"Orz..."

But he had already felt the stiffening of my muscles and was backing away, his head dipping low in an apologetic bow, again and again, as if he was horrified that he had scared me. Did he think I was repulsed by his embrace?

"Orz..."

He kept backing away, the set of his shoulders signaling abject misery.

I sighed, suddenly miserable myself, and I did not know why exactly. "I have to go. I shall find you when I return."

When I turned to leave, he did not follow again. But he called out in his ruined voice, the only word he could speak. "Orz."

I looked over my shoulder, at his shrouded, solitary figure. "I shall be back in a few days' time with Lord Karnagh."

I caught sight of Lord Brooker at the mouth of the cave. He looked after me with doubt in his blue eyes, but also acceptance. He thought the mountain would claim me, but he clearly consoled himself with the fact that he would still have my warriors and he could retake his castle with them, even without a sorceress on his side. In any case, a sorceress as foolish as one who would go up the mountain—in winter, no less—could be no great sorceress, but one quite possibly weakened in the mind.

I had overheard him talking with his captains just before dawn.

Tomron stood by him now and watched me with his usual quiet strength. He believed in my powers more than I did. If I said I was going to move the mountain, he would not have batted an eyelash, I was certain.

If I ever had a brother, he could not have been better to me than Tomron.

Then my gaze settled on Orz again, his head bowed, his face covered by the black hood of his robe. His hands were fisted at his sides. He did not like letting me go. I turned back to my path and strode forward before he could decide to follow after.

Marga bounded ahead.

We followed a trail made by wild animals. By midday, I had to stop, the climb a difficult one, not at all like climbing trees in my childhood. Rocks rolled under my feet; stones cut my hand when I reached out to steady myself. The cold wind chapped my face, making it difficult to breathe.

I ate and drank while Marga sniffed around. Then we moved on, continuing up and up. Things only turned worse the higher we reached.

The cold cut through my new furs. I had to keep my water flasks under my clothes, against my skin, so the water would not freeze. When darkness fell, we pulled under a ledge, but I could not start a fire. Trees were scarce and small; any broken branches were buried under heavy snow, frozen.

Only Marga, curled around me, kept me alive that night.

She must have been worried about me, because she did not go off to hunt at dawn.

As we walked up the frozen incline, now and then I saw tiger tracks on the trail. These Marga always carefully sniffed.

She did not rub against trees or try to mark anything with her urine. The side of the mountain was not her territory, and I suspected she did not want to be drawn into a fight as an intruder. We were simply passing through, she and I.

The following day, we did see a female tiger off in the distance, standing on a ledge, watching us. She was smaller than Marga and did not approach. I was grateful for that.

The next tiger we came across, a day later, was a large male. This one could have torn both Marga and me apart. But even if it approached growling, it did stop and sniff, then bounded forward in a more playful manner, straight toward me.

And then I recognized him. "Tigran!"

He was Lord Karnagh's battle tiger. We had met at Karamur. He had the habit of lounging under the table at Lord Karnagh's feet at the feasts. I had even tossed him bones now and then.

He greeted me first, then Marga, who showed her neck in submission. Then they moved as if to fight, but even as I looked on in alarm, Marga rolled on the ground, as frisky as I had ever seen her, making noises that were new to me.

She waved her paws, then finally rolled on her belly. Tigran stood over her and let out a series of roars that had me stumble back another couple of steps. Tigran grabbed Marga's neck from the back, but his enormous canines did not seem to pierce her skin.

And then he mounted her.

I looked away, understanding at last that I was not witnessing a fight, despite all the growling.

As noisy as they were, they were fast enough. Soon Tigran was leading us forward, up and up, until we suddenly broke out of the scraggly, sparse forest.

Here a stretch of incline began with nothing but low shrubs. But beyond that, I could see a squat, snow-covered building, the only man-made thing in sight.

"The Beast Lords' Chapel," I told Marga, forgetting my exhaustion and the numbing cold.

We hurried forward, following Tigran.

In the back of the chapel stood twelve stone sarcophagi in a half circle, each marked with a beast lord's name on the front, a carved, reclining tiger on top of each. Since the tigers were all different and distinct, I thought they were the replicas of the lords' true battle tigers.

In the middle stood the largest sarcophagus, and on top of it a giant statue of a battle tiger on his feet, maw opened in a snarling roar, the animal so lifelike I drew back for a second. *Bloodstorm*, I thought.

I had been so blinded by all the sparkling snow outside that I did not at first see Lord Karnagh's smaller figure in the dim interior, but I could hear a startled cry—Lord Karnagh's voice.

"Lady Tera!"

And I saw a lump move on a bed of dry grasses under the altar. I rushed forward.

Tigran bounded up to me with a growl. My sudden rush toward his master had caught him off guard and raised his protective instincts, but a soft chuff from Lord Karnagh stopped him in his tracks.

I proceeded more carefully and could make out the man fully at last. When I reached him, I fell on my knees in front of him.

He was but a shadow of his former self, his hair white like an old man's. I remembered well his golden mane, the color of his tiger, his handsome face that had set the women at Karamur atwitter when he visited. He'd had such a light and sparkle in his eyes...

He lowered his head. "I have suffered some injuries, my lady."

With my heart in my throat, I nodded. He was missing his sword arm. Never again would he lead an army into battle.

"Has Batumar come to free my lands?" Lord Karnagh asked and looked past me, eager to see the High Lord walk in behind me.

I swallowed painfully. And I told him about Batumar, feeling colder than I had felt out in the open, in the wind.

We both had tears in our eyes by the time I finished. And then Lord Karnagh insisted that I tell him about Batumar's wild plan to save our island.

Afterward, we sat in silence in the dying light, the two tigers copulating at the chapel's entrance, snapping and growling at each other.

"I have come up the mountain to die," Lord Karnagh said. Then, not without anger, "But the spirit of the mountain will not let me."

He paused. "There are places that have a spirit..." He looked at me questioningly, as if wondering whether I understood.

I nodded, suddenly feeling wooden. *Kratos*, I thought, and began to shiver uncontrollably, every muscle in my body screaming to flee.

"It is a good spirit at least, not a dark one," Lord Karnagh said grudgingly. "And it did allow you to come up the mountain."

I held my breath. Could he be right? For a moment, I closed my eyes and tried to feel for the spirit. I sensed no darkness, heard no hissing, smelled not the terrible, fetid smell of Kratos.

But I did sense *something,* a benign, feline presence, pushing against the edges of my consciousness with curiosity.

I drew in air as I opened my eyes. Maybe the spirit of the Beast Lords' Chapel *was* a different thing from the taloned god who'd left me bereft.

"I do not know for what reason I have been kept alive." Lord Karnagh gave a bitter grunt. "I can be no use to anybody. Mayhap the spirit of the chapel was lonely."

I hesitated. "May I see the rest of your injuries?"

For a moment, broken pride flared in his gaze. But then he looked away from me and threw back the battered cloak that had been covering him. His leggings were so tattered and torn that I could see his skin right through them as if he wore nothing.

His legs were twisted. They had been broken in several places and had healed badly.

"Not only will I never be able to hold a sword again, but I cannot stand, let alone walk, my lady. I have dragged myself up here clinging to Tigran's fur. The best tiger that ever lived. He is of Bloodstorm's bloodline, did I tell you that?"

He did not wait for my answer before saying, "I had two hands then, but the right one had been too badly damaged. It turned black soon after we reached the chapel. I had to cut it off with my own sword, then cauterize the wound."

I paled, trying to imagine.

He gave a half smile. "I tried to think of what you would do."

"I could not have done *that,*" I admitted.

He was silent for a moment. "I cannot cling to Tigran to go back down, not one-handed, and I cannot walk either." He gave a frustrated grunt. "Unless you can carry me down on your back, I am to die in this chapel whenever the spirit lets me go at last."

I kept staring at his legs. No herbs could help something like that. But if I could not carry Lord Karnagh down the mountain on his back, he could carry *me* down, I reasoned.

I laid my hands upon his left leg and closed my eyes, prayed to the spirits, then said, "I might know a way to heal this."

He pulled away. "I will not allow it."

I offered a weak smile. "You sound like Batumar."

"I have seen what healing during the siege did to you, my lady. I cannot let you take my pain upon yourself."

"I shall not die. You can help me down the mountain, and then I shall heal in Brooker's cave."

He raised a white eyebrow. "Brooker's cave? What happened to Brooker's Castle?"

And I told him.

When I finished, he asked, "Enough warriors to take the castle back?"

I nodded. "Then we could leave the common folk there, in the safety of the high walls. The main force of Emperor Drakhar's army has moved on. He only has roving bands of warriors here and there. He might not even find out until spring that he has lost the castle.

"By then, you, my lord, and Lord Brooker could move on with two hundred warriors to lift the siege from your own castle, Regnor. Then, joined with the warrior queen's army that holds the last free city to the south, you could push the enemy back and back, until the whole of Seberon was regained."

Lord Karnagh nodded. "Once the kingdom is free, we could cut off supplies to the Emperor's army."

"Yes."

He looked at me. "I shall confess, I had at times thought it strange that you were a healer *and* a concubine, but now I find even stranger that you are at heart a general."

I laughed at that. "I know precious little of war."

"Yet you brought a host of five hundred people to Lord Brooker. Through enemy land."

"Only because it had been willed so by the spirits."

He watched me, contemplating all we had said. "What do the spirits will now?"

"That you return to your people."

He fell silent for a long time. Then he held my gaze. "You could make it so I could walk again?"

"With the spirits' help."

His eyes brightened but then clouded again after a moment. "I could still not hold a sword."

*No.* I could not grow bones. But I said, "I led a host of five hundred through a war-torn land without a sword."

And he laughed again, but once more, his merriment did not last long. "Is there not another way? Can you not help without harming yourself, my lady?"

I shook my head. Yet an idea I did not much like, pushed into my head. "Maybe it could be accomplished differently," I admitted.

"How so?"

"To set the bones right and heal them the proper way, I must soften them first, move them out of their bad positions. This takes much strength," I said, with no small amount of reluctance.

"That will weaken you."

I nodded.

He watched me, and after a while, he understood. "But if the bones were rebroken, then you could save your strength for the healing itself. It would not be as dangerous for you, then."

I nodded again.

"But still dangerous?"

"Yes." The knitting together of bones required much from a healer.

We sat in silence.

I pulled out my food sack and shared some food with him, hard biscuits and cheese, which he ate with haste. I suspected Tigran had fed him nothing but snow hares since they had come up the mountain.

"You have a tiger," he remarked.

"I do not know how." I shook my head. "My mother was a pureblood Shahala; my father...Barmorid," I admitted. "A Kadar." A well-known Kadar at that, the High Lord before Batumar.

Lord Karnagh looked at me with much interest. "Barmorid was the son of a Kadar warlord by his Selorm concubine, if I remember right." He thought some more. "One of those times when the Kadar came to our aid. Our people have traded favors for centuries. Barmorid returned home with payment in gold and a Selorm princess to strengthen the alliance."

I blinked.

Lord Karnagh smiled, pleased. "We might be related. I would have to look it up in the annals of our people. If the enemy has not burned every scroll when they took our castles."

How strange that thought was, that I might yet have living family. I hid that small flicker of hope deep inside me. "But even Selorm women do not bond with tigers."

"You are no ordinary woman, my lady." He fell back again into deep thought as we finished eating. "In this healing...I want no harm to come to you at all. And beyond that, I fear Batumar's spirit will find me in a battlefield and slay me."

"I am a healer. I am supposed to heal."

"I am a warrior. I am supposed to die from deadly battle wounds," he countered.

"Not when a healer is readily available."

He scoffed. Glared. Then, "You will not die?"

"I will not," I promised. "Your people need you. *My* people need you," I added quietly.

And after a long while, he nodded.

"I will need a moment." I went to the doorway and lowered myself to my knees as I looked to the sky.

Why would the spirits bring me here if not to heal Lord Karnagh? And if they brought me here for that purpose, then they would not withhold my healing powers from me. Since the battle at the ancient temple, I had healed only with herbs, but now a skill beyond herbs was needed.

I thought of my mother until I had her face and voice and smell firmly in my mind. I let her kindness and love fill me, then I prayed and prayed. And I felt a flickering of my healing power awaken.

I gave thanks to the spirits and went back inside.

Lord Karnagh dragged himself to the steps that led to the altar.

"Let us break the bones, then." He stretched his legs out over the steps, then reached for a fallen block of stone with his one good arm.

"Tigran," he called out. "To hunt."

The great tiger looked at us, but then turned around and bounded out. Marga remained.

"If I cry out, Tigran might think you are attacking me, my lady," Lord Karnagh explained.

He held the stone over his right leg, the bone bumpy, the muscles mangled already. He swallowed hard. "I do not know where to strike."

I selected some herbs from my belt and traded them for the stone. "Chew on those while I decide what needs to be done."

He shoved a handful of herbs into his mouth. He chewed, swallowed, chewed again. When I saw his eyes becoming cloudy, I hefted the stone suddenly. I broke his thigh bone first, without warning.

He groaned.

The stone came down again.

Sweat rolled down both our faces.

I moved over to the other leg, hesitated.

But he growled, "Do it, my lady."

And I slammed the stone into his leg with all my strength.

When, at long last, I could cast that stone aside and lay my hands on the broken bones, the pain that hit me was so fierce, I swayed. I could not stay kneeling next to him. I had to sit.

Even with the badly healed fractures rebroken, I still had to do some softening. Pain flowed into me like a flooding river, washing away thoughts, our surroundings, whether it was night or day.

I knew nothing but pain.

And even as all that agony filled me, my strength flowed out. I had some of my healing spirit back, but not enough.

Handhold by handhold, I took Lord Karnagh's injuries upon me, knitting his bones and muscles. Healing the injuries once they were inside me was easier than in another body, but far more painful for me.

I did not mind giving my strength. Batumar was gone. My unborn babe was gone. In my numb grief over Batumar, I had not felt the new life inside me that early. I would have felt it in a handful more days, I thought. But more days the babe had not been given.

I wanted to go and be with them, the ones I lost but still loved. Lord Karnagh would be a better leader of troops than I, and I was certain that after freeing his own lands, he would hurry to my people's aid. So I healed him.

At that point, if Tigran returned and ripped me apart, it could not have hurt more; indeed, death would have been a welcome release from the pain.

When the chapel began spinning around me, I fell back and closed my eyes. In my heart, I sang to the spirits. Or tried. For the first time, I could not think of the words. Too much pain filled my mind.

The long climb up the frozen mountain had left me weakened. I had not eaten well since...*I have overestimated my strength*, I thought, even as darkness claimed me.

When I woke, Marga stood over me, licking my face. Lord Karnagh peered at me with an anxious expression. He spoke, but I could not hear his words. Behind him, Tigran looked at me solemnly with the eyes of an ancient spirit.

I could see the dark sky through the doorway. Night had come. I blinked. I had not felt the passage of time.

My legs felt as if they had been chewed to shreds, even the bones—as if some wild beast had sucked out the marrow.

My head spun. Darkness tried to claim me again. And I realized at last that I might not have enough strength to heal myself.

"You must leave me," I whispered to Lord Karnagh. "It is more important that you return."

He pushed to his feet, having to hang on to the altar for support, and scowled. "Not without you, my lady."

And then nothing but darkness again.

The next time I woke, I lay across Lord Karnagh's shoulders. The sky was light, and we were climbing down the mountain, his steps unsteady. I might have healed his bones, but he had to rebuild the strength in his muscles. He should not have been carrying me. But I did not have the strength to tell him this.

The world fell away again.

The next time I opened my eyes, I lay on Tigran's back. After that, I woke on Marga, who walked with me most gently.

Then I opened my eyes, and I was in a cave. Only for a moment, I thought we were back in the Beast Lords' Chapel and I had imagined the whole journey down the mountain. But no, I could hear children. We were in Brooker's cave. I was lying by the fire in the small chamber.

Orz stood at the opening with his back to me, his sword unsheathed, growling in warning like a tiger.

Beyond him, I spotted Tomron's shape.

"My lady?" Tomron called when he saw my eyes opened.

Past him, the cave was nearly empty save for a handful of mothers and their children. Marga padded by Orz, ignoring his sword and growl, and came to lick my face, then lay down next to me.

"My lady?" Tomron said again.

"Orz. Please let him in."

Orz came and sat by my feet, letting his naked sword rest on his folded legs.

Tomron carefully edged in and stayed far away from him, as if Orz had turned into a wild creature. I wondered what he had done while I had been sleeping.

People stopped by the opening, stared at me, then moved on. But then more people came.

"Why are they looking at me like that?"

Tomron smiled, keeping a careful eye on the hollow. "They had heard of sorceresses, my lady. But few have ever seen one. And they had neither seen nor heard of a sorceress who could bring a man back from the dead."

"Lord Karnagh was very much alive when I found him," I assured him weakly.

But Tomron shook his head. "They all believe he had been but a spirit. You have gone up the mountain, through the forest of the wild tigers, to the Beast Lords' Chapel, a place no man had dared approach in an age. And there you made a deal with the spirits for his return. You gave the spirits your strength for his life."

As even shaking my head was beyond me, I could only groan at such nonsense.

"There are already songs being sung about your great deed around the campfires," he said as if that was that. Once something had been sung in a song, it could not be refuted.

"Will you live?" he asked after a while.

Orz stilled, listening intently at my feet.

I checked the pain. Better. I did not think the darkness would claim me again. I tried to move my legs. They shifted under the furs, although I did not feel it wise to test them yet with trying to stand. "I will."

"Good." Tomron nodded solemnly, some of the furrows on his forehead smoothing out. "For the people believe you are a sorceress sent by the spirits to save the world."

# CHAPTER TWENTY-THREE

## LEADER OF THE FREE PEOPLE

The fire burned low in Lord Brooker's small cave chamber, but it filled the space with warmth. I lay on my bed of furs that protected me from the cold, hard cave floor, two more furs piled on top of me—the pelts of silver wolves.

"More water, my lady?" a striking young woman asked, slim as a doe, graceful, her ebony hair a mass of curls, her eyes full of compassion.

"Thank you." I sat up and accepted the cup, and she went back to her cooking at the fire.

Orz sat by my side, within reach. Marga was out hunting.

I had been back from the Beast Lords' Chapel for seven days.

A few steps away, Lord Brooker, Lord Karnagh, and Tomron sat cross-legged, discussing strategy. They were talking about the secret tunnel that led inside Brooker's Castle.

"The opening of the tunnel is in a copper mine a day's march from here," Lord Brooker said. "If we leave the women and children, the old and the sick here, the fighting men could reach it even faster."

Tomron and Lord Karnagh glanced my way.

Lord Karnagh said, "We cannot leave anyone behind unprotected," at the same time as Tomron protested, with full respect. The other two were lords, Tomron but a captain.

Next to me, Orz stiffened.

"But if we leave part of the fighting force behind," Lord Brooker responded, "we might not have enough strength left to retake the castle." Then he added, "And if we all go, we will go more slowly. We might have to spend the night in the open."

At this, the men fell silent. The north wind blew outside. An icy chill ruled the cave everywhere but near the many fires. Out in the open, few could survive the long, dark night if we caught a hard freeze.

"When?" Lord Brooker asked.

Again, Tomron and Lord Karnagh looked at me.

I sat up to prove my strength, then stood on shaky legs.

"Three days hence," Lord Karnagh said. "We bring nothing but our weapons, furs, and blankets."

Lord Brooker nodded. "And a day's worth of food and water." He looked toward the mass of people who filled every nook of the cave. "In the meanwhile, all able-bodied men must hunt, every time the weather allows it."

Then they discussed what would happen once they breached the castle, the position of guard posts, the location of the armory, what our men would have to take over first, all while the women and children, the old and the sick, kept hidden in the tunnel.

Lord Karnagh came to me once their meeting ended. I had sat back down by then, and he sat next to me. "You had promised me that my healing would not damage you badly."

His voice was roughened, his eyes filled with worry.

"I will recover."

"Why would you take such a risk?"

How could I explain? "Have you ever heard the Shahala myth of our world's creation, my lord?"

He shook his head.

"In the beginning, there was nothing," I began. "And in this nothing, the Great Mother floated. To ease her loneliness, she gave birth to the planets and the stars. They floated from her body and scattered across the universe."

In my mind, I could hear my mother's voice as she had told me this story many times over.

I continued. "Tired she was from her labors and slept for the first time. And when she slept, she dreamed. She dreamed of plants and animals and people, nations and races. And when she woke, she saw that all she dreamed had come into being."

Lord Karnagh listened.

"But as time passed," I said, "all she created did not please her, for her creations lacked spirit. So like a mighty wind, she rose and swept through all there is. And all who breathed her gained spirit, until the last of her was gone into the last of her creations."

We sat in silence.

At last, I said, "It is not that I do not know that overusing my healing spirit is harmful to my own body…I am not, on purpose, wasteful with the gift. But the Guardians think I am the one to end this war. Even if the last of my spirit has to go into my people and those I care for, those who can bring about the Emperor's defeat…I would but fulfill my destiny."

He shook his head, lips pressed together.

I held his gaze, willing him to understand. "If I die, but the world should live free, would that not be a victory?"

As the days passed, while I regained more strength, the others prepared for the journey. Lord Karnagh, Lord Brooker, and Tomron trained the men from the villages along with the warriors and patiently explained what breaching the castle and taking it back would entail.

By the time the morning of our departure arrived, we were ready.

I rode at the head of the column in a contraption Orz had made for Marga, an odd-looking saddle that helped me stay on her back. Orz stood by my side as always. Lord Brooker and Lord Karnagh walked with me, then behind us the warriors. Tomron walked at the end of our long column, protecting the rear with men from the villages. In the middle traveled the women and the children, along with the older people.

Only when we were halfway up yet another incline and I looked back at our long column snaking behind me in the fresh snow did I realize our true number. I could scarcely believe that I had left Ker with but Marga and Orz, not so long ago.

Now two lords, several captains, and the beginnings of an army followed behind me.

The mothers shushed their children; the old helped each other. Bitter winds blew over us, but not one person complained about leaving the cave or the dangers they would soon be facing.

They were from different Seb tribes, some who'd been enemies over the centuries, but they did not quarrel now. In Lord Karnagh and Lord Brooker, they had good leaders.

I smiled at the two Selorm lords with gratitude. "The people will follow you anywhere," I said, pleased.

Lord Brooker shook his head.

Lord Karnagh smiled. "They are following *you*, my lady."

"They do no such thing." I was no imposing figure. I needed straps just to keep me on my tiger's back.

Mayhap in the beginning, when they had no one else, they had looked to me. But they had proper warlords to lead them now, and I was but a woman so weak I had to be carried.

Lord Karnagh said. "If you would keep going, my lady. We need but a moment." And he walked to the side and stopped, Lord Brooker doing the same, the two of them quietly talking at the edge of the woods.

Marga walked on with me, her head down against the wind. The column walked after us without slowing, even if a few men and women cast curious glances at the two talking lords by the side of the road.

Soon the two lords ran to catch up with me, both of them grinning like boys.

"Now you stop, my lady," Lord Karnagh suggested.

With a pat on her shoulder, I directed Marga toward the trees. She went as I asked, then stopped when I asked, but the two lords kept on walking.

All alone, since the entire column stopped as soon as I left it. All eyes were upon me, as if they awaited instruction.

I sat in place, stunned for a moment, then I waved them on and urged Marga to walk the length of the column. Orz came with me.

I smiled at the men and women, looked them over, made sure the elderly had not become overly tired or the children too cold. Then I rode Marga back to the front of the line and caught up with Lord Karnagh and Lord Brooker.

"You are the leader of the free people, my lady." Lord Karnagh punctuated the words with a small bow.

And Lord Brooker said, "If you but wished, they would crown you their queen today."

A faint echo blew on the wind. *Have you come for power?*

"No!" I swallowed. "Thank you, but no." My heart racing, I urged Marga forward.

We marched until we found a sheltered spot surrounded by thick woods. Here we rested and ate but did not start any fires. All the dead branches around us were frozen deep under the snow.

I moved through the camp, checking for frostbite or other injuries, but found none. People huddled together for warmth. Hope shone on every face. Wherever I went, they blessed my name.

*My people*, I thought. And smiled—I could do that with my face, just not with my heart. I smiled as if I knew for certain that victory and safety awaited mere steps away.

As we started out again a while later, I prayed to the spirits to keep my people in their care and deliver us to our destination safely. This they did, for we reached the copper mine shortly after nightfall the following night, without being overcome by enemy troops or a snowstorm, or any other major difficulty.

Half-frozen and wholly exhausted, we crowded into the front section of the mine shaft. As long as we had a roof over our heads, nothing else mattered. We had no fire, but we huddled together for warmth.

"Tomorrow we shall take back the castle, my lady," Lord Brooker told me as he passed by.

I worried about that, about how many would die in the fight. But I did not worry about the night. I thought we would be safe in the mine.

We were not.

I woke in the middle of the night to a great din at the mouth of the tunnel. Both tigers were gone from my side. Orz stood by my feet, facing away from me with his sword drawn, ready to protect me.

I caught sight of Lord Karnagh running toward the sound of battle cries, and shouted to him, coming to my feet. "What is it?"

"A roving band of mercenaries found us, my lady."

I stared after him as he ran to fight in the dark.

*Of course.* Why had I not expected this? A thousand people walking through snow left a wide trail. If any enemy came across that, they would come to investigate. All they had to do was follow our tracks. Since they had no young and no sick, they had caught up with us easily.

But even if I had not anticipated attack, it seemed Lord Karnagh and Lord Brooker had, for as I hurried forward to see what was happening, I could see they had left full half of our warriors guarding the entrance of our tunnel and they had the attack well in hand.

Swords clashed, men sounded battle cries, and tigers roared. I could see some of the enemy, but in the dark, I could not make out how many of them were outside, seeking to fight their way in.

I spotted Tomron in the scant moonlight. He was dragging an injured warrior my way. "All he needs is the bleeding stemmed. Save your strength, my lady." Then he hurried off, leaving the man at my feet.

"It is nothing, my lady." The warrior clutched his side.

Blood spurted through his fingers, appearing black in the night.

I bent to him. "Let me see."

A woman appeared at my elbow with a torch the next second. Then another brought water and my bag of herbs. And another rushed up and began tearing the bottom of her long skirt into strips.

I bandaged up the gash the best I could, then the next wound and the next. Our losses were much lighter than the enemy's, the injured men told me. We had the protection of the tunnel. But no matter how many enemy our warriors cut down, the fight raged on and on, until the light of dawn.

Only then did we realize that faced not a roving band of mercenaries, but an entire army unit.

# CHAPTER TWENTY-FOUR

## BROOKER'S CASTLE

Despite our warriors' best efforts, the enemy pushed inside. The women carried the injured deeper into the mineshaft, three or four to a man. I splinted broken limbs and stemmed bleeding with my herbs.

For a moment, it seemed we might be able to stand against the tide, but then fresh enemy soldiers moved to the front, and they pushed us back another distance. And again and again.

We were half-frozen from the long night, none of us had eaten that day yet, nor did we have any more water once they pushed us past the trickle that ran down the tunnel wall. We had but a handful of torches.

We drew back like an injured snake, in staggered sections, the women carrying the wounded, then resting, hoping our warriors would hold the line at last, then moving again when the enemy attacked more fiercely.

We progressed through the dark shaft like that through an endless day, until one of the women hurried back to me from the deepest reaches.

"We cannot go farther, my lady." She fought back frightened tears.

I went to investigate.

Here the tunnel branched off into a dozen directions, and our people had poured in. As they were all packed in, unable to move farther, I knew these were all blind tunnels that dead-ended.

A timber door closed off the main tunnel, fortified with wrought iron bands. Even when several of us pushed, it would not yield. The door was somehow barred from the other side.

The sounds of fighting filled the air, mixing with the sounds of dying. I looked back at the frightened women, and our warriors behind them, fighting, falling.

My stomach churned, my heart heavy inside my chest. *I* had led these people here. We were all doomed to the grave. What healing powers I had were no help with this, nor my ability to sing songs to animals and sometimes make them listen.

Here, so close to our goal, was an obstacle we could not overcome. Here our valiant quest would end.

I wanted to cry out for the spirits' help, but I was afraid what would answer down here in the deep.

I looked at the torch in my hand. If we tried to burn the wood of the gate, the smoke would fill the tunnel and kill us all. Then I thought of a better solution.

I turned and ran toward the fighting men. "I need the men from the villages who brought their axes."

The word spread, and one such man appeared, then another. Soon I had a dozen. "Follow me."

As soon as they saw the gate, they knew why I had called them and fell on the great obstruction with all their strength. Wood beams creaked and splintered. Chunks as thick as my arm split away.

But when a hole had been cut in the gate, we did not see freedom on the other side. We saw a stone wall.

The enemy that had taken the castle had discovered the secret of Lord Brooker's disappearance and had walled in the tunnel to protect from just such an attack as we had planned.

The fighting mass of warriors reached closer and closer.

The women and the children, the injured and the old crowded around me, their desperate cries filling my ears.

"Save us, Sorceress!"

If only I had the powers they thought I possessed. I regretted bitterly not disabusing them of their high opinions of me before, not insisting that I was nothing but a healer.

I could not sing down stones.

Yet, as I looked at the desperate eyes, all dark in the dim, flickering light of the torches, I could not tell them that all was lost, I could not say *prepare to perish*.

I blinked back tears of desperation, and scanned the mine shaft. There had to be other branches. Even a small opening somewhere. We had to run and hide. The enemy would not find all of us in the dark. Some of our people might live.

But even as I thought that, I knew what would happen to those who escaped the enemy. They would starve and freeze down here.

Babes cried in their mothers' arms. The mothers rocked them, looking at me, waiting for me to save them. I closed my eyes, for I could no longer look upon their faces.

A true sorceress could bring down the wall. *How?*

In my frustration, I turned and struck it with my bare fist, which accomplished nothing but bruising my flesh. The wall was thoroughly unmovable.

My breath caught. *Or was it?*

The Kerghi were not city builders. They were horseback people who lived for war, all soldiers, marauding from one corner of the world to the other. They had no stonemasons among them.

Which meant that the wall before me had been erected by the castle's stonemasons, no doubt forced by the Kerghi. But would the castle's stonemasons not leave a path for future escape?

I pulled my little paring knife and attacked the mortar. Not much happened at first. But then I hit a soft spot.

I tested the mortar, and the blade slid right in. I scraped some out, rubbed it between my fingertips, smelled it. And realized that some of the stones were held in place by fine gravel mixed with half-frozen wax.

I needed something long and thin to work that wax out. "Hand me a dagger."

One of the women grabbed one from a fallen soldier and rushed it to me. I attacked the wall with all my strength and, after some struggle, removed a stone, then another.

Once a hole appeared, our men had someplace to wedge their axes and collapsed the rest.

The passageway's opening saved us from imminent death at the hand of the Kerghi soldiers who had pushed us to the tunnel's end, but not for long. Even as we rejoiced, our predicaments worsened.

Within a few steps, we found ourselves in the castle's dungeons, which were filled with men the enemy had taken captive. They were under full guard, and the guard sounded the alarm as soon as they saw us.

And then suddenly we faced enemy fighters on both sides.

Some of our warriors rushed to meet the new threat. Prisoners cried from their overcrowded cells, reaching through the bars, filthy, bloody hands, fingers disjointed from torture.

I saw the jailer—an old man with a whip and a row of keys on his belt—pressing himself into an indentation in the rock wall, trying to stay away from all the sharp swords around him.

"Marga!" I called the tiger.

And she appeared next to me.

I climbed on her back and directed her toward the jailer. "That one."

And as if she knew my mind, Marga rushed forward.

The fighting men cleared out of her way.

Then I was at the jailer, Marga's head level with the man's face. She showed her fearsome teeth.

The man whimpered as he soiled himself.

"The keys," I demanded.

He threw the key ring at me, then covered his face with his trembling hands.

Back to the cells we went, and I slid off Marga's back. While I worked on the locks, one after the other, releasing the prisoners, the tiger protected me. No enemy dared to come near.

The prisoners joined the fight with whatever they could first grab, a loose brick here, a chunk of wood there, a bucket. Then, as the enemy fell, the prisoners grabbed better weapons from the fallen.

The Kerghi who had followed us into the tunnel were defeated to the last man. Then our joined forces turned to the enemy inside the castle. And at long last, they too fell back.

Our warriors followed them up the stairs. The women and children, the old and the injured stayed in the dungeons. I stayed with them and healed.

We lost men. Too many. But many I could help.

I was still dressing wounds when one of Lord Brooker's men ran back down, covered in blood, gasping for air. "A message from Lord Brooker, my lady. We have the castle." And then he promptly collapsed.

I hurried to close the gash in his side.

When I finished with the last patient, I ran up the stairs to the castle yard. I looked upon the dead, the blood-soaked stones below my feet. Then at our men, smiles on their faces. We had the castle.

I turned around, dazed, and found Marga and Tigran together in a quiet corner, lying near each other, panting with exhaustion but with no serious injuries.

Lord Karnagh appeared at my side, holding a bloody lance. Maybe that was easier to maneuver left-handed than a sword would have been. "Marga fought well," he said. "From the looks of her, I would say she has some of Bloodstorm's blood in her, my lady."

"Is it truly over?"

"The castle is ours." Lord Karnagh beamed. "But I believe you had bigger plans."

I could not think about that now. "I need water boiled and as much clean cloth as possible cut into bandages. I would tend the wounded."

That night, we feasted. Lord Brooker's men found the larders full. The enemy had laid in ample stores for the winter, food stolen from the villages. But our feast was a mix of joy and sorrow. We lost over fifty men.

At least the walking wounded had not been so badly injured that I could not heal them. And we gained two hundred more warriors from the dungeons and other locked pits of the castle. The enemy had been planning to sell them at the slave markets of Muzarat in the spring.

They were skin and bones, but I expected a few weeks of three good meals a day would do wonders for them.

That night, I slept the sleep of the dead.

The next day's task was to take stock—of our people, of our supplies, of the castle. Teams were immediately assigned to the burial of the bodies. Since the ground was frozen, they were given to fire.

Another team worked on walling the tunnel back up again, without wax this time. We did not want the enemy to intrude among us through there.

Lord Karnagh and Lord Brooker talked to the prisoners, who told tales of battles fought far and near. At first, I sat in those meetings with the men, but the darkness they spoke of I could not long bear, so I went around the castle with Marga and Orz to see who needed my help.

I had enough wound dressings to change for the work to last all day, even with help. But as the days passed, the wounds healed.

Orz turned out to be a great helper. He was strong enough to lift the most badly injured, turn them over, move them. He carried bucket after bucket of water for me.

And when I worked myself into exhaustion, he would even carry me, to the bedchamber Lord Brooker had kindly given me. Orz was offered lodgings too, but he would have none of that. He slept outside my door on the cold hard stones instead.

The first men, nearly a dozen, appeared in front of our gate a week after we had regained the castle. They had women with them and one child, a newborn babe. They called up to tell us that they were from the other side of the Silver River, had been hiding in the woods. They had overheard Kerghi soldiers fleeing in the night and knew that the castle was now held by free men.

Lord Brooker had the gate opened for them.

Two days later, another small group came. Then another and another, as if the birds themselves were spreading the news.

Then small groups of Selorm soldiers arrived here and there, those left behind for dead on battlefields, then later recovered, those who escaped enemy ambushes.

By the next mooncrossing, the castle could not hold us all. Soldier camps had to be set up outside the castle walls, tents upon rows of tents.

I began to fear that our food stores, as plentiful as they were, would not be sufficient.

But the soldiers hunted. The villagers went as far as the river for fishing. One way or the other, we were able to feed the great host of people who gathered.

Before I knew it, we had a full army.

Lord Karnagh, Tomron, and I were standing on the parapets, looking at the warriors training on the new grass. We were, at last, at winter's end.

Orz was playing with Marga on the side of the training field. They made an odd couple, communicating with grunts and growls. I wondered if he might not have some Selorm blood in him. After seeing that he caused no harm, most people accepted him, especially when they saw Marga accept him. Both the Seb and the Selorm put great faith in the judgment of tigers.

Marga bounded away, twisting her head to check on me before she moved toward the forest. The sparring warriors switched positions, and one challenged Orz.

Without the slightest hesitation, Orz stepped into the fight. He held his own, despite his disfigured fingers that badly gripped his sword.

Lord Karnagh remarked, "The hollow is no stranger to war. If he had his voice, you could make him a captain."

"He might have been a captain once," I allowed, and told him about the disappeared captain of Ishaf's city guard.

We watched him as he fought, beating back his opponent little by little. Due to his uneasy grip, his blows were not as accurate as the other man's, but he had more strength behind them.

"Tomorrow, I set out for Muzarat," I said.

"And we set out to free Regnor," Lord Karnagh responded. "We have the men to do it. As soon as my city is free, I shall be coming to your assistance, my lady."

We had agreed the day before to split our new army. Lord Karnagh gave Tomron, who had once been sworn to the Selorm lord as his captain, into my service. I named Tomron my general, an honor the battle-hardened warrior had accepted with tears in his eyes.

And now we were ready to leave.

Up this far north, the river was riddled with rapids, unsuitable for barges, but below Muzarat, the waters calmed. I would march to Muzarat with my half of the army, and from there, the Silver River would take us to the sea; then we could sail to the islands of Landria and negotiate transport back to Dahru.

Batumar's cloak with the star map stitched into the lining was gone—my heart twisted with a sharp pain, even as I thought that—but since I stitched the map, I remembered it fair well. I was certain I could recreate it again.

"The most difficult part will be to convince the Landrian king to put his navy in our service. But in a world such as we live in now, even he must be looking for alliances," I told Lord Karnagh.

He grew thoughtful. "I might be able to help with that."

He pointed to the hills, covered in trees all greening for spring. "Landria is a nation of small islands and island fortresses. Their navy is crucial to their defense. But their arid southern islands lack the right kind of wood for shipbuilding."

I listened with budding hope as he continued.

"Seb loggers cut the cedar and fir for the ships, the oak for the oars, then the logs are floated down the Silver River to Uramit. The rapids do not damage the logs much. Wood for ships is our main trade with Landria." He smiled. "I shall write a missive you can carry to their king, to remind the old man just how much he needs our trade and let him know how fully we support your quest."

I embraced him as I would have a brother, and he embraced me back, awkwardly, one-armed, but with warmth.

So close was I to the end of an impossible journey, tears suddenly burned my eyes.

We would march from Brooker's Castle to Muzarat, where I hoped to find Graho and purchase the children from him to free them, then float down the river to Uramit, the nearest seaport to the Landrian islands.

And from there, home to Dahru to save my people. I smiled, but that smile soon wilted as I saw Lord Brooker approach with a grim look on his face.

"Bad tidings, my lady. I have word from the latest refugees. The main force of the Emperor's army was seen heading toward Uramit. They have the dark sorcerer with them."

My heart stopped. "Uramit has a Gate."

Lord Karnagh grunted with frustration next to me. "Can a dark sorcerer open the Gate of the World on Dahru from the Gate of Uramit?"

"I do not know." Desperation filled me. Who knew from whence the Emperor's sorcerer drew his power?

I thought of Kratos, the taloned god, and shuddered.

Our march south through enemy-controlled territory was most difficult. We fought skirmish after skirmish, battle after battle. What castles we passed, we freed.

It was after one such battle that I was nearly captured by retreating enemy.

We thought the Kerghi who had survived the last clash had run off. After I treated our injured, as I was covered in blood and gore, I wished to bathe. Our soldiers crowded around the castle well, trying to do the same.

I left the well to them, needing peace after the bloody battle, some silence for my ears that had heard too many death cries that day. I knew the forest outside the walls had a creek. With Orz and Marga, I walked out to seek its clean water.

I had bathed in many forest creeks with Orz and Marga standing guard. Marga liked splashing in the water with me. Orz would stand on the bank, sword drawn, with his back to me. I felt safe with him. He was protective of me. I did not think he thought of me as a woman.

About that, I was wrong.

I washed the blood of the injured off me, out of my hair, scraped it from under my fingernails. We were far enough south so that, although the water was bracing enough to make me not want to linger, I was not cold once I walked out of the creek and dried myself.

Darkness was falling on the forest. Marga padded off to hunt. She would have filled her belly on the battlefield, but I would not let her feast on the dead, not even our enemies, and never had.

"Let us go and find two unburned beds," I said to Orz, now alone with him in the clearing.

Part of the castle had caught on fire while we had fought, but the flames had since been extinguished, only the south tower badly damaged.

Orz turned toward me.

Tension sat in his movements, in his wide shoulders. I could feel him watching me from under his hood. Instead of heading down the path, he took a step toward me, then stopped, as if fighting with himself over something.

I tilted my head. "Orz?"

But I did not have time to puzzle out what bothered him. A moment later, voices reached us on the wind, guttural, Kerghi sounds. Some of the enemy were still in the forest. Judging by all the different voices, at least a dozen.

"Run," I whispered, not wanting Orz to try to take on that many. And since I darted down the path toward the castle, he had no choice but to follow me.

But the enemy heard our racket and gave chase.

While standing his ground in a fight, Orz's movements were fast enough. But he was not a fast runner, not with his broken gait.

The enemy gained on us. Orz knew it too, and when he saw a hollow tree a few steps off the path, he darted for the waist-high hole.

He slammed into the cavity backward, laying his sword on the ground in the same moment so I would not be skewered when I slammed in after him.

We filled the hole with no room to spare, and I scrambled to pull my robe in and around me. I hoped, if anyone looked in the falling darkness, my brown robe would be just a brown shadow on the brown bark, not easily noticed.

My heart raced as the enemy rushed by us. But then, since our footfalls had stopped, they stopped too. They doubled back.

I held my breath.

Orz sat with his knees pulled up, me on his lap, with a knee on either side of him, straddling him. My hands were braced on either side of his head. His hands were on my waist, under my cloak.

As the enemy searched around outside and I squirmed in fear, Orz's mangled hands came to grip my hips.

And then my heart raced even faster.

Plunged suddenly into darkness, our bodies were invisible, defined only by touch, reducing us to just a man and a woman.

His face was a hairsbreadth from mine. His hood had slid up, but in the pitch dark, I could not see his face.

My heart hammered away.

*Does he hear it?* Heat crept up my cheeks.

I tried to shift up a little, but my behind on his thigh slipped right back down, the joining of my thighs coming into hard contact with his loins.

The harsh catch of his breath sounded loud in my ears. A small moan escaped my throat. I hoped he recognized it as a moan of embarrassment. What would he think of me otherwise? For all I knew, he *was* the captain of the Ishafi city guard and had a wife at home and ten children.

But if he did, he was not thinking of them at the moment, because his hands tightened on my hips.

My hands dropped to his shoulders that were hard with muscles. For the first time in a long time, a faint yearning unfurled inside me, but, as soon as I recognized it, an ice-cold wave of guilt washed it away.

The moment I stiffened, Orz withdrew from me in the tight space, allowing a little more room between us, and I was suddenly cold enough to shiver.

His hands loosened on my hips. Before he could pull them away, I slid my own hands over them. And then I did something I had ached to do for a long time. I healed his fingers.

He growled low in his throat once he realized what I was doing, but I would not release him, and he could not escape. He had guarded me and had given me his friendship, his companionship through a difficult journey. I was determined to do this one thing for him.

I would have healed his entire body, but I feared that might truly arouse his anger. So I softened the ruined bones of his hands, then I knitted them together the right way again, using my own good bones as the pattern.

I grew tired by the end. The knitting of bones, even small ones, was never easy work, and I had already been exhausted by caring for the injured of the battle.

When I finished, I leaned against him, my head resting on his shoulder. And he folded his arms around me and stroked my hair with the hands I had just made whole again.

His heart beat steadily against my chest. I sighed. I had missed the feel of strong arms. Suddenly, I was blinking away tears.

Orz's arms tightened. In a dark hole, hidden away from the world, I let his comfort wash over me without questioning it for a moment, then another. Emotions I could not name swirled through me.

Then the enemy stalked off, swearing at having lost their prey, and we eased out of our hiding place and hurried back to the castle.

Day and night, men and women kept coming to us. The women and their babes, the injured and the old we left behind at the freed castles, with their men to protect them. But some warriors asked to join us, and these we took along. Our numbers swelled once again.

After a while, we did not have to fight as often as when we had begun our journey. Smaller bands of enemy soldiers would not engage us but often fled before us instead. The areas we marched through had already been conquered; the Emperor's main army had moved on, only enough soldiers left behind to hold key positions.

The worse their area had been ravaged, the more fighting men joined us. With their homes burned and their families killed, they had nowhere else to go. By the time we reached Muzarat, our numbers had doubled once again.

We camped on the low hill that overlooked the end point of the caravan trail. The Silver River flowed south just outside the city. Here, caravan goods were loaded onto barges and simply floated down to the port city of Uramit.

Tomron, Orz, Marga, and I stood in front of my tent.

Orz watched the river. Did it remind him of something? Was he from around here? Would he ever remember who he was and where he was from and leave me?

How much that thought bothered me took me by surprise. I had grown most used to his company. A hundred times a day, I was searched out by his gaze, or he was searched out by mine.

But he did not seek being as close to me again as we had been in the hollow tree. Part of me was disappointed; part of me was glad.

Then I thought of Lawana in my mother's tale, how she could not make her decision, turning back and forth until a great hole was created.

*"The hole, deep and wide, drank Bottomless Lake and swallowed Mountain of No Top. An endless swamp took their place, and to this day, it is called Lawana's Swamp,"* my mother would say.

*"What happened to Lawana and her parents and the man?"* I would ask my mother each time she reached this far in the story.

*"The swamp swallowed them,"* my mother would tell me, her voice deep and grave.

Now, having seen some of the world, I knew at last the meaning of the tale: indecision had a price. A lesson I would do well to remember.

I ran my fingers through Marga's fur, and she rubbed against me. I drew my mind from the past and considered the more immediate difficulties we faced.

From the scarce news we had gained from new refugees, I tried to calculate whether we or the enemy army would reach Uramit first. *And if they do, how large a force will we face?*

I kept scratching the tiger's neck. She knew to lean against me only partially. Her full weight would have tipped me over.

"The Emperor began this war with a formidable army," I said. "But some of his men were lost in the fighting. Others have to be left behind to hold territory while the main force moves forward."

Tomron nodded. "Which means his fighting force is decreasing."

This gave me some hope as I searched Muzarat, which stretched before us with its endless markets, the largest city I had ever seen. Oddly, despite its size, Muzarat had but a minor fortification in the middle.

Of course, I could not see what I most wished: Graho the merchant and his little beggars. We were too far away for that.

Tomron pointed at a procession leaving the city, a dozen men on horseback—all white horses of the finest breeding. Orz was moving already, calling Marga to him with a soft chuff and walking back toward the middle of our camp with the tiger. *Well done.* I did not want anyone from the delegation to be thrown from his horse when the animal panicked.

For this reason and others, we had learned to camp outside the cities we came across instead of marching in and causing distress.

"Here come the emissaries," Tomron said.

They stopped at a fair distance and remained on their horses, which pranced anyway, since the wind blew from the camp and they could smell Marga.

The men gave short bows and introduced themselves with names that were a combination of sounds and snorts. Luckily, the one who spoke next—the youngest of them—used the merchant tongue. "Greetings from the Merchant League of Muzarat."

They looked between myself and Tomron, trying to judge which one of us they should address.

Tomron solved this problem by saying, "The High Sorceress, Tera, accepts your greetings, merchants. I am her general, Tomron. We are on our way to the port city of Uramit. Our army will camp here until we can find enough barges to take us down the river."

He simply informed them of our plans, did not ask for permission or an opinion.

"Were you hired to defend Uramit?" another merchant asked, the one in the turban.

"We were not," Tomron said.

They smiled at that and slipped from their horses to the ground at last, stepped closer and bowed again.

"The Merchant League of Muzarat would hire the sorceress's army. Would you come into our city to discuss terms, my lady?" a man with a silver beard asked.

"The army is not for hire," Tomron informed him.

The emissaries looked at each other with frowns. They were merchants. Perhaps they did not trust that which was not for sale.

"Do you know of a merchant by the name of Graho?" I inquired.

Since they showed no recognition of the name, I added, "He traveled to Muzarat with the caravan from Ker, transporting nine little beggars."

The merchants murmured amongst themselves, then the young one mounted his horse and rode back toward the city.

"We will enquire," silver beard told me, then asked, "Why risk the spring river? Why not wait a mooncrossing here? Ice floes come from the northern mountains and sink barges this time of year. We would provide you with tents, food, and women for the men. And male pleasure slaves for you, my lady," he added hurriedly.

I nearly choked on my own spittle at the thought. I did not return his smile. "We hurry to Uramit."

The merchants looked at each other. Then the turbaned one said, "The Emperor Drakhar's main force is marching on the port city."

My very reason for wanting to reach the seaport in a hurry. "How soon will the enemy troops reach the port, do you think?"

"Five days at most," the oldest of the merchants said in a trembling voice, so many folds of skin above his eyes, he could barely keep them open. "They will sack Uramit in no time. Then they shall march on us."

"Can we reach Uramit in five days?" I asked.

Again they looked at each other. None would speak. A few gave noncommittal shrugs. They did not want us to leave.

"If we face and defeat the enemy at Uramit, they will never reach this far," Tomron put in.

This brightened them up. No battle anywhere near their city meant they need not lose a single man, a single home, a single possession.

The turbaned one was just about rubbing his hands together. "How many barges would you need, my lady?"

And so it happened that the Merchant League of Muzarat put their barges at our disposal. After a night of rest, our army began floating down the Silver River. The turbaned leader of the merchant league volunteered to travel with us and help us on the way.

By the time the barges pushed away from shore, I had word about Graho. He had been in Muzarat, but he had not sold his little beggars. Only a few days earlier, he had hired a barge to take him and the children to Uramit.

*Why was he going there?*

I pondered that question more than a few times during the five full days we spent on the barges, moving closer and closer to the sea. Few ice floes bothered our progress, none large enough to sink us. For this, I gave thanks to the spirits.

Once our barges reached Uramit's port, we disembarked and marched to the city gate. Unlike Muzarat, sprawling at the edge of the desert, the port city was well fortified with thick walls and guard towers.

As we had an emissary with us from Muzarat who was well known to Uramit's city fathers, we were allowed in without delay. Indeed, once I told the city fathers that we had come to help them, we were celebrated.

I was escorted to the Blue Palace of the leader of the city council, Mizrem, while the other city fathers assigned lodging to my army, adding them to their own defensive forces.

I was to be housed at the Blue Palace with Orz and Marga, as they would not leave me. Tomron was also offered chambers, but he wished to stay with the soldiers.

"Before I have the servants escort you to your quarters, my lady," said Mizrem, "allow me to show you something."

He was a pleasant man with a stubby beard and had the lean look of someone who ran around all day. He told me he owned the city's warehouses and was the type of owner to visit each every day to oversee the work of his men personally.

Mizrem was greatly worried that the enemy would breach the walls and erase all his wealth in a single day. He was most grateful for our timely arrival and promised to repay us for our aid.

He led me atop his tallest tower. Since the Blue Palace sat on the highest point of the city, the view was incomparable.

As we looked east, buffeted by the wind from the water, my throat tightened. The Kerghi hordes were spread out in the distance, a black pestilence that covered the ground as far as the eye could see. They were like a giant funeral shroud the uncaring gods were about to pull over the city.

"They will reach us tonight," Mizrem said, his voice pinched. "Then they will attack at first light."

They were a great host for certain, much greater than I had hoped. Fear tingled across my skin. How could we stand against them?

Orz watched them too. I wished he could tell me what he thought.

I turned away from the bleak sight with relief when Mizrem suggested that I should go and rest. I nearly stumbled down the stairs in my misery. Marga held me up, leaning against me.

My quarters were suitable for a queen, a spacious room with a large balcony, an iron tub in an alcove that had its own hearth, smaller rooms for my own servants, of which I had none. Mizrem swiftly offered me a dozen.

"No need," I assured him. "I will have Orz and Marga with me."

His eyes widened slightly but in no other way did he betray his surprise. He simply nodded and took leave of me.

Marga lay in the middle of the sumptuous carpet that covered the floor, the weaving depicting a flowering garden. I walked to the balcony.

"We have reached this far," I said to Orz. "Pray to the spirits to help us beyond this point."

I could not see over the city walls from here but could see most of the city, myriad houses pressed close, even built on top of each other. Uramit was crowded with people, filled to bursting, the streets barely passable. I suspected it had been so even before we had arrived. Like all other cities, they probably had their share of refugees.

I could see a blue temple—a popular color in Uramit from the looks of it—and in the temple square, the Uramit Gate: giant white stones set up in a circle, with other stones atop them, forming a series of entries to an empty space in the middle.

"It is a working Gate," I told Orz. "It must have a Guardian. I would wish to talk with him." My eyes were suddenly burning. "I miss the Guardians." I sighed. "How is it possible to feel this lonely in the middle of a crowded city?"

Orz moved closer. His presence truly was a comfort to me. I knew that if any danger threatened me, he would be the first one to reach for his sword. He had been willing to lay his life down for me, more than once. He had listened to all my doubts, all my complaining.

He stepped forward until he was in front of me, his head bowed as always. He had definitely filled out his robe, especially in the shoulders. None who saw him could doubt now that he had been a soldier, even a captain, before his affliction.

He reached for me and took my hands, smoothed his scarred thumbs over the tops of my knuckles. We had not been this close since we had been trapped in the hollow tree. His touch seemed to tingle through me.

Such longing swept over me, I swayed on my feet.

"I wish to see your face," I whispered. Even if his features had been monstrously distorted by the sorcerer, I could not imagine drawing back from him. He had been a true friend to me, a confidant, and even...

He let one of my hands go and reached for the edge of his hood, his jaw working as if he prepared to say something.

I held my breath.

But just then, the door burst open, and Orz's hand shot to his sword.

"Sorceress!" A familiar voice boomed behind me, and I turned to see Graho stride in, dressed like a prince, surrounded by the children, who were equally well dressed, smiles on every face.

Graho strode to me without hesitation, picked me up, and swirled me around, laughing like a child himself. "I found you then, the gods be praised." He set me down, keeping me close. "I have thought of you every day."

# CHAPTER TWENTY-FIVE
## THE UNEXPECTED PRINCE

The children greeted me with enthusiasm and unrestrained love, hugging me and chattering as we drew into the room. They were so changed from when I had last seen them, I could scarcely believe it.

Once I told them how much I had missed them and hugged them all back, one by one, they went to catch up with Marga, who was impatiently waiting her turn, nudging them from the back with her great head, eliciting peals of giggles.

"My lady," Graho said in a softer tone, his gaze darkening as he looked me over.

He was freshly shaven, his hair cropped, his clothes well-appointed indeed. He looked at me in such a way...

I wrapped my arms around myself, feeling naked suddenly, my face heating even as my mind scrambled to catch up with what was happening. "You are not a merchant."

He smiled.

Understanding dawned on me. "The children were no slaves."

"We do not practice slavery in Landria," he said, holding my gaze, his blue eyes sparkling with laughter.

"You are Landrian," I said weakly.

He bowed with the ease of a born courtier. "Grahomir, crown prince of Landria. At your service."

I gasped, then grabbed on to the first question I could catch flying around in my head. "Why are you here?"

"We arrived two days ago. We have been waiting since for favorable wind to take us to Landria, the Forbidden Islands. I was just in the harbor to see if we could sail out tonight, before the enemy reaches the port, when I heard news of a great sorceress, the sister of tigers, come down from the north to free the world. I wondered if it might yet be you, so I have come to see for myself."

*The crown prince of Landria.* I stared, having trouble comprehending this turn of events.

"And your slave marks?" I remembered suddenly.

He flashed a puzzled look.

"The tattoos on your side."

He smiled. "The royal house of Landria is marked so at a young age."

*Oh.* "What were you doing on the pirate ship?"

He said nothing for a long spell, then, "That is a story not many know." He paused. "I shall tell you, but at another time, my lady." He turned toward the balcony and looked out at the city overrun by my soldiers. "I see you found your army."

My mind was too stumbling to think. "In truth, they found me."

He looked at me carefully. "You do draw people." His lips turned up into a smile as to make maidens swoon. "You are the candle in the night. All things are drawn to light."

He could sing a sweet song for certain. If he had not been born a prince, he should have been born a bard.

"I believe you are mistaken, my lord," I told him, not intending to fall under his spell. "Only moths go to the flames. To their detriment, I believe."

The sound of his laughter filled the room. He took my hands without hesitation and held them. "I knew you had power. Had I known how great, I might not have given up looking for you in Ker. What happened? You disappeared."

I told him, finishing with, "I am not a true sorceress. That was... accidental."

I wanted the war to be over so I could go back to the cave on the beach where I had been born and raised, where I had learned healing at my mother's knees. I wanted the sunshine and the sea, to know the joy of helping those who came to me for healing. I wanted, more than anything, to have the life my mother had. I had never wanted great power, as I wanted no great riches or great beauty.

"People follow you. That makes you a leader," Graho said. "And when you are a leader, you become what your people need you to be." He smiled. "Or so the palace philosophers have been telling me from the time I can remember."

Of course. Because all his life, he had been taught as a prince, trained to be king someday. He knew more about leading than I could ever hope to comprehend.

"Will I ever be my own again?"

He watched me with a gentle gleam in his eyes. "I am afraid not, my lady." He drew me closer. "It is a service easier for two than for one. Come to Landria with me and be my princess."

A growl sounded behind me. In the surprise of seeing Graho and the children, I had forgotten about Orz. He still stood on the balcony, his face deep in his hood. I could not tell if he was looking at me or seeing something out in the city.

"I am safe here, Orz." I told him. "You may go if you wish."

But he stayed.

"I heard tales of you in the harbor," Graho said, drawing my attention back to him.

I wanted to ask what tales, but servants came to invite us to a feast. The city fathers wanted to talk with me about the morning's battle.

Two women were already pouring me a quick bath; another brought a selection of dresses, gifts from the city.

"I must prepare," I told Graho.

He let me go with a reluctant gleam in his eyes and headed for the door, but stopped and turned back from the doorway. "And the hollow? How is it that it still lives?"

"His name is Orz."

Surprise crossed the prince's face. "He speaks?"

"Only his name," I said with true regret.

"He is much improved," Graho allowed. Then he nodded toward the hollow. "A pint, then, old friend? I would reward you for guarding my lady."

But Orz did not move, nor did he acknowledge the prince.

"He usually stays with me," I put in.

The prince's gaze cut to me, widened. "Whilst you bathe?"

"By the creeks in the woods, he protected me." At first I had not looked at him as a flesh-and-blood man but as a lost wraith.

"Very well," the prince said. Then frowned. Then smiled. "I am jealous of a man without a spirit."

I wanted to argue that Orz had a spirit. I was almost certain. He had shown so much care for Marga, such care and loyalty for me...But by the time I found the words, Graho had left me, the door closing behind him.

"Your bath, my lady," one of the servant women called, and I headed to the alcove, glancing at Orz.

He took up position in the middle of the room, facing the door, his back to me, his hand near his sword. The servant woman frowned at him with disapproval but held her tongue when I did not send him away.

"If you allow me, my lady." The woman distracted me with stripping off my clothes, then unbraiding my hair once I was in the hot fragrant water that felt better than anything had in a long time.

I sank into the comfort and closed my eyes, let the woman rub soaproot paste over my body and into my hair.

The journey down Silver River had been a cold and distressing one. I had worried about our soldiers, about failing, about never reaching Dahru, about not being able to save my people.

The warmth of the bath seeped into my bones now, nearly lulling me to sleep. Then Orz gave one of his soft growls, maybe answering Marga, who was now sunning on the balcony. My exhaustion-addled brain drifted, idly wondering what it might feel like to have Orz's scarred fingers in my hair instead of the servant's.

A strange feeling flooded me, startling me so much that I sat upright in the bath, splashing water on the stones, upsetting the woman.

"Forgive me, my lady." She thought she had somehow hurt me, pulled my hair.

"All is well. I can finish this myself." I ducked under the water and held my breath for a moment, then another, trying to regain my composure.

Yet I still did not have it when I broke the surface.

Orz still stood as he had, his back to me, innocent of my strange imaginings, his attention on the door, giving no indication that he could hear me splashing around in my bath.

But I was aware of his presence as I had not been before.

I dressed in a hurry, in the nearest dress, barely allowing the servant to help me, which upset the woman again.

"I'm sorry, my lady," she kept repeating.

To calm her, I let her comb and arrange my hair.

Then I caught Orz, from the corner of my eye, looking at the tub. Did he wish to bathe? Even as I thought that, I grew embarrassed. Of course he did. He was no different than I.

Among the common people, sharing a bath was a habit. They started with the young and finished with the parents, the whole family of a dozen or more accomplishing their weekly bath in the same water.

Yet now, with Orz, sharing a bath seemed an oddly intimate thing. Still, I could not deny him the comfort.

"Would you like to use the water?"

He stilled as if I had caught him by surprise. But then he nodded.

I could *not* stay and watch him disrobe. Even if part of me wished to look upon his face. As the servant woman fled, I strode to the balcony, closed the doors firmly behind me, and looked out at the city.

The city fathers walked the parapets, assigning soldiers to towers. I could see Tomron. I saw many men who had come to the city with me, some with better weapons than they had arrived with.

The city merchants were putting away their wares, some nailing boards across their windows. The noise of the city rose up to me, but I suddenly heard another, muffled, noise behind the doors. Was that Orz, splashing into the tub?

I felt so many things. Longing, yes, and a great curiosity, but also great shame. I had allowed Graho to hold me earlier, and now I was thinking about Orz. Where was my loyalty to Batumar? What was wrong with me? I did not want any other man but him.

Orz's kindness had reached my heart. *As a brother*, I tried to tell myself. And yet...

My cheeks burned by the time he opened the door behind me and cleared his throat, signaling that he was ready. I turned slowly. Blinked.

He had shaved. I stared at the tip of his scarred chin.

I wished to see the rest of his face. "Orz—"

A rap on the door interrupted.

I stepped closer to Orz. But then the rap sounded again, and, with a small sigh, I hurried to the door.

Graho waited outside, his face immediately breaking into a smile.

"A lovely dress, but it pales in beauty next to the lady wearing it." He offered his arm. "Allow me to escort you to the feast."

"Thank you, my lord."

What else could I say? Even if Orz was making low sounds behind us that made me think he might shove Graho down the staircase.

"Uncanny how much he sounds like the tiger," the prince observed, oblivious to danger.

He entertained me all the way to the feast, then during the feast. And I did not receive respite after the feast either, for Graho escorted me back to my quarters and wished to come in.

Only because I wanted to know more about the children and the truth about their strange journey did I let him inside.

Orz stood guard by the door. I invited Graho to sit with me by the fire.

He looked toward Orz. "I think that hollow is in love with you," he said thoughtfully, then offered a sudden smile as he returned his attention to me. "Who can blame him?"

I did not want to acknowledge his words, much less think on them. "How does a prince with the best navy in the world come to travel on a pirate ship?" I asked instead.

Graho leaned back in his seat. "Why are *you* here?"

"I hope to hire the Landrian navy to sail my army to Dahru to free my island."

He offered a rueful smile. "I wish you had told me so when we first met."

"When we first met, you were a horrible merchant who traded in children."

He laughed, holding my gaze. "Not a very good merchant. A good merchant does not let go when he sees something he wants. He obtains it at any price." He fell silent, then looked toward the city outside the balcony. "You gathered an army. Not that I ever doubted you could."

"But I arrived here too late to sail."

He turned back to me with a pensive look in his blue eyes. "The Landrian navy does not sail the hardstorms. But I would try for you," he added. "Now that I have seen how it is done. I paid most careful attention."

That I could believe.

"Why were you on the pirate ship?" I asked again.

He cleared his throat. "My father, the king, had known for some time that the Emperor would reach our corner of the world sooner or later. We gave all our attention to our fleet, building more ships, so we might be able to defend our islands."

I waited.

He scowled. "While we worked in the shipyards, watching for an enemy fleet, a simple fishing boat slipped past our defenses. Some of our children were kidnapped."

"The nine?" I guessed.

He nodded.

His journey was beginning to make sense. "And you brought them back."

"They are not ordinary children," he confessed. "Many centuries ago, during a great war like this one, Landria had taken in a handful of refugees from a faraway land. Their men and women have special powers, most strong in childhood, then fading as they age, almost as if they are born with a certain amount and it runs out over the years."

I listened with great interest. Never had I heard such a thing. My own healing power was late to come to me but had strengthened over the years. Among my people, the older a healer was, the more skilled.

Graho continued. "A rival kingdom grew envious that we should have such guests among us, helping Landria prosper."

I guessed the rest. "So, using the chaos of the preparations for the coming war, they kidnapped the children. Was that when they were injured?"

Graho pressed his lips together, his expression most grim. "Their injuries were no accidents. The priests who held them believe that only the gods can be perfect. If humans tried to be so, the gods would mete out grave punishment. Among their people, if there is one of great beauty who also has great talent, one who might be too close to perfection, such a person is sacrificed to the gods. And with these children, who were fair of face and with such powers…"

My heart broke as I understood now what had happened. "The priests had to make the children imperfect."

"As you say." A hard look settled on his face. He cleared his throat again. "I found them, but I did not reach them before the high priest's knife."

I sat silent as horrific images washed over me. *Why do the spirits allow such darkness in the world?*

The prince said, "On the way back, we reached as far as Kaharta Reh on Dahru, but by then, Dahru's Gate had closed and we could travel no farther. We sailed to Rabeen, where pirates were rumored to provision for their longer journeys."

He gave a pained smile. "We had to travel in disguise, or they would have seized the children to sell them for their powers. So would have any common bandit. We could not safely reveal our identities until we were inside the walls of Uramit, among allies."

He would make a good ruler one day, I thought. He cared about his people. He could have sent a captain of his to the rescue; he could have remained protected behind his fortress walls. He hadn't.

"What are you thinking?" he asked.

"That you are a good prince."

He smiled. "From what I hear, you are a good sorceress."

I winced at the title. I wished nothing more than to be free of it.

"You are not comfortable with that word," he observed.

"No."

"Because you are not comfortable with your power."

"I have no great power," I protested. "And the only sorceress I know of is the dark sorceress Noona from the Kadar legends." And what disapproving whispers I had heard of my great-grandmother.

"You could be princess instead." Graho turned most serious. "Unless your heart is set on going back to Karamur and becoming the new High Lord's concubine." He leaned forward. "In Landria, a man chooses but one woman. For life. Agree to become my princess, and when this battle is over, I shall lead the Landrian navy myself to the shores of Dahru to save your people. Just promise that you will return to Landria with me when the war is over."

"That is a most honorable offer," I stammered. Then swallowed, my hand flying to my chest. "But my heart..." My heart was dead. I did not want to sound as stark as that. "It is asleep."

But he would not waver. "Then let me awaken it."

I did not think he could, even as kind a man as he was. I pressed my lips together, desperately trying to think of an answer that would not offend him.

"I have distressed you," he said. "Talk of love scares you more than talk of a siege, doesn't it?" His mouth curved into an amused smile. "Let us then discuss your army."

We talked long into the night. We should have rested instead, for the Kerghi did not wait until dawn. The sky was still black when they attacked.

I did not watch the battle from the top of the tower, nor did I lock myself into my quarters with Orz and Marga for protection. I walked the city walls, looking for injured soldiers to heal.

I found patients aplenty, but all in all, I did not think the siege was going badly. Until the wall next to me exploded, and a falling soldier knocked me off my feet.

I stared up, my spine fairly rattled. "What was that?"

"They brought siege machines, my lady," Tomron called as he came running.

"Can we hold against them?" I asked as Orz assisted me in standing.

"Not for long," Tomron told me with a grim expression. "Eventually, the wall will be breached. We are badly outnumbered. Once the Kerghi are inside, my lady, we cannot stand against them."

"How long?"

"Three days at the most."

But in that, he greatly overestimated Uramit's walls. They were breached by that evening.

# CHAPTER TWENTY-SIX

## THE SIEGE

The siege machines made all the difference. I watched in the twilight as the first tower crumbled. I ran to help the men buried under the rubble.

I was half-buried myself when strong hands seized me and pulled me back. Graho and Orz.

"What are you doing here?" Graho dragged me rapidly through a throng of soldiers, away from the wall.

Instead of growling at him, Orz was now helping him.

Dust and blood covered the prince's hands and his handsome face. He'd obviously been fighting among the soldiers. "You must stay in your quarters."

"I must help." I tried to dig my feet in. I couldn't. He was much stronger.

"You must live," he snapped at me, harsher than I had ever seen him.

I glanced around for Marga, but she was off. The bloodlust of battle was on her. The savagery of Bloodstorm sang in her veins.

I looked at Orz for support, but instead, he moved rapidly in front of us to part the sea of soldiers so Graho could drag me faster.

Between the two, they had me in my quarters in no time.

Then Graho hesitated. "I wish to stay to protect you should the worst happen, but they need me on the wall."

"Then go to the wall," I snapped. I wished nothing but to be on the wall myself where I was needed.

He was talking to Orz already. "Guard her."

And of all times, Orz picked this one to agree with him instead of ignoring him or doing his glaring-without-looking trick.

As soon as Graho left, Orz positioned himself inside my door. In his black robe, he looked as unmovable as a granite boulder.

I moved toward him. "You know I must go and help."

He made no sound, moved not a smidgen, just barred my way.

I stepped closer, a small thing against those strong arms and wide shoulders. The death cries of men in the distance twisted my heart.

"This is what I was called to do," I said, standing but a hairsbreadth from him.

I put a hand on his chest, palm flat against his robe. I meant to gently push him aside, but I could have more easily moved a mountain. Unlike Graho and the soldiers, Orz did not wear a breastplate. The heat of his body warmed my palm.

He stopped breathing.

Then he put his tortured, scarred hand over mine and held it in place.

My heart constricted. I could barely whisper the words, "This is my destiny."

His jaw worked. I held my breath. But all he said was, "Orz."

And all I said was, "Please."

He released me then and stepped aside. I opened the door and ran.

Of course, he was right behind me, always at my side from the moment I had found him half-dead in that ditch. At my side, rushing into battle to defend me, without armor.

The thought of losing Orz to an enemy sword stole my breath for a moment. I grabbed for his arm. "Be careful. Please."

He had become important to me. A friend, for certain, and in some ways becoming as if my family, and in others...I could not think of that. My heart would belong to Batumar. Always.

And yet even in that, Orz and I matched. At times, I felt as hollow inside as he was. Maybe that was why we got along.

Prince Graho had offered me his heart, but I had no heart to offer back to him. Orz and I were both broken, just in slightly different ways. If we survived the war and I returned to my mother's beach, set myself up as a healer...I was certain Orz and Marga would come with me. And with that thought, for the first time in a long time, the future did not fill me with dread.

But it did fill me with guilt the next moment. I wanted to love no other than Batumar, not even a little. Giving even my dust heart felt wrong, a betrayal he did not deserve.

Then we reached the fighting men, and I could have no other thought but healing.

Marga must have caught a whiff of my scent on the wind, because she came to me, bounding over dead bodies. I asked her for help, and she gave it, using her great strength to drag the wounded out of the way.

Orz too helped where he could but spent most of his effort on keeping the enemy far away from me. He cut down one Kerghi after the other—fierce blows, each lethal. His movements weren't smooth—his tortured body could not give him that—but he had great strength.

I had so much to do, so much bleeding to stanch, so many broken bones to set, I barely noted when the fighting shifted. Suddenly we were surrounded.

The enemy had broken the outer wall in yet another place, and so many of them poured in, our men were pulling back behind the inner walls of the city.

I charged as many as I could with dragging the wounded with them, and I did the same, staggering under the weight. Marga helped. Orz fought with one arm while holding up a wounded city soldier with the other.

We made it inside the inner wall's gate at the last possible moment. The wooden gate, as thick as my arm was long, was pushed closed behind us, then barred, giant beams dropped into place.

I glanced up at the stars as I collapsed with the man I held. The night was half-over.

I looked back, and I could see our men behind me on the safe side. There were more injured than hale. But at last, the spirits showed us mercy, for the Kerghi attacked no further. They took the remainder of the night to loot and burn the ground they had gained, then rest for the next day's attack.

I healed what wounds I could with the help of the city's herb women, then returned to my quarters after dawn, only when Orz picked me up and carried me, snarling at my commands to let me stay.

No sooner were we inside than Graho came, exhausted but unharmed. Orz withdrew stiffly to the balcony. The prince strode straight to me and drew me into his arms. I was too tired to resist.

He did not take me to task for leaving my quarters, as I expected. Instead, he said, "There is a secret passage from the palace to the back end of the harbor." He drew back, still holding on to my hands. "A boat is waiting for you there. I want you to go to the Landrian royal castle."

I shook my head.

"The enemy is focused on the siege," he said more forcefully. "They have already burned the ships. They are no longer watching the harbor."

I looked up into his face, which was lined with frustration. "Why don't you go? You are the crown prince. Your life matters a great deal to a great many."

"I will not be the craven prince of the ballads," he scoffed.

"You must take the children."

His expression darkened. "The children and I must stay."

"To what possible purpose?" I cried, and when he would not answer, I asked, "Will your father send the navy?"

His jaw tightened. "He would have seen the smoke from the outer city burning. If he sent ships, they would already be here."

"He does not know that you are in Uramit. If you send word with the boat—"

"Too late." From around his neck, he pulled a gold chain that had been hidden by his doublet, on it a royal seal. Before I could protest, he looped the chain over my head. "This will allow you admittance to the Forbidden Islands. You will be treated as my princess."

*Whether or not he survives the battle.* I understood his unspoken words as clearly as the spoken.

"The Landrian navy will not let the islands be taken," he said with confidence.

I offered a small smile. "I cannot be the craven sorceress of the ballads."

"You never wanted to be a sorceress," he argued with urgency in his voice. "Be a wise princess."

"I must be who I am. I must protect what was given in my care."

"A ragtag, mismatched army of peasants and soldiers?" His voice filled with frustration. "These are not Karamur's walls."

"And yet these are my people." Sadness washed over me as I said the words, for I feared they would all perish before long. "I must stay with them. I must stay with the Gate. If we can only hold the temple square…"

"We cannot."

I nodded, my heart twisting.

"Will you not go?" he beseeched me again. "There is nothing here but darkness. Save your light. Take it where it can make a difference."

I smiled. "A Guardian once told me that it is the darkest room that most needs a candle."

Graho dipped his head so suddenly, before I knew what he was doing, he had already brushed his lips against mine and was pulling back, letting my hands go at last.

He gave a quick bow. "I shall fight twice as hard, then, my lady. I pledge my life to your service."

He was gone before I could scold him to do no such thing.

Even as I looked after him, all the day's and night's exhaustion hit me at once, and I swayed on my feet. Orz was there with a hand under my elbow to hold me up. He did not speak, but disapproval rolled off him in waves. I could not tell whether he disapproved of the prince or my refusal to escape.

He steered me toward the tub in the alcove, which the servants were quietly filling. He seemed ready to bathe me himself, but at the servant woman's outraged shrieks, he let the women tend to me. Then, once I was clean and in my night shift, he used unmistakable gestures to order everyone out and carried me to the bed.

I fell into a dreamless sleep, dead to the world around me.

In what seemed like a blink of an eye, I awoke and knew some time had passed, as the sun was higher in the sky. I could hear the enemy outside the walls.

Marga was gone. She was probably fighting alongside the men. I had long since accepted that she had battle tiger blood. That she was untrained in war seemed to slow her little. When she was not with me, she could most often be found defending the Selorm soldiers.

For a moment, I caught a glimpse of Orz, sleeping sitting up at the foot of my bed, his sword on his lap. But as soon as I shifted, he was awake and on his feet. He checked the door, then strode to the balcony with his uneven gait.

I wrapped the covers around me and hurried over. The sky was gray, a storm coming from the mainland.

The part of the city that lay between the inner and outer walls was a charred wasteland. But at least the enemy was attacking without their siege machines. The outer walls, most of which still stood, were taller than the inner walls, so hitting the inner walls from the distance was near impossible, since they couldn't see what they were aiming at. They were just as likely to hit their own troops as ours.

Yet the enemy force was overwhelming.

We would be overtaken. I could already see the tops of ladders brought to scale the inner walls.

For now, our soldiers shoved them back, but they could not keep up with them all, not for long. Sooner or later, the first of the enemy would be in the city proper.

As I turned to go and pull my clothes over the simple shift I had slept in, I caught something outside from the corner of my eye and gasped.

Many more ladders tried to attach to the wall in the south section. *Near the temple.*

"The Gate!" I called to Orz, then dressed faster than I ever had and practically jumped into my boots that waited at the foot of the bed.

Orz had to remove the heavy table he had pushed in front of the door for protection. Then he swept some food from it into my old food sack and ran after me.

I rushed toward the Gate, running through the winding rows of the spice market. "Marga!"

I needed all the help I could summon.

She found me as I reached the temple square, loped by my side as I ran for the Gate, the giant stone circle.

"Guardian!"

I had meant to come to see him before this, but I never seemed to have a free moment.

He stood in the middle, leaning on his carved staff, his brown robe hanging on his bent frame, thinning gray hair streaming to his shoulders. He did not turn. Maybe he was working his gift—some spell, a protection. Hope tingled through me. I slowed and quieted.

But even as I circled him, I knew something was desperately wrong. And then I could see the blood on his robes. I stepped closer, fully facing him now.

He looked as ancient as our Guardian of the Cave. His eyes were glassy. The blood had run from his nose, a great deal. Only his staff, one end pressed into the ground, the other against his chest, held him up.

"Guardian?" I whispered this time, stepping even closer.

He seemed to be in some kind of trance. I was not certain if I should interrupt him.

Shouts sounded from the temple behind him, clamoring and banging on the doors. Something stopped me from going up the temple steps.

I sensed darkness behind the temple gate, coiled and waiting. A moment ago, I had been sweating from our desperate run, but now I suddenly shivered.

And slowly, the Guardian revived, looking at me. "You feel it," he said in a gravelly voice. "You met Kratos before."

I stared at him, dumbfounded.

"The old god has come back," he said, full of disapproval. Then he drew breath, the first time I saw his chest rising since I had found him. "No matter," he said. "His priests are sealed in. I am most accomplished in sealing gates. No dark priest will emerge from there, nor any dark spirit."

But the slimy whisper filtered through the temple door and called to me. *Have you come for power, Sorceress?*

The Guardian peered deeply into my face. "What does he say?"

I shuddered as fear turned my blood to ice. "He offers power."

Orz moved between me and the temple.

The Guardian's hand tightened on his staff. "He knows you."

"We have met before," I admitted as despair sliced through me. Nothing scared me as much as the old god. But had the heroes of legends not always marched toward fear?

My breath left me. Was this what I was supposed to do? Was my fate to serve the merciless god as my great-grandmother might have? She had taken the power for her own purposes. But if I took the power to save my people...

I had refused each offer of power thus far. Yet what did my refusals gain me? The god took and took from me anyway. *Kratos takes what he will.* If I did ask for power and saved the city, saved my people, what else could Kratos take?

"More than you are willing to give," the Guardian predicted with a troubled gaze, as if he had read my thoughts.

A strangled laugh escaped my aching throat. "My life? To save my people, I would gladly give that."

But the Guardian slowly shook his head, watching me as carefully as if measuring the weight of my spirit. "People who amass power rarely do it for the benefit of others, no matter what they tell themselves. One barely needs any power to be of great service."

"How can someone powerless stop the great darkness that is the Emperor when he has a sorcerer in his service?" I challenged.

"If you have a strong spirit and a brave heart, and you use them to stand up for what is good and right, it is all you need to make a difference in the world." The Guardian's voice held no rebuke, only kindness.

"What do we do, then?"

"I have been holding the Gate closed so the Emperor could not send his troops straight into the heart of the city. When all hope is lost, I shall destroy the Gate," he said.

261

I stared at him. Our Guardian of the Gate had to give his life just to seal our Gate, but our Gate was much larger, the Gate of the World. Holding this one closed did not require as much power, but destroying it would.

Yet the Guardian did not seem perturbed. "I shall fulfill my fate. You go and fulfill your own fate, Tera of the Shahala."

How did he know my name? I had not the chance to ask.

*Take your power, Sorceress,* the dark god hissed. *Serve me.*

I shuddered.

He laughed. *Safe passage for you and yours,* he promised. *Will you pay the price, of your own free will?*

I turned my back on him.

And the temple shook as if in an earthquake.

The soothsayer of Ker had said *only darkness can cast out darkness.*

He had been wrong. I knew with a certainty that allowing the ancient god's darkness inside me would only turn the whole world black. Only light dispelled darkness. We had to hold on to our light if we were to win.

Swords clashed in the distance, then suddenly, much closer, men shouted. Marga growled, pacing inside the circle, looking out as if expecting an attack.

Orz had the same body language, although he stood still. But his attention was fixed on the street leading to the temple square, his sword ready in his hand.

"We must save the city," I told him.

A hollow, an accidental sorceress, and an untrained battle tiger.

Against the most powerful army in the world.

To his credit, Orz did not laugh at me.

# CHAPTER TWENTY-SEVEN
## HOLDING TOGETHER

We hurried toward the sounds of battle, leaving the hissing god and his offers of power behind us.

"We shall do what we can," I told Orz.

I could heal. That had made a difference at Karamur's siege, although I had many Shahala healers there with me.

Then I thought, *I could, sometimes, communicate with animals.*

I had on the pirate ship when I had called the fish. But what good was that now? What could I do? Call fish onto dry land?

My spirits flagged.

I wished I could call to Lord Karnagh. Alas, my spirit song could not reach men.

Then my eyes popped wide with a sudden, dizzying realization. I could call their tigers!

I stopped in my tracks. And then I sent my spirit song north. Soon I felt the tigers, and through them, their masters. I knew that the animals heard me. I felt them stir. I knew they were coming.

On the river, they could reach us in but a few days. I asked them to hurry their bonded lords if they could.

When city soldiers rushed by, I sent news with them to the city fathers that reinforcements were on their way. Hope could double a man's strength. Or even triple it. I rushed, with Orz next to me, to also pass the good news on to our soldiers.

That hope was enough that day to hold the inner wall. The enemy could not breach it. When darkness fell and the fighting ended for the day, we were still safe.

That night, once again, Graho came to see me. He looked dead on his feet. I offered him food and wine the servants had brought, which he accepted.

He did not stay long. We both knew that the battle would start again the next morn. We needed to be ready for it.

And the following day *was* more difficult. The enemy had somehow sighted their siege machines so they could send their projectiles over the half-ruined outer walls and hit the inner walls more often than not.

When the first, small section crumbled, it did not seem as if we could hold out long enough for the Selorm lords to reach us.

But then Graho brought the children.

"Stay with us," he asked me. "They have never done this before. They are scared."

I had a feeling I was about to witness their secret powers. I went with them—with Marga and Orz—as the children scrambled straight up to the wall, to the base of the section the siege machines were hitting most frequently, near the temple.

With pinched faces, flinching from the loud battle noises, they placed their little hands upon the wall. And I could feel as they poured their spirits into that wall until the expanse of stone was almost like a living thing.

"They hold things together," Graho said next to me, his voice filled with worry.

I stared at him. *Hold things together.* A powerful skill indeed for a nation who lived on small islands covered in fortresses, nothing but walls, which every enemy would do its best to demolish.

That we had an unexpectedly easy passage through the hardstorms made sense all of a sudden. The nine had been holding the ship together.

And Graho's confidence that the makeshift barrel raft would not sink came from his knowledge of their gift.

"What can I do to help?" I asked.

He watched me with true desperation in his gaze for the first time. "Make sure they are not injured."

I sent my spirit to them. The next hit reverberated through my arms, through my very being, as if I was holding up the wall and not the children.

I cried out in anguish, feeling as if my bones were pulverizing from the inside, as if my body had fallen between millstones and the great stones were grinding.

The children remained standing, for I had taken the pain of all nine upon me.

If Orz had tried to pull me away, I would not have let him, but instead, he came behind me and wrapped his arms tightly around me to keep me from falling. He made soft sounds in his throat that might have been whispers, but if he was at last talking to me, I could not comprehend it, I was so overtaken.

When my knees buckled, he held me up. And the children stood. And the wall held, hit after hit.

At the periphery of my senses, I could feel the soldiers' spirits revive, and word spread through our defenses that some great magic was afoot, that the sorceress had once again wrought something.

They talked to me as some priests talked to their temple statutes. I could not respond. I could but take the pain. And Orz held me throughout the day.

I would only let him carry me back to my quarters when night fell and the siege machines went silent.

Graho came to see me some time later.

"The children?" I asked.

Orz was cleaning his sword on the balcony.

"Well and asleep, all thanks to you," Graho responded to my question.

"They do what they can. I do what I can," I told him. "So this is why you have not sent them away in the boat."

He nodded, his gaze haunted. "I still do not know whether I have made the right decision. I risk losing them. Yet if I sent them to safety, we risk losing the world." He paused. "We make our choices, do we not? Either we fight for light or let darkness creep in."

"And once we choose, we do what we must," I agreed.

"The sorcerer is not with the Emperor's troops outside." He said the very thing that I had been thinking about just before he had arrived. If the sorcerer had been here, he could have counteracted the children's power *and* mine.

"Where is he?" I asked, more than a little troubled.

"Mayhap he found out that you were in the city and fled."

This I very much doubted.

Graho bowed. "You truly are a great sorceress."

I could only shake my head. I was too tired to protest.

"I had seen you on the ship, bundled against the cold, weak with hunger. Then soppy wet, carried to shore and dumped in a heap by the tiger." He made a helpless gesture with his hand.

I raised an eyebrow. "Are you trying to say I did not look like much, Prince Graho?"

He held my gaze. "You looked like the woman my heart wanted," he said simply. "I saw that. But I had failed to see the power."

He watched me for a long time. "I want you to be my princess. And when I am crowned, I want you to be my queen. But whatever choice you make, when this siege is over, the navy of Landria shall be at your service, no matter how hard my lord father might object."

"Does a prince overrule a king in your kingdom?"

"I am the admiral of the navy." He gave a slow smile. "My captains will obey me above all others."

I thanked him, too tired even to be relieved.

He stood, and once again dipped close to steal a quick kiss, just a soft brushing of the lips.

"Prince Graho—"

"That takes more courage than you think, Sorceress. I am never altogether certain that you will not smite me."

His words turned my frown into a smile. The way he spoke, with that boyish look of pleasure on his face—how could I chide him? And why would I, when neither of us might survive the next day?

I had a lot to think about after he left me.

I had an army, even if our numbers decreased each day. But if the Selorm lords reached us in time, enough of the army might yet remain to save Dahru. And now we had the use of a navy.

How I wished that Batumar was with me.

Yet he was not. Nor would he ever be again. The thought echoed painfully around in my empty chest.

Someday in the future, I might face a choice: whether to live on my mother's beach with Orz, or as the princess of the Forbidden Islands with Graho.

Thank the spirits, I did not yet have to make that choice. First we had to repel the siege, then free Dahru from the enemy.

The days that followed turned out to be more difficult than I had feared. I tried as best as I could to help the children hold up the walls, but exhaustion weakened their strength and mine.

I rarely stopped to rest. When the siege machines were not attacking, and I was not needed to help to hold up the walls, I healed the injured.

Then the enemy thought of setting the wooden gate on fire. And even as it burned, they aimed their siege machines at it.

The children could not go into the flames.

So I tried. I thought somehow they could send their spirit to me as I had sent mine to them. I lay my hand on that gate and held it there until my palms blistered from the burning gate, until the smoke overcame my lungs.

But nothing worked. Not even when the Guardian showed up to help. The fire consumed the wood. We could not hold ashes together.

Orz and Graho dragged me away and absolutely forbade me to try again. As they stood over my bed, looking down at me, Graho's eyes clouded with worry. Orz's shoulders were stiff with it. They did not appear to be afraid of my great sorcery.

And, truth be told, I could barely speak to beg them to stop their badgering. My voice sounded as ruined as Orz's. Not that it ever slowed him down. He could badger me aplenty to stay in bed and rest without saying a word.

In the end, the spirits saved us, for they sent a night of heavy rain that put out the fires and soaked the remaining wood through so it could not be set afire again.

I was back out by the wall the next morning.

My help was not enough. Somehow the enemy had guessed our power and sought to overcome it by relentlessly attacking the very spot where the children stood. After the third missile in a row, I was shaking. By the fourth, I was doubled over with pain. The fifth missile had me fainting. The sixth missile demolished the wall, and the rocks buried us.

Orz was next to me in the rubble, protecting me with his body, while Marga roared and dug madly above us. The enemy soldiers pouring in the gap must have given her wide berth, for instead of fighting them, she kept digging. I could hear her claws scraping on stone as she roared for me furiously.

All I could think of were the children.

The sounds of more commotion reached us from a distance. Loud shouts from the direction of the harbor, I thought.

Orz pushed against the rocks with superhuman strength. I tried too, but my strength was thoroughly sapped. Still, between Orz and Marga, they broke me free. And I gave a sigh of relief when I saw the children safe.

Graho tossed a rock aside. He had been helping Marga, I realized.

"The children held up the section directly above them," he said, "but you were standing farther away."

A horn sounded far away, and Graho turned toward it, shouted something I didn't catch. But then he turned back, a ferocious smile on his face. "The Landrian navy is in the harbor."

Orz carried me, Marga clearing the way to the nearest tower that had but a small door and might yet be defendable. Graho and the children came with us. Help was here. We had only to hold out a little longer.

And the spirits smiled on us once more. Even as the navy attacked the enemy from the harbor side on the south, Lord Karnagh and his army arrived on barges from the north.

Later, I would remember little of that day. All I knew was that we had held out long enough for help to reach us, and that was sufficient.

Once the enemy was pushed back, out of the city, I did nothing but heal the wounded. And the next day, and the next day, and the next.

Graho came by often, sometimes with the children. His visits were a blur. Tomron reported our losses. Orz remained at my side always.

Then the worst of it was done, or enough so that the herb women could handle the rest. I slept for three days.

When I woke, the most beautiful purple dress waited for me at the end of the bed, a high-sheen satin that glistened like the waves. And a message from Graho that he would visit with me that day over the evening meal.

Orz stood over the bed, his shoulders stiff as the servant passed on the message.

"I am well," I assured him and slid out of bed. "I would like a bath," I told the servant woman.

I wrapped a blanket around myself and went to stand on the balcony while my bath was prepared.

"Are you sure you are not hurt?" I asked Orz, who stood next to me with a sullen tilt of his shoulders. He had not let me examine him, let alone heal him. As many men as he had cut down, I was certain that some of the swords had reached him.

Marga's tail twitched as she paced the balcony behind us, restless. The port city was no place for the tiger. And she would hate a ship even more. Yet I knew that I could not leave her behind, nor would she abandon me. Our fates were forever connected.

"I am going to ask Prince Graho to have his ships transport us as soon as possible," I told Orz and looked at his hooded face. I had to give him a choice, even if I held my breath as I did. "You are a man of Ishaf. Do you wish to return there?"

His response was to step closer to me.

I did not know why that should make me feel so much better.

The servant called. I went inside for my bath. Orz remained on the balcony with the tiger, turned toward the city.

269

He stayed that way until I was bathed and dressed. He came in just as the servant looped the prince's gold chain with the royal seal over my head. Graho had insisted that I keep it while I considered his proposal.

With my back to Orz, I only knew he came in by the sound of his footsteps. Without turning, without seeing his face, I knew he was scowling.

Then the prince arrived, and Orz returned to the balcony.

"My lady." Graho bowed, his face brightening as he looked me over. He smiled. "Sorceress."

I wished people would stop calling me that.

"Prince Graho," I greeted him as the servants slipped out behind him. I smoothed my hand down the front of the satin gown. "Thank you for the lovely gift."

He was equally well dressed, in black leather leggings and a purple satin doublet. "I thought we have both spent enough time going about looking like butchers."

I allowed a smile. "We have spent more than enough days blood covered."

He looked to the balcony where Orz stood, a dark, solitary figure. "Must he stay?"

I supposed Orz could take Marga out of the city. The tiger needed to run, needed to hunt if possible.

"Orz?" I called to ask him.

He did not move.

"I do not think he can hear us," I told the prince as I turned back to him.

He came closer and brushed his lips against mine. This time, I had expected it, yet I did not draw away. I did not move closer either. Flustered, I offered him a seat.

He smiled. He was an admiral. He did not miss my pitiful attempt at a military maneuver.

"How fares the city?" I asked. "Since the siege, I have seen only the injured."

"Most of the losses are among the city soldiers," he said. "Your army fared better. They had been bloodied before and battle hardened."

"And your people?" I moved some roasted duck over to my plate.

"My sailors performed as expected." The prince served himself as well. I liked that about him. He must have grown used to taking care of himself while pretending to be a merchant.

We talked about what would come next. Lord Karnagh and his warriors would come with me to Dahru. As would Graho.

Our meal was pleasantly spent.

"The ships are ready to sail whenever you are," Graho promised.

I thanked him.

"And that other matter?" he asked, taking my hands when we stood at the end of the meal.

He lifted my hand to his lips and kissed my knuckles. Then he drew me closer.

I did not fear his touch. I cared for him. He had become a friend during the siege, and maybe even before that. When he lowered his lips to mine, I did not protest.

"Be mine," he whispered against my lips. And then he kissed me. And then he kissed me more deeply.

It was a kiss to make maidens swoon, from a handsome prince. But I was no maiden. I was a healer, thought by some a sorceress, most certainly a woman who was not in love with the man kissing her.

Had it been Batumar's arms tightening around my body and pulling me closer, my knees would have melted.

"I cannot," I said as I pulled back a little.

"You have my heart," he said without letting me go. "All I ask is that you try. My love will carry us through until you grow to return it." And he kissed me again.

When I pulled back once more, he said. "Make your choice. To be a free woman, a queen someday in your own right. Rule instead of being locked away in a Pleasure Hall, inherited like an old suit of armor."

I bristled at the words, yet in many ways, he was right.

He kissed me again, harder, deeper, holding me tight, tighter than I liked.

"Let me go." I tried to move away, but he still held me.

He was not overly forceful but clearly thought I needed convincing, hoped that his own passion might awaken mine. I knew that was not possible.

I looked him square in the eye. "In life or death, my heart belongs to Batumar."

Then I heard metal scraping metal and I knew that somewhere, much closer behind me than he had been earlier, Orz had removed his sword from his scabbard.

He growled a tiger's warning first, but then spoke, his voice broken and rusty. "The Lady Tera said no."

My heart quickened as I recognized that ruined voice. I whirled to him. My knees weakened as I saw him stand before me, his hood back at last, Batumar wearing Orz's robes, his face nearly unrecognizable under a crisscross netting of scars, yet so very precious in my sight.

His gaze was on Graho's hand that still held mine, murder in his obsidian eyes.

Graho let go.

And I flew forward.

I was caught against Batumar's wide chest, my dust heart filling with blood and expanding until I thought it would burst, my throat impossibly tight. I clung to him like leaves to a branch in a storm.

If this was a dream, so be it. I wanted to waste no time questioning it, fearing that if I thought too much, I might yet wake. I wrapped my arms around him as tightly as he had when I was helping to hold up the wall and he was trying to make sure my spirit would not forever leave my body.

Sword in one hand, the other around my waist, he caught my lips in a searing, branding kiss that deleted all other thought from my mind and turned my knees to water.

*Batumar.*

I was laughing, and at the same time, I cried and was certain I was going mad.

When we broke apart, we were alone in the room. Graho had retreated.

Batumar let me go. Stepped back. He had not looked into my eyes all through our long journey from Ker, but he made up for it now, an overwhelming hunger burning in his gaze.

"The prince is right, my lady," he said, his voice rough. "You have not had your choice."

"I did," I protested feebly as my mind still scrambled to catch up with his presence before me.

"I took you to Karamur. I put you in my Pleasure Hall."

"I was not unhappy."

He took another step back and sheathed his sword. "I choose you. Over all others. Forever as one pair. According to your people's custom. No other concubines." He paused, then said, "Make your choice freely now."

He stood utterly still as he waited, a dark mirage with blazing eyes, battered and scarred.

"I choose you. Only you and no other." I watched as the tension drained out of his shoulders.

He communicated with Marga in their growls and chuffs, then opened the door. The tiger walked out and lay down outside, on guard.

Batumar closed the door and pushed the monstrous oak table in front of it with little effort. He laid his sword on top of the table, at the ready.

He looked at me, dark fires burning in his gaze. "Any man tries to come through that door, dies."

And then he swept me off my feet with the fierce look of a marauding barbarian.

# CHAPTER TWENTY-EIGHT
## ONLY YOU

Batumar carried me straight to the bed. But instead of laying me down on the covers, he stood me on my feet, my knees barely holding. He crushed my mouth under his while his hands went to the neckline of my dress. And then he rent the satin from top to bottom.

I gasped even as he tugged the material off my shoulders; then once the satin pooled on the carpet, he lifted me up and out of the dress, kicking Graho's gift away. The royal seal followed in short order.

He examined my shift with narrowed eyes as he set me down. "Is that too from the prince?" His voice was low and roughened.

I shook my head. "This came with the clothes the city merchants sent as gifts."

"Do you wish to keep it?"

Since I did not have much in the way of clothes, I nodded.

He reached to my shoulders and brushed the straps down. He did not have to do more. The slip glided easily down my body. And then I stood before him naked.

He unpinned my hair, then his callused palm cupped my face. He would not take his eyes off me. He kissed me again, like a man once dead come back to life, receiving another chance. And then I was suddenly in the middle of the bed, being kissed senseless.

Then his robe was gone, then his leggings, but his long shirt remained. When I reached to tug the shirt off him, he ground out a fierce "No," and grabbed my wrists to bring them over my head and hold them there. "The shirt remains."

"Scars cannot scare me. I am a healer."

But he would not let my hands go until I nodded.

Then he was ravishing my mouth again, then my breasts that ached for his touch alone, his mouth and hands all over my body. His fingers traveled the length of my legs. The fire burned so hot in his eyes, I felt enveloped in heat.

He did not take me in a slow seduction, but in as thorough a claiming as I had seen between Marga and Tigran, a feral, animal coupling that left me breathless and slick with sweat, aching for what only he could give me.

My back arched on the sheets, my body tightening around him. He moved hard and deep. I wanted harder and deeper and cried out my need, a wanton I barely recognized as me.

My very being pulsed with pleasure as my world shattered.

But Batumar growled, "More."

His teeth scraped the sensitive skin of my neck, his palms covering my breasts. "Mine forever," he growled the words.

I looked up into his fevered, possessive gaze. "Yes."

When at last he emptied into me, the sound he made was half-human, half-tiger.

Afterward, as we lay together, my head on his chest, I slid my arm around him as his arms were around me, holding me tight, as if we were both scared of being separated again.

"He kissed you," Batumar said darkly, and his great chest expanded. "More than once."

My pleasure-addled brain refused to work. I looked up at him. "Who?"

I must have said the right thing, because the corner of his mouth twitched. "Navy or not, Prince Graho came closer to dying in this room than he shall ever know."

I kissed Batumar's chest, wishing his shirt did not have to be between us. I longed to feel his naked skin against mine. "The prince is a good man," I said carefully.

Batumar grunted.

And I asked the question foremost in my mind. "Why did you not reveal yourself earlier?"

He looked toward the tall ceiling. "I did not want to saddle you with something this broken. You deserve more."

I buried my face in the crook of his neck. By the spirits, how I had missed this.

"If you had chosen him—" He fell silent.

And my reawakened heart twisted at the thought that he had watched the prince court me. If I had given in to Graho's kisses, Batumar would have let me have my choice.

Would he someday simply have disappeared? I did not think he could have long continued as my bodyguard and watched me with the prince.

He held me tight. "I will never be High Lord again."

I didn't know what to say. The Kadar elected the strongest and most able warrior among them. With what he had suffered at the sorcerer's hands, he was no longer that.

He looked back at me with questions in his eyes.

"I have made my choice," I reminded him.

His face clouded. "I might not be able to protect you."

I smiled. "I have my army."

And he smiled back, the scars dancing on his face. "That is an odd thing to hear you say."

Tears sprang to my eyes. I had thought I would never again see his smile. I ducked my head so he would not see me weep.

"I thought you were dead," I whispered against his neck.

"Close enough so few would know the difference." His arms tightened around me another bit.

"You sank into the ocean. What happened?"

He waited a moment or two. "I do not much remember." His chest rose as he filled his lungs with air. "I remember being cut down, but I cannot recall hitting the water. Then I remember drowning, water in my mouth, everything hurting so much I did want to die. And then a voice, calling my name. Your voice." He kissed the top of my head. "That voice drew me to the surface."

"I could not see you."

"The ship was moving," he said. "Maybe I had surfaced on the other side. I have some vague memories of Pek dragging me out of the water with a harpoon."

"And then?"

"Nothing. He must have talked the pirates into letting him keep me. I have a flash of him rolling me to shore in an empty barrel."

"He must have sold you to the sorcerer." If only I had known. I would have taken the red tower apart brick by brick with my own two hands to get to Batumar. "What did the sorcerer want?"

For a long while, Batumar said nothing. Then, "My pain to strengthen some spell."

I thought of his broken gait, the web of scars that covered what I could see of his body. Almost as if every bone had been broken. As if then he'd been flayed. Then put back together again. Because healing hurt too, especially the knitting of bones. More pain for the sorcerer.

I felt sick.

"I thought you were a hollow without a spirit." I blinked back tears.

"I was," he said quietly. "There was nothing but darkness."

"At the gate, in Ishaf, did you recognize me?" I blamed myself fiercely for not recognizing him.

"I do not even know that I was at the gate of Ishaf."

So then I told him how I had found him.

He shook his head. "I knew nothing but darkness and pain. I wanted nothing but death. Could I have talked, I would have begged for a swift lance through the heart."

He fell silent again. "Then, at the edge of that darkness, I saw the faintest of light, as if from a candle at a great distance. I had no hope of ever reaching that light, but like some reasonless animal, no, less than that, an insect, I moved toward it."

My tears wet his shirt.

He said, "That light was all I had, so I followed it. I knew that if I turned away, I would forever be claimed by the darkness." He trailed kisses over my brow. "Little by little, the light seemed to grow. And then little by little, some of it came inside me."

"When did you recognize me?"

He shook his head. "I cannot say. But one day, you were there, and it was as if you had always been there. But I could not talk."

"You could have shown yourself to me."

"I feared I would scare you. I was not fit to be seen." He swallowed. "I am barely fit to be seen now."

I could not imagine what that journey must have been like for him. I looked up at him again. "Why did you say your name was Orz? I thought you were Ishaf's vanished captain of the city guard."

He kissed away my tears. "Not Orz. Yours." He gave a lopsided smile. "You asked what I was."

"Yours," I whispered back as my heart filled with so much love it nearly burst. "I wish I had known."

"I had nothing to offer you. The only thing I could think of was to keep following you. If you were set upon by brigands, I could at least jump on their swords and give you a moment or two to escape."

I moved up to kiss him.

He kissed me back hungrily, but I pulled away after a short time to bury my face into his neck. "I lost our babe," I whispered against his warm skin. I did not know of how aware he had been back then.

His heart thudded like funeral drums. I clung to him in silence.

"There will be other babes," he whispered into my hair at long last, his tone soothing, but I caught a thread of grief in it. Then his voice roughened as he said, "You are here. You are well. We are together."

And then we found each other's bodies again.

We sailed out the next day, the Emperor's diminished army nowhere in sight. They had withdrawn to the east to recover from their losses. We had to secure the Gate of the World before they could attack Dahru. All my instincts said that the Emperor's sorcerer was even now working a plan for that.

Part of Graho's navy stayed behind to protect Uramit, a larger force to protect Landria's own islands. But we still had all the ships we needed to transport our army. And we had plenty of food, given to us as payment by the city for defending them. We had no shortage of weapons either, many taken from the fallen enemy.

While Batumar, Lord Karnagh, and Tomron trained the troops up on deck, I went to the captain's cabin to thank Prince Graho.

"A prince keeps his word," he said, sitting behind his desk.

It was the first I saw him brooding.

"You would have been better off with me," he said.

I smiled. "Batumar told me the same thing."

The prince frowned. "It is difficult to hate a wise man. And a hero. He came back from death for you. How is a prince to compete?"

"You will find your princess," I promised.

"There will be ballads, in any case," he said, his tone milder. "The crown prince leading the navy through the hardstorms and regaining the Gate of the World."

"Maidens will swoon."

He frowned. "They will not be you."

"But there will be one you will love more than you ever loved me."

He looked doubtful. But then he said, "Mayhap it is better this way. It is a dangerous business, loving a powerful sorceress. One little fight over dinner, and you could wilt my...sword."

I grinned even as I rolled my eyes at him. He grinned back.

And then Batumar burst in.

"You know, my lord, you do not have to drag me off to bed every time I talk to the prince," I scolded Batumar, lying spent across his body in our cabin a while later.

Truly, with his healed fingers, he could peel me out of my dress as fast as a beggar boy peeled a sweet, juicy dindin.

"I want to make up for our lost days." He caressed my rib cage, all the way up to my breast. "We will be entering the hardstorms tomorrow."

Somehow, when we were together now, everything was different. We had spent so much time apart, yet I felt as if we were closer in spirit. Of course, we were different people now than when we left Karamur. Batumar was no longer High Lord. I was no longer the High Lord's concubine.

Yet our bond was tighter than it had ever been.

He cupped my breast. And then he suddenly shifted me so I was under him, and he between my legs.

*Again?* But my body quickened with need. Yet I couldn't help teasing him, making a face as if I was terribly put upon. "Oh, what now?"

He claimed my lips. Then he was inside me in one smooth thrust. "In Uramit, the prince kissed you," he growled the words. "More than once." He growled again. "Only when I am here..." He ground himself into me, filling my body with pleasure. "Can I bear that thought."

He held my gaze. "I love you, Tera of my heart."

And my spirit sang.

— THE END —